Also by Dan Koboldt

Gateways to Alissia
The Rogue Retrieval
The Island Deception

THE WORLD AWAKENING

Gateways to Alissia Book 3

DAN KOBOLDT

HARPER
VOYAGER
IMPULSE

An Imprint of HarperCollinsPublishers

THE WORLD AWAKENING. Copyright © 2018 by Daniel C. Koboldt. All rights reserved. Printed in the United States of America. No part of this book may be used or reproduced in any manner whatsoever without written permission except in the case of brief quotations embodied in critical articles and reviews. For information, address HarperCollins Publishers, 195 Broadway, New York, NY 10007.

Map by Dan Koboldt

Digital Edition FEBRUARY 2018 ISBN: 978-0-06-265910-1
Print ISBN: 978-0-06-265911-8

Harper Voyager, the Harper Voyager logo, and Harper Voyager Impulse are trademarks of HarperCollins Publishers.

HarperCollins is a registered trademark of HarperCollins Publishers in the United States of America and other countries.

FIRST EDITION

17 18 19 20 21   HDC   10 9 8 7 6 5 4 3 2 1

To Audrey, Elliott, and Sam

ALISSIA
MAIN CONTINENT

FELARA

Wenthrop

LANDOR

Cambry

PIREA

NEW KESTANI

Crab's Head

The Enclave

Bayport

TION

CARALIS

VALTERON

Valteron City

"It is foolish to think that our presence in this world has gone unnoticed."

—R. Holt, "Recommendations for Gateway Protocols"

CHAPTER 1

SNOW

Sergeant Mitch Jackson, designation Charlie-3, made another sweep of the snow blanketed ridges with his binoculars for what felt like the hundredth time. Nothing moved up here on the frigid rim of the gateway valley. Nothing except the wind, which managed to chill him even through the synthetic fur cloak and flexsteel armor. He stamped his boots to try and shake off some of the snow. His eyes ached from the brightness. He put the glasses down and checked the progress on the vale below. They'd gotten most of the tents up to accommodate the latest batch of recruits, which would put them at about a hundred and fifty soldiers. The engineers should finish assembling the modular siege equipment within a couple of days. Maybe after that they could start the march south, out of this godforsaken cold.

Gods-forsaken, he corrected himself. Wouldn't want to make that slip in front of a native.

A dark, armor-clad figure appeared on the switchback trail just below him. That would be Corporal Ferata, better known as Charlie-4, coming up to take the next watch.

Jackson started one last sweep of the rim. He couldn't wait to get down to the mess for a hot meal. Even if it was rations. He glassed the wide half-moon ridge on his right, and spotted movement. What the hell? A shadow appeared over the ridge top, then another one. He squeezed his eyes shut for a second, and looked again. There they were. Two figures in dark brown cloaks. Even as he watched, they ducked down from the ridge and hurried out of view. "Shit."

Ferata appeared beside him. "Damn, the wind is cold. See something?"

"Could have sworn I did. Up there on the crescent ridge."

"What was it?"

"Looked like two people."

Ferata glassed the ridge himself for a minute. "You sure? All I see is snow."

Maybe he'd imagined it. Seven hours in this freezer could give you hallucinations. "I don't know."

"Well, let's go check it out."

Jackson glanced regretfully at the cheery fires below. "All right. Double-quick."

They climbed up another twenty yards on the switchback and then left the trail to push through the snow along the top of the rim. Nothing else appeared on the crescent ridge as they approached. It was almost a relief to climb over it and not find anyone.

"Guess I was wrong," Jackson said.

"Happens to the best of us, old man." Ferata started to turn back, then cursed.

"What?"

Ferata pointed to a wide impression in the otherwise pure snow. Like a couple of people had pressed it down. Two sets of furrows led away from it down into the boulders. Tracks. *Damn.* The snow was too powdery and deep to tell what they were, but there were definitely two sets.

"Call it in."

Ferata touched his ear. "Charlie-4 to base. Possible bogeys on the southeast ridge."

Jackson loosened his sword in its scabbard. "Let's go."

They followed the tracks down around a fallen tree and saw movement ahead. Two figures, moving south at a good clip. They disappeared into a patch of evergreens.

"See that?" Ferata asked.

"Yep."

They picked it up to a jog. Jackson circled left and signaled Ferata to go right. Definite movement in the trees. *We've got them.* He eased his sword out. Ferata did the same. They crept closer. Twenty yards. Ten. Ferata signaled a three-count and skirted around back, out of view.

One. Two. Three!

He raised his sword and charged through the thick evergreen branches. The falling snow half-blinded him, but he sensed his foes just ahead. Heard Ferata crashing in from the other side. He shoved through, brandishing his sword-blade so they could see it. "Nobody move a muscle!"

He brushed the snow out of his face, and found himself staring into a pair of wide-set yellow eyes.

Ferata burst out laughing. "I think we got 'em, Mitch!"

They were goddamn mules. Two of them. The animals stared for a moment, then resumed grazing on the green springs that poked up through the blanket of pine needles.

Jackson sighed and shook his head. "Could have sworn I saw someone."

"Yeah, you know how to spot a threat." Ferata put

a finger to his ear. "Cancel the alert. Just a couple of animals."

"You ever seen these before?"

He tilted his head to survey the mules. "They're ugly-looking things, aren't they?"

Uh-oh. "Careful, they're—" Jackson started.

"Ow!" Ferata swore. "The damn thing just kicked me."

"—Tioni smart mules," Jackson finished. He shoved his sword back in the scabbard and held up his hands to the mule. "Our mistake." He backed away through the evergreens. More snow showered down on him. "Damn it!"

Ferata tromped around to join him, and they made their way back to the valley rim.

"Sorry about that," Jackson said.

"No worries." Ferata shrugged. "It's the most excitement I've had all week."

"Never gamble more than you can afford to lose."

—Art of Illusion, February 2

CHAPTER 2

THE GAMBLER

Two hours into the game, Quinn Bradley had over-bet the pot and didn't have the cards to win it. Three of the other players, a man and two women, had dropped out before betting got out of hand. They watched in eager silence as the pile of coins in the middle of the table grew to a small fortune. Smoke from their untouched pipes curled up to join the hazy, acrid cloud that hung beneath the ceiling.

Quinn fought the urge to cough every time he inhaled. *Shallow breaths.* He'd have covered his mouth with a cloth, but that was against the rules. If he broke any rule, he forfeited the hand along with every coin he'd brought into this dive.

"It's your turn," his opponent said.

"I know." Quinn pretended to study his cards for a moment. "Defer."

The clean-shaven young man couldn't be more than thirty. He wore an embroidered jacket that glittered with silver fastenings. Each one had the shape of a different spider. He grabbed a fistful of coins from his still-considerable pile and threw them in. "Fifteen."

By Quinn's count, *seventeen* coins had in fact joined the pot, but he felt it best not to quibble over small details. You could tell a lot about a person by how they gambled. Some kept their stack close to their person, and let go of their wagers with reluctant fingers even when they led the betting. His opponent did the opposite, treating his pile of money as if it were merely a symbol of entertainment, not a means to put food on the table. Family money, probably. Never had to earn it, didn't care about spending it. Quinn saw marks like him in Vegas all the time.

Trust fund kids are the worst. Especially this one, because he actually played to win.

He counted out three stacks of five coins each and shoved them forward. "I'll see another card."

The card came, and only took his hand from bad to worse. He smiled, cursing himself for getting so deep into this hand.

The omnipresent ball of warmth in Quinn's stomach pulsed enticingly. It would be so easy to tap into his power and swing this game his way. But he didn't trust himself to do anything that precise when he hadn't practiced it a hundred times. Besides, it felt like cheating. Probably because it was. No matter how bad he needed to win.

Which, if he was being honest, was pretty bad. He'd spent his entire stash of lab-created jewels in a dozen Alissian cities from Tion to the Landorian coast. He hated to do it, but some were bound to have tracking chips embedded. And he didn't want anyone finding him. He tapped the table with his finger. "Defer."

His opponent shoved in a glittering stack of coins. "Twenty."

"That's a strong bet," Quinn said. *And also, twenty-two.*

"Thank you."

"It wasn't a compliment."

His opponent's chaotic betting strategies made his pattern hard to pin down, but when he failed to count how many coins he threw in, that almost certainly meant a bluff. So he didn't have the cards to win. Unfortunately, neither did Quinn, and he didn't want to take a chance on holding the high card. *Go big or go home.* "You know what?" He smiled at the man, and shoved the rest of his stack into the pot with his arm. "I'm all in."

The check-raise won him titters of amusement from the watchers around the table and a sour frown from his opponent. Now all he needed was for the other guy to fold. The trouble was, he was an ego player, the kind who never wanted to lose face at the table.

"You held out on me," the man said.

Quinn smiled. "I thought I should be polite."

"It is not customary to bet this way."

"It is where I'm from."

"Where is that?"

A little place called Las Vegas. For a brief second, he considered blurting it out. "None of your business."

His opponent scowled at his cards.

Check-raising was an aggressive move, to be sure. But Quinn had no way of knowing if it would be enough. Maybe he shouldn't have gotten so deep into this hand, but the promise of winning big had tempted him. Jillaine liked to stay in inns. Nice ones, too. All of a sudden she had this rule about separate rooms. Twice the cost, half the romance. *Wish I knew what made her so cold.*

Cold. The word gave him an idea.

He drew upon that little bit of power within him. He did it with exaggerated care, like a thief unshuttering a lantern. He stared his opponent in the eye, unblinking, and imagined the air growing cold around him. Pictured the sudden goose bump-prickling chill on the man's skin, as if caught in a sudden frigid draft from outside. Maybe that would give him pause. Maybe that would make him think that risking a showdown was a poor idea.

"What's it going to be?" Quinn asked. At this point in the game, given the size of the pot, a true odds player would call no matter what. But an ego player would care more about saving face.

His opponent snarled and threw down his cards. "Concede."

This feels too easy. Quinn didn't move. "Are you sure?"

The man rubbed his forearms, and wouldn't meet his eyes. "Take it."

"Very kind of you." It didn't hurt to reaffirm the sentiment that the guy had given him a gift. Maybe he had, maybe he hadn't. Quinn tossed in his cards. *Guess we'll never know.*

He wanted to leave right then, but stuck around for another hour to lose a little bit of the money around the table. His opponents regained some face that way, and hopefully they'd be less likely to wait for him outside with a couple of armed thugs. He had a sword in the rack just inside the door, and various smaller weapons stashed about his person, but he'd just as soon avoid any violent confrontations with a bit of human psychology. So much of it came by instinct: how to approach the marks, milk them dry, and make a clean break. Anyone who made it on the Las Vegas Strip had to be a fast learner.

Slow learners went broke, or dug their own graves out in the desert.

When the game ended, Quinn thanked the other players, and made promises of returning the next night that he'd almost certainly be breaking. He pressed some silver into the palms of the attendant, the barkeeper, and the proprietress. The latter was a redhead named Ava, and the tallest woman Quinn had seen in this world. She operated a syndicate of gambling houses in southeast Caralis. If her portion of tonight's winnings was any indication, she might be the wealthiest woman he'd met in this world as well.

"You did well tonight, Mr. Thomas," she said, referring to the alias Quinn had given when he met her. That introduction had been memorable for two reasons: first, the shock of learning that the matriarchal head of the syndicate was so young, and second, the casual way that she'd pointed a crossbow at his groin.

"Beginner's luck," he said. "How much did you say it was?"

"One in eight, or in your case, twenty-two silvers."

"Right." He counted them out, marveling at the woman's counting abilities. He'd come with thirty silvers and left the table with two hundred and four. Technically, the house's cut was slightly *less* than twenty-two, but he found it best not to argue math with someone who enjoyed pointing weapons at crotches. He counted out twenty-two pieces. Then he added another five. *A token of my esteem.* "I'd like to come back tomorrow night, if it's all right."

"The buy-in will be thirty-five."

He blinked. "I thought it was thirty."

She offered a smile as cold as Felaran streamwater. "We're progressive like that."

He bowed his head. "Thirty-five it is." He'd be long gone by tomorrow night, but if Ava expected him back tomorrow, so much the better.

"Until then, Mr. Thomas." She swept the coins into a steel-banded strongbox behind the bar, and nodded to the enormous mute who guarded the door. Only then did he step aside.

Quinn buckled on his sword-belt, then threw on his cloak and drew the hood. "Pleasure doing business." He gave the mute a wide berth and slipped out into the night.

Crown, the capital city of the Caralissian monarchy, made claim to the best nightlife in Southern Alissia. Part of that came from the wealth of a city that traded wine for double its weight in silver. The focal point of nocturnal activity lay in the six-sided plaza in the heart of Crown, where dozens of lighted tents drew revelers of all stripes with noise and merriment. Quinn saw the crowd and felt even more conscious of the weight of silver against his person. He'd taken care to spread the money around to various hidden pockets and purses beneath his coat, but it wouldn't be hard to find if he was unconscious. Or dead.

No less than three patrons of Ava's establishment had departed after his big win. Maybe that was co-incidence, or maybe they'd given his description to some cudgel-wielding friends. Crown might seem clean and refined on the surface, but the city had a sordid underbelly just like any other.

He saw it in the countless armed guards outside of high-end shops, and the regular patrols of city watch-men. He heard it in the whispered conversation of hooded figures behind a charcoal-gray tent. Hell, he even smelled it, in the occasional whiff of caustic chemicals that lingered near the windowless tents on the periphery of the night market. Few people emerged from those tents, but they probably were in no condition to go walking about anyway.

The perceived value of the tents increased as one approached the center of the plaza: from cheap food to luxurious sweetmeats, from rough ale to imported liquor. Not wine, though. Caralissians were picky about how they sold their precious wine. A night market like this, even in Caralis, didn't pass muster. Besides, most of the people here couldn't afford it. With all the silver from the night's take, Quinn might be able to buy a single bottle, but not a very good one. And something told him it would pale in comparison to the vintage Anton had shared at the Enclave.

There was no order or system to the tents, which were assembled haphazardly each night as darkness fell. The narrow passage wound its way among them like a drunken snake. It doubled back on itself more than once, which is how Quinn first noticed the man following him. The mustache certainly helped—it was a handlebar, thick and dark and glistening with some kind of oil. When Quinn saw it three times in five minutes, it might have been a coincidence. But five times in ten minutes, even after he'd changed directions a few times, made it something more sinister.

One way to know for sure. He paused at a stall that sold liquor in palm-sized bottles of colored glass, like the airline booze but much fancier. He inspected a few bottles until he found one that would suit, an opaque material the Alissians called *mirrorglass*. He held it up to catch the right angle of the lamplight, and spotted the mustache right on his six, staring at his back. "Well, shit," he muttered.

"Beg pardon, sir?" asked the vendor, in a rather indignant tone.

"How much for this one?"

"For you?" The fellow eyed him up and down, taking in the crushed velvet collar and the fine silk shirt. "Six silvers."

"Three," Quinn said.

"I could do five."

"Done." Quinn tossed out the coins, palmed the bottle, and moved on.

He didn't look over his shoulder, though his neck itched with the desire to. The euphoria of his big win at cards had ebbed. He walked faster, weaving against the flow of the crowd and through little gaps as they came up. Every now and then, he held up the bottle as if trying to see what it contained. In truth, he was looking for the mustache. And he found it every time, no matter how fast he walked, no matter how many quick turns he took. In fact, it loomed ever closer. *He knows he's been made.*

He reached the center of the plaza, where the night market's most opulent wares basked in soft lamplight. The visible presence of armed guards every booth or two offered testament to the wealth on display here. Surely his tail wouldn't try anything here, not with so many witnesses around.

Then again, this *was* Alissia, so . . .

I'd best be ready.

He made sure his sword-handle was clear of the cloak. There was an open area about ten feet ahead, with enough room to confront the guy, but keep some space between them. Right before he reached it, a couple of shoppers abruptly gave up on the table in front of them and stalked away, right across his path. He had no choice but to stop. It was either that or bowl right over them. The man muttered something about ridiculous prices as they shuffled out of the way. Quinn waited on the balls of his feet. His tail would be nearly on top of him by now. Finally the way was clear. He took one step. A hand fell heavily on his shoulder. He tried to twist away from it, but the grip tightened.

"Easy, friend," said the man. He had a high voice with a slight lisp to it.

Quinn went for his sword. He got his hand on it, but felt a sharp pressure against his lower back. A knifepoint. He froze.

"Ah-ah," the man said. "Wouldn't want to bloody this fine garment of yours."

Quinn sighed and straightened. "What do you want?"

"For starters, keep your arms down, and your hands where I can see 'em."

"And then?"

"Start walking. Nice and slow."

Quinn obeyed, and the man followed on his heels. They marched in lockstep with the flow of the crowd that moved away from the center of the market. The sharp pressure against his back never wavered. Neither did the hand on his shoulder.

Got to get him talking. "Want to tell me what this is about?"

The man grunted. "It's about you doing what I say, and not trying to get cute."

Quinn kept walking, but didn't rush. The more time he had to figure something out, the better. The sword was a no-go. He'd never get it out in time. Whatever this was, probably wouldn't be worth getting stabbed in the kidney. Especially in a world without antibiotics. The belt buckle zapper wouldn't help him unless the man moved in front, which didn't seem likely.

All that remained was the magic, the *real* magic. It tantalized him. There was almost limitless power there, but he had little knowledge and even less control. *Maybe I should have stayed at the Enclave.* That gave him a thought.

"I should warn you about something," he said.

The man made no reply.

"I'm a magician," Quinn said. "An Enclave magician."

"Are you, now?"

"Yes. And I think we both know what it means to cross one of us."

"Oh, I'm shaking in my boots."

So much for the dangerous reputation.

They skirted around a blacksmith's booth, and Quinn pondered grabbing for one of the many daggers that lined the front of the table. It was risky, though. The other guy *already* had a knife, and Logan had informed Quinn definitively that getting into a knife fight with a native would only win him a slower and more painful death. In the end, he didn't have the stones to make a grab for something, and the moment passed. The next booth held only candles and wax soaps. *Less than useless.*

They reached the periphery of the night market, and the crowd began to thin.

"Where to?" Quinn asked.

"Keep walking."

Another thirty paces would put them past the drug tents and out into the night. Then it would probably be down a dark alley, where gods knew what would happen to Quinn. He focused his thoughts on the power deep in his gut. He didn't have a plan, really, other than trying something with that source. He had the most luck with fire. He didn't feel very confident about summoning a ball of fire behind them, where he couldn't see it, but it was the best thing he could think of. He bit his lip and made ready as they marched between two high-walled tents. *Screw it. It's now or never.*

Maybe the guy saw it coming, because he fell a step back. His hand slipped from Quinn's shoulder.

Quinn spun out and away from the knifepoint, ready to hurl some kind of magical hell right in his assailant's face. But the man stood stock-still, one hand in the air palm down, and the other close to his hip, concealing most of a small, kindjal-type dagger. Behind him, the air shimmered slightly, mangling the glow of lamplight from the market. Something was there. *What the hell?*

Then he smelled roses, and he knew. *Jillaine.* Gods bless her, but she had great timing.

Quinn tugged his right ear in one of their prearranged signals. *Stay back.* He'd just as soon not let this man know about his backup. Instead he stretched, and smiled. "That's much better, isn't it?"

This brought no reply, but the man glared daggers at him above a snarl of mute fury.

"Now we can revisit some of my questions," Quinn said. "I suppose I should free your mouth so you can offer some answers."

The man's mouth fell open beneath his mustache. He worked his jaw once or twice, then demanded, "What did you do to me?"

"Did I forget to warn you that I was a magician? Ah, no—I didn't. So, this is only the beginning. Who are you?"

"No one."

"Come on, you can do better than that."

The man lurched forward, as if struck from behind. "Ah! All right. Name's Burro."

"Why did you attack me?"

"I wasn't going to hurt you."

"You had a knife to my back!"

"Not a real one. Just a pigsticker."

They love that word here. "What did you want with me, then?"

"Money."

"Did one of the other players tip you off?" He wouldn't put it past them, either. No one liked a new guy coming in for a big take.

"Not sure what you mean," Burro said.

"How did you know I had money?"

"Didn't know that for sure, but the reward's a tidy sum."

"What reward?"

Burro tried to move, but remembered he was immobile. "There's a parchment. Inside of my cloak, on the right."

Quinn hesitated, because getting closer to the guy who'd put a knife up to his back didn't hold much appeal. But his curiosity got the better of him. He took a cautious step forward. "I'll take the pigsticker." He grabbed the knife by its hilt and pried it free of the man's grip. It was a small but nasty-looking dagger with a curved blade, like something you'd buy at a market in the Middle East. He used the tip of the blade to lift Burro's cloak up away from his chest. Four parchments were sewn to the inside of the hem, each with a sketch of someone's face. "What *is* this?"

Burro looked down. "My assignments, you might say. Folks I'm looking for."

He's a damn bounty hunter. "Interesting line of work."

"Puts food on the table."

"And people into harm's way." Quinn cut off, because he'd spotted the parchment that bore his likeness. It was a surprisingly detailed sketch, like a caricature, but more accurate. There was written text on the paper, too, though he couldn't read it. He gripped the parchment and ripped it free of the stitches. "Where did you get this?"

"From the boss man."

"Who's that?"

"He's the one in charge."

Quinn sighed. "What's his *name*?"

"He's a miller. That's all I'm going to say."

Quinn wasn't cut out for torture, and there wasn't time anyway. "Fine. Tell me this. How many of you are there?"

"In Caralis, about fifteen serious lookers. Maybe twice as many hobbyists you don't really need to worry about."

"Will they all be looking for me?"

"Probably."

Sweet Jesus, how does this keep happening to me?

Quinn jammed the parchment into his pocket. "I want your word that you won't follow me, or tell anyone that you saw me here."

"In exchange for what?"

Quinn held the wicked dagger in front of the man's face. "How about keeping all of your extremities?"

Burro gave a sharp nod. "No following or talking."

"I knew you'd see reason." Quinn went to tuck the dagger into his pocket. That was standard procedure, according to Logan. *Disarm the incapacitated foe.*

Burro crinkled his forehead. "Listen, do you have to take the pigsticker?"

"I was planning to, why?"

"It's kind of a family heirloom."

"Seriously?"

"Used to be my granddad's."

He's got guts, I'll give him that. Quinn lifted the nearest tent-flap and tossed the knife in, to the satisfying shouts of alarm and tinkling of glass. "It'll be right there."

"Wasn't exactly what I had in mind," Burro muttered.

"But it'll keep you busy. Goodbye, Burro. See you never."

Quinn turned on his heel and walked off, not daring to look at Jillaine again. She caught up with him outside of the market, and their agreed-upon rendezvous point. They set off into the quiet emptiness of the open square. The orange haze of the night market faded, enveloping them in darkness. After the tight press of the crowd, the solitude was a comfort.

"Well, that was interesting," she said.

"Thank you for saving me." He sighed. "Again."

"You don't sound very grateful."

"No, I am." He caught her hand with his own and held it. Sometimes she'd pull away when he did that, and other times she'd allow it. This time, she let him. *Small victories.* "I just wish I could rely on magic when it's important."

"You need more practice."

"I suppose." What he probably needed was to return to the Enclave, but Jillaine wouldn't hear of it. She'd spent most of her life trying to get away. Kept reminding him that he'd promised to show her the world. "Well, at least there's good news."

"Such as?"

"I won tonight. We're up about one fifty."

"That's good."

"Also, I'm a wanted man."

She snorted. "It must be a mistake. Why would anyone put a bounty on *you*?"

"I'd rather not start guessing." In the last few months, he'd orchestrated the removal of Richard Holt's magical protections, outed himself to Kiara's sister at the Enclave, and dropped out of contact with CASE Global. That last bit hadn't been his fault, but the lieutenant probably wouldn't see it that way.

"What should we do?"

"Oh, we're *we* all of a sudden?"

She let go of his hand. "Don't push your luck."

"All right, all right." *Still in the doghouse.* At least she was willing to help him. "Well, someone's looking for me. I say we find out who it is."

"No sailor can serve two ships."

—**Valteroni proverb**

CHAPTER 3

UNCHAINED

The sailors brought Veena Chaudri up on deck as the ship made ready to dock in Valteron City. The bay surface looked like glass, reflecting a sky that seemed almost too blue. She couldn't see a single cloud, but the faint column of dwindling smoke marred the picture if she looked south. She still didn't understand what started the fire in the admiral's keep. That was never part of the plan.

Yet another thing she'd have to answer for today.

Captain Mansfield appeared beside her, coughing politely into a gloved hand to announce his presence. "We'll make port in a matter of minutes."

"I appreciate the lift, Captain."

"Yes. Well." He held up a length of rope. "If you'd be so kind."

"Right." She turned and put her arms behind her back.

The captain looped the rope around them in a figure eight. Thank the gods, it was a new rope of soft hemp, not one of the rough tar-covered lines from the rigging.

"Is that loose enough for you?" Mansfield asked.

"Perfectly so."

"Will you excuse me?" He jogged up to retake the wheel as the ship neared the docks. The mate shouted for men to reef sails. Mansfield steered them in, and nosed the ship right up against the pilings as it drifted to a stop.

"Make fast!" the mate shouted.

Mansfield reappeared beside Veena. "It seems you're expected." He nodded to the dock, where a party of fresh-faced guardsmen waited. They wore the livery of the Valteroni Prime, and held their halberds in awkward grips.

"They look new," Veena said.

"Greener than spring seedlings," Mansfield said. "Every fighting man with an ounce of experience got sent—" he broke off, and glanced at her, and cleared his throat. "Well, no need for you to worry about that."

The sailors lowered a ramp to the dock and secured it.

"I suppose that's my cue," Veena said.

"Let me help you." The captain took her elbow, and helped her climb the ramp.

"What's the name of your ship, Captain? I nearly forgot to ask."

"We're the *Prime Directive*."

"A fitting name." She hid her smile behind her hand as they reached the dock. "Thank you for plucking me from the water."

"Good luck to you."

She stepped onto the dock and appreciated the firmness of it. *Dry land at last.* The guards awaited her in silence. They hadn't brought a sedan chair this time. Good. She addressed the closest one, a fair-haired young man whose uniform looked two sizes too big. "Shall we?"

They escorted her off the docks and into Valteron City without a single word. Now and then, one of the guards cast a furtive glance at her. Not a one of them could have been older than twenty-five. Halfway across the great city square, the one in front fumbled his halberd and they all had to stop while he picked it up.

Veena bit her lip and kept her eyes down. Just a meek prisoner, nothing more.

They marched her up the long marble staircase to the front gate. Sailed past the guards at the top, and beneath the portcullis behind them. Within minutes, she stood in the wide throne room with the tall windows where she'd met Richard the first time.

And there he was, standing at the very same window. Looking out of it like his mind was a thousand leagues away. *At last.*

She'd have run and thrown her arms around him right then, but the other man in the room gave her pause. He looked of an age with Richard, but taller and completely bald. He appeared to be staring at the floor, but his eyes burned with a strange intensity.

Her escort guards must have sensed it, too. They left her standing in the entrance and hurried out, pulling the heavy doors shut behind them.

"Richard?"

He turned at the sound of her voice. His face lit up like a burst of sunlight. "Veena!" He strode over to her, arms spread wide. He took her by the shoulders—a slight disappointment, that—and squared her to him. Then his brow furrowed. "Why are your wrists bound?"

"Hmm? Oh, I'd forgotten." She felt suddenly flustered, under the weight of his close attention. She turned so he could see them. "Would you?"

He untied the bindings, his long fingers making deft work of the knot. "I didn't tell them to do this."

"It was my idea. I thought it best I look like a prisoner, in case anyone's watching."

"Clever. Very clever." Richard got the rope free

and spun her around. "Now, what happened out there?"

She began to answer, but paused, because he hadn't even mentioned the other man. "Richard." She nodded in his direction.

"What?"

"I believe the young lady is wondering who I am, and what I'm doing here," said the man behind him. His voice was deep, but strangely soothing.

Richard put a chagrined hand to his forehead. "Where are my manners? Veena, this is Moric, one of my oldest friends."

"Pleased to meet you," she said.

He gave a gracious nod. "Equally so."

Richard leaned in. "He's from the Enclave."

Veena gasped softly.

Moric pointed at her, and looked to Richard. "See, this is the proper reaction." He smiled at Veena. "It's nice to be appreciated for a change."

"Yes, yes, you're very impressive," Richard told him. "Would you give us a moment?"

"I'll be outside. Take as long as you need." Moric stalked to the door, which flew open at the crook of his finger. It slammed behind him.

Veena stared. "I wasn't sure I believed you."

Richard waved a dismissive hand. "Ignore him. He's just showing off. So, what happened out there?"

She grimaced. "I suppose the plan got away from me a little."

"The fire in the admiral's keep *was* a bit of a surprise."

"Is he all right?"

"Truthfully? No, he is not. He was burned very badly, trying to save some of his household servants from the blaze."

"I feel terrible about that," Veena said. "I still don't understand how or why it was set."

Richard put his hand on her shoulder, a comforting gesture. "It's not your fault. I'm sure that was Kiara's decision."

"I still think it was a mistake to let them have the backpack."

"That little bit of leverage wasn't going to hold them forever," Richard said. "More importantly, it's kept their attention while I put some other pieces in place."

Veena marveled at his confidence. Even in the face of disaster and near-impossible odds, Richard always had a plan. *And now I'm part of it.* "It was a close thing, getting away from them."

"Good. It was meant to be."

"Should I be offended that they didn't try to come back for me?" For a moment, she'd believed they would. The boat had started to turn around, and Julio was shouting her name. But they went on, and Mansfield scooped her up instead.

"Kiara will put the mission first until the day she dies," Richard said.

That was true—Logan and Julio followed her orders. Sometimes a little too well. "Oh, that reminds me." Veena dug out the tiny metal snuffbox she'd borrowed from Mansfield. "My comm unit."

He started to reach for it, but paused. "Are you certain you're ready to hand this over?"

"Yes." Not only because she didn't want the company tracking her, either. She just couldn't listen to Julio's attempts to reach her anymore. He tried once every two hours, like clockwork. Every transmission brought a pinprick of guilt to her stomach. *Poor Julio.* He was her main regret about how this played out. Even here, in Richard's awe-inspiring presence, she rather missed him.

"Very well." He took the little case from her, but then it tumbled from his fingers and clattered to the floor. He gasped. His legs gave out. He crumpled to the floor before she could catch him. "Richard!"

The doors to the chamber burst open. Moric practically flew in. "What happened?"

"I don't know." Veena knelt beside Richard and turned his head toward her.

His eyes fluttered open. "That was strange."

Thank the gods. "Are you all right?"

Moric appeared beside her. "Move away from him, Veena."

"Why?"

"Because this is not a natural affliction."

Suspicion flared in her. "How do you know?"

"I felt it. That's why I came in."

Not natural. He must have meant *magical*. She took her hand from Richard's chest and moved back.

Moric took her place. "Richard?"

"Moric." Richard licked his lips. "I feel strange."

"May I examine you?"

"By all means."

He put his hands on Richard's chest and closed his eyes.

Richard gasped again, and arched his back. Moric lifted his hands. Confusion knotted his forehead. "I don't understand."

"Is he going to be all right?" Veena asked.

"Well, there's no physical injury, but . . ." He trailed off, and shook his head. "It doesn't make sense."

"What doesn't?"

"His arcane protections are no longer in place."

Richard coughed. "I thought we had a bargain."

"So did I. Unless . . ." He tapped a finger against his chin, then stood suddenly. "I must go."

"Where are you going?" Veena demanded. "You can't leave him like this."

"He'll recover in a few minutes."

"What about the protections? Can you restore them?"

He shook his head. "It's not a simple enchantment. Which raises the question of why it seems to have been undone." He strode toward the door. "I'll return as soon as I can."

"And until then?" Veena called.

Moric paused long enough to look back at her. "Until then, he's as vulnerable as you and I."

Well, it figured. Veena traveled all the way across the Alissian mainland to join her former mentor, probably just in time to see him assassinated. He'd recovered quickly enough after Moric departed, and now seemed perfectly hale. But when she looked at him, she imagined she saw a target on his back. He stood and wandered over to the window again.

"Richard, get away from the window!" Veena snapped.

"It's perfectly safe."

"It *was* perfectly safe. Why would the magicians revoke your protection?"

He frowned. "They're normally not so capricious. I'm sure it's a simple misunderstanding."

"What is the nature of this deal you have with them?"

"It's been in place for decades. Their arcane protections on the Prime, in exchange for our navy patrolling the seas around their island."

"But you recalled the navy."

"Temporarily."

"Did you *tell* them it was temporary?"

"You know the saying, Veena. Loose lips sink ships."

She put her hands on her hips. "In this case, tight lips lost you the single best defense against CASE Global."

"I still have my guards."

She rolled her eyes. "I've seen your guards in action." Logan could cut his way through them without even breaking a sweat. "Don't you have any more experienced soldiers?"

"They're needed elsewhere."

"Maybe you can hire some."

He laughed. "I've already conscripted or bought every experienced soldier in Valteron City."

"Well, you can't walk around unprotected." He wouldn't be safe out in public. He might not even be safe here in the palace, given CASE Global's motivation.

"What do you propose?" he asked.

"I *propose* that we find some fighters who know which end of a spear to stab with."

He shook his head. "I'm telling you. There isn't a decent fighting man within two hundred leagues."

"That's true. But there may be fighting *women*."

He blinked at that, and then realization crept over his face. "Surely . . . you don't mean the Tukalu."

"That's precisely who I mean."

"I've tried negotiating with them. It went nowhere."

"Maybe it needs a feminine touch."

He blew out air across his lips. "If you'd like to try it, be my guest."

"I'll need a few things," she said. "A letter of rights, of course. So that I can negotiate on your behalf."

"No problem."

"A ship with a reliable crew."

"You can have Captain Mansfield's, if he's still in port."

"That will do."

"Anything else?"

"Yes, actually," she said. "I will need you to remain here in the palace until I return."

"I have a lot to do, Veena. I can't simply—"

"I'm sorry," she broke in. "Are you arguing against common sense? I didn't give up my life and career so that you could run off and get stabbed by some beggar that the company has brainwashed. You'll remain here until I return."

He opened his mouth as if to protest, but seemed to think better of it. He coughed into his hand instead. "Yes, ma'am."

She smiled. "Now *that* is more like it."

He shuffled over to a small writing table where parchment, quill, and ink stood ready. "What shall we call you?"

"Sorry?"

"We can't very well have you announcing yourself as Veena Chaudri."

He had a point; there was no sense in making it easy for Kiara to learn that she'd survived. *A chance for a new name.* "You know what? Call me Dahlia."

The *Prime Directive* made good time on the journey south. Veena had just finished reviewing the scant notes on Tukalu when calls of "Land, ho!" drifted in.

Captain Mansfield knocked on her door a moment later. "M'lady Dahlia?"

She savored the sound of her new name. "Come in."

Mansfield entered almost timidly, with his ridiculous feathered hat in his hands. "We're in view of the island, m'lady."

"Already?"

"We kept full sail all night."

"Bravo, Captain." That wasn't normal operating procedure for Valteroni ships. Her remark on the urgency must have come across well. Funny how a little sheet of parchment with the Prime's personal seal transformed her from captive to honored guest. If Mansfield thought her sudden elevation unusual, he hid it well. He'd even insisted she take his cabin.

She followed him to the deck, where the rising heat promised a sweltering day. A hot breeze filled the sails, which were perfectly taut. The deck sloped at a slight angle, but the ship was making five knots, possibly more. A few points to starboard, a dark peak jutted from the water.

Tukalu.

"Have you been here before?" she asked the captain.

"Once, on a seasonal trade run. That was enough."

Technically, the volcanic island was a protectorate of Valteron, but the relationship was a distant one.

Valteroni ships came twice a year for trade and tribute, but otherwise left the Tukalu alone.

"What are they like?" Veena asked.

"In a word? Terrifying."

She laughed softly. "This I can't wait to see."

"We'll drop anchor well offshore and run you in the tender, if you don't mind."

"Not at all."

The sailors drew lots to see who'd have to row her, which did not reflect well on what they thought of Tukalu overall. Veena put that at the back of her mind, and focused on what she saw. A dense jungle canopy formed the shoulders to the volcanic peak. She counted at least forty palm-frond huts along the narrow strip of white sand on the island's northern shore. There were even more behind them, but it was hard to get a good count with the way they blended into the jungle. Various small watercraft plied the shallow waters close to shore. Canoes, mostly. On the surface, all of it suggested a fairly primitive society, but something bothered her about it. The Tukalu themselves paid little attention to Veena and her boat as they approached, but the canoes and the net-fishermen and the people on the beach all found a reason to be elsewhere as she neared the shore. The two sailors hopped out to pull the boat up to shore. They helped Veena out, touching their foreheads in odd salute, then shoved the boat back into the bay and hopped in.

"Stay close, please," Veena told them. With how fast they were rowing, she wasn't sure they heard her.

She turned to find a figure striding to her across the now-deserted beach. A woman, tall and lean, with her hair in long narrow braids. The shell-beads in them rattled against the rib-bone shirt. *Are those* human *bones?* Veena straightened and faced her, trying not to think about it. "Hello."

"It is not a trading time," the woman said.

"No." Veena swallowed the lump in her throat. "I'm here for other business. My name is Dahlia, and I speak for the Prime of Valteron."

"I am Alethea." She rested a hand on the hilt of a long knife on her hip. It looked well-used. She waited with a perfect air of calm.

Veena wasn't sure how to begin, so she thought it best to be direct. "The Prime's life is in danger."

"All lives are in danger."

"But he matters more than most."

Alethea shrugged. "He can hire guards."

"None that are good enough." *Or that I trust not to be CASE Global assassins.* "I want the best. I hear that's your people."

Alethea shook her head, rattling the beaded braids. "We do not fight for Valteron. That is outside the agreement."

"This is protection, not fighting."

"They are the same."

"We're prepared to pay for your assistance."

"No."

"A lot of silver. Or gold, even. We can pay gold."

Alethea spread her hands out in either direction. "Look around you. Do you believe we are in need of shiny metals?"

Veena began to understand why Richard had made little progress with these people. "All right. What *can* I offer you?"

"The Tukalu need nothing."

"There must be something you want."

"We honor the agreement. That is all we want. Go home, Dahlia." She turned and started to walk away.

Veena wanted to scream. This was her first chance at actually *doing* something for Richard. *If I fail at this, how will he trust me with anything else?* She thought furiously for some other bargaining chip. Nothing came. She had the full power of Valteron in her hands, and it was worthless to these people. It's as if they weren't Valteroni at all. "How about your island?"

Alethea halted. "What of it?"

"This island belongs to Valteron, does it not?"

"In name only. *We* live here."

"Possession is not ownership. Or independence, for that matter," Veena said.

Alethea took a few steps toward her. "You would grant us independence?"

"No more tribute. New trading terms, with both sides as equal partners."

"In exchange for what, exactly?"

"Twenty fighters to protect the Valteroni Prime, for two years."

Alethea pressed her lips together. "Two years is a long time. Let us say, one year."

Veena sighed. How long would the conflict with CASE Global last? Probably even longer than that. All that mattered now was that she bought some time. *And that I push back a little.* "A year and a day."

Alethea nodded. "But we cannot give up so many fighters. That will leave the island bare."

"How many can you spare, that will be enough to keep him safe?"

"A dozen and one."

How cute. "Very well, a dozen. But I want your very best."

"You will get them." Alethea smiled like a feral cat. "Starting with me."

"Some of my military-minded colleagues think that Alissian instability is our ally, but I fervently disagree."

—R. Holt, "Alissia Retrospective: Fifteen Years"

CHAPTER 4

BAIT AND SWITCH

Logan had yet to find a part of Tion that he didn't despise. That certainly applied to the central marshes where CASE Global had an emergency bunker. Well, *used* to have an emergency bunker. Holt had blown it up using the built-in security mechanism, and destroyed two more bunkers the exact same way. That left few safe havens in the southern half of the Alissian mainland.

The port city of Bluewatch offered little comfort,

either. Two ships flying Valteroni colors were docked when Logan and Mendez made port. They had the broad hulls of merchantmen, but their presence made Logan nervous. The Valteroni Prime had recently recalled its entire fleet. These ships were either the last stragglers on their way home, or on an outward mission with Holt's orders. *But when opportunity knocks, you take it.*

"We need a new ship," Logan said.

Mendez glanced up from honing his knife, which he'd done incessantly for the last week. "What's wrong with this one?"

"Nothing, except we took it in Valteron City."

"You think Holt's put out a medieval A.P.B.?"

"I wouldn't put it past him. But I'm more worried about Blackwell," Logan said. From a mission standpoint, the raid on the admiral's island keep had technically been a success. They'd recovered Holt's bag of contraband, which was already on its way back to the gateway. Even so, the admiral got a good look at Logan's face. That made it personal.

But that wasn't the worst part about the mission. That wasn't the scene that played over and over in Logan's head whenever he closed his eyes. Instead, he saw Veena's look of surprise and alarm as the grappling hook dragged her overboard. That was hardly a safe topic for conversation, though. Neither was the pneumatic sniper rifle and box of venomous darts he'd picked up in Bayport.

As an unspoken rule, he and Mendez were sticking to safe topics.

"We should probably ditch it," Logan said.

"Fine by me. I'd love to get off this death trap."

"I'm betting you've sailed on worse." *Come on, give me a smile.*

Mendez didn't oblige him. "Just the one."

Logan eyed the smaller of the merchantmen, which looked to be around forty feet long, with a couple of sails. "You think we could sail one of those?"

"By ourselves? Probably not. Need at least two more sets of hands."

"We could hire them, in a pinch."

"Why, what are you thinking?"

Probably something foolish. "It'd be a lot easier to get into Valteron City if we had one of their ships."

"Or an Apache, as long as we're daydreaming."

"I think we could pull it off," Logan said.

Mendez snorted. "You've been spending too much time around Bradley."

"I don't think I spent enough."

"Still no word about him?"

"The lieutenant has a team en route to the beacon he lit up, but I'm not optimistic," Logan said.

Everybody had a different theory as to why Bradley fell of the grid. Kiara suspected he'd gone A.W.O.L. just to annoy her. Mendez was thinking technical issues with Bradley's comm unit. Logan took a darker view: the magician let his guard down, or overplayed his hand at the wrong moment, and got his throat cut. He'd never really taken things seriously, despite all the warnings about what a brutal world Alissia could be.

Bradley wasn't a safe topic. Neither was Holt, for that matter. *Remove the threat* had been the lieutenant's orders. When Logan balked at it, he learned that CASE Global had effectively taken his wife and daughters hostage to guarantee his compliance. He had a feeling they'd done the same with Mendez's family, too.

"We can stand to look into it. Unless you got a better plan for slipping into Valteron under Holt's nose?"

Mendez returned to honing his knife.

Didn't think so. "Grab the gear," Logan said. "We're five minutes out."

The hiring of local mercenaries was a grand military tradition dating back to the Roman Empire. Logan had brought on Alissian contractors before, though they'd always had Holt's team to find and vet appropriate candidates. With Veena gone, CASE Global's research program had no visible leader. The lieutenant hadn't mentioned finding a replacement, and frankly Logan didn't care. It would be preemptive in any case, since they didn't know for certain that Veena had perished. She might have made it to one of the ships, which meant that she'd be a prisoner. *Holt's* prisoner. That might explain the radio silence.

One mission, two casualties. Both of them were Logan's fault, too. He should never have agreed to let Bradley off the leash. And Veena, well . . . that one would haunt him for a long time. He'd been two steps away when she went overboard.

Mendez had taken it hard. He followed Logan's orders without question, but never cracked so much as a smile. There was a darkness in him, and it was growing.

"Which role do you want?" Logan asked, as they sauntered along the Bluewatch waterfront, looking for the right kind of establishment.

"I'll play backup. You can be the dope."

"Thanks."

"Don't mention it."

They passed a couple of routine alehouses that catered to sailors, then a much nicer establishment that had the look of a captain's bar. That would likely be where the Valteroni ships' officers were holed up, so Logan figured it best to give them a wide berth. Instead, he and Mendez traveled up a narrow lane off the waterfront strip to where several unshaven men loitered outside a ramshackle building. Mendez hung back and took up a position against the wall. Logan swept back his cloak enough that his sword was plainly visible, and ducked inside.

He paused just across the threshold to let his eyes

adjust to the lamplit dimness, and to check his corners before he committed to the room. Two tables, both unoccupied and still not cleared of last night's ale glasses. Another pair of tables in the middle of the alehouse lay similarly empty. Fourteen stools at the bar, eight of them occupied, with plenty of space between the drinkers.

Logan slid onto an empty stool and made contact with the bartender, a stout man with a cudgel on his belt and the bearing that said he knew how to use it.

He took Logan's measure a moment, then limped over. "What'll it be?"

Logan plunked a fat silver coin down on the table—easily worth ten drinks, in a dive like this one—and slid it across. "Ale and introductions."

"If yer looking for companionship, try the next alley over."

"Not that kind of introductions. Looking to hire a couple of hands."

"What kind?"

"Seaworthy types."

The bartender spat, directing it just enough to the side to not mean an insult. "That applies to just about every man in town. Except maybe you."

Ouch. "I need the kind who aren't afraid of a scrap. And can keep their mouths shut."

"Now you're narrowing it down. Trouble is, I don't know anyone like that."

Logan put down another silver coin. "Sure you do."

"It's starting to come back, but I can't put names to faces."

Logan sighed, and put a third coin on the table. "How about now?"

The bartender had a theatrical revelation. "That's right, I remember. Snicket and Ralf, down at the end of the bar. They've got twenty years on the deep blue between 'em."

"Do they have a berth now?"

"No. Their last one went down with most hands in a storm."

Logan grimaced. He'd experienced Alissian storms before, and couldn't imagine trying to weather one in a wooden ship. "How'd they survive?"

"Buy them an ale, and maybe they'll tell you."

Half an hour and four ales later, Logan knew more about Ralf and Snicket than he ever wanted to.

"So we clung to that bit of timber all night, until a fishing boat happened by and plucked us free," Snicket was saying. "Just us, out of thirty-six crew."

"That's rough. I feel for you," Logan said. "How do you even go on from something like that?"

"The ale helps," Ralf said. He never seemed to utter more than four words at a time.

"We get by, picking up a little work here and there," Snicket said.

"Have you found much?" Logan asked, though he knew the answer. Alissians considered a shipwreck bad luck, and a sailor who survived one carried the stigma with him. Somehow the good fortune of not drowning came with the curse of never finding steady work again. Yet another backward concept brought about by this world's superstitions.

Both men looked at their ales, not answering.

"I ask because I'm looking for a couple of hands right now."

"For a berth?" Snicket asked. "What ship?"

"We'll get to that," Logan said.

Ralf set his tankard of ale down for the first time in half an hour. "What about pay?"

"That I *can* tell you about." Logan set a fist-sized purse on the table, untied the top, and tilted it so they could see within. Lamplight glinted on dozens of silver and copper pieces. Normally, he'd never be as careless as to flash this amount of coin around an unsavory place like this, but he had to bait the hook for the right kind of contractor.

Snicket licked his lips. Ralf simply stared. Then they met one another's eyes. A brief, unspoken thing passed between them.

"We'll do it," Ralf said.

"I haven't even told you about the berth yet," Logan said.

"Doesn't matter. If you've got coin and are willing to take us, we'll sail anywhere you want us to," Snicket said.

"I should have details in the morning." Logan shook out two coins, both of them silver, and tossed one to each man. "To hold your interest overnight."

Snicket pocketed his coin straightaway, but Ralf tried it with his teeth. He saw Logan looking, and shrugged. "Never was one to trust in good fortune."

"No offense taken," Logan said.

"Where you staying?" Snicket asked.

"An inn down on the waterfront, forget the name," Logan said. "It's got a bird on the sign, I think."

"The Needlebill."

"Yeah, sounds right." There was always a bird inn on the waterfront. In truth, he and Mendez would take rooms at a company-vetted manor house in the hills overlooking the bay, but the more misdirection, the better. "But no need to come to me. I'll find you here tomorrow."

"Great," Snicket said.

"We'll be here," Ralf added.

"Until then." Logan slid down from his stool and flipped one last coin to the bartender, who'd lingered nearby for that exact reason. He snatched it out of the air and gave Logan a nod of thanks.

Logan sauntered to the door and shoved it open, whistling to himself. Like he hadn't a care in the world. The door slammed shut behind him.

Five, four, three, two, one . . .

A soft creak, as the door whispered open. Logan passed the loiterers, ignoring them. He didn't look at

Mendez but flashed a hand signal. *Two bogeys.* He kept whistling, kept walking. Turned the corner along the waterfront row, which was all but deserted this late in the evening. A boot scuffed the cobblestones as someone came up behind him. A hand caught him on the shoulder.

"Say there," a man said. Ralf, judging by the word count.

Logan halted and turned to find Ralf and Snicket right up on him. He feigned surprise. "Gentlemen. Something wrong?"

"Not exactly," Snicket said. "Just occurred to us that maybe we'll collect our silver up front."

"That's not the way it usually works. How do I know you'll still do the job?" Logan asked.

"You don't."

"Then I'm sure as hell not paying you now."

"Matter of fact, you are. All of it," Snicket said. He brandished a stout knife with a curved blade that Alissian sailors called a *throatcutter.* "Then we go our separate ways."

"But this isn't right." Logan began backing away, one step, then another.

Ralf moved around to fence him in. He had a narrow dagger in one hand, brass knuckles in the other. Looked like he knew how to use them, too. "It's not about fairness."

"It's about who's holding the steel," Snicket said. *Couldn't have said it better myself.* They'd passed the psychological examination. Now it was time for the final exam. Logan sighed and untied the purse from his belt. He held it out toward Ralf. The man reached for it. Logan let it tumble to the ground. Ralf bent to retrieve it. *And there's my opening.*

Logan grabbed the man's head with two hands. Drove a knee into his face. He groaned and toppled backward.

Snicket changed the grip on his knife. "You'll pay for that, you bastard."

Mendez swung around the corner, sword drawn. Snicket glanced back at him, suddenly uncertain. Logan drew his own sword. He kicked Ralf in the midriff before he could stand again. Snicket tried to skirt sideways. Logan jabbed the point of his sword into the wall right in front of his face. Mendez boxed him in from the other side.

"All right, easy now!" Ralf let his dagger clatter to the cobblestones and held up his hands in the universal sign of surrender.

"On your knees," Logan said.

Snicket sank to his knees and bowed his head. "Listen, I'm sorry. We got mouths to feed, and no one'll hire us."

"I told you—I'm paying you when the job is done," Logan said. "Not a moment sooner."

Snicket blinked a few times, as if not trusting his ears. "You're—you're still going to pay us?"

"Generously." Logan put away his sword and hauled Ralf back to his feet. The nose was bloody, but didn't look broken. He mumbled curses, but couldn't come up with three intelligible words. "Sorry about the nose."

"But why?" Snicket asked.

"Like I said, I need a couple of hands." Logan offered a crooked grin. "No conscience required."

Mendez sheathed his sword, and kicked the dagger back toward Snicket.

"This here's Rico, one of my associates," Logan said. "He's here to emphasize that you will do as I say, and you won't make the mistake of trying to cross me a second time. Is that understood?"

"Clear as spring water," Snicket said.

Logan looked to Ralf, who nodded.

"Good. Now, get some rest so you'll be ready to work tomorrow."

"Might be easier if we knew what we were in for," Snicket said.

"We're going to steal a Valteroni ship."

"Gods above," Snicket whispered. "We *are* cursed."

"You don't really believe that, do you?"

"I didn't until now."

"Look at it this way. If we pull this off, it's a good sign you've got your luck back. And you'll have the silver to prove it."

"Suppose there's that," Snicket said.

"So, you're up for it?"

"Suppose so."

Logan turned back to Ralf. "What about you?"

Ralf hawked and spat a bloody mess to one side. "Almost rather you kill us now."

Logan chuckled. *I'll be damned, he does know more than four words.*

"Good assistants keep the audience entertained and engaged. Great assistants distract so well that the magician can do whatever he wants."

—**Art of Illusion, January 15**

CHAPTER 5

THE FAMILY BUSINESS

Goldensong, the summer seat of the Caralissian queen, lay nestled among the sloping vineyards of central Caralis. Quinn had gotten the briefing on the monarchy's governing structure, but the details lay beneath cobwebs in his mind. Overpriced wine, terrifying monarch, that sort of thing. Honestly, Logan's description on the soldiers who escorted the wine caravans had proven far more memorable. He'd always delighted in speculating about the various ways in which Quinn might meet an untimely demise in violent fashion. Caralissian mercenaries meant serious business.

Then again, the more time Quinn and Jillaine spent in Caralis, the clearer it became that they took few things lightly. For starters, the number of bribes, threats, and interrogations required to track down the head of the Caralissian bounty hunters defied belief. Several days of legwork and a host of un-cooperative sources had finally led to the name Mott the Miller, who ran this unassuming mill-station on the banks of the Diamond Ribbon.

"It doesn't look like much," Jillaine said.

"I think that's on purpose." Quinn lifted his cup of tea to blow on it, and stole another glance at the wooden structure across the lane. The windows were shuttered tight, and looked like they hadn't been open in years. Cobwebs draped across the top of the iron-banded door. In contrast, the great waterwheel—which was nearly as tall as the structure itself—spun with a subtle urgency.

No one had come or gone from the mill since they'd begun their surveillance this morning. The riverside café offered a perfect cover. They'd claimed a table on the outdoor terrace with a clear view of the mill's entrance. Even better, the place served only tea and biscuits, two things that made for slow dining. Enough foot traffic passed up and down the avenue for them to mill-watch while seeming to people-watch. A few of the passersby gave them second glances, but Quinn guessed that probably had something to do with the dress Jillaine wore. It was the color of daffodils, light and low-cut. Distracting as hell. Either she failed to understand the point of covert surveillance, or she simply enjoyed tormenting him.

Probably both.

"Maybe this isn't the place," she said.

Quinn shook his head. "It has to be."

"Why?"

Because otherwise this was a massive waste of time and money. "All of our leads point here, and Burro said he was a miller." He tilted his head at the building on the other side of the street. "That looks like a mill to me."

A trio of figures approached down the street, walking close together. Their lockstep gait drew Quinn's eye first, and the stiffness between them made him stare. The man and woman on either side held the arms of the brute in the middle. He wore a black-dyed leather jerkin and an open snarl.

Quinn inhaled sharply and looked away.

"What's wrong?" Jillaine asked.

"Get a look at these three coming up the lane."

She brushed a strand of hair behind her ear, and turned her head to steal a glance down the avenue.

When the big fellow in the middle spotted the mill, the snarl fell from his face. Something more desperate and uncertain replaced it. He halted, and fought to escape his escorts. They struggled for a few seconds while everyone in the café—Quinn and Jillaine included—pretended not to notice. He shook off the woman. The man struggled to keep hold of him.

He might break free after all. Quinn silently rooted for him to do so.

Then the woman produced a cudgel and cracked him smartly in the temple. The big man slumped, and they half-dragged him the rest of the way up the avenue. They knocked on the iron-bound door to the mill, waited for half a minute, and then were let in by someone Quinn couldn't see.

Jillaine picked up the delicate teapot and poured more tea for both of them. "It could still be a coincidence."

Quinn bit back a smart-ass remark. Jillaine had made it expressly clear that she wasn't fond of those. At the moment, things were a little fragile between them. No need to rock the boat. He itched to retort, but simply smiled and said, "Maybe. It depends on what happens next."

A few minutes later, the iron-banded door opened to disgorge the man and woman. They made no obvious gesture, but something about their manner had the look of a late-night roulette winner leaving the casino floor. A bounce to the step that only newfound riches can convey. *Looks like somebody got paid.*

More importantly, the other man didn't leave with them.

He kept his face down until they were well past, to make sure they didn't get a close look. For all he knew, they'd just been sent out to search for *him*. No need to make it too easy.

"Well, what do you think?" he asked.

"I think we're, what is that phrase you like?" She made her voice gruff. "In business."

"Oh, you're imitating me now?"

She shrugged, but it was playful. "You have an odd way of speaking."

He smiled, basking in the way her voice put a shiver on his spine. "You're not the first to say that."

"Oh? Who else?"

"Moric, on the first day I met him."

"Oh."

The mention of her father's name brought the shadows back to Jillaine's face.

Damn, shouldn't have said that. "Sorry."

"It's all right," she said.

"I really hoped we'd find him here," he said.

"Me, too."

Quinn couldn't ignore Occam's razor on where Moric probably was—at the palace of the Valteroni Prime—but he dared not take Jillaine there, let alone risk going himself. Richard Holt would peg him for an outsider in about two seconds. And even if he didn't, Kiara and her team almost certainly had eyes on Valteron City.

"Look at the bright side. You get to see more of the mainland."

"Oh, yes." Jillaine gestured to the mill where the unwilling fugitive had been forcibly dragged a few moments before. "It's all very glamorous."

"I did tell you that the Enclave was my favorite place here by far."

"Yes. But then again, you told me a lot of things."

Ouch. "And most of them were true."

"It's the 'most' that's been the problem."

Touché.

"Well, what do you want to do?" she asked.

"I'm thinking we go with the fake bounty hunter routine," Quinn said.

"Never heard of it."

"Oh, it's a classic. And you get to be the bounty hunter, which will be more fun."

She cringed a little. "I'm not sure I can pull that off. What do I even do?"

"And there's costumes, too," he said, pretending not to hear. He leaned back and gave her the up-and-down survey. "For you, I'm thinking leathers. Maybe a little chain mail to really sell it."

She giggled. "I've never worn either of those."

"All the more reason to try them. I'll bet we can find something in that market down along the river." They'd spotted the colorful pavilions on their way here. Quinn still had a pang of discomfort at the idea of crowded marketplaces, but at least they'd go in daylight.

"What about you?" she asked.

"I'm the prisoner, so I don't need much. Just for you to tie me up."

Her eyebrows shot up, and she put on a pensive expression. "This begins to offer some appeal."

Bright and early the next morning, they stalked down the avenue toward the mill, looking like two completely different people compared to the day before. Quinn wore a dirty cloak he'd borrowed from the innkeeper. Its only redeeming feature was a hood that concealed most of his face. It gave him no peripheral vision, but as a presumptive captive in chains he probably shouldn't be looking around much anyway. They'd bound his wrists together in front of him with a length of cord, and secured it with a complex-looking knot.

Jillaine had pulled back her hair into a tight bundle, held in place by two slender bone-pins as long as pencils. The leather shirt was about a size too big, but she'd cinched it tight over the leggings with Quinn's sword-belt. Sword on one side, dagger sheath on the other. She rested her hand on the sword's handle as they walked like it'd been there her whole life.

Quinn gave her another side look and fought to keep from smiling. *She looks like a badass biker chick.*

She caught him looking. "What?"

"Nothing."

"No, what?"

"It's a different look for you, that's all."

"I feel strange wearing all this."

"You look good," Quinn said. "I kind of dig it."

"Dig it?"

"Like it, I mean."

"But only kind of," she said, with an air of accusation.

"Yes, kind of." He couldn't resist a little dig. "As in, we're *kind of* together."

She shushed him. "You're going to ruin our scheme."

He clamped his mouth shut, because she was right. The mill lay fifty yards distant, windows still shuttered, the door still shut tight. Only the waterwheel showed any signs of movement, spinning slowly with the ever-present rush of the current. Quinn affected the reluctant shuffle of a three-year-old being sent to the bath. *Really got to sell it.*

"Gods, how can you do this?" Jillaine whispered.

"Do what?"

"Pretend to be something you're not when it might very well get you killed."

"I have a lot of practice. Don't worry. It's going to be fine."

"Unless we're discovered, and whoever's in there decides to put a crossbow bolt in each of us."

"There is that. But listen: when people want to believe things, they do. Especially when it means getting paid."

"I hope you're right."

Time to change the subject. Quinn nudged her with his shoulder. "How much do you think they'll pay for me?"

She rolled her eyes. "Undoubtedly more than you're worth."

They lapsed into silence as they stepped up onto the wooden entryway. The boards creaked underfoot with each step. The noise made Quinn's shoulders tense. He kept his eyes downcast in what he hoped was a hangdog expression. Jillaine pounded on the door three times with a mailed fist. It occurred to Quinn that maybe they should have invested in head-to-toe mail, or even armor. It would have been heavy as hell, but offered her more protection if this went south. At least he had the flexsteel suit on beneath his cloak. Push came to shove, he could put himself in the way. *And I would do it, too.* She'd saved his life at least twice. He'd be damned if he let anyone hurt her.

Boot steps echoed softly from the other side of the door, moving closer. They stopped, followed by the soft whisper of leather against wood. What was that sound? A peephole cover being removed, perhaps. Whoever stood on the other side stared at them a long moment.

"Go away," a voice said at last.

"I will, the second you pay me the ransom," Jillaine said.

Attagirl.

Another pause. "Who you got there?"

Jillaine jabbed Quinn in the side with her elbow. "Stand straight!" She yanked back the hood so that the man inside could get a decent look.

Almost immediately, metal clinked on the far side of the door. *There's the lock.* Wood groaned against wood. *And the heavy bar.*

The door slid open easily, soundlessly. The man behind it could have been a heavyset monk, were it not for the thick leather apron wrapped around him. His skin folded over itself on the neck and jowls, giving his head a frog-like appearance. Quinn took that image in with a glance, but dropped his gaze almost immediately. The man's eyes . . .

They were the kind of eyes you didn't want to look at for long.

"Get moving." Jillaine shoved him across the precipice.

He stumbled and almost fell. *Jesus.* He managed not to shoot her a dirty look.

Long timbers and massive wooden gears cramped the interior of the millhouse, making it seem much smaller than it had from the outside. The semi-darkness no doubt added to that. Sunlight streamed in from small windows overhead, but their narrow beams did little to cut through the gloom. The gears rotated at a speed that matched the flow of the water-wheel outside. Well-oiled though it was, the wood creaked and groaned in cacophony. The air smelled of sawdust and mildew.

It was mesmerizing, watching those great chunks of wood in motion. They both stood staring at it for a bit while the miller re-barred the door. Then Quinn turned to check on him and found himself facing the business end of a heavy crossbow. He hissed and held up his hands, tied as they were. He'd have backed away, but there was no room to maneuver past the millworks. *Shit.*

"The name's Mott," the man said. "Who the hell are you?"

Jillaine did a double take at the weapon, as if she couldn't believe what she was seeing. "I'm a friend of one of your . . . associates."

"Which one?"

"One of the Caralissians. Big fellow, bearded, carries his grandfather's dagger around with him." She shook the wanted poster. "Where do you think I got this?"

Mott lowered the tip of the crossbow. "Who *are* you?"

"Someone who wants to get paid," Jillaine said.

"Very well."

He still seemed on the fence. Quinn watched his shoulders as they followed him around the wheel-works to the back of the building. There was definitely a hunch to them. *We need to sell it more.* "Listen, I've got money. Whatever they're paying you, I'll double it."

"Save your breath," Mott said.

"I'm talking about gold."

"Don't care." He drew out a key on the chain around his neck. Beside it dangled an angular stone pendant with a familiar shape.

Son of a bitch. Quinn nudged Jillaine and nodded toward it. Her jaw dropped, which meant it wasn't his imagination. *A wayfinder stone.* Well, this was getting more interesting by the minute.

He'd kill to know how this guy managed to get a hold of one of those, but some instinct warned him against asking. Better to see how this played out first.

Mott opened a heavy steel lock on a strongbox that rested on a table against the back wall. The grating from the largest mill wheel was louder here. Distractingly so. Quinn had to remind himself not to look at the wheel, or he'd think too much about the stains on it.

Mott extracted a black-dyed leather purse. It was smaller than Quinn had hoped. *If there's a bounty on me, I at least wanted it to be a decent one.*

Mott shook out the purse into his open palm. A single, heavy object tumbled out. Too dull to be coins.

What is that? A small statuette in an animal shape. He couldn't make out the details.

"I didn't think anyone would collect this bounty.

Been saving it." The miller held it out toward Jillaine.

She reached for it . . . and he let it tumble to the floor. Where, naturally, it shattered into a hundred pieces. And less naturally, gave off a flash of green fire. Something *changed* in that moment. Quinn's skin tingled with electric fire.

"A summons!" Jillaine hissed.

Uh-oh. They had to get out of here. Quinn tugged loose a certain line in the bindings at his wrists, and the knots fell away. He grabbed Jillaine's arm and pulled her toward the door, ignoring her indignant squawk. A summons probably meant the Enclave, or at least someone powerful enough to call in favors with them. Whoever it was, he didn't want to meet them like this. But his flight with Jillaine seemed to slow down as the air in the millhouse thickened. First it was like trying to move underwater. Then he might as well be pushing through Jell-O.

"What's happening?" he shouted to Jillaine. Even his words came slowly, and took nearly all his breath to force out.

"Enchantment," she managed through gritted teeth. "Tied to the summons."

"Can you do anything about it?"

"I'm trying."

Quinn tapped his own well of power, or tried to, but it slid aside from his grasp. Not that he had a plan for using it, even if he could take hold. No matter how he tried to tap into that ball of warmth, it eluded him. It was no use. If Jillaine couldn't break this enchantment, he had no shot anyway.

Worse, he sensed something approaching. A wave of overshadowing *presence* drew near. They were trapped in this damn mill, unable to flee. He reached for his sword-handle on Jillaine's waist, but his arm wouldn't even respond. The room grew dark. The roar of the approaching thing filled his ears. Then blinding white light flashed, and a man walked out of thin air right into the middle of the room. He was tall, gaunt, bald, and immediately recognizable.

"Father," Jillaine whispered.

Oh, shit.

"Bad luck and criminal activity seem to go hand in hand."

—R. Holt, "Understanding Alissian Ethics"

CHAPTER 6

NEW PERSPECTIVE

Even when the enchantment dissipated, Quinn couldn't move. Some deep, primal survival instinct kept telling him that if he kept absolutely still, Moric wouldn't see him. Jillaine must have had the same thought. She remained behind him, clenching his hand tightly with hers.

Mott had retreated to the far side of the mill when Moric arrived. He lowered his crossbow to the floor with exaggerated care. The motion drew Moric's eye.

"Well-done, Mott. May I have a private word with these two?"

Mott nodded and fled out the door, leaving it wide open with a slash of bright sunlight. Moric flicked a finger and it slammed shut. *Not a good sign.* Quinn had to look at the magician—there was no avoiding looking at him—but for the first time in recent memory, could not think of the right thing to say.

Jillaine, though, had no such interdiction. She pushed past him. "Where have you *been*?"

Moric blinked, and then scratched his chin. "Where have *I* been? Now there's an interesting question." He walked over to study the spinning water-wheels, his arms behind his back. The casual air was an act, though. His tone had the undercurrent of a spring ready to snap. "I have been at the Enclave, trying to understand what in the name of the gods happened when I left for Valteron."

"*That's* where you were?"

"Yes. For a few days only, to render assistance to the Valteroni Prime," Moric said. "Imagine my surprise to hear that most of the Enclave thought me missing or dead. And that during my brief absence, my daughter took my place on the council, casting the deciding vote to break our alliance with the world's most powerful leader."

Whoops, Quinn thought. Well, he was going to have to pay the piper sometime for helping make that happen.

"But that was not the only surprise," Moric continued. "Apparently someone saw fit to tie up our dear harbormaster and make her a prisoner in the boathouse." He continued his wandering inspection of the mill, not looking at either of them. "She wouldn't tell me who'd done it, of course, but I can't help but notice that my daughter, the Valteroni Prime, and the harbormaster all have one thing in common."

Gulp.

Moric came over at last, and put the full weight of his gaze on Quinn. "What do you have to say for yourself?"

Oh, but Jillaine was not done with her piece. She stepped neatly between them. "He doesn't need to say anything. *I* did those things."

That made Moric's brow furrow. *"You* did?"

She stood up straight before him and lifted her chin. "I took your place on the council, cast the final vote, and tied up the harbormaster."

"Why in the name of the gods would you do that?"

"I'm allowed to have my own opinion, aren't I?"

"You are. I'd just like to know how you arrived at it," Moric said.

"And I'd like to know what Valteron has ever done for us," Jillaine said.

"They patrol the seas around our island."

"Except for when the Valteroni Prime recalls his entire fleet."

"He had no choice in that," Moric said. "There were . . . extenuating circumstances."

"If the Prime can recall his fleet, I see no reason why we can't recall our protections," Jillaine said.

"There's far more to this than you realize."

"I'm sure there is, but how could I have known? You never tell me anything."

She scored a point with that one.

Moric flinched as if struck. He gathered himself, and said, "Perhaps you're right. I haven't been as forthcoming as I should have. Particularly now that you're representing Pirea on the council."

"I'm not anymore, now that you're back."

Moric snorted. "Don't be so sure. More than a few people were glad to see someone other than me on the council for a change."

"It was only meant to be temporary."

"What's done is done, at least for the moment." Moric glanced back at Quinn. "And no matter the reason. But I will need you to come back to the island immediately. Both of you."

Jillaine shook her head. "I don't think so."

"Beg pardon?" Moric asked.

"I'm not going back so that you can keep me there another twenty-five years."

Oh boy, here we go. Quinn really wished someone had taught him the disappearing spell—he had little desire to come between a father and his daughter. And yet, the worst part wasn't how their little domestic drama would play out, but how much time the whole thing was wasting. Having solved the mystery of who'd put a bounty on his head, now he had to face the music: the most important threat right now was the mercenary army CASE Global had brought to this world.

Even so, he wasn't quite ready to garner Moric's attention. Luckily, Jillaine still had all of it.

"You left quite a mess behind at the Enclave. They want answers," Moric said.

"If you want us to go back there, you'll have to bind and gag us," Jillaine said.

"I can arrange that."

"Oh, I'm sure you'd *love* to."

Well, this had spiraled out of control nicely. The noise didn't help. Something about the mill's many moving parts and their creaky wooden cacophony put Quinn on edge. It provided a tense backdrop to this argument, and it was probably distracting both Jillaine and Moric from what was truly important.

I guess if I can't be invisible . . .

The power welled up inside, egging him on. He held out one hand, splayed his fingers, and clamped down on the great wooden turnstile with the strength of a hundred men. It screeched and groaned to a halt, fighting him. He clamped down harder. Drew more of the warm source inside of him, shaping it into an invisible fist. It squeezed the wooden wheel and held it fast. All of the wooden cogs and gears went still.

Silence fell. He looked up to find Jillaine and Moric staring at him.

"Gods, but you've come a long way," Moric said. "How did you do that?"

Jillaine made a dismissive noise. "He's just showing off."

Ouch, talk about a mixed crowd. Quinn forced his pride aside. "We have a lot to talk about, and there isn't much time. I'm sure I owe both of you apologies, so I'll start. I'm sorry for the mess we made when we left. It wasn't ideal, and if I could go back I'd have done it differently."

Moric pressed his lips together, and gave a little nod. "That's a start. I'll add my own apologies, for keeping you in the dark when I should not have. For leaving when I should have stayed."

"I'm sorry that we thought you were dead, Father," Jillaine said.

"Thanks," he said dryly.

"But I don't regret sitting for you in the council, or the way I voted. Quinn thought it was the right thing to do. Didn't you?" she asked him.

"Well, here's the thing—" Quinn said.

Moric hushed him suddenly, rudely.

Jeez, don't even let me explain or anything. Quinn released his hold on the mill wheel. Or started to, when Moric snapped his fingers and gestured imperiously for him to hold it fast. A noise intruded from outside—the pounding of many sets of hooves, followed by the shouts of several men.

"What is that?" Jillaine asked.

"Soldiers. Mott must have sold us out, hoping to double his fee."

"To whom?"

"Her Majesty."

Jillaine's eyes widened so much, Quinn could see the whites around them. The effort of holding the mill wheel fast taxed his will, as if he were holding a heavy sack in an awkward position. "I can't do this for much longer. Someone please explain."

"The Caralissian queen is not one of the Enclave's most ardent supporters. If she's gotten wind of our presence here, we could be in danger." Moric drew a palm-sized circle in the air in front of him, whispered something, and caused it to turn opaque. One of his scrying windows, no doubt. Quinn leaned around for a look, and caught a glance of several horsemen, armed with lances and swords. Their bright yellow cloaks against the dark gray armor gave them an odd honeybee appearance.

"They've got some colorful outfits, don't they?"

"Goldcloaks," Moric said. "Caralissian royal guards."

"Are they as bad as the wine caravan guards?"

"Worse."

Delightful. Quinn ran to the door and slid the bar down behind it, quietly as possible. He slid his fingers over the wood, but couldn't find the hidden locking mechanism. "Might be a good idea to take us out of here."

"Tempted as I am to give Mott a stern lecture, I'm inclined to agree." Moric beckoned. "Come in close."

Quinn gave up on the door, just as someone tried it from the outside. A muffled shout came next, and then a heavier hit against the door. It shuddered, but held. It wouldn't hold if they really wanted to come in, though. He ran over to Moric, who'd already begun an incantation.

Moric put a hand on Jillaine's shoulder. Quinn cleared his throat. He sighed, and then brought Quinn into the circle. Like it was a big favor or something.

The magic brought a tingle to Quinn's forearm. He braced himself for the sudden chill as the spell reached its climax. But the tingle faded, and the chill never came. Moric gasped.

"What's wrong?" Quinn asked.

Moric began to answer, but broke off as something heavy thudded against the door.

"It . . . it didn't work."

"I gathered that. Why not?"

Moric looked up in the rafters. "The mill must be warded."

"You got in just fine."

"Some wards prevent one from entering. Others, from leaving."

Quinn could guess the kind of ward a bounty hunter operation would want on its main base. "We'd better think of something. That door won't hold for very long." He searched in vain for the heavy crossbow Mott had pulled on them, but the man must have hidden it well or taken it with him. *He's a lot more clever than he pretends to be.* He loosened his sword in its scabbard, and grimaced at the thought that he might need it. "If we surprise them, we might be able to fight our way clear."

"Whatever our plan, we must take care not to harm any goldcloaks," Moric said.

Quinn figured he must have heard wrong. *"What?"*

"It's a capital offense to assault a goldcloak."

"What if they attack us first?"

Moric shrugged. "The law still applies."

Quinn groaned. *Why can't things ever get easier instead of harder?* "So no fighting, and no escaping. Can we at least hide, or is that illegal, too?"

"You gave me an idea," Jillaine said. "You're not afraid of heights, are you?"

Two goldcloaks kicked open the mill door, ripping the bar right out of its frame. They fell back as three others charged in, halberds at the ready. Quinn would have admired this military precision if he weren't fighting to keep absolutely still against the roof of the mill. It was either that or risk falling twenty feet to the floor. Jillaine had lifted them up here. Her magic held them spread-eagled against the underside of the roof. Moric had done something to conceal them here, but cautioned them not to move. So Quinn's job, apparently, was to keep perfectly still and not freak out about dangling in midair above a growing number of well-armed soldiers.

So . . . no problem.

The goldcloaks swarmed the mill's interior, efficiently searching every hiding spot and blind corner. If they'd hidden down there, they'd have been found in less than a minute. The goldcloaks found no one, of course, and began grousing to one another. The officer in charge shouted something out the door at Mott, asking about the wards. The muted reply confirmed that they'd been set, just as Moric had suspected. Then the worst happened: the goldcloaks expanded their search upward, probing the walls with their spear-points. It was only a matter of time until one of them decided to chuck a spear up at the ceiling.

Judging by the sweat dripping from her face, Jillaine was fully taxed with just keeping them aloft. Moric seemed no better off. Which meant it fell to Quinn to do something creative. Fighting was out. His best bet was some kind of distraction that would give them a chance to escape. *Gods, I wished I'd had time to actually* learn *some magic on the Enclave island.* The massive mill wheel continued its soft grind, just a few feet away from his head. Well, he'd stopped it once, and he didn't have any better ideas.

The magic didn't come as willingly this time. He was already near his own limit. He forced it upward and imagined a massive hand gripping it like a doorknob. Holding it fast. It was strange, how the magic conveyed a feeling of exertion for this feat. It drained him as if he were the one holding the wheel fast.

The great wheel's newly imposed stillness was not lost on the royal guards, who nudged one another and shared nervous whispers. They edged away from the stone wheel. One of them made a sweeping gesture as if to ward off evil. When nothing further happened, they continued their search. Even if all of them found an excuse to keep far away from the mill wheel.

It's not enough. Well, if the guards wouldn't get out, Quinn would have to make his own way. He caught Moric's eye and whispered, "Will the wards still work outside?"

"Shouldn't," Moric said, his voice strained.

"Get ready." Quinn took a breath and focused his attention on the mill wheel. He added to the pressure that held it, and forced it to turn the other way. *Against* the flow of the river. The pressure of the water grew, fighting him. The wheel began to slip forward again. He dug deep, and forced it backward. The wooden framework groaned in protest.

Just a little more . . .

A deafening *crack* announced the snap of the wooden spine that connected the millworks to the wheel outside. The massive stone grinding wheel shifted down six inches, then a foot, as it crushed the supports beneath it. Then it broke through to the water, and a wide crack split the building's frame to either side. The goldcloaks shouted in alarm and shoved against one another to flee out the open door. The wheel tottered inward. Then the bottom part of the outer wall gave way, and it tipped back out. It crashed through the outer wall, taking most of the structure down with it into the river. The roof split along a seam right above their heads. Blue sky showed through the gap.

"Jillaine, get us out there!" Quinn shouted.

She'd already gritted her teeth and done something with the spell that held them, shifting them over and up as the rest of the mill began to collapse. Timbers from the frame slid against the soles of Quinn's boots.

Damn, that's close.

A cloud of dust rose up as the mill crumpled into a pile of debris, half of which fell into the river and began drifting downstream. Quinn, Jillaine, and Moric dangled precariously some forty feet above it, with her magic the only thing preventing a perilous fall. And she was waning; Quinn could see that from the grimace on her face. He'd have tried to help, but feared he'd disrupt her concentration instead.

And he'd taxed himself almost completely with the mill wheel. He doubted he could lift a blade of grass, much less three grown adults.

"Can you get us over the water?" he asked Jillaine. It almost certainly meant capture, since their splashes would alert the guards. The current was strong here, but not fast enough to carry them away before the goldcloaks could grab them. But it beat falling into the mill debris.

She nodded, and began shifting them out over the water. Then she gave a little sob, and faltered, and suddenly they were falling. Quinn squeezed out the last bit of his magic to nudge Jillaine close. He got an arm around her and pulled her tight against him. Maybe he could cushion the blow. But that little bit pushed him over the edge. His vision blurred . . . and then a strong hand clamped around his wrist. A sharp, sudden chill washed over him. He tumbled into darkness.

"The rift between Valteron and Caralis runs far deeper than we realized."

—R. Holt, "Alissia: Political Overview"

CHAPTER 7

STRANGE BEDFELLOWS

Veena thundered down a narrow road at the head of a pack of horsemen. Theoretically, they were her security detail, but the captain of the guards had made the mistake of suggesting that they "maintain a slow pace so the lady can keep up." That was about two minutes before she emerged from the palace stables with the biggest, meanest gelding in Valteron City. They'd stabled him down at the end, solitary confinement as it were. He had more meat on him than most of the poor excuses for horses that Richard had brought in, but stamped and snorted with the pent-up energy of an animal that needed exercise.

He *twice* tried to bite Veena as she saddled him. Once she'd mounted, he shook like he might try to buck her off. She pulled the reins taut to bring him under control. Didn't let up the pressure as they rode away from the palace. Nothing but consistent, firm discipline. By the time they'd reached the outskirts, she had him well in hand. She had to keep him to a walk, though, or risk trampling the stream of refugees that still poured into Valteron City.

At last, they turned north-northeast on a wider, less-traveled road. The guard-captain set them at a canter, spreading the riders out. Veena nudged her gelding up front, dug her heels into his sides, and never looked back.

She continued to savor Richard's surprise and slight consternation at receiving a complement of Tukalu guards.

"As long as you're achieving the impossible, perhaps you should meet with a delegation from Caralis," he'd told her.

"Why not?" She'd glanced at the Tukalu, who'd taken up a position around him and then gone perfectly still. "Looks like you'll have your hands full in any case."

The meeting, if it could be called that, took place on disputed lands at the boarder of Valteron and Caralis. The Caralissians had less of a ride from their capital, and thus had already made camp at the coveted two-notch hill that overlooked the border vale from the northwest. She ordered her escorts to make camp on the southeastern hill, but to raise no banner yet. The men eyed the Caralissians and grumbled about their uphill position, which she chose to ignore. Thus far, everything had gone exactly as Richard predicted.

Richard.

She basked in the luxury of using his name, of becoming part of his carefully laid plans for Alissia's future. He'd given her a vital but near-impossible task: brokering an alliance with Valteron's chief economic rival. A trial by fire if there ever was one. At the root of the conflict was Caralissian wine, the nation's chief export and one of the most valuable substances in Alissia. Caralis controlled every aspect of its commerce, from manufacture to delivery, including transportation.

That last bit was the sticking point. Caralissians distrusted sea-travel. They only shipped their wine overland, which prevented Valteron's trading empire from sharing in any of the enormous profits. That's what would have to change. She only hoped that the Caralissians would not demand too high a price.

Precisely one hour after Veena's men raised the banner over her tent, a lone rider detached himself from the Caralissian camp. Veena pretended not to watch as he rode down the little valley between their two hills and approached her tent. Everything about the man said *genteel*: from the high-stepping horse to the riding crop to the crushed velvet jacket. Even the posture belonged more at a polo match than a parley between nations. The hat really sold it, though. She couldn't help but think that the ridiculous velvet hat would do little to stop a sword blow.

"Good day," the man said. "My lord the Baron of Summertree bids you welcome, and asks if you would join him in the vale in an hour's time."

Veena nearly replied, but caught herself. She beckoned her guard-captain over. "Tell him we're just arrived, and it will be two hours. But you know . . ." She made a vague spinning gesture with one hand. "Make it sound fancy."

The guard-captain blinked, but offered her a short bow, the first he'd shown since meeting her. He cleared his throat and strolled over to the courier, with a casual hand on his sword-hilt. "Well met, good sir. Would it terribly inconvenience the baron to make it two hours? We would certainly like the time to put our best foot forward for his lordship."

"I will ask." The courier backed his horse a suitable distance so as not to cause offense—no small show of horsemanship in that—and spun about. He trotted back up to the Caralissian encampment, tarried for a few minutes, and then returned a few moments later.

"The baron would be honored if you could join him in an hour and a half's time."

So it begins. Veena nearly smiled to herself. The guard-captain looked at her. She gave a minute nod.

"Tell the baron we'll be there," the guard-captain said.

Veena spent the next hour and fifteen minutes in her tent looking up Summertree in Richard's archives. He'd catalogued the entire Caralissian peerage system to an impressive level of detail, even before going rogue from the company. Now, with most of his intelligence network reporting to him and the might of Valteron behind him, he was as good as the CIA. Better, perhaps, because so many of his sources gave their information voluntarily. There were Valteroni sympathizers in Caralis and vice versa. Richard knew how to use that.

The Baron of Summertree, it seemed, commanded some of the most productive vineyards in all of southern Caralis. That made him a man of some influence. Even better, he was a cousin to the queen and either fourth or sixth in line for the throne, depending on whose rules of succession you believed. The fact that Caralis had sent a member of the royal family said that they gave this meeting some importance.

Now all that remained was for her to steer it to her will.

They met at the appointed time in the shallow vale between the hillsides: Veena, the guard-captain, and three of his soldiers and an equal number of Caralissians. Summertree rode a horse that Veena

had heard about but never seen. Its coat was white as
Felaran snow, the mane jet-black and long enough to
be braided.

She forgot all propriety and blurted out, "Gods
above, is that a Percheron White?"

Summertree's eyebrows shot up, but he smiled in
a pleasant way. "I'm surprised you recognize it." He
dismounted and patted the mare's flanks.

"I've heard enough about them, but I never
thought I'd see one in person." Supposedly, only the
Caralissian royals were permitted to ride them. She
got the feeling that fourth in line for the throne might
be the more accurate calculation.

"Then I'm glad I brought her." He straightened
and tossed his reins to a soldier. "I am the fourth
baron of Summertree, of the Caralissian queendom."
He accompanied this with a short, formal bow.

"And I am the minister of cultural affairs for Valteron." She mimed a curtsy, but in jest, because the
gesture would be ridiculous in her tight breeches and
riding jacket. "You may call me Dahlia."

"A lovely name, for a lovely woman, to be sure."
Summertree's face clouded. "Though I must admit that
I hoped the Prime himself would be at this meeting."

Ah, yes. Caralis would *so* enjoy that mismatch
of station. She wrinkled her forehead. "I'm terribly
sorry. Is Her Majesty the queen here as well?"

He coughed into his hand. "Alas, the queen does
not travel much outside of her capital."

"Nor does the Prime." Especially now that Richard's magical protections had been revoked. Veena still didn't know for certain why the Enclave had made that sudden decision, but if she had to guess, she'd say Quinn had somehow instigated it. He could charm the rattles off a snake. No matter the cause, the effect was all that mattered. Richard was more vulnerable now than ever before. He'd doubled his personal guard, but that might still not be enough. So for now, he stayed put.

"I see," he said.

"It falls to you and I to conduct the business of our nations."

The baron let his disappointment show for just a moment before his smile returned. "So it does. And I admit that your invitation came as something of a surprise. Nearly as surprising as your generous new trading terms."

"It's nothing. We *are* neighbors, after all," Veena said.

"And yet I have the distinct feeling that you're going to ask for something in return."

"We ask for nothing."

He gave her a look that said *we both know that's not true.* His eyes were a color of charcoal she'd never seen before. Another perk of the royal family, no doubted.

"In fact, we would like to *offer* something," she said.

"If you are going to offer to ship Caralissian wine,

you needn't bother. The wine must ever be transported overland. Never over water."

"By law?"

"By royal decree."

"May I ask why?"

"First and foremost, it's a matter of caution. The integrity of our process ensures that every bottle lives up to the reputation of Caralissian wine. This is the promise we make to those who drink it."

"To those who can afford to drink it, you mean."

He allowed a smile. "The finest of things do not come cheaply."

She conceded this point with a gracious nod. "Surely there's a more practical reason for never shipping the wine. Other than caution, I mean."

"Did you know that every wine train travels with an experienced vintner, who ensures its quality and authenticity upon arrival?"

"I'd heard that, yes," Veena said.

"Did you also know that no shipments of Caralissian wine have ever been lost or stolen during Her Majesty's reign?"

"None at all?"

"Not even once."

"Well, the armed escort doesn't hurt." Veena had seen a Caralissian wine transport before. If memory served, there were more guards than barrels. The grim look on Logan's face had said something about their abilities, too.

"Believe it or not, there are those who would try to take our wine by force, or by treachery."

Veena spread her hands out. "It's a dangerous world."

"We consider it a point of pride that no shipment has ever been lost. Can you say the same of Valteroni ships?"

"You know I can't." Valteron had lost two ships in the past month alone. Even close to shore, the Alissian oceans were unforgiving.

"Then you must understand why Her Majesty insists on shipping the wine overland."

Veena sighed. "I do."

"I'm sorry. It seems we'll both be going home empty-handed."

"Perhaps we don't have to."

"Oh? What did you have in mind?"

"If we can't settle on an economic partnership, what about a strategic one?"

"A military alliance?" His brow furrowed. "For what purpose?"

"To combine our strength, should a common enemy threaten either of us."

"Why would you ask such a thing now, when we're at peace?"

"Let's call it an overabundance of caution."

He did not smile at her clever little joke. "Do you know something that we don't?"

"We have our suspicions of things that are happening in Felara. There are reports of an army. Well-trained and moving southward."

"Felara's a long way from here."

"A long way as the wine trains go. A much shorter way if one travels by sea."

"Is that why you called all of your ships home?"

"It's one of the reasons." Other things, like the census, were just a flash of Richard's inspiration. "If these invaders come south, they will find Valteron no easy harvest."

"How comforting for you," he said. A newfound concern traced lines on his face.

"I'm sure it's the same with Caralis. You employ more mercenaries than anyone else on the continent."

"That may be, but we hardly keep them all in the same place."

Because they're escorting wine caravans all over the continent. "Spread a little thin, are you?"

"We can certainly recall a considerable number of soldiers. But that will take time."

"How much time?"

"Weeks."

Now it was Veena's turn to offer a dubious look.

"Months," he admitted.

"You may not have that long." She made her tone casual. "If only you could find an ally with the strength to ward off an attack."

"Even with necessity, I'm not sure the Caralissian people will like the idea of an alliance with Valteron. I mean no offense, of course."

Veena laughed. "The Caralissians will like whatever Her Majesty tells them to."

"Perhaps." He rubbed his chin, as if pondering.

"How far is her palace from the border again?" Veena asked.

Summertree's lips quirked downward. "Not far enough."

She smiled, because she had him. "It's time we put the past behind us. Caralis and Valteron are more alike than they are different."

"I will still need to verify what you've said, and convince Her Majesty to agree." His tone implied that this was only a formality.

"Yes. And you should still recall your mercenaries," Veena said.

"Why?"

"I'm afraid we're going to need them."

"There's no way to sugarcoat it. We underestimated them, and we paid the price."

—R. Holt, "Assessment of Alissian Militaries"

CHAPTER 8

TROJAN HORSE

Logan crouched beside Mendez in the shadow below the docks, waiting for perfect darkness. Waves lapped gently at their feet. The briny sea breeze nearly covered the pungent, sulfurous swamp stink for which Tion was known. At least there weren't flies here, like there were inland. He still had occasional nightmares about the flies.

"You sure about this?" Mendez asked.

"I'm sure."

"It seems like overkill to me."

"The less Holt knows about our movements, the better," Logan said.

Apparently part of the reason Holt had recalled the fleet was to take inventory. Valteroni ships were appearing in ports up and down both coasts again, but with a slight modification: a wooden panel on the stern with hand-painted numbers. *Like a medieval license plate.* As technological advances went, fleet inventories were pretty tame. Logan was far more worried about the disruptive tech they hadn't yet seen.

"You ready now?" Mendez asked.

"Let's give it ten more minutes."

They waited in silence for a couple.

"You want to talk about it?" Mendez asked.

"About what?"

"You *know* what."

Not really. Logan still couldn't believe that the lieutenant had brought his family to the island facility as insurance of his cooperation in taking out Holt. *Guess I didn't know her as well as I thought I did.* The worst part was that he had no one to blame but himself. He'd not taken steps to protect Sharon and the girls as he should have. And somehow, he'd given the lieutenant reason to question his loyalty. Hell, she might very well be listening in on this conversation. Bravo Team had brought all new comms equipment, supposedly to offer better range and superior encryption. Yet given the recent draconian measures against insubordination, it was always possible that the new comm units had other enhancements as well. Like passive listening capability.

He gave Mendez a hand signal. *Comms not secure.* "Oh, you mean Bradley?"

Mendez crinkled his brow. "Right, Bradley." He signaled back, *why?*

"He wasn't ready for this." *Distrust. Lieutenant.*

"You say that about everyone," Mendez said. *Action plan?*

Logan shrugged. *Family danger.* "Should have seen it coming. I'm just saying."

"There has to be something we can do."

"All we can do is wait," Logan said. *Opportunity.*

Mendez put his left hand on Logan's shoulder. *Got your back.*

They lapsed into silence again, as darkness crept across the water. There was nothing to do but follow orders, for the time being. Logan hated that, but at least he had lots of practice.

At last it was dark enough to cover their movements. Lamps and bow-lanterns sparked into existence out across the bay. Two similar gold-hued blobs of light appeared on the Valteroni vessels.

Logan stood and stretched his legs. "Ready to get moving?"

"Thought you'd never ask," Mendez said.

They stepped into the canoe that they'd rented from a local fisherman. It wasn't the sturdiest craft, but the low profile would make them hard to spot, and nothing was quieter on the open water. Logan wouldn't risk it in high seas, but the winds had faded with the sunlight, leaving the bay's surface smooth as glass. They slipped out into the open water, paddles whispering into the water.

For a moment, it was just like half a hundred maritime raids Logan had done in his career. Half a hundred quiet missions on moonlit nights. A lot of them dangerous jobs, too. Really touch-and-go. He'd always been able to keep focus for three reasons: his training, his brothers-in-arms, and the knowledge that his wife and daughters were safe at home. Now that last part wasn't true. As long as CASE Global held his girls at the island facility, they were far from safe.

Meaning he was far from focused.

It didn't help that they were right on the other side of the gateway, too. And the gateway was half a world away. He didn't have a prayer of going near it until they'd taken care of Holt.

But God, once I do . . .

All he needed was one little opening. Once he had his girls back, and they were safe, nobody could touch him. And he'd make sure CASE Global didn't make the mistake of threatening them again. That helped him focus again, because he had an operational objective that mattered.

It would have to be enough.

They hit some chop as they got out to where the

Valteroni vessels had dropped anchor. Not so heavy as to make Logan scrap the mission—too many pieces were already in play anyway—but enough that he had to concentrate so the canoe wouldn't capsize. He hoped Ralf and Snicket had found something sturdier or knew what they were doing. Without the two additional crewmen, they'd never get a ship out of this harbor. They'd literally be dead in the water.

"Which side do you want?" Mendez whispered.

"Whatever's out of the wind."

They paddled faster as the hull of the vessel grew near. No movement on deck, other than the amber lantern swaying back and forth at the bow. Twenty yards out, Mendez stashed his paddle and readied the first grappling hook. These were self-extracting hooks with padded tips; they landed silently and sprang open on impact. By the time Logan brought the canoe alongside the ship's hull, Mendez had two lines secured. He took one and handed Logan the other. Then it was a quick, quiet climb up the paracord, a drill Logan must have practiced a thousand times.

Mendez beat him to the rail, the scrawny bastard. He held position until Logan was ready. They vaulted the rail simultaneously, landing with a satisfyingly minimal sound on the wooden deck. Logan crouched low against the rail and drew his pneumatic pistol. With his free hand, he secured the climbing line to the rail with a half hitch. Didn't have to look—his hand tied it by muscle memory—allowing him to scan the deck for the crew. There *would* be crew. Even in a friendly port with a sister ship nearby, the captain would have left a couple of men on board.

So where are they?

He signaled Mendez to proceed toward the front of the ship. The lantern light in that direction should make for easy hunting. That left him with a far more difficult zone to cover. Even with the sails furled, the masts and rigging made the deck a nightmare to traverse in darkness. He moved in a half-crouch toward the stern, eyes straining to pick any humanoid forms out of the darkness.

A distant click and hiss from the direction of the bow signaled that Mendez had found his mark. No thud followed it, which meant he'd gotten close enough to catch the man before he fell. *Sneaky son of a bitch.* He turned back around and walked right into a chain that dangled knee-high across the deck for some unknown reason. It clanked and rattled, right in the middle of a lull in the breeze. He froze, hoping it hadn't been noticed. No such luck. Boot steps pounded the deck to his right, heading toward the quarterdeck.

Where the ship's bell would be. *Damn.*

Logan rushed to intercept whoever it was. Two or three strokes on that bell would alert half the harbor and blow this whole operation. He tripped on a hatch cover, stumbled, but kept his footing. He saw the runner now, a narrow blob of gray against a patch of darker background. Almost to the quarterdeck rail. Logan's dart-pistol came up. He fired, but heard the soft *thunk* as the dart struck the deck instead of its target. *Double damn.*

He clambered over a beam and made a rush to close the distance. The sailor swung up on a piece of rigging to vault over the quarterdeck rail. The grayish form hung in midair for a moment. Logan skidded to a halt, drew a bead, and fired again. The dart hissed away. Felt like a good shot. He didn't hear anything but running boots for a second. *Did I miss?* If so, he was out of darts and too far away to keep this man from raising the alarm.

Wham. Something heavy crashed into a barrel just below the quarterdeck. Then it was quiet for three seconds before Mendez came hauling up from the bow.

"You get him?" he asked.

"I think so." Logan signaled him to move starboard and advance on the quarterdeck. He did the same, sliding to port a bit since that's where the crash had come from. Ten paces up, he stumbled on a pair of boots pointed half-skyward. The rest of the unconscious man lay across the quarterdeck rail. His arms were both pointed forward, reaching. Logan looked past them and saw the milky white tendril of a string that ran up to the ship's bell. He'd come within two feet of reaching it.

Mendez approached with his dart-pistol raised, spotted the fallen man, and eased up. "Cut that one a little close, didn't you?"

"I missed on my first shot."

"You *missed*?"

"He was running full tilt toward the quarterdeck. You try hitting a moving target like that, in the dark on an unfamiliar ship."

Mendez whistled. "Never thought I'd see the day, man."

"Yeah well, I got him with my second shot."

Mendez snorted.

Logan pointed his gun casually in Mendez's direction. "It occurs to me that I've got another round chambered," he lied.

Mendez held up his hands. "All right, all right. You got him."

They worked quickly to clear the rest of the ship. Logan hated to sacrifice the time, but it beat discovering more crew were on board once they'd hoisted anchor. The hold was empty, which he'd guessed when they were casing it, based on how high the ship sat in the water. It wasn't a hard-and-fast rule, of course—spices and other lightweight cargo could fool the best-trained eyes. Still, the fact that the captain and most of the crew had gone ashore made more sense now.

"Let's make the signal," Logan said.

They jogged to the stern, where Mendez extracted a lantern from the gear bag. The metal-and-glass construction resembled in-world lanterns closely enough, though a close inspection would reveal some key differences. Like the ten-thousand-candlepower amber LED, which would let it "burn" for eight hours continuously on the lithium battery.

Logan hooked the device to a taut halyard near the ship's stern at about head height. He hit the activation switch on the bottom. Amber light bloomed, casting its glow on the ship and masts and even the water. Probably a bit on the bright side, for an oil lamp, but Logan didn't want them to miss it. Once he was confident it wouldn't peter out, he and Mendez left it and set to work. Mendez climbed up in the rigging and began to unfurl the sails one at a time. There were four on the mainmast, another two on the mizzenmast. Once unrolled, they luffed quietly in the breeze and would keep doing so until pulled taut. Right now, that would be a little more work than he and Logan could handle.

Instead, Logan climbed up to the cockpit to acquaint himself with the controls there. Valteroni captains preferred a spoked wheel to control the rudder, and this ship lived up to that expectation. Once they hoisted anchor, a half-turn of it should point them out of the harbor, almost perfectly downwind. At least one thing might go right tonight. No surprises or concerns in the cockpit area—the logbook was missing, but he'd probably find that in the captain's quarters—so he moved on to securing the crew he and Mendez had knocked out. His mark had been a young man, no older than twenty. Probably the most junior lad on the ship. He'd been brave to go for the bell rather than try to save his own skin.

He was a light kid, maybe sixty-five kilos, so Logan dragged him over the rail to the deck without any help from Mendez, who was still playing acrobat up in the rigging. "You going to wrap that up anytime soon?"

"Hey, don't blame me. It's a lot of sail." Mendez ran quick-footed along the topmast and leaped around the main to the other side.

Was I ever that young and stupid?

Logan's comm unit buzzed in his ear. He hit the button to transmit. "Go for Logan."

"It's Kiara. What's your status?"

"We've got our Trojan horse and we're getting ready to roll it out of the workshop."

"Good. Anything unusual to report?"

"You looking for something in particular?" It wasn't like her to ask vague questions.

"Holt is up to something."

"Tell me something I don't know," he said. "What is it this time?"

"He's been meeting with the leaders of other Alissian nations."

"Which ones?"

"All of them."

"Where the hell does he find the time?"

"I'd like to know. The rumor has it that he's hired ambassadors, and they're just as good as he is at figuring out what people want."

"The only thing unusual here is that the belly of the horse is empty, if you know what I mean."

There was a slight delay; she was probably pulling up the latest intel on Tion and its exports. Logan had to admit that he'd never seen Valteroni trading ships sit idle while their crew lived it up in port. Every day they sat at anchor cut into the captain's profit margins: he had to feed his crew, pay their salary, and probably pony up for some port fees.

"How many crew were on board?"

"Two. The rest are on shore leave."

"Will they know anything?"

He heard the unspoken suggestion, that he and Mendez *extract* whatever information they could from the captured sailors. "Doubt it. They just drew the short straws."

"Make sure, and then get rid of them."

He hesitated. *Surely she doesn't mean that the way it sounds.* "Say again."

"You're to leave no witnesses," she said.

"We took them down clean. They never saw us."

"What would pirates do, if they captured the ship instead of you? What would Marundi tribesmen do?"

"We're not like them."

"Holt knows that. If someone steals a ship without any bloodshed, he'll guess exactly who was behind it."

"So?"

"I'd rather keep him guessing. This is war, Logan. No one gets information for free."

There was no point in arguing. Once the lieutenant got her back up about something, she wouldn't listen to reason. *Be the good soldier she thinks you are.* "Copy that, Lieutenant."

"I want another update before you reach Valteroni waters. Kiara out."

Logan sighed and walked down to the stern to brief Mendez. Ralf and Snicket had come aboard, and the three of them were making good progress with the sails. The breeze had picked up a bit, too. "How long until we can get moving?"

"We're just about ready," Mendez said. "What about the sleeping beauties?"

Bind their wrists and throw them overboard. It would be easy to give the order. No witnesses, just like the lieutenant ordered. No complications. How many people would she order him to kill before this was done? He couldn't predict that, couldn't control it. All he had was the occasional small act of defiance.

"Give them another dose, and put them in the canoe," Logan said.

Mendez frowned. "What happens when they wake up?"

"We'll be long gone, so it won't matter."

Thankfully, Mendez didn't argue. Ten minutes later, they hoisted anchor and slipped out into the open sea. The wind picked up as they cleared the narrow peninsula that protected the harbor. Logan ordered full sail and turned the ship south, toward the seas of Valteron.

"The best weapon against one enemy is another."

—**Felaran proverb**

CHAPTER 9

FRIENDS AND ENEMIES

Veena had done what Valteroni and Caralissian ambassadors had failed at for decades: brokered a formal alliance between their two nations. That wasn't even the part she enjoyed the most. It came instead when they'd broken camp and were preparing for the ride back. The guard-captain approached to hold her horse's reins as she mounted.

"Thank you, Captain," she said.

He looked around, and lowered his voice. "I can scarcely believe what I witnessed back there."

She smiled. "I'm in disbelief myself."

"Did you know that you might do this, when you came here?"

"I had some inkling," she admitted. "But I gave it low odds."

"It was really something, watching you work." He held on to her reins and looked at her. "Might be the second time we underestimated you."

"Let's hope there's not a third."

He put on a pained expression. "I know I'm not in a position to ask favors, but would you consider setting a gentler pace on the ride back? My men won't let you out of their sight, but I'd just as soon not kill their horses."

He almost sounds respectful. "I'll do my best, Captain."

She floated back to Valteron City on a cloud, basking in the glow of her accomplishment. She couldn't *wait* to tell Richard. Only he could fully appreciate the magnitude of a Caralissian-Valteroni strategic alliance. Undoubtedly, he'd been laying the groundwork toward this for months. Improving the trading terms that Valteroni ships offered to Caralissians. Building a military strength that could answer the looming threat. Summertree had never questioned Veena's claims about it, which meant that Caralissian intelligence sources in Valteron were at least as good as Richard suspected.

She passed no less than three new security checkpoints between Valteron City's outer limits and the palace itself. That was good. Maybe Richard had begun to give credence to the rumors of an imminent attack. She passed through the last security checkpoint and rounded a corner to the entrance of the Prime's offices. At least, that's what it should have been. Instead, she came face-to-face with a broad, featureless stone wall. "Whoops." She retraced her steps to the checkpoint and tried again. Left at the shell fountain, right at the bust of the former Valteroni Prime that looked uncannily similar to Albert Einstein. Then around the same corner and . . . no, a stone wall again. Odd.

She thought she must be going crazy, until she started back a third time and bumped right into Darius Blackwell. He grunted and took a step back, with a face that said he'd smelled something unpleasant. It brought a flush to the crescent-shaped burn scars on the side of his face, a casualty of the fire that ravaged his compound after Kiara's raid.

Veena still felt that pang of guilt when she saw the scar. She'd played a part in that raid.

"I thought you were in Caralis," he said.

"I've just returned."

"Weren't gone long, were you? I assume they said no."

"Oh? Why do you assume that?"

"Caralissians only care about themselves."

Veena couldn't speak for all Caralissians, but Baron Summertree hardly fit this description. "You don't give them enough credit."

"Or perhaps you give them too much."

"Caralis and Valteron want many of the same things. It's long past time that both sides recognize that."

"Are they willing?"

She didn't want to tell him the whole story yet, because Richard should hear it first. And Blackwell should perhaps not hear it at all. "I think they'll listen to reasonable discourse."

"So our enemy now claims to have our best interests in mind." Blackwell gave her a feral smile. "You'll forgive me if I'm dubious."

Veena didn't think the admiral was still talking about Caralis. She hadn't been certain if he recognized her from the raid on his island keep, but it sure seemed like he did. Yet it didn't matter right now. Maybe it was the saddle sores or her exhaustion, but the thinly veiled accusation in his comment irritated her quite a bit. She couldn't resist offering a little jab in return. "Still don't trust anyone, Admiral?" She tsked. "What a *fine* Prime you'd have made."

He growled something unintelligible and shoved past her to the stone wall. She remained there, savoring both her poke at him and the fact that she wasn't alone in getting turned around in this place. Then he did something, and a faint *click* sounded from the stones in front of him. A vertical crack appeared to the side, then widened as a seamless panel of the stone wall slid aside. Lamplight glowed in the space within. Familiar lamplight. It *was* the Prime's chambers. So it wasn't her imagination or absentmindedness that brought her to a stone wall. It was a new security feature.

Unfortunately, Blackwell happened to glance back and must have seen the surprise on her face. He snickered. "Seems like I'm not the only one with trust issues."

Veena glared at his back as she followed him in. Then she had to suffer the indignity of being held back by the two Tukalu warriors who were stationed outside Richard's inner chamber. Their hair hung in bead-laced braids to their waists, where each had two mean-looking axes tucked into their belts. The dark tattoos on their cheeks made her want to cringe.

They relieved the admiral of his sword, but let him pass without a second glance.

Veena would have followed, but the taller one with the scar on her cheek leaned in to block her way. "Who are you?"

"Veena." She caught herself. "Dahlia, that is."

The woman examined her fingernails, completely unhurried. "Is it Veena, or is it Dahlia?"

"It's both." She felt a wave of irritation. "I need to see the Prime."

"He's in a meeting."

A meeting that started all of ten seconds ago. She took a breath. "I'm aware of that, but this is important."

"Is he expecting you?"

"Yes."

"He said nothing of it. Best wait until the admiral is finished."

So Veena stood there tapping her foot outside the thick double doors, listening to the rumble of Blackwell's and Richard's voices from beyond and casting the occasional glare toward the Tukalu. They ignored her. Their chitinous bone armor seemed out of place here in the midst of Valteroni opulence. It was like encountering hyenas in a five-star restaurant. At last the doors opened. Blackwell took his sword and walked past without a glance, as if Veena were one of the wall fixtures.

"You may enter," the Tukalu woman said.

How generous of you. "We were on a ship together for an entire day, you know." She composed herself and walked in.

Richard—the Valteroni Prime—paced behind a sturdy wooden table that bore a hand-painted scale map of the Alissian mainland. The level of detail outshone even the company's parchmap design, though clearly they were the basis for this. Strange that Richard had never shown this to anyone when he was still working for the company. The research team would have killed for it.

He glanced up, as if sensing this burning question in her mind. "Veena! I didn't realize you were back."

"I've just arrived. I came straight here. Would have been here sooner, but your new *guards* kept me out."

The corners of his mouth curved upward. "By that you mean the Tukalu warriors you dumped on me before running off to meet the prince."

"Are they working out?"

"You didn't get in, did you?" He laughed. "I've never felt safer and more terrified in my life. Come, sit." He gestured to the table and chairs on the side of the room, a plain wooden set that might be found on someone's patio, if this world had patios. "Tell me of your visit with the Caralissians."

So she did. They sat at the little table, with her giving the report and him interjecting with the occasional burst of energetic insight. If she closed her eyes, she could imagine herself back in the research lab with him before he went rogue, giving the same sort of briefing in the very same way. Only he was a different person back then, and so was she.

"If we'd gone there to negotiate about shipping wine, the meeting would have been over even sooner," she finished.

"They may eventually come around on that, but it's less important," Richard said. "We implied that's what the meeting was about for two reasons. Can you guess what they are?"

"First, because a summit on trade is far less dangerous than a discussion of a military alliance."

"Good. What's the other reason?"

She really didn't know, so she considered what she

knew of Caralis and offered her best guess. "Because they care about the wine?"

Richard shook his head. "They know what they have, with the wine. They won't be bullied over it. No, we implied this would be about the wine so that they'd send someone who can speak for the royal family."

"Summertree rather implied he could do so, though he didn't say it outright."

"He was being polite. For the past several years, he's been Maya's principal advisor on foreign policy."

"Maya?"

He cleared his throat. "Sorry. Her Majesty, the Queen of Caralis."

"You're on a first name basis with her?"

"Ah, no. Not in public, at least. But I've known her a long time." He shook his head. "I still can't believe you got them to agree. First the Tukalu, and now this." He put his hand on top of hers. "I'm *proud* of you, Veena."

She enjoyed two warm feelings: the soft one from his hand, and the fiercer one in her belly. At last, someone who admired her work, her abilities. *If only I could freeze this moment forever.* If only she were brave enough to tell him how she really felt.

Richard's smile faded. He lifted his hand. "I wish my news were half as good."

Veena's warm feelings faded. "What happened?"

"Two things. First, that the loss of my arcane protections was no accident. The Enclave council voted to discontinue their quiet agreement with us."

"Why?"

"It's not entirely clear, but I suspect it was under the influence of your former colleague."

"Oh." She didn't want to say Quinn's name. It felt like a betrayal—which, of course, it was. He'd only been doing his job. "Gods, I'm sorry, Richard."

"As am I. It means we can no longer trust the Enclave magicians. I've asked Moric and his colleagues to stay away from Valteron."

"Is that the other piece of bad news?"

He laughed, but there was no humor to it. "No, we're still on the first one. The second is that over the last two weeks, nearly all of my sources in Felara have fallen silent."

"Where in Felara?"

"Everywhere within a hundred leagues of the gateway. My last update was from Silas, who runs the common room in Wenthrop. He said there was talk of an army to the north of them."

"Let me guess. Well-armed mercenaries in dark armor." *Armor that fit them perfectly and never rusted. Weapons that never needed sharpening.*

"I think we must assume the worst: that this is a full-scale invasion aimed at quelling any resistance to CASE Global's plans for Alissia."

"We both knew this would happen eventually," she said.

"Yes, but I'd hoped to have more time. Especially now that we have Caralis on our side."

More time. She stood, and studied the continental map. "How will they come?"

"By land, almost certainly. Kiara knows we control the seas, and they don't have nearly enough ships to move an army."

She ran her finger down across Felara to the border of New Kestani. "Nevil's Gap."

"That would make the most sense," he said. "The Felarans and Kestani have ended hostilities, so the Gap is open. They'll have no trouble moving men through in small groups."

"Unless the Kestani closed the Gap."

"I don't see why they'd change their minds so soon after coming to terms."

"What if we told them the truth? That there's an army of foreign invaders coming south?"

He shook his head. "They won't believe it. They'll consider it a Felaran trick of some kind."

"Maybe it *is* a Felaran trick."

"I don't follow."

"If they're more likely to believe Felara is the threat, let's plant those seeds of doubt."

"That's not a bad idea," he said. "Even so, it's a long way to Nevil's Gap, and I'm needed elsewhere."

"Then I will go."

He pressed his lips together. "New Kestani is not the safest of places."

"Believe it or not, I've been there before."

"I'll provide you a full complement of guards."

As tempting as it was to ride at the head of a column of armored guardsmen, she shook her head. "No."

"I'm sorry?"

"That will send the wrong impression. I think it might be better to borrow one of your Tukalu."

"*Two* Tukalu."

"Done." She strode for the door. She'd need to leave almost immediately, but she wanted a bath first. *No rest for the weary.*

"If you have to get out, do it before someone ups the ante."

—**Art of Illusion, September 4**

CHAPTER 10

ARTIFICIAL RETIREMENT

Quinn woke slowly, in a place so bright that it hurt his eyes even though they were closed. The ground felt soft beneath him. The air smelled faintly of salt and fish. None of it made sense. Then he remembered the mill and the fall, and forced his eyes open. He lay sprawled on a sleeping pallet in a one-room cottage. Clay walls, thatch roof, dirt floor. Someone had taken off his boots and sword-belt, and left both against the wall by the door. It was wide open, allowing near-blinding sunlight to stream in. *Not much of a prison, if that's what this is.*

He squinted against the sunlight and made out the shapes of a few small cottages. Beyond them lay a rock-strewn shoreline with waves crashing upon it, and then a seemingly endless expanse of blue-black water. A shadow darkened the doorway.

"You're awake," Moric said. "It's about time."

Jillaine. He tried to ask where she was, but his tongue was dry and cracked. All that came out was "Jill'n."

"She's down in the village, getting to know her cousins."

Thank the Alissian gods. Quinn sagged back against the pallet. "How long?"

"Since our run-in with the goldcloaks? About two days. You've slept the entire time."

"Then why am I still tired?"

"You overextended yourself, which obviously can be dangerous."

Quinn tried to wave this off, as if unconcerned. "I've seen you do it."

"Because I know my limits. Because I've been practicing magic since before you were born. You, on the other hand, are like a child who's found his father's sword."

He sounds like Logan. "I'm touched that you're so concerned."

"Don't be. I'm concerned insofar as you're one of my students, and a person that my daughter seems inexplicably inclined to spend time with."

"I thought that's what you wanted."

"I asked you to look after her, not *run away* with her."

Quinn sat up. He'd always known he'd have this conversation at some point, but he wanted his wits about him. He offered his carefully prepared response. "Leaving the Enclave wasn't my idea. It was hers."

"Why?"

"To search for you, for one thing."

"I was in Valteron. You knew that."

"I did," Quinn agreed. "But you asked me not to tell anyone."

"So you let her go on a wild chase instead."

"She wanted to see some of the world. She'd never been outside the Enclave."

"The Enclave is *safe*. You should have kept her there."

Time to push back a little. "She's not a child, Moric. She's a grown-ass woman."

Moric blinked. "I'm sorry, what did you say?"

"If I tried to stop her, she'd tie me in a magical knot and leave anyway. How would that be keeping an eye on her?" Quinn spread out his hands. "So I offered to come along and help protect her. I figured you'd want me to."

Some of the heat drained from Moric's cheeks. "You could have let me know of your plans."

Now he's not angry, he's offended. Quinn could work

with that. "There wasn't time. You know what she's like when she gets an idea in her head."

Moric snorted. "You have an answer for everything, don't you?"

"She was alive and well when you found us, wasn't she?"

"I suppose."

Quinn made his voice reasonable. "See? You've got nothing to worry about."

"Perhaps. But she seemed overly concerned with you."

"When?"

"In the past day. She never left your side, until I convinced her to go eat something an hour ago."

"Oh." That was a surprise, and a pleasant one, but he dared not let it show on his face. "Well, we've spent a lot of time together. We're friends."

"Do I look like a fool to you, Quinn?"

Uh-oh. "Um, no."

"You worked very hard to win my daughter's attentions, then you left the island with her, and now you're *friends.*"

He wasn't far off the mark, but the underlying reasons weren't ones that Quinn wanted to trot out right now. *Still, I've got to give him something.* "Maybe I hoped it would become more than that. But she's keeping me at arm's length."

That, more than anything, seemed to mollify the man. "Well, at least it wasn't a total loss."

"Glad I could cheer you up," Quinn said dryly. He rubbed his eyes and tried to squint past him through the door. "Where are we, anyway?"

"The safest place I know. That was my only thought, when we fell."

Quinn put that together with the cousins, the crashing surf, and the pervasive fishy smell. "Pirea."

"My home village, believe it or not."

"Your old stomping grounds? Oh, I can't wait to see this." He started to find his feet, wincing at the protests of pain from his legs.

Moric held out a hand to forestall him. "Before you get too excited, I should warn you that we're close to the Tip. I trust you understand what that means."

He meant the Pirean Tip, the northernmost part of the city-state. "Leward gave me a pretty good idea," Quinn said. *Not a good place to learn you have magic abilities.* Leward and his brother had barely gotten out.

"I am a mapmaker, which is why my work usually takes me far away from here." Moric's tone said that this was not to be questioned.

"Of course. And it explains why you're so . . . quirky."

Moric huffed. "I don't feel it needs to go so far. I'm perfectly normal."

Quinn snorted. "Don't give me too many lies. I'll get them mixed up."

"It's a good thing you've had so much practice," Moric said.

Touché. Quinn's stomach grumbled. "Is there anything to eat around here?"

"The boats should return in about half an hour. We'll eat soon after that."

"Let me guess. Fish."

Moric smiled. "As fresh as it gets."

"I can't wait."

"Which reminds me, it's my turn to get the cookfires going." Moric winked at him. "I'm pretty good with flint and steel."

Quinn laughed. "Oh, I'll bet."

Moric turned away, then paused. "That was a brave thing you did, to protect her as you fell." He strode away without waiting for a response.

Quinn wanted to follow, and to check on Jillaine, but his entire body ached like he'd been used as a punching bag. In spite of Moric's claim that he'd slept for two days, he still felt drained. The ball of magic within him felt muted, and used up. Well, as long as he had another hour . . .

He laid back and closed his eyes. *Just for a few minutes.*

He woke again in the dark of night. Starlit sky showed through the cottage's open door, and orange firelight flickered on the frame. Voices and laughter drifted in, atop the whisper of the ocean surf. *Damn, I was more tired than I realized.* He stretched and rolled to his feet. He took the boots but left the sword. It might be nighttime, but if someone wanted to hurt him, they'd have done it while he slept for the last two days.

Moric, Jillaine, and a few of their apparent kinsmen lounged around a fire-pit dug in the sandy earth between the cottages and the ocean.

His boots squelched faintly in sand, which rose up in small puffs at every step. That alerted everyone around the fire to his approach. Moric greeted him with less of a scowl than usual. Two men and woman, all of a similar age to him, gave him guarded looks.

"Well, finally." Jillaine offered a warm smile and beckoned him to sit beside her.

Quinn put on his walking-out-onstage grin. "Sorry I'm late to the party." There was a spot on the far side of Moric as well, but he gambled and took the one beside Jillaine. That bet paid off huge when she slipped her arm through his and snuggled up against him. *I might have snuck my way out of the doghouse.*

"You hungry?" she asked.

"Starving." He lowered his voice. "But introduce me first."

The two men were Sennic and Ulron, both cousins to Moric. They were tall and rangy like him, but darker from years of sun out on the water. The full heads of ash-gray hair raised the possibility that Moric was either unlucky, or chose to shave his own scalp clean. The woman went by Nicoletta, and it wasn't clear if she was married to Sennic or Ulron or both.

"This is Quinn." Jillaine squeezed his arm. "You *are* still calling yourself that, aren't you?"

He coughed into his hand and wasn't sure if she was kidding. "Yes."

"Are you a mapmaker, too, then?" Ulron asked.

"More like an apprentice. Trying to learn the ropes, as they say."

"What's it been like, having Moric as a teacher?"

"Sometimes I feel like he's more of a torturer, but there's never a dull moment."

Both men guffawed and slapped Moric's back. He smiled, though it looked forced.

I'm going to pay for that one later.

"What sort of things does he have you doing?" Ulron asked.

Nicoletta broke in. "Let him eat before you interrogate him, Ulron. The pot's ready." She looked at Moric as she spoke, though, in a furtive kind of way. Almost as if she knew a story about their real work would involve very little mapmaking at all.

She passed out wooden bowls to each of them, and they all six moved closer to the fire. A wide kettle rested on a metal grate above the coals. Quinn expected a soup or stew, but the creamy paste within lay perfectly flat, almost like a bowl of cooked rice. Maybe he'd missed the main course, and this was dessert. He was hungry enough not to care either way. His mouth was watering. Nicoletta broke the crust with a heavy ladle—and swiveled the handle around so that it faced him.

Ravenous as he was, he took the ladle and served Sennic who crouched to his left. Then he passed the ladle right to Jillaine.

Sennic gave him a side look. "You're not Pirean, are you?"

"No."

"But you've learned some of our ways," Sennic said.

Quinn held his bowl steady while Jillaine filled it. "It's a small price to pay, for food this good." *And it keeps paying off.*

That won him an approving nod from Moric's cousins, and even a little smile from Jillaine as she passed the ladle. He dipped a spoon into his bowl, tried it, and nearly burned his tongue off. The thick paste really held in the heat. It was thick but had a nice grainy flavor to it, almost like bread. "This is new to me, and here I thought I'd tried every Pirean dish."

"This isn't one," Nicoletta said. "It's Kestani sweet-grain."

"Oh, an import?" So Pireans did eat things other than fish. Quinn nudged Sennic with his elbow. "The fishing must be going well."

"Couldn't tell you. I don't even have a boat any-more." Sennic tilted his head at Ulron. "Neither does he."

Well, now I feel terrible. Here he was chowing down on a double portion, and these people didn't even have fish to eat. "I'm sorry. I didn't realize . . ."

Sennic waved this off. "No, it's not like that. I got to retire early, that's all."

"Oh? Well, then. Congratulations." Relief flooded him. He leaned back to rest while the stuff cooled. "How did you manage that?"

"Sold the boat to some foreigners."

"Yep." Ulron gestured around at the huts in the rest of the village. "All of us did."

"We kept a couple skiffs, just for getting around," Sennic said. "But the Felarans were desperate for deepwater boats, and they paid well."

Alarm bells rang in Quinn's head. He took a breath, and forced himself to keep his voice casual. "Felarans, you said?"

"A noblewoman showed up last month, looking for ships. Said they lost most of their fishing fleet in a storm."

Ulron gave a low whistle. "She was a stern one, too. Didn't take no for an answer."

"Very stern," Sennic agreed.

"You're just mad that she wasn't intimidated by you lot," Nicoletta said. "I kind of liked her."

Maybe it was all a coincidence, and a turn of good luck for some well-deserving Pireans. Quinn wanted to believe that, but the timing worried him. He looked at Jillaine. The crinkles on her brow said that she was troubled by it, too.

Moric held up his bowl so that Nicoletta could ladle in a portion. "So a woman shows up claiming to be Felaran nobility, and you sold her all your ships?"

"I know what you're thinking, Moric, but we asked around about her. Nicoletta's cousin sailed to Felara last year on a trade run, and knew about her back then."

"But hadn't met her," Moric said.

"Don't worry," Ulron said. "She even showed us her papers, to prove who she was."

"Convenient that she had her papers on her."

"I looked at them myself," Nicoletta said. "Everything was perfect."

Of course everything was perfect. Quinn knew he should finish his meal, but he couldn't make himself eat. He had to say something, though, because Moric clearly wasn't buying this. The man took a breath.

Quinn cut him off. "I'm sure it was." He lifted his bowl. "Cheers to your good fortune."

Moric's eyebrows shot up. Quinn gave him a subtle but clear shake of the head. Moric pursed his lips, and echoed the toast along with the others. He'd want an explanation for that, the second they were alone.

Quinn kept the smile plastered on his face. *I have a lot of explaining to do.*

"Talking to the audience is all about controlling the narrative."

—Art of Illusion, July 31

CHAPTER 11

RETURNS

Of course, it wasn't enough for Quinn to tell Moric that he came from another world. It wasn't enough for Jillaine to describe the scene at the gateway. Moric had to see it all for himself.

That's how Quinn found himself knee-deep in snow once more, leading his smart mule up an unforgiving mountain slope. Somehow he'd been *voluntold* to take the lead. Jillaine walked in the middle. Her mule followed without being asked. How she got a rapport like that with the animal, he still couldn't understand. Moric rode at the back, watching the mountaintops and doing something with magic that Quinn couldn't figure out. It made the hair on his arms stand up, though. At least, he thought so. It was kind of hard to tell beneath the two sets of borrowed furs that he wore to keep warm.

It's a mistake to come back here. He knew that, and had tried to convince Moric of it as well. They had no idea what the company had been up to over the month. Now, Quinn was beginning to imagine all of the ways that this could go wrong.

"How far would you say it is?" Moric called.

Quinn halted, grateful for the respite. He even remembered to ask his mule to "Stop, please," so the damn thing wouldn't run him down into the snow. He took a minute to count the mountain peaks and reconcile that with the mental picture he kept in his head. "I don't think it's far. Maybe a couple of hours until we'll have a visual."

"Good," Moric said.

"I still say this is a bad idea, for the record. The place could be crawling with mercenaries."

"You've said a number of things, many of them untrue. I'll be convinced when I see it myself."

I guess I deserve that. Even so, convincing Moric would be pointless if they were captured by CASE Global. He sighed. "Can you at least use a scrying window?" Moric had done so before, when they were hired by Richard Holt to escort Kiara and company back to Felara.

"I suppose so." Moric nodded in the direction of a copse of scraggly evergreen trees. "Let's try over there."

Quinn patted his mule's flanks. "This way, please." He took two steps toward the copse of trees and fell chest-deep into a snowdrift. "Jesus!" He scrambled back to the makeshift trail, cursing to himself, while Moric and Jillaine had a nice long laugh about it. His mule even snorted a couple of times.

"Mind the snowdrift, Quinn," Moric said.

Now you tell me. Quinn shot him a dirty look, then felt his way around the ditch. They shoved through the snow to the dubious shelter of the trees, where at least it wasn't as deep. The mules set about to cropping the few springs of undergrowth that managed to poke through.

Moric muttered to himself and held his hands in front of him, palms out. Light bloomed between them.

Quinn took a sharp breath. Pins and needles danced on the back of his neck.

Moric spread his arms wide, opening an opaque rectangle in the air in front of him. An image appeared on it, but that wasn't what got Quinn's attention. He'd seen this trick before. But this time, he felt like he might actually understand how to *do* it. He'd wait until he was alone to try it, though. *The less he knows about my breakthrough, the more he might be willing to show me.*

"Anything look familiar?" Moric asked. Snow-capped ridges scrolled past in his scrying window. Much of it looked the same as the wintry landscape they'd been riding through all day.

Then a kidney-shaped boulder appeared, and it rang a bell. "Keep going," Quinn said. Up that long, evergreen-studded slope. Just to the right of the twin peaks. *There.* "Slow down," he said, not knowing if that was even possible.

Moric made no visible gesture, but the landscape slowed to a virtual crawl. Which might be for the best, because if memory served, there was one more outcropping and then . . . bingo.

The tableau laid out before them, and even Quinn had to look twice. The gateway cave was entirely obscured by multiple interlocking walls. They were wood-colored, but had the unnatural sheen of a synthetic material. Blockish guard towers pockmarked the structure at regular intervals, and they were manned. Every guard cradled a nasty-looking crossbow with the casual readiness of born soldiers. They'd also built a prefab structure around the cave entrance. Quinn's heart sank when he saw all this. There was an air of grave intent to all of that infrastructure. A permanence.

It was a statement that CASE Global had come to stay.

"Now do you believe me?" he asked softly.

"Why couldn't you have been lying about this?" Moric asked, almost to himself.

"I'm sorry. I wish I was."

"Who are they?"

"Mercenaries from another world. From my world." It felt strange to admit that to Moric, even though his daughter already knew. Confessing to her had felt like a grand gesture. Confessing to him felt like a setup for disappointment.

"How did they get here?" Moric said.

"You can't see it now, but there's a cave in the hill-side behind those walls. You go in that cave, and there's a dome-shaped gateway that leads to our world."

"Gateway?"

"A portal, so to speak. Between this world and ours."

Moric nodded as if this were perfectly normal. He made no gesture, but began doing *something* through the scrying window. Quinn could feel it. He closed his eyes and tried to sense what this new spell accomplished, to no avail. He wanted to ask but figured that might be impolite.

"I make around fifty soldiers, give or take," Moric said.

"There were more last time we were here." Quinn looked at Jillaine. "Weren't there?"

"You dragged me away before I could count," she said.

"I'm sure there were more. Hundreds."

She shrugged. "Maybe they went back where they came from."

He shook his head. "More likely, they've gone somewhere else. Maybe on the boats Ulron and Sennic sold. They came here for a reason."

"I don't suppose you'd care to tell us why?" Moric asked.

"They didn't really loop me in on everything, but I know their top priority."

"Which is?"

"Removing Richard Holt from power."

Moric's lips quirked downward at this revelation. "And then?"

"And then no one will be able to stand in their way."

Moric let his scrying window fade, and said, "I've seen enough."

"What now?" Quinn asked.

"Now, we return to the Enclave."

"I'm not sure how warm a welcome they'll have for me, what with your . . . not being dead and all."

"How they welcome you is not important. This is a threat to our entire world, and the council must know about it."

Quinn looked at Jillaine. It was really her call, because she'd been the one who'd been so eager to escape the Enclave in the first place. She already had her chin tilted up, which wasn't a good sign. But she chewed her lip and finally said, "I agree, they must know."

"How soon do you think you can take us—" Quinn started.

But Moric was already chanting.

The crenellated spires of the Enclave towers cast long shadows across the island. Quinn rubbed his arms and sneezed. He'd still not gotten used to the magical teleportation thing, though this time had somehow felt different. As if he were starting to sense the enchantment Moric used to move them from one place to another. There were these *threads* tying the two places together. Like a tin can telephone, but with a magical tether instead of string.

But piecing that together could wait. Moric was already striding toward the crest of the hill that looked down into the Enclave's little vale. The last time they were here, Moric had conjured some kind of a platform and zoomed them down the slope. It seemed like half a lifetime ago. Sure enough, Quinn felt the distant tingling sensation as the air beside Moric's feet became an opaque square. He stepped on and looked back at them expectantly.

Well, it can't be that hard. Quinn stalked over to the crest to give it a closer look. The odd part was that the platform *was* air, somehow solidified into a block structure. The well of magic in him sang a note of encouragement. *I can do that.* He drew on the power until his ears buzzed. Electric spiders danced on his temples. Then he molded it into a platform of his own, a round concave saucer three feet across. It was solid, too. He tried not to think too hard about how he knew that.

Moric pursed his lips, looked down at the saucer, and up at Quinn. "Well, that's new."

Quinn nearly ruined the moment by trying to step on. It wobbled under his weight a little. He spread out his arms like a tightrope walker and fought for balance. Then he got his other boot on it, and the thing seemed to hold.

"You all right?" Jillaine asked.

"Yeah." He didn't dare look as he felt her summon a platform of her own. He was too busy trying not to fall.

"Shall we?" Moric glided forward and shot down the hill.

"Go ahead," Quinn told Jillaine.

"Are you sure?"

That I don't want you to watch me? Absolutely. "I'll be fine."

She glided away down the slope, light and elegant as a feather.

"Well, here goes." He nudged the saucer from behind. Gently at first, which made it drift forward encouragingly. Then he tried it too hard, and nearly shoved the thing out from under himself. "Whoa! Damn." Once he had his balance again, he gave the saucer a slow, steady push. It crept forward to the edge. A little more. He reached the edge, tilted over, and started gliding down the slope. Gravity took it from there, pulling him down the incline faster and faster. His cloak flapped behind him in the wind from it.

That's what I'm talking about. He tilted the saucer down a bit on one side, then the other, testing his ability to steer. It took a bit to get the hang of it, but he figured he could at least avoid major obstacles. He centered it again and then bore down on the front edge. It shot him forward, and the wind in his ears became a roar. "Woo!"

Moric and Jillaine, previously two specks against the distant greenery, grew larger as he gained on them. Which he seemed to be doing quickly and rather recklessly. He eased back on the saucer and let the lip come up, which helped a little. The slope plunged downward. He gained on them fast. *Too* fast. He leaned to one side to give Moric a wide berth. Otherwise he'd have plowed right into him. He shot past, startling the man as he careened down toward the bottom of the hill.

Flat ground raced up to meet him. At the very bottom, the edge of his saucer scraped the ground and almost sent him tumbling. He pinwheeled his arms backward, overcompensated, and fell right on his ass. "Oof!" His saucer dissipated into a cloud of dust.

Moric and Jillaine glided to a stop beside him, both wearing identical expressions of amusement.

So much for the grand entrance.

"Are you all right?" Jillaine asked.

Moric chuckled. "Not as easy as it looks, is it?"

"I like to learn things the hard way." Quinn stood and brushed himself off. The magic had fled when he fell, and now he lamented the hint of emptiness it left behind. "Where are we going?"

A chime sounded. It sounded like it came from above, only there were no overhead speakers here. A second, identical-sounding note followed.

"I was about to say to 'find the members of the council,' but it seems they're expecting us." Moric stepped off his platform and dismissed it with a wave. "It might be safer to walk."

"If you want to win big, you have to bet big."

—Art of Illusion, June 25

CHAPTER 12

INTERROGATIONS

The first time Quinn saw the Enclave's amphitheater, he had to prove his abilities to the crowd. Even with the dire threat of execution looming over it, the whole occasion had felt more like a carnival than a life or death trial. Now, as he approached the west entrance with Moric and Jillaine, he got another vibe entirely. It was already crowded with magicians, and all of their faces were grim. The last few stragglers who entered just before them avoided eye contact. The normal hummingbird-buzz of light conversation was notably absent, replaced instead with low mutterings of discontent.

If this were a theater in Vegas, Quinn would have taken one look and decided to call in sick.

"Something doesn't feel right," Jillaine said.

"I know," Quinn said.

Moric said nothing. His face might as well have been chiseled in stone.

Quinn yanked him to a halt by his sleeve. "Moric?"

He halted and looked down at Quinn's hand until he let go. "There were a lot of questions after your abrupt departure," he said. "The Enclave wants answers." He strode in.

Quinn turned to Jillaine. "I think he's still mad at me for spiriting you away."

"That's not why he's upset."

"Why, then?"

"He's the one who found you, and argued that you should be taught with the other students. He vouched for you more times than you realize."

"I've kept my promises to him. Even he admits that."

"Maybe he's still not sure where your loyalties lie."

We're not talking about Moric anymore. He had to say this just right. "I'm a magician, and I'm loyal to the Enclave. I can't say that was always true, but it is now."

She rewarded him with a smile, and a little sparkle to her eyes. "You still have a lot of trust to rebuild. This is how you go about doing that."

"All right, lady." He pointed a finger at her. "But stick around, because you're next."

She half-rolled her eyes at him, but she kept smiling. "Just go."

"I'm going." He turned and marched into the amphitheater with all the false bravado of a stage performer.

The scene within proved even worse than he'd predicted. Virtually every magician of substance at the Enclave waited there, seated in row after row toward the front. All of them wore dark robes with their hoods drawn. The unhappy murmur of conversation fell away to silence as he entered. They were looking at him. No, not just looking. He could *feel* their gazes, but every time he saw a face he recognized—Sella, Anton, even good old Leward—none of them would meet his eyes.

Like jurors with a guilty verdict.

Captain Relling, former head of Alissian operations and now the Enclave harbormaster, sat in the second row, all the way to one side against the wall. She looked so like her sister Kiara that he did a double take. She stared at him with open ferocity. Moric had gone to take a seat beside Sella. He didn't have to squeeze in; there was a gap in the front row there. As if she'd saved the seat for him. Which was either extremely polite guesswork, since Moric had arrived with him, or . . . *oh, shit*. They'd already known. *He'd* known. And he'd brought Quinn here with virtually no warning to face them all.

Damn, at least the last time Moric had brought

him here for trial, he'd given him the courtesy of a heads-up. *How far I've fallen.*

Given the face of such hostility, he felt that bluster was his best friend. "Well, it's good to be back here. How are you all?"

Not so much as a flicker of a response rippled over the audience. They sat in silent judgment of him, waiting for something. An apology, perhaps, or a confession. It depended on what they'd figured out since he'd left, what Relling had told them, and what Moric had revealed. Hell, even Anton could have shed some light on things if he cared to. There was no way to be certain. The only thing he knew was that this crowd needed some major winning over.

"I suppose you have questions." He took a breath, and let it out slowly. "Ask, and I will do my best to answer them."

A few heads turned to look in Sella's direction. The white-haired, matronly woman sniffed, and fixed him with a hard stare. "Why don't you start at the very beginning? What's your name?"

"It's Quinn, actually. But my family name is Bradley, not Thomas." That one cost him nothing. Lots of people knew both his stage name and his real one.

"Are you actually from Landor?"

"No." There was no point in sticking to his cover identity any longer, useful as it had been.

"Then where are you from?" Sella demanded.

"Felara." He saw Moric's frown, and knew he wouldn't get away with that one. "But I was born on another world. We call it Earth."

"How did you get here?"

"There's a portal between Earth and Alissia."

"What do you mean by *portal*?"

He shrugged. "I don't know. It's a doorway of sorts. A threshold. You walk through it, and then you're in the other world. Both sides have a sort of cave around them."

An odd thing happened then. Sella looked over at Moric, and something passed between them. They seemed in a rather intense—albeit quiet—conference with each other.

Anton took the opportunity to step in. "Is it a natural phenomenon?"

Quinn shook his head. "I don't think so. At least, we wouldn't call it such on my world. And it gives off a strange sort of energy when you're around it. A buzzing feeling." He couldn't describe it any better than that, but the sensation of being near the gateway was unique and inexplicable. Almost like standing near a powerful electrical transformer, hearing the hum, but not being able to see inside the box.

"Magical?"

"I guess it could be. Honestly, we've been studying the damn thing for years and we don't know."

"Who is this 'we' you speak of?"

Uh-oh. This had strayed into dangerous territory.

For him to blow his own cover was one thing. Burning Kiara, Logan, Mendez, and Veena was quite another.

Sella came to the rescue. She broke off her sidebar with Moric to demand, "How long has this gateway been in existence?"

"At least fifteen years, but maybe longer. It's well hidden on our world."

"Did you feel anything when you walked through it?" Moric asked.

"Cold. Like one of Sella's lessons at the stream," Quinn said.

"He wouldn't have felt it," Sella said to Moric.

"He might have."

"He's still a student."

"Not any longer, I should think."

Sella gave him a cool glance. "Only because he's been deceiving us."

"He has," Moric said. "But he's also been using magic."

She snorted. "You're as blind as I was."

Moric gestured vaguely in Quinn's direction, but didn't look at him. "Check him yourself."

"Fine." She stood with a huff, and set about straightening her robes. Which wasn't necessary at all, but spoke to her current mood. Then she fixed her predatory gaze on Quinn and marched right up to him. "Show me your magic, boy."

For the first time that he could remember, Quinn

had everyone's eyes on him and absolutely no inclination to perform magic. "Um, I don't feel like—"

"I'm not interested in your *feelings*. Show me!"

Quinn sighed, and lacking any better idea, he opened himself up to the magic enough to summon back the flying saucer. It took shape in pure white form beside him. He didn't want to risk climbing on it, given how badly that had gone before, but he gave it a little push and set it gliding around the amphitheater for effect. *Let no one say Quinn Bradley refuses to entertain.*

Sella sniffed in apparent disdain. "A little flashy for my taste. Do something about this." She made a casual twisting gesture and set Quinn's cloak on fire.

"Oh, come on!" He started to yank it off, but caught himself. She wanted magic. And the flames that licked up the edge of his cloak, while alarmingly close to the crotch, didn't emanate nearly as much heat as true fire should have. The magic welled up inside of him almost on its own. He imagined it became the frost of Felaran mountains, and sent it whooshing down his body like a wave. It snuffed out the flames with a soft *whump* and a brush of ice-coolness down his legs. He might have just given himself frostbite, but at least the fire was out.

"Satisfied?"

Sella grunted. "Doesn't mean he can tell us if the gateway is what you think it is." She turned her back and marched back to take a seat beside Moric.

"Wait, what do *you* think it is?" Quinn asked.

"That is not your concern," Moric said. "We will be asking the questions."

His wooden tone was irritating. He'd been so eager to get Quinn and Jillaine back here, apparently to facilitate this little interrogation. "Then ask one."

"Why did you come here?"

"You know why. So that I could learn magic."

"Is that the only reason?"

Damn. So much for getting away with half-truths. "My former employers told me to come, to learn about your relationship with the Valteroni Prime."

Stark realization passed over Anton's face, and disappeared just as quickly. If he made the mental leap to Quinn's involvement in the vote, he didn't bring it up. *Doesn't want the aiding and abetting charges.*

"Why are they so interested in the Valteroni Prime?" Sella asked.

"They want to remove him from power." That was the truth, if not the whole of it. Maybe it was the stage magician in him, but he thought he should hold back a little.

A few of the magicians began muttering to their neighbors. The distress was palpable, as was the displeasure. They really didn't like the idea of aliens meddling with their local politics. *If only they knew.*

Relling took the news stoically. The snarl had disappeared from her face, replaced with something closer to thoughtfulness. Quinn would have killed to know the reason why.

Moric stood and made his way to the front. "I would like to say something about Richard Holt, since I didn't have the *opportunity* to do so before the council took its vote." He shot Quinn a dark look. "Richard Holt has done more for Valteron than the past three primes put together. He came to power in the midst of a civil war, put an end to the violence, and made his adversaries into trusted allies. What other political leaders can we say that about?"

The audience had gone still. No one offered up an answer.

"Exactly," Moric said. "He also opened his gates to thousands of starving refugees, providing them food and shelter. His navy protects our ships and shores from piracy. And his *discretion* helps ensure that no one can find our island unless we wish it." He turned to Quinn, but asked the question loud enough for all to hear. "Why in the name of the gods would anyone want to remove this man from power?"

Quinn was beginning to wonder that himself. Yet he'd promised to give answers, so he offered up the best one he could think of. "Because he's from my world, too."

"At this moment, there are too many unknowns. What happened to the *Victoria* being just one salient example."

—**R. Holt, "What Is Our Endgame?"**

CHAPTER 13

UNEXPECTED PARTIES

The magicians told Quinn to return to his quarters in the Landorian tower while the council talked things over. It wasn't a prison sentence *per se*, but it had the ominous feel of one. *Return to your quarters until we come for you.* Jillaine promised she'd come to him later; she wanted to put her role as a council member to good use.

At least I have one champion in there.

At least, he thought he did. Because two hours had

passed, and no one had come. He took that as a bad sign. The last time he'd been here, he'd had three visitors before he set his saddlebags down. This time, not so much. Not everyone had been in the amphitheater when he made his confession, but rumors spread like wildfire in the Enclave. No one here could keep a goddamn secret.

Other than me, I suppose . . .

The only upside of returning to the Enclave is that he could openly practice magic without worrying about being burned at the stake. The trouble was, he didn't know how to do much that was practical. Hell, he didn't know how to do much that was impractical, either. So he focused on what he could manage: pushing small objects around, levitating things, making a flame appear and disappear. The process was surprisingly similar to mastering sleight of hand tricks. He got better with repetition. It gave him something to practice, something to focus on. Something to keep his mind off the fact that his fate might be decided in a room on the far side of the island.

Of course, it being Alissian magic, it also made him drowsy. He must have drifted off at some point, because he woke to the sound of an insistent knock on his door. *About time.* He tucked his spread of gold and silver coins—a small fortune by this world's standards—back into his purse, stumped to the door, and yanked it open. "I was beginning to think you'd forgotten—"

His words fell away, because the last face he expected to see was Captain Relling's.

This can't be good. He took an instinctive step backward, and tried to remember where he'd put his sword. Maybe she'd come to finish the job she started in that shack near the harbor. "What do *you* want?"

Uncertainty warred with the usual scowl on her face. "Just a word in private, if you don't mind."

"I *do* mind, actually. I haven't forgotten what a private conversation with you is like."

She held out her hands so that he could see they were empty. "I'm not armed."

He should tell her to get lost, and to keep the hell away from him. But he was bored, and frustrated with the council's silence. "I suppose I have a minute."

She checked both directions down the hall, entered, and pushed the door shut behind her. Almost like she was worried someone would see. Which she didn't need to worry about, because everyone on this island was avoiding him like the plague.

Quinn took up a position on the far side of his room, which wasn't nearly enough distance to make him comfortable. He'd seen how fast Relling could move. She had her sister's sense of efficient brutality. Warily, he said, "So, Captain Relling. Here we are."

She grimaced. "It's been a long time since I've been called that."

"At least five years, if I'm not mistaken. That's a long time to stay under cover."

"You can't begin to imagine."

"So, are you here to ask me whose side I'm really on?" *That's all anyone seems to ask me lately.*

"No, I think you made that obvious when you blew your own cover today."

"I'm putting my cards on the table."

She nodded, and the thoughtful look returned to her face. "What I can't figure out is why you didn't blow mine."

"Oh. Did you want me to?"

"Of course not. But calling me out could have taken some of the heat off, and strengthened your cause. It would have been good strategy."

"In the short term, maybe." He gave her a wink and a smile. "I'm more of a long-term guy."

"What's your objective? Blackmail won't work with me."

He nearly laughed out loud. *That's exactly the sort of thing Kiara would say.* "You've been part of the community for a long time. I didn't think calling you out would help anyone."

She gave him a measuring look. "Well, I appreciate it. And that makes us even."

He did laugh, that time. "By my count, you owe me one."

"You left me hog-tied in the boathouse."

"But I also didn't kill you."

"True." She gave him a flat look. "Then again, you haven't got the stones for it."

"Ha! Now you sound like Logan."

"Well, you've kept my secret, so I'll keep yours," she said.

He spread out his hands. "I don't have any more secrets. I'm an open book."

"What about your crush on Moric's daughter?"

Whoa. He coughed, to recover himself. "I wouldn't call it a crush."

"What would you call it?"

Quinn shrugged. "Admiration."

She shook her head, not buying it. "Just don't let it cloud your judgment."

He gave her a toothy grin. "It's a little late for that."

Quinn continued to wait in his quarters after Relling left, but no one else came. Which was probably for the best. Anyone seen associating with him now would probably end up with their own troubles. At last, he began tinkering with the magic again. He didn't have the concentration he'd enjoyed before Relling's surprise visit, though, and soon he was frustrated. He stretched out on the bed. It felt strange to be back in his bed here, alone and essentially imprisoned just like he'd been the first time.

He dozed off but slept poorly, and woke up feeling like he hadn't slept at all. It was early enough that patches of fog still swirled around the base of the Landorian tower and cast a gray pall over his window. He sat up and rubbed his eyes. He didn't re-member his dreams, but the sense of fear and panic lingered after them.

Morning already, and they still hadn't come to get him. Well, he sure as hell wasn't going to sit around here all day doing nothing. He tugged on his boots and stalked down the hall to the common kitchen, praying that someone had started the coffee. Sure enough, the sharp, bitter scent of it reached his nose before he even got to the end of the hall. *At least some of the Alissian gods still look after me.*

Then he walked into the commons to find Moric, Sella, and Anton waiting for him. They sat at the little four-person table by the coffee bar, blowing on mugs of the dark hot liquid and speaking in hushed tones. A hefty burlap bag sat on the table between them. Anton had a few wrinkles in his shirt, which was about the most disheveled Quinn had ever seen him. He sat across from Moric and Sella, who both had rings under their eyes.

Quinn bit his lips on the verge of wishing them a good morning, and went straight for the coffee. He knew he'd need it, and if they couldn't deign to knock on his door, they didn't get the regular pleasantries. He borrowed the same chipped ceramic mug that he usually did. At least that would be something normal. He cradled it in both hands for the walk over to their table, and used his magic to push the chair out far enough to sit in. This won him a raised eyebrow from Moric and a stern look from Sella.

That's right, just a friendly reminder. He might as well get the ball rolling. "You three look like hell."

Sella's mouth fell open. Moric choked on his sip of coffee.

Anton gave him a sidelong glance. "You're no morning rose, either."

Moric regained control of his faculties. "You've also given us a lot to talk about."

"Apparently so." Quinn blew on his own coffee, considered trying it, and forced himself to wait. These people brewed their coffee at a boil, and he'd just as soon not burn his lips off.

"I still have trouble believing that Richard Holt is from another world."

"Well, believe it," Quinn said.

Sella shot him a dirty look at that, but before she could bite his head off, Moric said, "I'm certain that they looked into his past before electing him Valteroni Prime."

Just as you looked into mine. But it seemed inadvisable, at this moment, to remind them that he, too, had put one over on the natives. "I'm told he's a persuasive guy."

"And the Valteroni can be careless," Anton said, predictable as ever.

"They weren't careless. Our people are just that good," Quinn said.

Sella sniffed loudly, the way she did before handing out verbal punishment. "Maybe they are. The fact remains that this conflict is between Holt and his former colleagues. It has nothing to do with the Enclave, and we see no reason to get involved."

That was good news, but strangely made Quinn a little bit sad. Without the Enclave, Holt didn't stand a chance against CASE Global. "I think that's wise."

Sella half-closed her eyes, an expression that said she plainly didn't care what he thought about it. "There's less of a consensus about what should be done with you."

Crap. "All right," Quinn said. "What sort of things are being discussed?"

"Everything from censure to execution," Anton said.

Quinn bristled at the casualness in his tone. "Execution?"

"Yes."

"For what crime, exactly?"

"Lying to all of us, for starters," Anton said.

"Oh, because you're all *so honest* to one another? Give me a break. You're going to have to do better than that."

"*We* are not on trial here. *You* are the one who came here just to spy on us."

"I didn't come here voluntarily." Quinn jabbed a finger toward Moric. "He kidnapped me."

"Because you led me to believe you could use magic," Moric said.

"I *can* use magic." Quinn forced himself to take a calming breath. The caffeine was kicking in, and reminding him of things more important than crabbiness. *I want to* help *these people.* And he had wronged them, so he supposed it was only fair to show a bit of humility. "Look, I don't deny that I came here with official orders. But I didn't have a choice. And when I did, I chose to do things to *protect* the Enclave. Is it really so bad that you've severed ties with Valteron, given what's coming?"

Anton shrugged in agreement. Moric seemed troubled, but didn't offer a counterargument.

Sella cleared her throat again. "Putting that aside for the moment, there's also the matter of you assaulting our harbormaster on the night that you left."

"She attacked me first."

"What?" Sella's eyes narrowed. "Why?"

Here was yet another dangerous path of conversation. He could tell them the full story, but the moment he mentioned how Relling had zapped Jillaine with the belt buckle, Moric would probably blow a gasket. Quinn still harbored the occasional dark thought when he remembered sitting in the chair, powerless, as Relling raised the club over Jillaine's unconscious form. Even though that was what gave him his breakthrough. At least he'd been able to stop her, and to save Jillaine. But if he didn't put this issue to bed, he might have to tell them about the harbormaster's origins. *Better to steer clear.* "It was a misunderstanding. She came by last night, and we straightened it all out. No hard feelings."

"Are you serious?"

"You can ask her."

Sella harrumphed.

Moric pursed his lips. "That's a serious issue resolved, then." He looked at Sella. "Surely someone who makes peace with the harbormaster deserves a bit of credit."

"Fine," she snapped. "I withdraw my suggestion of execution."

Now it was Quinn's mouth that fell open. "Sella!"

"You lied to me, boy."

"So the penalty for lying to you is death, now?"

"You did it *several* times."

Quinn was still in shock, but he didn't miss the undertone of hurt in that remark. "Gods, I said I was sorry."

"And I said I withdraw it."

"You've been a really great teacher for me. I'd never have broken through if it wasn't for your lessons. Near-fatal as they often were."

Sella waved off the compliment as if she didn't want it, but she sat a little straighter, and the sourness on her face softened to her usual level.

Two down, one to go.

"I have one more question for you." Anton pulled open the burlap bag and extracted a bulky object. "What is this, and why did you leave it on an island a hundred leagues south of here?"

When Quinn saw what it was, his blood ran cold. It looked like one of the crude weather vanes that Alissians sometimes mounted atop buildings, but this one was crafted in the R & D lab back on Earth. In theory, this was to boost the signal of in-world communications, but he'd long suspected—and Relling had confirmed—that it would let the company pinpoint its location. "Where did you get that?"

"I followed you and Jillaine when you left the Enclave. Your trail took me to that island, where I found this." He held it up and examined it on all sides. "I found it . . . curious, that you'd go to such trouble to leave a weather vane on a featureless island."

Of all the moronic things to get curious about. "I wish you hadn't done that," Quinn said.

"Why? What does it do?"

"It lets me communicate with my former employer. But more importantly, I think it's designed to help them find me."

"No one saw me take it. I'm sure of that."

Quinn shook his head. "It doesn't matter." He tried to think of a good way to explain modern tracking technology. "You know the wayfinder stone?"

"Of course," Anton said.

"It's like my employers have one, but it points to this weather vane. If you've had that since we left, then they may be able to follow it to this island."

A sonorous tone sounded from outside. Much like the summoning chimes, but deeper. The three magicians tensed, listening. It rang again, then fell silent. Anton cursed under his breath. Moric and Sella shared a look of dread.

Quinn stood. "What is that?"

They ignored his question, but pushed back their chairs and left their mugs on the table. Quinn trailed them as they hurried outside. All of them looked west. Moric spoke an incantation and brought up his scrying window. It looked like featureless ocean on the other side, nothing but water and sky with a blanket of fog obscuring the horizon. He and Sella seemed intent on this, so Quinn grabbed Anton by the shoulder. "What was that bell?"

Anton cast an irritated look down at Quinn's hand. Maybe he wasn't accustomed to people touching him.

"You might call it our border alarm," Anton said.

"I've got it," Moric said.

A dark shape had appeared in the scrying window. Moric did something with his hands to enlarge it. The single-masted ship turned almost broadside, skirting along just inside of the wall of fog behind it. At least a dozen dark-clad figures swarmed on the deck.

"What is that?" Sella asked.

"A Pirean coldwater sloop," Moric said. He gave Quinn a serious look. "They're a long way from the Tip."

He shifted the view again, and the deck of the vessel leaped into view. The men lining the foredeck rail wore close-fitting armor and swords on their belts.

"Are Pirean fishermen always this well-armed?" Anton asked.

Quinn stared at the figure who stood above them, on the higher deck beside the wheelhouse. He said something to the woman who held the wheel. An order, perhaps. She made an adjustment. The ship swung wide. The man reached into his cloak, pulled out a pair of binoculars, and swept them across the shoreline of the Enclave island. *Binoculars and flexsteel armor. Oh, shit.*

"Those aren't fishermen." Quinn looked at Anton. "You really should have left that where you found it."

"Never show the same trick to the same audience."

—Art of Illusion, March 9

CHAPTER 14

BORDER SECURITY

The *Victoria*'s bow crashed into another wave, send-ing up another cloud of salty spray that drenched Quinn where he stood in the bow. He wiped the water from his eyes, cursing, and tried to peer through the fog. *Where is it?* A blocky shadow appeared ahead and somewhat to the left. They'd made another turn.

"Ten points to port!" he whispered over his shoulder.

"Got it." Leward turned and jogged back to the wheeldeck to relay the new heading to Relling.

Thirty seconds later, the bow eased over left, put-ting the vague shadow more or less at their twelve o'clock. They still hadn't gained, though. *Damn, this is frustrating.* He probably should have been grateful to have cobbled together this pursuit at all. Moric, Sella, and Anton didn't understand the urgency, and there hadn't been time to explain. He'd given up on them and run pell-mell down to the harbor, picking up Leward and Jillaine along the way.

Relling, to her credit, didn't need a ten-minute explanation of what had triggered the border alarm. By the time the three of them reached the harbor, she'd already drafted five able-bodied sailors to crew the ship and made ready to get way.

"What set off the alarm?" she shouted, when she spotted Quinn on the docks.

"A Pirean sloop, but they're not Pireans."

She cursed. "Where are they?"

"Southwest, by the fog." He reached the gangplank. "Permission to board?"

"What for?"

"We want to help."

She paused long enough to give them a brief inspection. "On this ship, I'm in command. You do what I say, when I say it. Agreed?"

Quinn looked over at Leward and Jillaine, who both nodded. "Agreed."

"Hustle aboard, then. We're shoving off."

They jogged up the gangplank and helped cast off the lines. The *Victoria* was slow to get moving, but picked up speed as they left harbor. Relling sent

Quinn up to the bow and ordered Leward to act as ship's runner. She didn't try ordering Jillaine about, which maybe was for the best given their history.

That was maybe half an hour ago. The moment they'd pulled out of harbor, the CASE Global ship had fled through the fog. Now it was a game of cat and mouse to catch them before they slipped away. Quinn fought to keep them in sight through the grayness, which wasn't easy. The swirling fog played tricks on his eyes.

"What exactly is your plan here?" Jillaine asked.

"To stop them before they can reveal our position to CASE Global."

"How?"

"That's not up to me."

Leward jogged back down to the deck. He had the look of a nervous hare on his face every time Quinn made him relay something to Relling. "The harbor-master wants to see you."

"Keep an eye on that ship." Quinn ran down the middle of the ship and up to the wheeldeck, where Relling stood at stoic attention. "They're fifty yards out, but we're not gaining much."

"That may be close enough. Did Logan teach you how to shoot a bow?"

"He wishes. I already knew. Why?"

"This is why." She pulled a little wooden lever on the side of the wheelhouse. A faint mechanical whirring came from the foredeck. A panel slid aside on the deck, revealing a wood-and-metal machine the size of a motorcycle.

Quinn stared. "What the hell is that?"

"Self-loading bow ballista. All you have to do is point and shoot. Think you can handle that?"

"I guess, but I can barely see their ship at all. It's going to be tough to hit anything important."

"It won't be in a minute. Try to punch a hole in their hull at the waterline. The ocean will do the rest."

"Aye, Captain." He ran back up to the bow and gave the ballista a once-over. It looked like an over-size crossbow mounted on a rotating platform. A steel-tipped bolt already rested in the long slot that ran up the middle of the weapon. He tested the movement of the base and looked down the sights.

"What did Relling say?" Jillaine asked.

"That we're about to come out of the fog." Better not to tell them the rest. He joined her and Leward at the rail. "Let's see what we're dealing with."

The fog receded, and with it, the muted silence. Canvas flapped as the wind shifted. Sunlight encroached on the grayness, and painted the world in color. Quinn shaded his eyes to get a look at their quarry. It was sixty yards out, on an almost identical bearing. Two soldiers stood at the stern of the other ship. Something about their side-profile stance caught his eye. Another spray of seawater blinded him for minute. He wiped his face, looked again, and saw the telling bit of movement.

They're drawing bows . . .

"Down!" He threw Jillaine to the deck and fell on top of her. Fire lanced along his back. The arrow glanced off his hidden armor and skittered away. *Sweet Jesus.*

Jillaine whimpered beneath him; he was crushing her. He groaned and rolled onto his side. He put a hand to his back and felt torn clothing, but no wetness. Good. It still hurt like hell.

"Are you all right?" she asked.

"Yeah." He grimaced. "I just need a second."

She looked up past him, and the color drained from her face. "Leward!"

The young magician sat back against the foremast with a dazed look of surprise. A white-fletched arrow jutted from his chest. A dark stain was spreading where it went into his chest.

God, no. Quinn scrambled up next to him, his own pain forgotten. The arrow had hit the left side of his chest, away from the heart, but there was a lot of blood. "Leward. Stay with me."

Another arrow slammed into the rail above their heads. They ducked and tried to shield poor Leward from the splinters.

"Damn it!" Quinn put his hand on Jillaine's shoulder. "Get him to the infirmary."

"What about you?"

"I have orders. Go!"

She opened her mouth as if to argue, but then

threw an arm over Leward. They disappeared, leaving only dark bloodstain behind.

Quinn crawled around the ballista and crouched behind it. He put a hand on the trigger and stood, taking aim. The two bowmen spotted him. One nocked an arrow while the other drew. He put the sights on the latter and jerked back the trigger.

Clack-THRUM!

The machine shook as it hurled the missile across the gap. It struck low, punching a basketball-sized hole through the deck at the soldiers' feet. One of them went down, clutching his leg. Nothing serious, but it put him out of play. The other scrambled behind a bulwark for cover.

Damn, didn't compensate for the yardage. But a double-click announced the arrival of another bolt in the ballista's slot. The second mercenary didn't realize this. He probably thought Quinn had to re-crank the ballista. He stood and nocked an arrow. Probably the bastard who shot Leward. Quinn drew a bead on his chest, eased it up a few degrees, and let fly. The bolt struck the man center mass and hurled him over the far side of the ship, taking out a few halyards on the way.

"We're losing ground on them!" Relling shouted. "Go for the hull!"

The next bolt was already loaded, waiting to fire. Part of Quinn's brain wondered how many more the machine had left in its magazine. He picked a spot amidships on the other vessel's hull, just above the waterline. The bolt would tear a gash in it the size of a basketball. Even on these gentle swells, the ship wouldn't be able to stay afloat for long. An hour, at most. Then it would sink, taking the soldiers in their flexsteel armor with it.

He'd been in the water once, in armor. He'd never forget the way the water pulled at him, tried to suck him down into its depths. He wouldn't wish that fate on anyone. So he brought the sights up and took aim at a different part of the ship, held it there, and pulled the trigger.

Clack-THRUM!

The base of the mainmast exploded in a shower of wood and metal. Their mainsail plummeted over, tangling up most of the crew in a mess of canvas and rigging. The vessel lurched to starboard, its momentum falling off. Relling veered the *Victoria* hard to port to keep from ramming them. She stormed up to the bow a second later. "What the hell is going on up here?" She saw the dark bloodstain against the timber. "Oh, hell. Who was it?"

"Leward. He took an arrow."

"Damn."

"I got their mainmast," Quinn said. A woman in flexsteel armor—presumably the captain—raised a white scarf and let it flutter in the wind. "Hey, look! They surrender. Who'd have guessed?"

"I told you to put a hole in their hull," Relling said.

"Isn't it better for us to have captives? I know how much you love interrogation."

She jabbed a finger at the opposing vessel. "That's a search and rescue team. They're not going to know anything of value."

"Well, still—"

"They've not only located the island, but now they've seen my ship. More importantly, they've seen me." She shoved him out of the way and took aim with the ballista.

"Captain—" he started, but she ignored him.

Clack-THRUM. Click. Clack-THRUM.

The missiles punched two gaping holes in the hull of the other ship. One right on top of the other. Cold, dark seawater rushed in. The vessel groaned and began to split right in the middle. Quinn could only watch, speechless, and the ends rose up and sank slowly, inexorably, into the abyss.

"You didn't have to do that," he said at last. His tongue felt thick in his mouth.

"This is war, Quinn," Relling said. "The sooner you realize that, the better."

Quinn dozed alone in a chair outside the Enclave infirmary, waiting for news about Leward. The young man was white as a ghost by the time they'd gotten here. Still breathing, but raggedly so. *What am I going to tell Everett?* Leward's little brother was a fellow student. A good kid, without any other family on the island. Quinn knew he should find him, but didn't have the strength.

A shadow fell across the open door to outside.

"How is he?" Relling asked.

Quinn forced his eyes open and sat up. "They got the arrow out. I don't know more than that."

She teetered on the threshold, then came in and sat down across from him. "What a goddamned mess."

He tried to laugh, but it made his stomach hurt. *There can't be anything left in there.* He'd gotten sick on the way back. Sicker than he ever remembered being. Mostly because he'd known that Relling was right. This *was* war. He just didn't think he was cut out for it.

The distant buzz-feeling of magic that he'd felt through the closed infirmary doors faded at last. That was either a good sign, or a very bad one. The doors opened. Sella, Moric, and Jillaine emerged. They looked exhausted. Ragged.

"The boy will survive," Sella said without preamble.

Relief flooded Quinn. "Gods be praised."

"Are you certain no one escaped?"

Quinn felt like he might throw up again. "I am."

"Good." She crossed her arms. "I don't like the way it happened, but at least we've contained the problem."

Relling caught Quinn's eye and gave a little shake of the head. *She doesn't think so.*

"I can't promise that," Quinn said. "They may

have gotten word to their superiors. Even if they didn't, the company will be suspicious when their men don't return."

"Then they know not to trifle with us," Sella said.

"Or they see us as a legitimate threat," Relling said.

Sella whirled on her. "What do you know of it?"

Relling shrugged, and looked away.

"That was just a search and rescue team," Quinn said. "Next time, they won't send another ship. They'll send an armada."

Moric looked at Sella. "It appears that neutrality may no longer be an option for us."

"I'm sorry," Quinn said. "I never meant to drag the Enclave into this."

"It's a little late for apologies, boy," Sella snapped.

"It's not his fault, Sella," Moric said. "These invaders have harmed a member of the Enclave. It must be answered."

"How do we go about doing that?" she asked.

"I don't know," Quinn said. He looked at Moric. "But I know who to ask."

Quinn stood in the crow's nest of the *Victoria* and tried not to think about how high up he was. He'd made the mistake of telling the captain that he was still spry. Apparently, this was her idea of a joke. Lookout duty. At least it gave him a bit of isolation from the likes of Moric and Anton. They'd been in a foul mood since leaving the Enclave. Maybe they didn't like leaving Sella in charge, though it made sense.

Jillaine had volunteered to stay back and keep an eye on Leward, who remained in serious condition. At least, that's what she said. She looked at Quinn differently since he and Relling came back without any prisoners. She didn't ask what happened, and he didn't volunteer it.

I hope she doesn't think I'm a cold-blooded killer. Maybe she just needed some time.

The council had kept things quiet, but ordered Moric to arrange a meeting with the Valteroni Prime. Of course, Holt had reasons not to welcome a sudden overture from the Enclave, given their recent falling-out. Yet Moric had somehow prevailed on his old friend to agree to a rendezvous. With conditions, of course, because both parties understood the capabilities of magicians all too well. Thus, magical transport was off the table for the delegation.

They should make landfall on Valteroni shore sometime today. That was Quinn's supposed duty up here, to watch for land. And to keep an eye out for the sails of other vessels as well. These might be Valteroni seas, but if CASE Global mercenaries were posing as Pirean fishermen, all bets were off. Until they worked things out with Holt, even Valteroni ships couldn't be trusted.

The mast trembled as someone climbed up beneath the crow's nest. *Watch doesn't change for another hour.* He tore his eyes from the unchanged horizon long enough to recognize the clean-shaven head. "Hey, Moric."

Moric scrambled up into the nest with surprising agility, caught his breath, and spun to take in the vista. "Quite a view up here. I can see why you like it."

Quinn snorted. "More like it's what I get for opening my mouth."

Moric smiled. "And here you were just telling me how you and the harbormaster had worked things out."

"I like to think she's got me up here out of respect for my seamanship."

"Oh, I'm sure."

"You know, I got a job offer from the ship that brought me to the island last time." Quinn put his hands on the rail and let out a long breath. "Sometimes I think I should have taken it."

Moric nodded. "It *would* have saved us a lot of trouble."

"I'm sorry about that, for what it's worth."

"Is that all you're sorry for?"

"No, probably not. But hey, I stuff my sorries in a sack."

"Now there's an odd expression. I suppose I shouldn't be surprised, given your peculiar origins."

"It's funny, isn't it?"

"What is?" Moric asked.

"The fact that we can understand one another when we're talking, even though we don't speak the same language."

"The polyglossia."

"Right." *Even the word for it translates. Unbelievable.* "I still have trouble wrapping my head around the whole idea. I'd kill to know how it works."

"You don't know?"

"No." Quinn did a double take. "Wait a minute. Do *you* know how it works?"

"I should hope so."

"Oh, you've got to tell me."

"How can I be certain you won't run off and tell this to your employers?"

"*Former* employers. I don't work for them anymore."

"Would you tell me if you did?"

"I've got my cards on the table," Quinn said. "I'll lose a lot more than my job, if they find out what I told you." *Or if they realize what I've done.*

"Oh?"

"There's no going back now." And now that he said it out loud, he realized how true that was. He could explain away the radio silence as having lost his comm unit. He might even be able to explain away the beacon, which they'd dropped off at yet a third island a few days ago, just to keep the company guessing. But now the Enclave knew about Holt and Kiara and the gateway. There was only one possible source for that leak. Kiara would see it right away.

"In that case, I'll let you in on some history that's little known outside the Enclave," Moric said.

"Oh, good. I like history."

"Have you heard anything about how the Enclave was founded?"

"We didn't even know the Enclave *existed* until you brought me there."

"There were once three magicians who were contemporaries of one another. Aran, Callum, and Maddalena. They lived in a time when most Alissians feared magic, when even claiming to be a magician brought persecution."

"Sounds familiar," Quinn said.

"In spite of the danger, in spite of the constant fear, these three found each other. That happens sometimes, among those of us with the ability. We're drawn to one another."

"Like when you found me."

"Just so. They were strong enough to defend one another, and managed to find more of our kind. They settled on the island, but they weren't done. Aran, Callum, and Maddalena set out to create three long-lasting enchantments to change the world's perception of magic." Moric looked at him. "Two of them, you know already."

"The polyglossia is one of them?"

Moric nodded. "The idea, I think, was to help us talk to one another."

"That's a hell of an enchantment."

"Well, the three forebears were, by all accounts, some of the greatest magicians our world has ever seen."

"I can't imagine what the other miracle might be, though."

"And yet you live in it, as do most of us."

Of course. "The Enclave towers."

"Their bones were pulled up from the bedrock. Each one styled like a country in the mainland, so that everyone at the Enclave feels a bit at home."

I knew there was something odd about them. "All right, then what's the third?" Quinn asked.

"Pardon?"

"You said the magicians created *three* enchantments."

"Oh, we've no idea."

"*What?*"

"We don't know what the third enchantment was."

"Then how do you know there is one?"

"Because—" Moric began.

"Just a minute." Quinn put a hand on his arm, and used the other to shade his eyes. A pale, fuzzy shape broke the perfect flat plane between the ocean and the sky. He leaned over the edge of the crow's nest. "Land ho, Captain!"

Other members of the crew took up the call, and word reached Relling on the foredeck. She looked up at Quinn; he pointed in the right direction, and she swept that way with her spyglass. *Oh yeah, I saw it first.*

And three of the crewmen owed him silver, because he'd gotten closest on the hour. He smiled to himself, then remembered Moric. "Sorry, you were saying how you knew there was a third enchantment?"

"We know it was cast, because it was the last thing the three magicians ever did."

The meaning sunk in, and Quinn regretted having pushed on this matter. "Oh. Sorry to hear that."

"We'll figure it out eventually. Hopefully while I'm ahead in the betting pool."

"You took *wagers* on the third enchantment?"

"Oh, you think you're the only one who knows how to gamble?" Moric smiled. "That's cute."

Quinn snorted to himself. "Just when I thought I understood this place."

"Now that we're close to land, I feel there's something I should tell you about my most recent trip to Valteron. It seems that, not long ago, there was an attack on Admiral Blackwell's keep, on an island in the harbor."

That can't be a coincidence. "Go on."

"I'm told the assailants took something of value from the admiral's vault. Granted, the details are murky. Most of this I gleaned from rumors circulating in the city itself."

"What did Holt say about it?"

"Nothing. Then again, the Prime was tight-lipped about most things when I saw him last."

"I thought you two were close," Quinn said.

"We are, but given recent developments, he's become far more circumspect. It was all I could do to set this meeting."

"Maybe someone should remind him that trust is a two-way street." Holt hadn't exactly been forthcoming about his true origins when he accepted the Enclave's protections.

Moric grunted in what might have been approval, or disagreement. "In any case, the attack on the admiral's compound left at least a dozen dead, and twice that number burned."

"Burned?"

"They set fire to the keep to cover their escape."

Kill, steal, and burn. If he ever needed proof that Kiara and Relling were sisters, there it was. "So they got away with it?"

"Not entirely. They lost one member of their team. A woman."

The news hit Quinn like a punch to the gut. "What did you say?"

"She fell overboard as they fled. Rumor is, the ship might have been able to come back for her, but fled instead."

"Gods." *And now I know which woman fell in.* Only Lieutenant Kiara would be hard enough to make that call. Which meant that Veena had gone into the drink.

Quinn had fallen overboard in full clothing and flexsteel armor once before. It didn't matter how strong of a swimmer he was. The weight pulled him down like an anchor. He remembered the feeling of the water closing in on him, and shuddered.

"I take it you know who it was," Moric said.

"A friend." *Jesus. Veena.* How had this happened? It was a mistake to bring her on the mission, to put her in the crosshairs of veteran soldiers. "Someone who didn't deserve it."

"I could say the same of Admiral Blackwell."

"Is he all right?"

"He's alive. I don't know more than that."

"That's a relief." Not only because someone hadn't died, but since Quinn was the one who'd helped put the team on to Blackwell in the first place.

"What I wasn't able to find out is why anyone attacked Blackwell's compound." Moric had a casual tone, but there was a question buried in there.

"He was holding something for the Valteroni Prime."

"A hostage?"

"Contraband. Things that could be dangerous to your world."

Moric drummed his fingers on the rail. "It seems out of character for Richard."

"I don't think he meant any harm. He only wanted to give us pause."

"To deter anyone from coming after him."

"Exactly." It surprised him a little that Moric saw the Machiavellian angle so quickly. *I keep forgetting he's the Enclave's enforcer.* All the more reason to get back on the man's good side. "Without that leverage in play, Holt's in greater danger."

"Believe it or not, the Prime can take care of himself."

"You don't understand, Moric. They'll stop at *nothing* to remove him from power."

"A fact the admiral can attest to, no doubt. All that remains for us is to convince him to let us help."

"Let's hope we can," Quinn said.

"Which reminds me of the second thing I meant to tell you," Moric said. "The Prime asked for certain conditions in order to take this meeting."

"So you told us. That's why we're taking the slow boat to Valteron."

"The Prime also wanted you to be there."

"He asked for *me*? By name?"

"More by description. But it was clear who he was referring to."

"And you're only telling me now?"

"If I'd told you this before, would you still have come?"

Now there was a tough question. "I want to say yes. But I don't know. What does Holt want with me?"

"We'll find out soon enough."

"The true test of sailors here is living through a storm."

—R. Holt, "Alissian Superstition"

CHAPTER 15

THE NEED TO KNOW

Logan took over the wheel from Mendez an hour after sunrise. A few white puffs dotted the horizon to the west and south. Thankfully, none had yet diverted course to make Logan's day more difficult. The closer they got to Valteron, the more ships they encountered flying colors that matched their own. It became a cat-and-mouse game of keeping his distance from them without giving the appearance of doing so. Once, another vessel came close enough that he put up the signal for *sickness aboard*. That turned the eager-to-chat captain around right quick. Trouble was, they left the signal flags up and then encountered a ship full of Valteroni chirurgeons. The damn vessel dogged them for half a day with their offers to come aboard and treat the sick until he'd lost them in the predawn fog.

"Get some shut-eye," Logan said.

Mendez shook his head. "I'm fine."

"You look like crap. I'll wake you in four."

Mendez didn't argue, and Logan watched as he trudged belowdecks. The ship life was taking a toll on him. Taking a toll on all of them. The air felt thick as water, and the lack of wind added to the stifling effect. Even under full sail with a decent tack, they were only managing ten knots. *At this rate, Holt will die of old age before we find him.*

His comm unit buzzed with an incoming, startling him. He wasn't due to check in for another hour.

"HQ to Alpha Team," came the lieutenant's voice.

He hit his transmit button. "Go for Logan."

"This is Kiara. What's your twenty?"

"We're headed south, close to the Valteroni border."

"Still?"

"The wind's against us, and I've only got a four-man crew."

"Anything unusual to report?" she asked.

Other than you calling me an hour before check-in? "No. Why?"

Logan couldn't believe it. Not only the death

count—and that was pretty bad—but the logistics that the numbers suggested. CASE Global rarely sent that many personnel in-world at once. The only other time it had happened was the search-and-rescue for the *Victoria*. So for almost forty men to be hurt or killed meant there was almost certainly more than that here. "What was this? A training exercise?"

"No. They're part of a strike force that we've been assembling for new strategic operations."

"How big is this strike force?"

"Two companies."

Christ, that's nearly four hundred soldiers. Easily ten times the number that Logan himself had trained, in his entire tenure on the project. "Where in the hell did we get so many?"

"We've ramped up the recruitment program since you left."

"Who's running it?" The last he checked, Logan was in charge of training, and was pretty sure he'd remember training four hundred new recruits.

"External contractors."

And that's why you didn't want to tell me. Logan had opposed bringing in private security forces or other third parties for in-world operations. Not enough vetting, and far too much risk. Raptor Tech, the main commercial rival, probably planted operatives in the private security companies CASE Global was most likely to hire. He was sure of it, mainly because that's what he'd do in their position. Clearly he'd been overruled on that front, so there was nothing he could do. But he didn't have to like it. "I hope you can trust them."

"Trust is a luxury. We need the manpower."

"For what, exactly?"

The delay stretched out to an uncomfortable length. Too long for her to be picking her words. That meant she was clearing something with the top brass. Either to put him on a need-to-know list, or maybe to cut him loose. Logan hoped for the latter.

She dashed those hopes a moment later. "I'm reading you in on a new operation. Tiger Paw."

Finally, an op name Bradley would appreciate. Or would've, if he'd survived. The thought brought a twinge to Logan's gut. He sighed. "Go ahead."

"We're assembling the forces required for a major military incursion."

"When were you planning to tell me about it?"

"When it became necessary, which is this moment," she said.

Thanks for the heads-up. "What's the operational objective?"

"Removing the leadership structure of our most powerful adversary."

"That's my job." He didn't like that she'd already made contingency plans.

"You're the tip of the spear. But Holt has built an entire organization of ambassadors and advisors. We can't afford to let someone else carry on his plans after you complete your mission."

"Like Admiral Blackwell."

"He's at the top of our list," Kiara said.

"Mine, too." Logan had faced him in combat once. The bruises still hadn't fully healed. On his arm *or* his ego. "But still, that's a lot of collateral damage. Valteron will probably end up in another civil war."

"Instability serves our purposes."

"Tell that to whoever sank your ship."

"Is that a joke?"

"It's an observation. A ship disappearing near the beacon that Bradley set can't be coincidence."

"As much as I dislike your tone, I reached the same conclusion. That's why we've moved up the timetable."

"How are you moving them south?"

"By sea."

"Is that wise?"

"It's our only option. Our advance teams report that the Kestani have closed the Gap again."

"Why?"

"We don't know."

The timing made Logan suspicious. "That's a long way to come across waters you don't control."

"I'm aware. That's why I have another mission for you."

He bit back a sharp reply before it could leave his tongue. "What now? We're already halfway there."

"I want you to find a safe harbor in Valteroni territory from which we can stage our operations. You can do it on the way."

Find your own damn harbor, he wanted to say. "Where does it fall in priority?"

"Number one."

"So we can forget the other thing, then." He kept his tone casual, but prayed she'd agree.

"I never said that."

Damn. "One and done, Lieutenant. That's what we agreed."

She was silent a moment. "This is not a negotiation, Sergeant Major. These are orders. You know what's at stake."

He knew, all right. But he wondered if she did. This entire conversation pissed him off. The potential breach with the private contractors wasn't even the worst of it. That honor fell to the fact that this half-ass strike force now required him and Mendez to run as the advance team. Which only gave Holt more time to find new protections. And, more importantly, made it longer until Logan could get back to his girls. "Isn't there anyone else you can ball-bust do to this?"

"You're the only team close enough."

He gritted his teeth. "What kind of ships are we talking about?"

"Flotsam. Every half-decent hulk I could cobble together on short notice. My flagship is a Felaran icebreaker with two feet of water in the hold."

"Wait, *you're* with the fleet?" He'd expected her to return to Command. To quarterback things from afar.

"Like I said, it's priority one. We're bringing about everything we've got."

She's coming right to me. The thought sent a ripple of cold calculation through him. A lot of bad things could happen out on the ocean. And she wanted him to tell her where to go. He took a breath and steadied himself. Pretended to think it over, when he'd already made his decision. "I'll see if I can find the right place."

"Let me know when you do. Kiara out."

Logan put his comm unit back into standby mode and rolled his shoulders, trying to ease out some of the tension. Plans and deceptions wanted to take root in his head, but he pushed those traitorous thoughts aside. Step one was to do as she wanted. *I'll worry about step two later.*

He summoned Ralf and Snicket to the cockpit.

"What's the story, boss?" Snicket asked.

"How well do you know the ports along the Valteroni coast?" Logan asked them.

"We used to work on a trader in those parts," Snicket said. "Took us from south Tion around the bend, a few days past Valteron City."

"Sounds like a pretty good berth."

"Yep. Was a shame when she foundered in a storm."

Wow, these guys *did* have some bad luck. "So you've seen some of the harbors in southwest Valteron," Logan said.

Ralf grunted. "Some more than others."

"Good. I want to stop somewhere before we make the press to Valteron City to resupply. Someplace *quiet*, if you take my meaning."

In other words, where no one would recognize a stolen Valteroni ship.

Snicket rubbed his chin. "Reckon we do." He looked at Ralf. "What about Kidney Cove?"

Ralf shook his head. "Too crowded."

"Lamphorn Bay?"

"Too shallow for us."

"Gustenmire," Snicket said.

"There's a navy outpost."

"Well, you know any better places?"

Ralf looked away. "I know one."

"Come on, *that* one?"

Ralf shrugged.

"I promised I wouldn't go back."

Logan had never seen the man look so discomfited. "Where are you talking about?"

"Nowhere," Snicket said.

"Ralf?" Logan asked.

"Port—"

Snicket broke in. "Ralf, *don't* say it!"

"Morgan." Ralf finished.

Snicket threw up his hands and stomped away, muttering.

"Port Morgan?" Logan asked. "Never heard of it."

"Most haven't."

It sounded too good to be true. "What's wrong with it?"

"Nothing. You'll like it."

Logan pointed at Snicket. "What's his problem?"

Ralf barked a laugh. "How much time you got?"

"Just tell me that Port Morgan will be private."

"Private as they come."

"Good." *The fewer witnesses, the better.*

"Stage magic makes money, but street magic makes friends."

—Art of Illusion, August 23

CHAPTER 16

TURNABOUT

Easton Dell, the port village on the Valteroni coast where the meeting was set, was the strangest Alissian settlement Quinn had ever seen. Not that he hadn't encountered a walled-in village before, but this one had been carved entirely in stone, as if a massive hand lopped off the top of a mountain and then carved out neat rows of houses in the stone below it. Relling took one look at the village's narrow harbor and proclaimed that the *Victoria* would drop anchor offshore. She left her first mate in charge of the deck with explicit instructions to flee if any ship but their own tender tried to approach. The ship was to be preserved at all costs.

She, Moric, Anton, and Quinn climbed down a rickety ladder into the tender, which was nothing more than a rowboat with room for six. Relling took up one of the long oars. Quinn volunteered for the other and quickly regretted it; he was winded after less than twenty strokes while the captain had hardly broken a sweat. She stared at the *Victoria* unblinking while she rowed, as if willing herself to be back on board it the whole time.

"I still don't see . . . why we couldn't . . . sail up to the pier," Quinn huffed. The three Valteroni ships, which were already in port when they'd arrived, had docked without issue. "Looks . . . deep enough . . . to me."

"It's plenty deep. It's the width of the harbor mouth that concerns me."

"I'm sure . . . we could fit," Quinn said.

"We could sail in without issue. But I doubt we'd have room to turn, and that makes for a slow departure."

"Are we in a rush . . . to leave?"

"We might be," Relling said.

"I thought this was a friendly rendezvous."

"It's a meeting with a former ally on his turf. We should be ready for anything."

They lapsed into silence as the roar of salt water on

stone announced their proximity to the docks. Relling began issuing terse orders. *Pull harder. Half-stroke. Steady on.* Half the time, he was guessing what she wanted, but she was quick to correct him whenever he guessed wrong. Funny how they'd been adversaries just days ago, and now he jumped to her orders without a second thought. A week on the *Victoria* was all it took.

Two men, sailors judging by their garb and posture, waited on the dock in silence. One of them threw a rope when the skiff drew close enough. Moric caught it, and wrapped it in a figure eight around a cleat on the bow. Relling stowed her oar, so Quinn did the same. The other sailor waited near the back of the boat, so he climbed into the stern and found a line there. He estimated the size of the post on the dock, tied a quick bowline, then tossed it to him. The man on the dock had the salt-and-pepper in his beard and the rolling gait of a lifelong sailor. He caught the rope, examined the knot, and gave Quinn a faint nod of recognition.

Oh, yeah. Nailed it. No one knew knots better than magicians.

Moric accepted a sailor's offered hand and clambered up onto the dock. Anton vaulted himself up unassisted, though Quinn could have sworn he felt a twinge of magic. He accepted the salt-and-pepper sailor's hand; the man had a strong grip cased in rawhide. Quinn was glad to let go of it. The sailors set off down the dock, and Moric and Anton followed. Quinn made to as well, until he noticed Relling wasn't moving. She stood as if glued to the dock, her eyes still fixed on the *Victoria*.

"Captain?" he asked quietly.

She tore her gaze from the water. "This had better be worth it." Then she stomped off in the direction the others had gone.

Quinn hurried to catch up with her. "Look at the bright side, Captain. It's our first away mission together."

"So?"

He made a grand gesture with one arm. "So now you get to see me in action."

"How delightful. Just try not to get us all killed."

"Copy that."

For the first time in recent memory, Quinn regretted not having Logan around to cover the security angle. The Valteroni ships were moored beneath the walled city of Easton Dell by the time they arrived. No one looked to be aboard, though there were men on the walls. Sentries. Probably just city watchmen, but he couldn't be sure. Logan would know. Aside from them, the village seemed all but deserted— doors closed tight, windows shuttered, and narrow streets devoid of people.

Moric, Anton, Quinn, and Relling walked down
the main avenue and through yet a second gate in an
interior wall, this one made distinct by the iron teeth
of an actual portcullis. Beyond that lay a cluster of
buildings around a sort of village green, where several people lingered under a tented pavilion. Relling
fell back a little. Quinn quickened his steps to catch
up with Moric and Anton. *Richard Holt at last.*

The former head of CASE Global's research program sat in the shaded pavilion with his legs propped
up on a long wooden table. He wore what Quinn had
come to recognize as merchant's garb: fitted breeches
and a light woolen shirt beneath a long belted jacket.
The leather boots seemed period-appropriate from
every angle except the bottom, which revealed soles
with the unmistakable tread of company-issued foot-
wear.

Those soles just happened to be visible as Quinn
approached, which probably was no accident. *That's
a message meant for me.* A gentle reminder that Holt
had the best of both worlds: the knowledge and tech
of the company's R & D lab, plus the considerable resources of Valteron's supreme leader.

Richard spotted them, but didn't get up. He put
his fingers to his lips and whistled. A squad of exotic-
looking fighters formed a protective ring around
him, their long, beaded hair rattling against chitinous
armor. They were taller than most Alissians Quinn
had seen, but unless he was mistaken, they were all

women. Regular soldiers in Valteroni livery appeared in windows and on rooftops all around the green. Everyone had a crossbow. Locked, loaded, and aimed at the Enclave magicians.

Well, son of a bitch. Quinn wanted to edge closer to Moric and Anton, who stood just outside the edge of the pavilion. But he also didn't want to be shot with a crossbow. The flexsteel armor was no guarantee of protection at this range.

"Richard, what is this?" Moric asked.

Holt put down his feet, stood, and stretched. His tone was casual. "I hope you'll understand our need for security, given recent events."

A dull thump echoed down from one of the over-looking windows, followed by a whimper of pain. Then a body fell out of the sky, thudding heavily on the grass of the village green. Must have been one of the crossbowmen in the windows. He appeared un-conscious. They all looked up to the window above, where someone else had taken up the crossbow, and pointed it unambiguously at Richard Holt.

Quinn smiled to himself. *Nice work, Captain.*

"You have your security. We have ours," Moric said. "And I should remind you that the consequences of harming a member of our guild apply to *everyone.* Even the Valteroni Prime."

"There's no need for theatrics, Moric. It's not you that I'm worried about." Holt sauntered past him and Anton—which caused visible irritation on the latter's face—and approached Quinn where he stood. His exotic guards floated after him like orbiting moons. Relling kept a bead on him with the crossbow, which basically meant she ended up pointing in Quinn's direction, too. *Perfect.* Hopefully she wouldn't get an itch near her trigger finger.

"You must be Quinn," Holt said. Emerald fire burned in his eyes, but whether it was curiosity or simmering anger was difficult to tell. His guards spread out to encircle both of them. None had drawn weapons, but they looked capable of doing plenty of damage with their bare hands.

Quinn did his best to ignore them, and put on his stage grin. "You must be Richard."

"I've heard a lot about you."

"Not as much as I've heard about you, I'd wager." It was strange, because after reading so many of his reports, and hearing so many stories about him from the rest of the team, Quinn almost felt like he knew him.

Holt stared at him. "Well, at least they didn't exaggerate. You *are* a handsome devil."

Quinn laughed in spite of himself. "You're not so bad yourself."

The tension that had settled on the village green eased a little. "Do you mind if I search you?" Holt asked.

"Why not?" *It beats dying in a hail of crossbow bolts.*

Holt stepped close and looked into Quinn's right ear, then moved around to check out his left. "Where's your comm unit?"

"Smashed into pieces, and scattered in the ocean." Sure, it had been Relling who'd done the first part, but he elected not to offer that little detail.

"Well, that's a point in your favor."

Quinn shrugged. "I don't need it anymore."

Holt continued his up-close inspection. He poked Quinn's chest and didn't seem surprised at the flex-steel armor beneath his shirt. Then his eyes fell to the hilt of Quinn's sword.

"A short sword?" He chuckled. "Well, Logan's consistent as ever."

Hearing the big man's name spoken here so casually was surreal. "For the record, I asked for a rapier," Quinn said.

"You any good with this thing?"

"I'm trying not to find that out."

"Smart man." Holt pushed up Quinn's sleeves next and checked his wrists. He found nothing there but the sleeve of the flexsteel armor. His bushy eyebrows knitted together.

"Something wrong?" Quinn asked.

"Not wrong, but mysterious." Holt patted him down around the waist, still looking for something. Which put him in nice and close for a light-fingered move Quinn had just been dying to practice. A minuscule slice of air to part the leather cord, a three-fingered catch, and the tuck up his sleeve.

"When your ship appeared out on the harbor, I thought I'd seen a ghost," Holt said, low enough that only Quinn could hear. "And up there behind that crossbow, I could swear I see another."

He hadn't so much as blinked when Relling took out his crossbowman. Quinn would have to be careful in telling him anything.

Damn, what a cool customer. "No one else knows."

"Not even our former colleagues?"

"Especially not them."

Holt paused to regard him with a hawk-like stare. "More and more curious." He stepped back, finished with his inspection.

But still worried about me. "Satisfied?" Quinn asked.

"Not in the least."

"What exactly are you looking for?"

"Answers," Holt said.

"Are you going to tell me the questions, or do I have to guess?"

"You've been working against me for some time. Why the sudden change of heart?"

"Because I don't want anything to happen to the Enclave."

"And yet you put them at risk."

Touché. "Well, in my defense, so did you."

"You're not ex-military, and almost certainly not a spook."

"How do you know?"

"You're too chatty."

Whoops. Quinn smiled. "You've got me there."

"That leaves few rational possibilities. My best guess is that you're of a stripe with Penn and Teller."

Damn, he's good. "Two for two."

Holt nodded, as if this were only confirmation of something he already knew. "You must be very good, to have carried on the act this long."

"Oh, it's no act."

Holt chuckled. "Come now, Quinn. You can't expect me to sell me on this ruse, given what I know."

"Then can I ask you a question?"

"Certainly."

"Where's your purse?"

Holt's hand went to his belt. His eyebrows shot up. They climbed even higher when Quinn produced his purse and offered it back to him.

He accepted it with a nod. "That's pretty good. But it proves nothing."

I'd like to see you pull that off. A jaded witness was always the hardest to convince.

The magic inside pulsed willingly, so Quinn sighed and let it flow outward. He shaped it in a familiar way, so that a grapefruit-sized orb of golden fire bloomed in the air between him and Holt. It shimmered and danced there, more of an ornament than a threat. Still, the Prime's fierce bodyguards shrank back from it like they would a leper.

"Extraordinary," Holt breathed. He leaned closer to inspect the orb, curious where the others were afraid.

"Maybe don't get too close," Quinn said. "I'm still new at this."

"The fact that you can do it at all is simply astonishing." Holt shook his head, almost in disbelief. "This world continues to surprise me."

"That's saying something, considering that you know it better than anyone." Here was the world expert on Alissia, and acted like a kid in a candy store at the merest hint of Alissian magic. That innocent zeal carried no small weight in Quinn's estimation. *This guy gets it.* He was beginning to understand how such a man accomplished all that he had.

Holt looked at him carefully, as if sizing him up in the context of new information. "You raise questions more quickly than you answer them, but for the moment I'm satisfied." He made an open-handed gesture to his guards, who took a step back and came down from the balls of their feet. The crossbowmen, too, lowered their weapons.

Quinn took what felt like his first full breath in a long while. In the direction of Moric and Anton, a faint but notable tingling of magic that he'd hardly noticed dissipated into the void. The feeling was so subtle, he almost missed it.

They were ready for anything. The thought disturbed him more than a little. They'd both acted like reconciling with Holt was a given. The fact that they'd been unsure told Quinn how close a thing this was.

"Come and sit." Holt gestured grandly toward the pavilion. "I believe we have a great deal to discuss."

Quinn's top two goals were to avoid a violent death at the hands of Holt's exotic guardswomen, and to make sure he was present when the Valteroni Prime reunited with the former head of Alissian operations. Richard Holt and Captain Relling, oddly enough, had been among the first CASE Global employees to enter Alissia. Now, the company listed one of them as "Missing, presumed dead" and hoped to put the other into that category as well.

Once Holt invited them into the pavilion, it signaled to most of the weapon-carrying folks in the stone village that bloodshed would be avoided, at least initially. The guardswomen congregated in a distant corner of the village green. One of them produced a palm-sized leather ball, and they began a vigorous juggling game to prevent it from touching the ground. Feet, shoulders, knees, and the building could touch the ball, but hands could not. There was a song that went with the game, apparently, and if there actual words to it, they didn't translate. Quinn couldn't decide which was more distracting: the astonishing dexterity that these lithe women seemed to take for granted, or the massive pile of weapons they'd tossed aside before they started to play.

Relling eventually appeared at ground level, the crossbow still in her hand. She carried this over to the shady section where the man she'd thrown out the window had been propped against a wall. He appeared shaken but conscious, accepting his weapon back and exchanging some quiet words with Relling. At one point, they even shared a laugh about something. Quinn couldn't imagine what.

Then Relling approached the pavilion at the green's center. Her normal purposeful stride faltered into an uncertain kind of tiptoe. Her gloved hands twitched, already missing the comforting handle of the crossbow. Quinn watched her coming out of the corner of his eye. He flashed her a hand signal drilled into him by Logan, the one that meant *five by five*. In other words, everything's good here. She saw it, got the message, gave him a strange look, and then lurched into the pavilion.

Holt stood and smiled at her, a friendly expression that made no assumptions. Moric stood as well. "This is our harbormaster. She goes by Relling, and we still haven't gotten her to tell us her first name."

"In that case, I'll offer mine." Holt extended a hand. "Richard Holt."

Relling hesitated a heartbeat before she shook it. "Good to meet you."

Their handshake lasted a moment longer than

usual, and something passed between their faces, but Quinn would have missed these things if he weren't watching for them. He was almost disappointed. Holt had reason to be the most surprised—Relling had certainly gotten word of his defection, for lack of a better word—but he seemed to take the information in stride. That either made him about the coolest customer Quinn had ever met, or suggested that he knew more than he let on. After all, he'd certainly withheld information about the Enclave from his reports to CASE Global. Moric claimed that Holt never set foot on the island himself, but he still might have gotten wind of a certain ship anchored in its harbor.

Curiouser and curiouser indeed.

"Let us agree on a few common principles," Holt said, once everyone had taken a seat around the table. "First, that we are united in one penultimate goal: defending Alissia from a powerful enemy. Second, that we are almost certainly outmatched in technology and resources. And third, that this is war. It will demand sacrifices of all of us."

War. Right up until Holt said the word, Quinn hadn't thought of it that way. A conflict, perhaps. An invasion, certainly. But war took it to a whole new level. War meant death, destruction, and heartbreak. *Maybe I made a mistake to bring the Enclave into this.* But CASE Global knew where it was. And it was probably his fault.

"The Enclave has usually avoided conflicts on the mainland," Moric said, as if reading his mind. "For as long as I've been on the council, I've believed our greatest safety lies in obscurity. Others have had different opinions." He looked from Anton to Quinn.

Quinn winced, but Anton made no reaction.

"Even so, that is a luxury of the past," Moric continued. "The council feels that the threat is too grave for us to ignore. If you can use our help, you will have it."

"And mine," Relling said suddenly.

Quinn felt like his eyes would bulge out of his head. *Relling stepping up on her own?* He really should look into this person she'd met who'd swung her so firmly over to the Alissian side.

Even Holt looked stunned. "Really?"

"I may remember a thing or two from a past life that could be useful."

"She's got a pretty nice ship, too," Quinn said.

"Well, I'm certainly not going to decline such generous offers, because we can use all of you," Holt said. "We have also secured an alliance with our easterly neighbor."

Anton choked on his wine and had a coughing fit. "When did this happen?"

"Less than a fortnight ago."

"Gods." Anton sat back with a stunned look on his face.

Holt smiled. "Their militia will nearly double our numbers."

"And give you control of the largest army on the continent," Moric said. "Will that be enough?"

"I believe it will." Holt unrolled a large map of the Alissian mainland. "Here's what I have in mind."

"Successful magicians are always learning, always practicing. Hidden skills are how we stack the deck."

—**Art of Illusion, October 30**

CHAPTER 17

PLAYING WITH FIRE

They talked for almost two hours, while the shadows grew long across the village green. Holt did most of the talking, laying out his position with surprising frankness. He *had* been building an army as Kiara suspected, though Quinn doubted she had any idea of the scale of his ambitious operations. In the few months since taking over as Prime, Holt had rebuilt Valteron's economy into a machine of war.

There was no sign of the stone settlement's inhabitants until later in the evening. Right around when Quinn's attention span had begun to wane, and his belly grumbled in complaint at having not seen food in hours, the wonderful aroma of baking bread touched his nose. He thought it a mirage at first, a trick played on him by his exhausted senses. Then the guardswomen flooded the pavilion with no warning, forming a loose ring of weapon-bristling female badasses around the meeting table.

Their concern, it seemed, was the appearance of three men and four women in the corner of the green. Each one carried a tall wicker basket lined with cloth, and approached them with timid smiles. The men wore colorful vests over loose-fitting linens. The women wore long flowing skirts, and had tied up their hair in bright scarves that neatly complemented the vests. Two of Holt's guards loped over to inspect the baskets, eventually deeming them safe to approach.

"Our hosts were good enough to prepare an evening meal. I hope you'll join me for it," Holt said.

His offer was met with a murmur of enthusiastic agreement. Even Anton looked pleased at the prospect of a hearty meal. *No doubt the wine won't be up to his liking, though.*

The villagers said nothing, but set down their baskets, smiled, and disappeared back in the direction they'd come from. Quinn started to untie his purse—the least he could do was throw some coins their way—but they just laughed and waved him off.

"We may not be Pirean, but we know the importance of hospitality," Holt said.

Moric offered a nod of thanks at the words.

Quinn felt a little warm comfort himself. Holt always knew the perfect thing to say.

The baskets held a wealth of delicious-smelling pastries in the shape of half-moons. Quinn grabbed one and noted the heft, the density. *Meat filled. Oh, yeah.*

Everyone broke off into somewhat random little groups to enjoy the meal with quiet conversation. Anton and Moric moved off for a private discussion at one side of the green. Holt invited a reluctant Relling to join him at his table to catch up on old times. It would have been awkward for Quinn to play third wheel with either of those pairings. He felt an odd spike of nostalgia for those meals in the Pirean tower where you were squeezed in so tight you could eat off your neighbor's plate.

He could have taken the meat pastry on his own somewhere, but eating alone was neither fun nor challenging. *When in doubt, do the least expected thing.* He walked over to where Holt's exotic guardswomen had seated themselves in a loose circle, their weapons still within reach. "May I join you?"

Several of them cast a glance at the woman opposite him in the circle, whose oil-black hair hung in an intricate array of beaded braids. They *click-clacked* together when she moved her head. "If you wish it. Quinn." She said his name slowly, as if it had an unfamiliar sound. "I am Alethea."

"Good to know you." He sat down cross-legged in their circle, with his back to the pavilion, to the bemusement of the warrioresses to either side. He made his voice conversational. "So, where you from?"

"We are of Tukalu." Alethea must have seen the blank look on his face. "It's an archipelago southeast of Valteron."

"I've not heard of it, but I hope you'll forgive me." He offered his best smile. "I'm not from around here." Whether he won any of them over with that was hard to tell. He tried a bite of the pastry. The crust was light and flaky, the filling a delightful meld of cheese, meat, and savory sauce. After a week of basic ship's fare, it tasted like heaven. *God bless those villagers, whoever they are.* The fact that Holt's presence won them meals like this spoke volumes to his reputation, even in the distant reaches of Valteron. These warrior women remained a mystery, however. They'd lapsed into silence since he joined them, but occasionally made little gestures and expressions at one another. So they *were* still talking, but not in a way that he could hope to hear or understand. Well, he might as well try again. "So, how is it that you know Rich—the Valteroni Prime?"

"You ask a third question, but have answered none," Alethea said.

"That's a fair point. Then again, you haven't asked me any." He tried the smile again, but might as well have been using it on a stone. Alethea's control of her face was masterful.

"How do *you* know the Prime?"

A complicated question, but he felt like it was also a test. "I met him for the first time today. But we come from the same place, so we know many of the same people."

She nodded, accepting this answer despite its vagueness. She bought herself time by taking another bite. Then she asked, "Why did you choose to eat with us? Are you not liked by your companions?"

"They like me well enough. Most of them, anyway." *At least they haven't killed me yet.* "But I came here because I wanted to get to know you."

"For what purpose?"

"Fun, mostly. You *do* know what fun is, don't you?"

"Another question," she said.

"In my defense, I answered three."

She offered a feral smile. "Our idea of it is different from yours."

He should probably have let it go, but she'd opened the door for him and he couldn't resist. "You don't know that. You just met me."

"You're a mainlander, aren't you?"

"Not really." An idea came to him. "I live on an island, too."

This statement caused a few second glances from the women to either side of Alethea, who'd been thus far ignoring him.

"A volcanic island?" she asked.

"No, a regular one."

"That hardly counts."

"Come on, an island is an island," Quinn said.

Alethea unfolded her legs and stretched them toward him. "Do you have feet like this?" She was barefoot, but the soles of her feet looked like old leather.

It caught him off guard, and he laughed. *No wonder they never wear shoes.* "Gods, no."

"So you have soft feet. That leaves out the coal walking." She looked him up and down. "Perhaps you have other redeeming qualities."

He winked at her. "I like to think so."

The woman beside Alethea leaned over and whispered something to her. They looked very similar, though this one appeared a few years younger. Quinn caught himself, because he couldn't go around assuming people who looked similar to his inexperienced eye were related.

"My sister has offered a good suggestion," Alethea said.

Or maybe they're sisters. "Let's hear it."

"Do you know how to throw a knife?"

He was careful to keep his face neutral. "I do."

Alethea clicked her tongue twice. All of the women wrapped up their meals and stood. One of them produced a circular wooden plank about a foot in diameter. Alethea's sister held it tight in both hands, perpendicular to the ground. Alethea moved back about ten feet, drew her belt knife, and flipped it almost casually. *Thunk.* It stuck right in the center of the wood. A good thing, since her sister's face was only about a foot behind it. The other women all snapped their fingers in a sort of chorus. A miniature applause.

Then another woman moved up, drew *her* knife, and threw. *Wham*, another bull's-eye. More snapping fingers. They went right after one another like that. Not every woman hit the exact center, but no one missed the board. The next thing Quinn knew, Alethea held out the knife toward him, handle-first. "Your turn."

"Whoa, hold on. I'm not a professional like you." And if he so much as scratched Alethea's sister, he could only guess at the unpleasant fate that awaited him.

She pouted at him and somehow made it look predatory. "You *did* say you wanted to have fun."

He sighed. "Guess I had that coming." He took the knife and tested it. It was a bit heavier than the flashy props he'd used onstage, but the balance was perfect. Ten feet. Three and a half rotations. He flipped the knife over and took it by the blade. Whispered a prayer, and threw it before he thought better. He didn't even think to use the magic. He relied completely on muscle memory. The knife flailed through the air and buried itself in the board. A little high and off center, but close enough. He grinned, more relieved that pleased with himself, while the warriors snapped their approval.

Oh, but it wasn't over. Another woman took the board. Alethea's sister threw first. *Thunk*. A perfect throw. The other women followed in turn, many of them using their left hand this time. Quinn sort of eased back a little. He'd done it once, but didn't trust his luck to hold a second time. Even the best magicians never tried the same illusion twice on the same night, with the same crowd. That was just asking for it.

Alethea spotted him. "You've one more throw to make."

"I wasn't going to press my luck."

"In Tukalu, it is bad luck to throw once."

"Oh, sure, now you tell me." He took the proffered knife, and set himself up exactly as he had before. Same hand, same distance. He could do this. He put the blade between his finger and thumb. Nice and easy. *Just hit the wood*. He wound up.

Alethea leaned close and breathed, "Don't miss, handsome."

He missed the board by about two feet. The knife didn't hit anyone, mercifully, but clanged loudly against the low stone wall that bordered the green. He cursed while the women roared with laughter. Alethea laughed hardest of all. He glared at her, but she returned this with a mocking wink. His face had to be bright red. He smiled, feeling sheepish, and shook his head. *They set me up for that one.*

Moric appeared at Quinn's shoulder while the women were still chuckling to themselves. "I hate to tear you away from this," he said, his tone dry as papyrus.

"Oh, please do," Quinn said.

"We're starting again."

"Thank the gods." He turned to Alethea, whose eyes still twinkled with merriment. No doubt, she'd been the mastermind of the little prank. "Thank you for the hospitality, but I have to go."

"Aw, that is unfortunate. We were just starting to like you."

"I'll see you around." He made his tone firm enough to suggest a veiled threat. Not that he ever wanted to have his ass handed to him in a fight or anything, but because he felt it was the right thing to do.

She smiled, showing her teeth. "I look forward to it."

He turned with Moric and walked away, forcing himself to keep a relaxed pace.

"Interesting lunch?" Moric asked.

"That's an understatement."

"What possessed you to join a Tukalu knife-throwing contest?"

"The more they like us, the less likely they are to kill us."

Moric gave him a side glance, maybe to see if he was serious. "You're a surprising man, Quinn. Entirely wrong about the Tukalu, but still surprising."

They spoke late into the afternoon, until Quinn's brain could no longer absorb details of Holt's troop movements or Relling's proposed countermeasures. They'd come to dominate the conversation in any case, to the point where he and Anton merely offered the occasional polite observation but otherwise stayed out of the way.

At last, Holt apologized that the meeting had to end—he needed to get back to Valteron. He stood, and they all did likewise.

"I'm glad you came, Moric. This bodes well for the future of Alissia."

"Let us hope so," Moric said.

"May I have a moment in private with your . . . apprentice?" Holt looked meaningfully at Quinn.

"Take as long as you need," Moric said.

Quinn followed Holt out of the pavilion and across the green, heading west. Alethea and one of her guardswomen shadowed them, close enough to be noticed but not to eavesdrop.

"So," Quinn said. *Alone at last.* There were so many things he wanted to ask the man who'd defected from CASE Global to start this whole mess.

"So." Holt smiled in a way that said he was thinking exactly the same thing. "I suppose it's no accident that the Enclave's vote involved circumventing my arcane protections."

"You're probably giving me a lot more credit than I deserve," Quinn said. "There was already momentum toward reconsidering the agreement with Valteron. I just gave it a little . . . push in the right direction."

"That much I understand. My former employer has a proven ability to recruit people who can get things done."

That almost sounds like a compliment. "You ain't kidding." He had to admit, he rather enjoyed being able to slip back into casual speech, without fear that something would be lost in translation.

"I'd love to know how you managed to infiltrate the Enclave in the first place."

"Well, it started when Moric kidnapped me." He went on to recount the story of his kidnapping, trial, and eventual acceptance as one of the Enclave students. Holt listened to it all without comment or interruption. It nearly seemed as if he were making a mental recording of the entire affair for future entry in one of his reports. *Wouldn't that be something?*

"So basically, it's through a little bit of cheating and a lot of luck that I'm still alive," Quinn finished.

Holt barked a laugh. "Now you're giving yourself too little credit, I think."

"I'm serious," Quinn said. "I've only been here a few months, and I've lost count of the times I was a sneeze away from a violent death." He couldn't resist adding a little jab. "Some of which was your fault, by the way."

"*My* fault?"

"The wyvern, for starters."

"Ha! I'd nearly forgotten about that. If it's any consolation, you've been a thorn in my side as well."

"I've been a thorn in a lot of sides lately. Just ask Moric."

Or Kiara.

"Yes, well. You've answered a number of nagging questions for me, but one remains. What made you turn against the company?"

Quinn knew this one would be coming, but his carefully rehearsed answer felt insufficient. "It's a number of things, really. Spending time at the Enclave. Learning that I could use magic on my own. Getting a glimpse of what CASE Global would do, if they considered us a threat."

"What about Captain Relling?"

"What about her?"

"Did you know who she was, when you first went to the Enclave?"

Now Quinn had to chuckle. "Oh, yes. She's hard to miss. And so is the *Victoria*."

"Yet you chose not to tell the company about her. May I ask why?"

It was interesting that he chose this line of questioning, and when Quinn put it together with Holt's muted reaction to seeing her, it pointed to a surprising theory. "Probably for the same reasons you did."

Holt put his lips together, and hesitated just long enough.

Gotcha. "So you *did* know what happened to her," Quinn said.

"I had some suspicions. The fact that you also concealed her from the company will work to our advantage. And it certainly brings a point in your favor."

"I can sense a *but* somewhere ahead."

Holt nodded. "Withholding information is something one can easily correct. But revealing your identity to Alissians, to magicians no less, was a far more serious act."

"I know," Quinn said. "But I wanted to earn their trust."

"May I ask why?"

"Come on, do you really have to know *everything*?"

"Understanding your motivations will help me trust someone who, if you'll forgive me for saying so, seems to enjoy playing both sides."

"Touché." Quinn looked behind them, to make certain they were well and truly alone. "Well, the thing is, there's also this girl."

Holt raised an eyebrow. "A native?"

"Yes. She started out as a source, and she shouldn't have been more than that."

"But you fell for her."

Quinn smiled. "Yeah, the whole thing kind of got away from me."

Holt squeezed his shoulder. "Believe it or not, I understand how it can happen."

"Now you know the catalyst for my change of heart," Quinn said. "Now you know pretty much everything."

"Oh, I doubt that. You seem like the kind of man who always keeps a card up his sleeve."

"Old habits die hard."

"Ha! I imagine they do. Even so, I think you've satisfied my concerns for the moment," Holt said. "And I believe that, if you're willing, I could make use for you in the campaign against CASE Global."

"What do you have in mind?"

"From what I understand, you have a penchant for finding trouble."

"So they tell me," Quinn said dryly.

"How would you like to do it intentionally, on behalf of this little coalition we've formed?"

"To what end?"

"To make things difficult for the company, in the same way that I did for your retrieval team."

With mercenaries, magical barriers, and wild dogs. "I have to admit, that kind of sounds like fun."

"I can think of no better role for an ambitious young magician."

"I'm going to need help, though. I'm still a beginner at this."

"Moric seems like a good teacher."

"He is." Quinn glanced back at the pavilion. "But the recent flip-flopping, as you put it, has won me a sort of unofficial suspension."

"Say no more. I'll take care of it," Holt said.

Oddly enough, even though he'd just met the man, Quinn believed him. Holt got impossible things done like some people changed their clothes. More and more, it was apparent why he'd so easily taken control of Valteron.

"Come let us return to the group," Holt said. "It will be dark before long, and my Tukalu guards get jumpy as wildcats when they can't see any threats before they come."

They turned back toward the pavilion, where Moric and Anton stood watching them with guarded looks of interest.

Wondering what the Prime and I might have to discuss in private, no doubt. Quinn smiled, just to throw them off.

Alethea and her sister doubled back, running soundlessly, to take up a position flanking him and Holt.

"They seem very capable," Quinn said.

"The Tukalu are among the finest warriors in Alissia."

"Are they all women?"

"Alethea's group is. As for the others, I couldn't say." Holt gave him a knowing look. "I've found it's best not to ask too many questions."

"Right. Apparently they'll just start asking you ones right back."

"Got a taste of that, did you?"

"My curiosity got the better of me," Quinn said.

"I admit that surprised me."

"That I played their game, or that I came back in one piece?"

"Both," Holt said.

They reached the pavilion, which the guardswomen began to dismantle in haste. They pulled the stakes, wound their ropes around them, and broke down the main structure in about thirty seconds. Quinn did his best to stay out of the way while Holt bade farewell to everyone.

"You said I could have Quinn as long as I liked," he said to Moric. "Were you serious about that?"

"I should point out that he is still a student of our arts," Moric said.

Anton jumped right in. "If you need a magician, we will provide one who has more experience."

Now I know what they had to discuss in private. Quinn could guess the thrust of that conversation, too. *Keep him out of the way, however possible.*

"He may be new to the study of your arts, but I think we can all agree he has a certain set of skills," Holt said.

Moric chuckled. "That's one way of putting it."

"Perhaps another more experienced member can accompany him, then? As a chaperone, and to continue his education."

Oh, well-done, Quinn thought.

Anton made a conciliatory gesture with one hand, like a king granting a request. "Moric can do it."

Moric shot him an irritated look. Apparently *that* wasn't part of the plan.

"That's fine with me," Quinn said quickly, before an argument could take root.

Holt smiled. "It will provide an opportunity for him to prove himself. To you, and to me. If he succeeds, I'd like to find other uses for him."

Moric's lips twisted like he'd swallowed a lemon. "Very well. How would you like him to do that?"

"Nothing too difficult, I should think." Holt smiled. "I want him to borrow an egg from a neighbor."

"When it comes to Tioni mules, manners come first, and all else comes second."

—R. Holt, "Overview of Alissian Husbandry"

CHAPTER 18

NATURAL FEARS

Felara seemed to get colder every time Quinn went there. He rode west from the southern tip of the mountain range that concealed the gateway cave a few hundred leagues to the north. Moric had taken him here, with a promise to return two days hence to pick him up again. This would be his test mission for the coalition, his tryout. *A cake walk*, Holt had called it. Meeting a trader in exotic native creatures. *Sounds like a recipe for an untimely death.*

The farm he sought was exactly where the Prime had promised—at the end of a long, straight road paved with porous volcanic rock. Black rock. Little puffs of ground ash drifted across the road and swirled around the mule's hooves. He'd specifically requested a horse for this little mission. *Specifically*. But no, Holt claimed that all decent mounts were already committed elsewhere.

But he could spare a Tioni smart mule, of course. There never seemed to be a shortage of *those* whenever Quinn needed to ride somewhere.

A pungent, familiar odor crossed his nose.

"Stop, please."

The mule plodded forward a couple of steps and then deigned to halt. Quinn caught another whiff of it, and then he was certain. The farm smell came mostly from manure, but also a mix of hay and animal musk. When Quinn was a boy, his grandfather used to take him on hunting trips in rural areas outside of Vegas. Quinn used to complain about the smell. His grandfather would always chuckle and say, *smells like money to me*.

"All right, continue, if you'd be so kind," he told the mule. It grated him a little to be so polite, but if the animal detected a hint of sarcasm or impropriety, it would be a long walk back to the rendezvous spot.

North Felara had a short growing season; most farmers had better luck with livestock than crops. Holt's contact here, Callan Rainswood, was unique among these; he ran a sort of menagerie specializing in exotic animals for security, sport hunting, and "other forms of entertainment."

Quinn hadn't pressed for details, but kind of wished he had.

The road here ran across the top of a rise, with the land falling away to either side. Clumps of evergreen trees gave way to more open terrain, most of it snow-covered. He hadn't seen any sign of civilization for half a day, and was beginning to wonder if this was some sort of prank arranged by Moric, when he encountered the fence. It ran in on either side of the road, a wooden stockade job that had to be eight feet tall. Mounted and up on the road, Quinn was just high enough to see over the top. That's how he first noticed the animal tracking him on the right-hand side. It looked like an ostrich, but taller and with thicker legs. The beak, too, was curved downward like a bird of prey.

It paced languidly alongside the fence, peering at Quinn with overlarge eyes. It made no sound. It didn't even blink. Disconcerting as this was, it paled in comparison to what appeared on the left side of the road. Four Alissian wild dogs appeared out of the woods and loped alongside the fence. Their coats were mottled browns and grays, the perfect color to blend into the Felaran undergrowth. They were built like Rottweilers beneath their shaggy coats. Veena had said that even if captured as pups and raised in captivity, Alissian wild dogs eventually turned on their owners. They would not be tamed. Were it not for the ten-foot fence keeping them back from the road, they'd be trying to hamstring Quinn's mare right now.

Veena had assured him that wild dogs were mostly nocturnal, but these ones were tracking him in broad daylight. *Guess she didn't know everything.* She'd still known so much, though, and it was clear he'd not taken enough advantage of her encyclopedic knowledge of this place. Too late to change that now.

Ahead, he began to pick out the buildings of several low-set buildings. More fencework appeared, partitioning off the landscape in ever more complex delineations. The good news was that it forced the Alissian wild dogs away from the road; they melted into the woods and disappeared from view. The road ran straight up to a story-and-a-half cottage with white siding and a thatched roof. A man leaned against the frame of the open door.

Callan Rainswood was just as Holt had described him: tall, bearded, and built like a wrestler. He wore rawhide chaps beneath a woolen shirt, but the clothing faded into the background. In the foreground was the arbalest tucked under his arm. This was a heavy crossbow used against cavalry. Quinn had never seen one in this world; Logan had told him that most soldiers couldn't carry one for distance. Rainswood cradled it as if it were a child's toy.

Gods knew what he might need that for, among his menagerie.

"You must be Rainswood," Quinn called. He whispered to the mule. "No sudden moves, please."

"Who are you?"

"My name's Quinn. I'm here on behalf of the Valteroni Prime."

The man looked him over with a distrusting eye. "Prove it."

Jeez, he's as paranoid as Holt made him out to be. Worse, even. "You met him for the first time in the Tioni marshes, when you were hunting log lizards."

"Go on."

"The second time you met him, he gave you a book. *Compendium of Poisonous Snakes*, I believe it was called."

"*Compendium of Venomous Snakes*, actually," Rainswood said. "But close enough."

"Good. Thank you." Quinn started to dismount. "I'm here to—"

Rainswood snapped the crossbow up and took aim faster than seemed humanly possible. "Stay where you are, stranger."

Quinn froze with one foot in the stirrup and one in the air. "What's the matter?"

"Need a third assurance," Rainswood said.

Uh-oh. Holt had given him only two. "Come on, man. Who else would even know to find this place?"

The man said nothing, but shifted his crossbow in his massive hand.

Quinn racked his brain, but couldn't remember any other details that Holt had told him. Certainly not something private enough to act like a passcode. It didn't seem like Holt to make a careless mistake. *This must be part of the test, too.* "Well, what about this? A few months ago, you helped him put something in a wyvern's nest. And you loaned him a few of your Alissian wild dogs."

Rainswood grunted. "Didn't get all of them back, either."

I might have had something to do with that, Quinn didn't say. This guy seemed a little attached to his animals. "So, are we all right now?"

"Sure." He set the crossbow on a table inside the cottage door. "Say, you didn't happen to see a very large snake on the way in here, did you?"

The question caught him off guard. "Uh, no. Why do you ask?"

"No reason."

"It sounds kind of important."

"Eh, don't worry about it." Rainswood spread out his massive hands in an inviting kind of gesture. "So, what can I do for the Valteroni Prime?"

Quinn felt like he should get a bit more information, but time was short. *Remind me to ride twice as fast out of this place.* He cleared his throat. "He's sent me to ask if we can borrow an egg."

"What kind of egg?"

"The biggest one you've got."

"The biggest one I have belongs to a wyvern. Is that what you want?"

"Gods, are you serious? I'd love to know how you pulled that off."

"I have my ways."

"Apparently. So, where's the mother?"

"Up in the mountains, but not far enough away for my comfort." Rainswood spat to one side. "The moment that thing hatches, it'll put out a siren call for its mother. I should've destroyed it."

"Why haven't you?" Quinn asked.

"Can't bring myself to do it."

"So let me take the egg off your hands. I think we can put it to good use."

Rainswood considered a moment, but shook his head. "Too dangerous. It's close to hatching."

"Don't worry about it. I can travel faster than most people."

"If you let it get cold and the thing hatches, do you know what to do?"

"I can take a guess."

Rainswood frowned at him. "Go ahead."

"I get it as far away from me as possible."

The big man grunted. "That's half of it."

Damn, this guy never gives full credit, does he? "What's the other half?"

Rainswood stared at him with a gaze so intense

that Quinn couldn't match it. He looked down at his boots, then back up.

"You run," Rainswood said. "Fast as you can, low as you can, and pray that the mother doesn't see you. Even when she has her brood back, if she thinks you came near it . . ."

"The territorial thing. I get it," Quinn said.

"I don't think you do. A wyvern can outpace a horse at full gallop. On a smart mule, you won't stand a chance."

"I said I get it." He had to move this along, too, or risk being caught out here at nightfall with the Rainswood menagerie. *No thank you.* "The longer we stand around talking, the closer that thing gets to hatching. You going to give it to me, or should I tell the Prime you refused?"

Rainswood stared at him a moment, and then shrugged. "Your funeral, bub." He went inside the cabin and emerged a minute later with a large, cloth-wrapped bundle. He stumped down and thrust it into Quinn's hands.

"Gods, it's so *warm*," Quinn whispered. He could feel the heat even through the wrappings.

"Best keep it that way," Rainswood said. "Wyverns roll an egg out of the nest to hatch it, so you let this thing cool, and it'll take that as a signal."

Quinn tucked it beneath his cloak to keep off the snow. "I'll tell the Prime you were helpful."

"Tell him we're even." Rainswood strode back into his cabin without another word.

"He's a polite one." Quinn tapped his mule on the flank. "Take us back the way we came, please."

The mule did an about-face and set off down the road. The flurries in the air thickened to a dedicated snowing. Quinn had trouble keeping the right balance with the thick bundle tucked under his cloak. He'd just found a good position and looked up when he saw a big log lying across the road. "That's new."

The log rippled sideways, scraping across the gravel. Quinn nearly fell out of his saddle. *It's a god-damn snake.* Easily as thick as his leg, and twenty feet long. He froze. The mule stopped on its own accord at a respectful distance. He had to admit, maybe smart mule was an accurate name after all.

The snake shifted again, grinding through the gravel as it slid off the road. Its head reared up till it was level with Quinn's. The eyes were amber, and as big as silver dollars. Jet-black pupils narrowed to slits as it looked at him. Quinn's chest hurt. He couldn't breathe. He wasn't any more afraid of snakes than the next guy, but this thing was a monster.

The snake flicked out a vein-blue tongue that had to be a foot long. Its eyes fell to the bulky shape beneath Quinn's cloak. As if it knew what it was. Quinn considered going for his sword, but thought better of it. *Maybe I should say something.* "Rainswood gave it to me."

The tongue flicked out and back in again.

Quinn took a cue from the mule and kept stock-still, waiting. Trying not to show how terrified he was. Trying not to think about the ever-cooling egg underneath his cloak.

The snake lowered its head to the ground and slithered off the road into the woods on the right-hand side.

Thank the gods. The mule trembled beneath him. Its neck was taut, and the ears lay flat against its head. Quinn leaned down and put a hand on the back of its neck. "We're all right. Let's go before it changes its mind."

The mule lurched forward.

Quinn took a breath, and smiled. For once, he didn't even have to say please.

Quinn made the rendezvous point as the sun began to slip below the horizon. There hadn't been a good contingency plan for if he missed the meeting. Knowing Moric, he might zip back to the Enclave and forget about him for a couple of weeks.

The gods must have taken pity on him, because Moric waited at the rendezvous point on a smart mule of his own.

"I was beginning to worry about you," he called when he spotted Quinn. Then he did a double take. "You're pale as a ghost. Have you taken ill?"

Quinn shook his head and glanced behind him for what must have been the hundredth time. "I just saw a really big snake."

"You're afraid of snakes?"

"Not usually." Quinn shivered, and it wasn't from the cold. "It was a hell of a snake."

"Did you get what the Prime requested?"

Quinn hoisted the bundle. Its unnatural warmth trickled into his fingertips, even through the gloves. "Right here. A mountain wyvern's egg."

Moric's eyes widened. "*That's* the egg he wanted?"

"I think so. It's biggest one Rainswood had."

"What kind of a fool are you?"

Quinn smiled. "What, are you afraid of eggs?"

"Eggs, no. The mother of those eggs, absolutely. Have you ever encountered a fully grown mountain wyvern?"

"Believe it or not, I have. And it was—" The rest of the boast died on his lips as the egg shuddered. "Uh-oh."

"What's wrong?"

"I think it might hatch."

"*What?*"

The egg shook again, then went still. "Never mind. I think we're all—"

There came a loud *crack* as a fracture appeared in the top of the egg.

"Or maybe not so much."

"What are we supposed to do if it hatches?" Moric demanded.

"Get it far away from us and then run really fast."

"Oh, that's superbly helpful."

"Well, I don't think we're getting this back to Valteron. At least not while it's still in egg form."

"What do you propose?"

"Hang on, I'm thinking." There was no getting this egg back the way Holt wanted it. Yet a wyvern egg was a rare thing. A potentially destructive thing. *Alissia's answer to bioweapons.* "We need to take it near the mountains. That's where the mother is."

"If that's where the mother is, shouldn't we do the opposite?"

"No. The Prime wants us to cause trouble for CASE Global. I know just the place."

"Alissians may not be able to match our technology, but that advantage only gets us so far."

—R. Holt, "Ramifications of Technological Disparities"

CHAPTER 19

DELIVERY

A frigid northerly wind blew out of the mountains, cutting through Quinn's heavy cloak like it wasn't even there. His feet, too, sensed the encroaching chill from the knee-deep snow. The egg trembled against his chest. *Hold on, little guy.*

He took a second to get his bearings. The ridge overlooking the gateway cave's valley was just uphill. Moric had brought them right to it. "Hey, not bad. You saved us a walk."

"It'll be dark before long. Where do you want to go?"

Quinn pointed at the ridge. "Up there. I need to see the valley."

They asked the mules to stay put. Quinn let Moric go first, and clutched the egg against his chest as he trudged along in the furrow Moric made in the snow. Near the top of the ridge, he tried crouching, but couldn't do that and keep his balance with the egg. So he sank to his knees, ignoring the bite of the snow through his pants.

The sun had already dipped below the line of mountain peaks to the west, casting the valley into twilight. They'd driven stakes into the ground at regular intervals to hold artificial lanterns, which provided enough light to see by, but didn't create an unnatural glow that might draw attention. Smart. Neat rows of familiar pup tents were arranged in a grid across most of the valley floor, from the fenced-off horse enclosure all the way up to where they'd parked the siege engines.

"It's more crowded than I remember," Moric said quietly. "Do you think the missing soldiers returned?"

"Maybe." But Quinn thought it more likely that this represented a new wave of mercenaries on CASE Global's payroll. Jesus, they must have spun up a major training program months ago. Right after the second mission got under way, most likely. Yet another piece of Kiara's master plan clicked into place.

Now I know why she was so eager to make Holt vulnerable. "Either way, there's a hell of a lot of men down there, so I hope this works." He unwrapped the cloth around the egg. The shell was off-white, almost yellowed, and had a dull shine. He put a palm on it. It was slick under his fingers, almost like ceramic. Still warm, but cooling fast.

"All right, what's your plan?" Moric asked.

"We're going to put this right in the middle of the camp. If you can lift it—"

"Oh, I'm not lifting anything."

Quinn did a double take. "Why not?"

"Richard mentioned that you felt like you need more instruction." Moric gestured at the egg. "This seems like an excellent opportunity."

The egg shifted again, and almost fell over. *Jesus.* Quinn heaved it upright again. "We don't have a lot of time for this."

"Then quit stalling."

Quinn stifled a groan. *I asked for it.* "I feel like I should practice on a rock first."

"Absolutely not. We learn best by doing."

"I'm worried I'll break it."

"Do you routinely break eggs when you pick them up?" Moric asked.

"No, but I know to be gentle. It's instinct, you know?"

"The same thing applies here. Just think of your

magic as an extension of your hand. That's essentially what it will be."

Quinn sighed, closed his eyes, and reached for the magic. It filled him with pulsing warmth. He opened his eyes and focused on the egg. Imagined a soft hand lifting it from underneath. The egg wobbled and almost fell. He cursed. *All right, two hands beneath it.* The hum of magic filled his ears with buzz. The egg steadied, and lifted up from the ground. He could feel the smoothness of the shell, the warmth of it.

"Unreal," he breathed. They *were* his hands. Now he understood why it felt the way it did, when Moric or Sella used magic to smack him back into line. Or when Jillaine held him so he couldn't move. Like a massive hand wrapped around his body.

That realization gave him the confidence to keep going. He carried the egg out from the ridge, beyond the safety of its snow-blanketed landscape. Better not to think about what would happen if he lost control of it now. But that wouldn't happen. He held it in his hands, now, and he was *good* with his hands. Certainly good enough to keep an egg from falling to the ground.

This is child's play. He maintained the self-delusion as he floated the egg farther out over the vale.

In the fading light, it was harder to keep his eye on it. The strain of keeping it steady intensified until his real hands began to shake. "I think it's getting harder."

"The greater the distance, the greater the cost to the magician," Moric said.

Quinn guided the egg over the first rows of tents. It was hard to even see it. His entire world was the pinpoint of the pale, round shape that floated fifty feet above the ground. Most of the mercs had already bivouacked for the night in their cozy pup tents, no doubt preferring the warmth of the self-contained nuclear heaters to Felara's frigid night air. Still, a couple of two-man patrols walked up and down the rows at random intervals. Any one of them might look up and spot the egg hovering unnaturally overhead, if he let it go much lower. Not that going lower would help things much: a fall from twenty feet would be no less devastating than a fall from fifty. Even if the egg somehow survived, the impact of a large heavy object in the middle of a soldier camp would set this wide open.

The mercenaries had shoveled the top layer of snow into long waist-high snowdrifts between their rows of tents. These ran roughly east-west, so Quinn had his pick. He aimed for the widest one, smack-dab in the middle of the mercenary encampment. The strain of holding the egg that long began to gnaw at him from the inside out. *Jesus, this is hard.* He began lowering the egg, taking care not to do so too

quickly. It drifted silently down on his magical fingertips, down to where the snow was. At this distance,
he couldn't gauge the height with too much accuracy.
All he could do was lower it slowly, while his abdomen shook and his arms burned with invisible fire. At
last, he felt a chill on the back of his right hand, the
sharp-cold feeling of snow against bare skin. "I think
that's it."

"Well done," Moric said.

Quinn let the lifting-hand fade away, but held on
to the flow of the magic. Tired as he was, the flush
tingling of it coursing through his body had an addic-
tive sort of hold on him.

Moric put a hand on his shoulder. "Let it go, son."

Quinn frowned, but complied, and didn't manage
to hide his disappointment at the void it left behind.
"Sorry."

"The magic will tempt you more each time, beg-
ging you to hold on a bit longer."

"I hadn't noticed." In truth, he'd simply pegged it
for the elation of being able to call upon magic whenever he wanted. How many times had Sella tried
to beat or frighten the ability out of him? He'd lost
count. Now, to think he could summon it as a whim,
brought a twinge of excitement. "Should I be worried
about that?"

"Most magic users learn to control the impulse as
children, in the same way that we control hunger and
thirst."

Perfect. "Yet another thing I missed out on."

"You seemed to spend your youth in other productive ways."

"Was that a compliment?"

"Don't let it get to your head."

He's a good teacher. Probably better than Jillaine, if truth be told. Maybe because he'd had to learn this stuff himself, whereas Jillaine simply grew up with it.

The wind picked up as they waited. Moric drew his cloak tighter around himself. "How long will it take for the egg to—"

He cut off as a crackling noise echoed in the chill night air. They could see the fracture down its midline. The creature within struggled for another couple of minutes. All Quinn could do was watch. At last, the two halves of the shell broke apart, revealing the curled reptilian form of an infant wyvern.

By a stroke of luck, both patrols had wandered to the far end of the encampment when the egg hatched. No one seemed to have noticed. The wyvern unfolded itself into a crouch and took a couple of shaky steps. It scanned left and right, taking in its surroundings. Then it lifted its snout to the sky and crooned two sharp, staccato notes somewhere between a grunt and a gull-cry. The lanterns of the two patrols went still. *They must have heard.*

The wyvern crooned again, louder this time. The sound echoed up and back from the mountain peaks. Now the patrols' lanterns began bobbing in its direction. It crooned again. They picked up their pace.

Quinn looked up at the dark sky, but saw nothing. "Come on, mama wyvern," he muttered.

The nearest two-man patrol came within about twenty yards of the snowdrift and halted, their hands on sword-hilts. A brief debate ensued, which Quinn couldn't make out, but he guessed the gist of it might have been *what the hell is that thing* and *I have no fricking idea*. The wyvern hunkered down in the snow among its egg fragments, watching them. Its tiny pink tongue flicked in and out. The second patrol ran up, bringing the number of confused bystanders to four.

The wyvern crooned again, a single drawn-out note that started low and ended with a sort of high-pitched whistle. A whine, perhaps. It was a pitiful little sound, really. The mercenaries let go of their sword-hilts and approached it from two sides. Like dogcatchers approaching a nervous stray.

The wyvern let them come within a couple of paces. Then it reared up and snapped at the nearest man, nearly catching his arm. They retreated a few steps, muttering to each other. The hands went back to the sword-hilts. The wyvern snapped again, and now the swords came out of the scabbards.

"I think playtime is over," Moric said.

"No kidding."

A hissing scream shattered the chill night air from

above. It had the sound of an eagle's cry, and made Quinn duck his body protectively to the ground. Sheer instinct, that. He froze against the snow and prayed the mother wyvern wouldn't see him. Light bloomed in dozens of tents as the mercenaries roused to this new sound, and small wonder. The next scream sounded lower, and louder, and when it faded, the *whump-whump* of massive wings sounded above the din.

"Sweet gods," Moric whispered.

Maybe he was still looking. Quinn had already buried his face in the snow. The current of air buffeted him like a sudden tempest as something massive heaved past them. Only then did he chance a look over the ridge. The dark outline of the winged beast blotted out most of the encampment lights below. Mercenaries boiled out of tents, many of them armed, and took up defensive formations in between the tents, eight or ten soldiers to each one. Distant *clack-thrums* marked the firing of the first crossbow volley. The bolts slammed against the wyvern's flanks—they could hardly miss at this range—but rained back down in shattered pieces to the valley floor. Then the wyvern swept down low across the tent-tops, ranking down men and tents with the claws of her hind feet.

She glided up past the gateway cave and turned for another pass. This time, the soldiers only got off a few crossbow bolts. Most of them hit the ground as she rushed past. Someone began shouting orders, trying to bring some structure to this chaos. Lanterns bobbed and wove toward the far corner of the vale.

"They're going for the siege equipment," Quinn said.

"I should think so."

They buried their faces in the snow as she shot right past the ridge, showering them with snow. She dove again, screaming. The ground shook as she landed. Quinn felt the impact and stole another glance. The wyvern had landed right near where he'd dropped the egg. Eight or ten mercenaries advanced on her in a wedge formation, spears bristling. She swung her tail like a mace, swatting them aside.

The hatchling lifted its little head and crooned at her. She nuzzled it, tenderly. Everything moved in slow motion for that moment. *It's kind of beautiful.*

An alarm Klaxon rang within the cave on the cliffs above. Soldiers poured out of the entrance, their swords glinting in the moonlight. Boots pounded down the hardpacked snow path from the mouth of the cave into the vale. A distant *clack-thrum* sounded. They'd gotten a ballista into position. The massive spear shattered against a boulder well short of the wyverns, but it sure got the mother's attention. She screeched so loud that Quinn had to cover his ears, then nudged her hatchling to get it moving. It walked on shaky feet, heading south.

Crap. It's coming right at us.

"I think that's our cue," Quinn said. "Let's get out of here."

No one answered him. He tore his gaze away from the carnage, and didn't see the man. *Where is he?* "Moric?"

He scrambled to his feet. Looked around. Nothing.

A crash of timber and the screams of animals drew his gaze back to the valley. The wyvern had smashed open the horse pens. The horses scattered and fled off into the snow. The hatchling had started climbing up the ridge. It couldn't be more than thirty yards down. Distantly, he became aware that the mother wyvern had gone still. She was staring right at him.

"Oh God." He backed up a step, then another. *Not again.*

She reared back and spread her wings.

"Shit!"

Suddenly Moric was beside him again. "I believe that's our cue."

"I already said that—run for it!"

They fled down the ridge, stumbling in the thick snow. Quinn's legs burned with the effort.

"Where'd you go?" he panted.

"I had to take a look at something."

"You could have told me!"

The mules had edged away from the vale. Maybe they smelled the wyvern, maybe they heard its screams. Either way, the whites of their eyes were showing. Another distant *clack-thrum* sounded from the other side of the ridge. The wyvern trumpeted her fury.

Quinn threw himself on top of his mule. "Can we go now?"

"With pleasure." Moric grasped his hand and took them away.

"Good people will be cheated, just as good horses will be ridden."

—**Kestani proverb**

CHAPTER 20

COLD ASSESSMENT

Port Morgan proved just like Ralf described it: a sleepy fishing village on a small but deep harbor. No serious ships in port, only a few skiffs and fishing dories. Logan relaxed a little on seeing that. No ships meant no puffed-up Valteroni captains hoping to catch up with a fellow countryman. It was isolated, too. Logan had to admit that. Natural cliffs encircled the harbor and hid the village from the wider ocean.

"Little smaller than I expected," Logan said, as he and Mendez glassed the village from the wheeldeck.

"Never heard that before."

Logan chuckled. "Good one."

Mendez took the updates from Kiara with characteristic stoicism. He'd said so little, Logan almost worried he didn't understand. Right up until he gave a single hand signal. *Opportunity.*

Exactly, Logan signaled back. "Harbor's wide enough to turn around."

"Looks deep, too. We can probably get right up to the dock."

"Nah, we'll take the skiff. I don't want anyone poking around."

They took the ship into harbor nice and slow, giving everyone time to spot them and get comfortable with the idea of a large Valteroni ship bearing down on their tiny village. A few hundred yards from the dock, Logan told them to reef sails and drop anchor.

Snicket dropped out of the rigging. "How about I stay aboard, keep an eye on things?"

"No. Get the skiff ready."

Snicket sighed. "It's already on the crane."

They drew lots to see who worked the oars. Logan and Mendez ended up with both of the short sticks. Ralf had held them, which made Logan a little suspicious. He didn't mind the work, though, and it was hardly the first time he and Mendez had taken on some hard manual labor together. They fell into a steady rhythm: the skiff, the swells, and the two men rowing.

Snicket elbowed Ralf. "Who do you think's going to collapse first? My money's on the boss."

Mendez snickered between strokes.

Ralf cast a dubious eye over both Logan and Mendez. "I'll take Rico."

"Wager?"

"Half-silver."

"Done."

They spat and shook. Logan locked eyes with Mendez. Both of them began rowing a bit faster. The boat lurched down one swell and up another, kicking up a cloud of seawater that drenched Ralf and Snicket.

"Gods!"

"Damn, that's cold!"

Logan laughed so hard that he *did* have to stop rowing.

"Told you, Ralf," Snicket said. "Pay up!"

They pulled up alongside the dock, where a small fishing vessel had just disgorged its crew and a decent catch. Logan recognized the indigo cigar-shaped fish. A shallow-water predator with nasty teeth. Good eating, but heavy fighters. The fact that these parchment-ancient fellows had brought them in on hand lines spoke to the kind of fishing village Port Morgan probably was. Family trade and all that. Very *The Old Man and the Sea*.

They'd hardly tied up to the dock when a rangy fisherman with a gray-and-black beard ambled over. "That your ship out there?"

Snicket tossed him the bowline. "Who's asking?"

The man guffawed. "Watery gods, is that Snicket?"

"In the flesh."

"Thought you were dead." Then the man pulled them in and tied off to an empty cleat. A perfect bowline, and he tied it one-handed.

Snicket hopped out onto the pier. "Hello, Jass."

They stood face-to-face for a minute, sizing one another up.

"Thought you were your dad," Snicket said.

"He's been dead ten years."

"Oh. Sorry."

"Gods above, you picked up a new earring or six, didn't you?"

Snicket cracked a smile. "This kind of beauty deserves embellishment."

Logan chuckled to himself as he climbed out behind Mendez. That kind of talk only happened between old friends or family members.

"Looks like you brought some friends," Jass said.

Snicket tilted his head at Mendez. "The quiet one's Rico. This here's the boss. Gentlemen, meet my uncle Jassup."

Logan smiled and offered his hand. "You can call me Denzel."

Mendez gave him a double take.

Logan winked at him. *Play it cool, man. Play it cool.*

"Well, Denzel and Rico. Welcome to Port Morgan," Jass said.

"Nicest port you never heard of," Snicket said.

"Hey now, mind your manners!"

"I said it was nice, didn't I?"

Jass beckoned. "Bring your friends, and you can see how much better the place is with you gone."

"We can't stay long," Logan said.

"My wife's got a roast on the hearth. Should be done around sundown."

Logan's mouth watered at just the thought of roasted meat. "We wouldn't want to impose."

"There's plenty to go around."

Well, if you insist. "Very kind of you," Logan said.

They set out down the docks.

Snicket glanced over at Jass. "Speaking of kindness, who'd you finally convince to marry you?"

"Your sister."

"What? She's your niece, man!"

Jass shrugged. "Only by marriage."

They kept up the banter all the way into the town proper, which included about two dozen stone-sided houses with slate roofs. The boats and skiffs in the harbor outnumbered the houses at least two to one. Not a major ship among them, though. That, along with Snicket's apparent notoriety, suggested that most of the people born here never left. Many called out to him from afar. Men and women both. Everyone wore a smile. None of them were armed, and they cast the occasional bemused glance at the swords Logan and Mendez wore on their belts.

Logan ignored them and gave the place a cold assessment. The harbor was deep, and had room enough for twenty ships like his. No wall or stockade between the coast and the settlement itself, but the cliffs behind it provided a natural shelter from elements and enemies both. That wide cylindrical building near the pier would be a granary, and the villagers themselves looked well fed.

A good place to land an army.

Mendez cast the occasional look around, but kept his expression neutral. He was sizing the place up, too, probably thinking along similar lines.

The next few hours offered a blissful respite from the monotony of life aboard ship. They also confirmed everything Logan had guessed about the village's strategic value. There were only three passes in the landward cliffs that separated Port Morgan and its outlying farms from the rest of the mainland, and only two of them were wide enough to let a wagon through.

CASE Global could capture this village without even trying. The villagers were farmers and fishermen, not soldiers. With a few modifications, they could turn it into a virtual fortress.

Logan probably should have called it in and let the lieutenant know. But Port Morgan kept offering him reasons to put it off.

The first was supper at Jass's house, where his wife had been slow-roasting an enormous haunch of meat since daybreak. He smelled it the moment they set foot on land, and his legs would have carried him there even without an invitation. Then there was a quiet offer from one of Jass's boys to sample his latest batch of moonshine out back. It looked like motor oil and burned an eye-watering path down Logan's throat and was exactly what he needed. The night sort of spiraled from that point onward. Logan allowed himself to unwind a bit, for the first time in what felt like a while. He had seconds on the moonshine, and thirds on the roasted meat.

Finally, he excused himself from the table and stepped outside to get some air. The harbor's glass-like surface still held some light, but darkness cloaked most of the village proper. Warm light spilled from half a dozen windows. He took a few deep breaths, enjoying the calmness of this moment, this place. Then he activated his comm unit.

"Logan to HQ."

"You've got Kiara. Go ahead."

"I found you an LZ. It's a place called Port Morgan. Deep harbor, good layout."

"Defensible?"

"With some modifications."

"Tell me about the village," she said.

"It's tiny. Probably less than eighty people. Nothing bigger than a fishing boat in the harbor."

"Is there a militia?"

"Negative."

"How many young men of age?"

"I don't know, six? Most of them are out at sea."

"Take them out before you leave."

She couldn't have just said that. "Can you repeat that, Lieutenant?"

"Take them out. Any man between eighteen and sixty years old."

Her casual tone made him go cold in his belly. "You're not serious."

"Of course I'm serious. I don't want any resistance when we arrive to make port."

"Lieutenant—"

"This is not up for discussion, Logan. Get it done, set a beacon for us, and proceed to your main objective. Kiara out."

Logan fumbled for his comm unit and switched it back to standby. He couldn't move after that. Couldn't believe what the lieutenant had just ordered him to do. Removing Holt was one thing. He'd made a conscious choice to go against the company. Odds were, he knew the risks. These villagers, though . . . they were innocent. Their only crime was living on a nice harbor within striking distance of Valteron.

The problem was, Logan couldn't refuse, either. The company had his family. Mendez's family. All of them hostages against their compliance. How many atrocities would Kiara put on his hands before this was over? He didn't want to think about it.

I need another drink. He went back inside, already feeling numb. Snicket was entertaining the crowd with stories of his shipwrecking career, which had the feel of a local legend. There was even a quiet betting pool someone started on how long it would take for Logan's ship to find *its* final hidden reef.

Logan found his chair again and forced a smile. "Can I get in on that action?"

Jass laughed. "Should you be betting against your own ship?"

"Come on, I'll pay double."

"Sorry, but we can't have you filling a one-holed bucket on us."

One-holed bucket? He'd never heard that one before, but it sounded like a no. "Fine, have it your way."

"How about some consolation?" Jass offered him another slice of meat from the haunch.

Logan shook his head. "If I eat any more, I'll regret it. But thanks."

"Beats hardtack and dried fish, doesn't it?"

"There's no comparison. If I could eat only meat, I would."

Jass barked a laugh. "You and me both, Denzel." He lifted his glass of moonshine. "To meat eaters."

"To meat eaters." Logan touched it with his own.

Jass sighed with contentment. "You a hunter, by chance?"

"I guess you could say that."

Jass leaned in like a conspirator. "We got a little day trip tomorrow, to hunt some goat up in the cliffs. You're welcome to join."

"I'm not sure we can stay that long."

Jass's eyebrows went up. "Leaving so soon?"

"We're on a schedule."

"Probably for the best." Jass took a long pull of moonshine, and smacked his lips. "Those cliffside trails aren't for the meek."

What the— "Did you just call me 'meek'?"

"It's all right." Jass patted his arm. "You don't want to go, you don't have to go."

"How long is this little trip going to take?"

"A few hours. We'll be back in time to fry some fish at midday."

"Who's going?"

"Every able-bodied man sober enough to pull a bowstring. We leave at first light."

Every able-bodied man. He tried not to think about the words, but they repeated in his head, over and over. "You know what? That sounds like fun."

"That's the spirit, Denzel." Jass slapped him on the shoulder. "You any good with a bow, by the way?"

"That's for the goats to worry about," Logan said. *And maybe Lieutenant Kiara.*

"All great illusionists know how to build trust in people and use it against them."

—Art of Illusion, April 7

CHAPTER 21

SIDE ENTRANCE

Quinn and Moric returned to Valteron City in the dead of night. It had to be two or three in the morning; even the gas lamps over the street corners had gone out. Law-abiding Valteroni citizens were in bed behind locked doors. No one else moved as they slipped across the city square toward the base of the palace steps.

"Do you remember this place?" Quinn asked.

Moric grunted. "It's where we first met."

There had been *thousands* of people in the square

that day, to see the announcement of a new Valteroni Prime. "What were the odds of that happening?"

"Too slim to believe," Moric said. "I must have offended the gods."

They kept to the shadows as they skirted the wide stone staircase that led to the palace's main entrance. The walls surrounding the palace proper had to be twenty feet tall, with steel spikes jutting from the top like fangs. Quinn felt fairly certain he'd have remembered fortifications like that last time. It looked more like a maximum security prison than the centerpoint of Alissian capitalism.

"Do you know where we're going?" Quinn asked.

The white stone wall seemed to have no end. He'd even lost sight of the palace by this point, and wouldn't be terribly surprised if they ended up in the harbor.

Or in Tion.

"A side entrance. The fewer people who see us here, the better," Moric said.

A minute later, he paused at an unremarkable section of wall and slapped it three times with the palm of his hand. Quinn thought maybe he saw a spider, and did it out of instinct. Except for two things: Moric was creepily fond of spiders, and a little cutout opened in the wall at head level.

"Moric and Quinn, to see the Prime," Moric said.

"Security question," said a husky female voice from the other side. "What nickname did the Prime give you?"

"Must we do that one?" Moric glanced back at Quinn. "I'm with company."

A guardswoman materialized behind them in the street. She crouched low and brandished a wicked-looking spear at the small of Moric's back. Quinn considered himself a decent hunter and woodsman, but he'd no idea how or when that woman snuck up on them. One second they were alone, and another she was there. *Where did she come from?* The nearest building was no less than fifty yards away.

"Fine," Moric said. He turned to the window in the wall and whispered something.

"Louder."

Moric sighed. "Raincloud!"

Quinn snickered faintly, and Moric shot him a look that quelled any humor. The little door banged shut. Then a vertical crack appeared, and a narrow door swung open. Maybe two feet by six feet, just enough for them to enter one at a time. Orange firelight flickered in the courtyard beyond. Moric entered first. Quinn followed, with the warrior right on his heels. He looked back and thought he recognized her from the knife-throwing game, but couldn't remember her name.

Not that it would have helped. She shoved him the last couple of steps so that he ran into Moric. They stumbled out into bright torchlight. Quinn tried to shield his eyes, but rough hands pinned both arms to his sides. More guardswomen. One of them pulled a wide band of cloth over his eyes and tied it firmly against the back of his head. Another one frisked him with absolutely no sense of propriety, confiscating both of his knives.

"Good to see you again," a woman said.

Alethea. "Wish I could say the same."

"Would you like a gag as well?"

"Never mind."

"That's better." She slid a hand beneath his shirt, and brushed her fingers across his abdomen.

"I'm pretty sure you already searched there."

"One can never be too careful." She put her lips close to his ear. "Did you miss me?"

Uh-oh. He cleared his throat. "On second thought, I'll take the gag."

Quinn would have killed to see what the Valteroni palace looked like, but that wasn't in the cards, at least for this visit. The heavy cloth and tight knot suggested that Alethea knew her way around a blindfold—a useful tidbit he filed away for later—and prevented him from using any of the tricks stage magicians could deploy to sneak a peek. Still, he had enough practice to pick up on some key details—mostly by focusing on his other senses instead.

The temperature warmed a few degrees as they crossed a threshold, which meant they'd come indoors. Their boots clicked on a hard, unyielding surface. Too smooth to be tile, which meant marble or waxed granite. They took two left turns, walked up sixteen wide steps, took a right. Walked down a long corridor past the soft tinkling of a fountain—a sound he'd recognize anywhere, given how pervasive *that* was in Vegas—and past a room with a familiar musty smell. *Old books. We must be getting close.*

At last they were told to halt while the guards knocked on a door. The mustiness was fainter here, and nearly masked by the overpowering smell of burning lamp oil.

Then someone untied Quinn's blindfold and pulled it away. They stood in a sort of study chamber, four rectangular tables with four ladder-back chairs each. Holt sat in one of these, perusing a hide-bound book like the world's oldest graduate student.

He finished reading something, closed the book with exaggerated care, and smiled. "Welcome, friends. I trust my guards were not too rough on you?"

"They've frisked me so many times this week, I'm—" Quinn began, and broke off at the sound of a soft thump against the far wall. A muted shout followed it, then silence. *Maybe I'm imagining things.* "Losing track," he finished.

"And we hardly expected to be bundled in here like common thieves," Moric said.

Richard spread out his hands in apology. "Unfortunate necessities, I'm afraid. We've had some security concerns of late. Apparently I've lost my magical protections . . ."

"Good point," Moric said.

"Maybe we should have Richard out to the island sometime," Quinn said. "Let him try our security practices for a change."

Moric tapped a finger against his lips. "That's not a bad idea."

They both spoke in jest, but Richard's mouth fell open. "I would *love* to visit the Enclave," he said.

"I was kidding," Quinn said.

"What if you weren't kidding? I've always wanted to visit there."

"Unfortunately, the Enclave is for magic users and their families only." Moric gave a tight smile. "We have security concerns of our own."

Richard's face fell, like a kid who lost his ice cream cone. "Maybe someday."

"Maybe," Moric said, though his tone made it clear the world would have long gone cold when Richard set foot on the Enclave island.

Richard stood, and gestured to the three empty chairs beside his table. "Come, sit. Tell me that things went well in Felara."

They settled around the table while a pair of liveried servants brought in refreshments—smoked fish, puff pastries, and gods be praised, a silver pitcher that steamed with the promise of caffeinated brew.

"Rainswood was holding a *wyvern's* egg," Quinn said. "You could have told me that's what it was."

"I could have, but that wouldn't have been much of a test, now would it?"

"He's missing a snake, by the way." Quinn shuddered just thinking about it.

"He's usually missing the odd creature or two." Richard poured coffee into a delicate porcelain cup and slid it across to Moric, in the manner of old friends. "So, where is it?"

"It hatched before we could get it here."

Richard's face fell. "That's a shame. I had plans for that egg."

"It started to hatch on us, so I had to call an audible. We dropped it into the middle of the camp outside the gateway."

"Oh, ho!" Richard grinned. "Not a bad idea. What happened?"

"What do you think?" Moric asked. "The mother showed up and tore the place apart."

"Fascinating creatures, aren't they?"

"That's one word for them," Moric said.

Richard poured a cup of coffee. Bless the man, he slid it over to Quinn. "I think we can both agree that Quinn's proven himself reliable."

"His sense of mischief knows no bounds," Moric said.

Sounds like a passing grade to me. Quinn paused. "CASE Global still had a lot of soldiers in the valley.

And siege equipment. More of both coming through every day, I'd imagine."

"They have a significant investment to protect here," Richard said.

"I'm worried about what happens when they decide to move south."

"Yes. Well." Richard took a sip of his own coffee. "If they try to move south, they'll find the Kestani border closed."

"How did you manage that?"

"A simple matter of diplomacy. Yet another strategic tool that our former employer never learned how to use."

Kiara might find that inconvenient, but it won't stop her. "They'll try another way."

"We only need to stall them. Captain Relling will have the fleet in position soon."

"You've co-opted my harbormaster?" Moric asked.

"She volunteered, and we can use her." Richard looked at Quinn. "In the meantime, I hope you'll continue making life difficult for them."

"Absolutely." Quinn flashed a grin. "Raincloud and I can handle it."

Richard chortled. "I believe you."

Moric pretended not to notice. "I'm afraid I won't be able to participate in the troublemaking this time around. I have an urgent mission of my own."

"May I ask what?"

"Research."

"It can't wait?"

"This pertains to the gateway that brought you here in the first place. I may know something of its origins."

"Oh, do tell," Richard said.

Moric shook his head. "It's too soon to say. But important enough that I should pursue it."

"I'd argue that defending ourselves against an invading army is important, too," Richard said.

"Anton can take my place. He and Quinn get along rather better than I'd realized."

Whoops. Quinn didn't look at him. *How much does he really know?*

"Anton is overseeing the assembly of the Caralissian forces," Richard said. "Alliance or no, they'll take orders better from one of their own."

Quinn cleared his throat to break in. "What about Jillaine?"

Moric's glare could have shattered a mirror. "Absolutely not."

"Who is Jillaine?" Richard asked.

Moric looked suddenly uncomfortable. "My daughter."

Richard's mouth fell open. "You have a *daughter*?"

Moric wouldn't look at him.

Strike while the iron's hot. "She's very talented," Quinn said.

"I'm sure she is," Richard said.

Moric's jaw tightened. "All the more reason to keep her as far from this as possible."

"Why?" Quinn asked. "We're a good team."

"Too good, I should think."

"Relax, Moric," Richard said. "You needn't worry. Quinn already has a girl he's head over heels about. He told me as much when we met."

Well, crap. Quinn felt his cheeks heating. He looked down at the floor, but not soon enough.

An awkward silence ensued.

"Oh," Richard said. "I see. Well . . . all the more reason to believe he'll look after her."

"This does not persuade me," Moric said.

"We need all the help we can get, Moric. And I daresay that any daughter you've raised will be able to take care of herself."

Moric sighed. "Very well. But I want her well protected by mundane means as well. An armed escort."

Quinn couldn't help but notice that Moric wanted *her* protected, not *them* protected.

"I can arrange that," Richard said.

"Not some half-asleep green recruits, either," Moric said. "Experienced fighters who know what they're about."

"I'll give you my very best," Richard said.

Quinn saw it coming a moment too late. *Oh, please don't say it.*

"The Tukalu warriors," Richard said. "There is no finer protection than that."

"Well, I'm satisfied." Moric clapped Quinn on the shoulder. "Are you?"

Quinn forced a grin. "Absolutely."

As in, absolutely screwed.

"Collaboration fosters deeper insight."

—R. Holt, "Research Team:
Budget Justification"

CHAPTER 22

EAVESDROPPING

Veena waited impatiently in a tiny room in the Valteroni palace, doing her best to ignore the Tukalu warrior who lounged beside the door. She didn't know the woman's name, but thought it might be Alethea's younger sister. The quiet one. The one who, until recently, had often volunteered for nightly guard duty outside of Richard's chambers. *Now there's a downside I never saw coming.*

She lifted the leather flap in the wall in front of her and peered through the dime-sized hole beneath.

The room beyond had four wooden tables cozily lit by oil lamp, an exorbitant yet delightful policy Richard had instituted when he took over as Prime. The man himself hunched over a table with his back to her. Someone who didn't know him well might think he was sleeping, but Veena knew his deep-in-a-book pose anywhere. He didn't even need the reading glasses from the prototyping lab—he'd been fluent in native Alissian script for years.

She let the leather flap fall back into place, and continued to ignore the Tukalu temptress. *A body-guard*, Richard had called her, without saying why he suddenly thought her in danger. She hounded Veena's steps like a stalking wolf, everywhere she went. Even here in the palace. Now she shifted away from the door and up against the wall, as if she knew how irritating her proximity could be.

The door banged open a moment later, making Veena jump. Admiral Blackwell halted midstep and began to apologize. Then he recognized her, scowled, and squeezed past her to the empty chair. "They're here."

"Finally. I was beginning to wonder." Veena reached up to lift her flap again.

Blackwell caught her arm at the wrist, and not gently. "Give it a moment."

"You're hurting me."

He held her in his iron-vise grip for a few more seconds, then released it.

She settled herself again, and resisted the urge to rub her wrist. She settled for a glare before she nudged the leather flap aside. There was Alethea, shepherding some blindfolded people into the room to meet with the Prime. Two of them. The only thing that Richard had told her was that these were important visitors, and he wanted her to listen in to the meeting. *To see and hear, but not be seen or heard*, he'd said.

"Why aren't you in there, anyway?" she asked.

"The Prime didn't want me to be."

"Hm. Surprising."

"For some reason, he seems to pay far more attention to his new advisers than his old ones." He turned his head enough to openly look her up and down. "Can't imagine why."

"Maybe if you offered a less violent suggestion for a change, he'd be more inclined to listen," Veena said.

"Some problems can't be solved by talking."

"We need every tool at our disposal. And every ally we can trust."

Blackwell looked like he wanted to spit again. "If you think we can trust these magicians, you're a bigger fool than I thought."

"You sound as if you've been burned by one before," Veena said, and instantly regretted it. The admiral winced at hearing the word "burn."

"We should put a crossbow bolt into each of them while we have the chance."

"Shoot first, and ask questions later." Veena shook her head. "That's your answer for everything."

"It's kept me alive this far."

He was so condescending with every word that she couldn't resist making a little snort of amusement. "Barely."

She went to lift her flap again, which is why she wasn't looking when he lunged at her. The Tukalu warrior moved faster than she thought possible. One second she was leaning against the wall. The next, she'd caught Blackwell's arm two inches from Veena's face. *Gods, he almost hit me.*

"Let go of me, you heathen—" he started.

He broke off with a bellow as she changed her grip on his wrist and bent his hand backward at a right angle. "How dare you!"

"I think you should step out for some air, Admiral." She dragged him bodily from the chair to emphasize the suggestion. He had no choice but to stumble with her, or fall and risk breaking an arm. Veena ducked out of the way as she dragged him out the door. Somehow, the warrior even managed to hook a foot and pull it closed behind her. Veena took a moment to catch her breath. She'd known the admiral blamed her for the mishap at his keep, but never imagined he would resort to violence against her.

The door opened again to admit the Tukalu woman. She closed it quietly, and then resumed her slouch against the wall like nothing had happened.

"How did you know he was going to do that?" Veena asked.

"Big men move a certain way, especially when they're about to strike a woman."

"What did you do to him?"

She shrugged. "I helped him find his way out."

Veena's head still spun with the idea that the admiral had openly attacked her, tried to strike her right here, fifteen away from Richard. *No wonder he assigned me a guard.* If she hadn't been here, if she hadn't been ready for him . . . Veena didn't want to think about what could have happened. "Thank you."

The other woman shrugged.

"What's your name?" Veena asked.

"Belladonna."

Nightshade. "It suits you. I am Veena. And I owe you one." She lifted the flap in time to see the blindfolds come off. She recognized Moric. The other man looked familiar, too.

She leaned closer to the peephole. "Oh my God," she whispered.

"Don't you mean gods?" Belladonna asked.

"Right. Gods." She really couldn't care about that right now.

Quinn Bradley. There was no mistaking CASE Global's inside man on the Enclave. How far he must have come, to be here as one of their representatives—it was impressive. Veena had seen him in action. She knew he was good.

But not *that* good.

They were talking about something that happened in Felara. Veena only half-listened. Quinn looked tan and a bit rough around the edges, but there was something different about him that she couldn't quite put a finger on. He'd always had confidence to spare, but now he seemed completely at ease in his surroundings. Even face-to-face with the Valteroni Prime. And Richard, bless him, showed no signs of recognizing him. Of seeing the danger that sat right in front of him. Veena let the flap fall, and stood quickly enough that her chair tumbled backward.

Belladonna shifted. "What's wrong?"

"We need to get in there."

"No interruptions. The Prime was very clear about that."

Of course Richard said that, but if Quinn was here, Logan wouldn't be far. "I don't care what he said. Figure out an excuse to go in there, or the Prime will be dead within the hour."

Belladonna hissed under her breath, but pulled open the door. Veena made to follow, but the other woman held up a hand. "You'll stay here, and bar the door behind me."

"This is important—" Veena ignored this and tried to brush past her.

Belladonna grabbed her wrist. Her grip was like an iron vise. "And so are you."

She slipped out before Veena could argue.

Someone knocked on the door. Veena forced herself to wait. Two knocks, then one, then two. Richard's knock. A knock she kept hoping that she might hear some night, when she went to bed alone in her sumptuous quarters in the west wing of the Valteroni palace. Still, it was a relief to hear it now. She unbarred the door.

Richard strode in. "What's wrong? I trust this is important."

"Where do I even start? The admiral just attacked me."

"He did *what?*"

She waved off his concern. "Belladonna handled him."

"Why would he do that?"

"I think he blames me for what happened to his keep."

Richard pursed his lips. "Even so, I'll have to send him away. Early retirement. You're too important to lose."

"You have more immediate problems." Veena pointed at the wall that separated them from the sitting room. "That man in there, he's . . ."

"Bald? He has been as long as I've known him."

She slapped his arm. "Not him. The other one, the young man."

"What about him?"

"He's a magician."

"Both of them are," Richard said.

"No." She wasn't making herself clear, and the rising sense of panic didn't help with things, either. "He's *our* magician. The one that Kiara recruited to infiltrate the Enclave."

Richard laughed. "Relax, Veena." He caught her trembling arms and stilled them. His hands felt warm, reassuring. His tone slowed her racing heart. "Quinn is on our side."

"I'm sure he's made you believe it, but that's what he's good at."

"He's proven his loyalty. Even Moric agrees with me on that point, and you won't get a tougher sell than Moric."

"You think we can trust him?"

"One hundred percent."

"How can you be sure?"

"Because he's told me everything."

She lowered her arms so that he let go, and then shoved him back. "Why didn't you tell me?"

"Two reasons," Richard said. "First, because he hadn't yet proven his mettle for doing what needs to be done. And second, because I wasn't certain I wanted to see you two reunited."

"Why not?"

"He's a handsome fellow."

"So what?"

He looked away from her and didn't answer.

"Wait a moment, are you *jealous*?"

"No, not at all." He looked away. "There's just . . . something about him."

Of all the foolish things for you to feel now. For so many years, it had been her role to play the jealous one. "You're not wrong."

Richard's face fell. "I'm not?"

"Not at all." She let him suffer a moment more. Then she smiled at him. "But he's not really my type."

Richard let out a long breath. "Well, thank the gods. It sounds like he's got his hands full in any case."

"With whom?"

"Moric's daughter."

"Isn't Moric a . . . fairly powerful magician?"

"One of the most powerful magicians on the island, if my sources are to be believed. Your friend lives a dangerous life."

She clucked her tongue. "Says the man who went rogue against a billion-dollar corporation."

"I have my reasons."

She leaned in a little closer. "As do I."

For a long and beautiful second, she thought he might kiss her. Instead, he cleared his throat and looked away. "In any case, I think we can make use of Quinn."

"He might still be playing you, though. Are you sure he's not reporting back to Kiara?"

Holt gestured at the wall. "Why don't you go in there and ask him yourself?"

"My favorite illusions defy both explanation and expectation."

—Art of Illusion, November 22

CHAPTER 23

DAHLIA UNMASKED

Quinn watched Richard stride from the room. Two of his guards followed, but Alethea and her sister took up positions inside the door. *Probably to keep an eye on us.* "What do you think that's about?"

"I'm not certain." Moric frowned at the door.

"I guess he is running the entire coalition."

"Still, something tells me it's not good news."

Quinn grinned at him. "Now I understand how you got that nickname."

Moric's eyes glittered. "If I were you, I'd forget that I ever heard it."

Yes . . . Dad.

Whatever was going on, it didn't matter. He got to see Jillaine again. It surprised him how much he was looking forward to that. Even with the unofficial friend zone she'd placed him in. If he could get her alone for a little bit, both of them working toward a common purpose, he could probably break out of it. Granted, that would be a lot harder with Tukalu warriors around. Especially if one of them was Alethea, who seemed to have taken a predatory interest in him.

Richard reentered the room. "My apologies for the interruption, but my chief ambassador has asked to meet you."

"Ah yes," Moric said. "The legendary Dahlia."

Quinn didn't have a strong urge to stick around and meet some dry ambassador, but maybe it would give him a chance to talk his way out of the armed escort. He was racking his brain for an excuse when Veena Chaudri walked into the room. No amount of stage training, no locked-down game face could have prepared him for that. He not only let his mouth fall open, but gasped.

"Hello, Quinn," Veena said.

Oh. My. God. For the first time in probably everyone's recent memory, Quinn Bradley didn't know what the hell to say.

She offered her hand. He shook it, laughing in silent disbelief. He'd have pulled her in for a hug right there, but one of the Tukalu guardswomen standing nearby cleared her throat rather pointedly. "What in the world are you doing here?"

"You're not the only one who can play two sides." Her eyes sparkled with amusement. "I hear you're still calling yourself a magician."

She wasn't even surprised to see him. *Somehow, she already knew.* Richard had probably told her, and they'd kept it quiet just to have fun with him.

Well, two could play at that game. He reached for the pulsing font of magic inside and imagined a tiny ball of light forming in the air between them. Not fire, but pure cold light in brilliant, blinding glory. Veena covered her eyes, as did everyone else in the room. A high, keening note pierced the air as well. Then he let go of the magic. The ball winked out, and the keening noise faded to silence.

"It's no longer an act." He held out his hands to show they were empty, and delighted in the puzzlement on her face.

"That's incredible, Quinn."

Quinn looked over at Richard and Moric. "Do you mind if we have a minute?"

"As long as you promise not to run away with her," Richard said.

Quinn laughed. "I won't."

"Right up until he does," Moric said, somewhat grumpily.

Richard beckoned. "Come on, Raincloud, I've got a new book to show you."

They wandered off to the reading table.

"So, what's it like?" Veena asked.

"What's what like?"

"Using real Alissian magic."

"Wonderful and frustrating." He sighed, but then put on a smile. "I understand you've been working some magic of your own, on the diplomatic front."

"Hardly. I'm filling in for Richard wherever he needs."

Because he can't be two places at once. He had a flash of realization. "You're the reason Valteron and Caralis are suddenly allies, aren't you?"

She blushed and looked away. "Everything lined up just right."

"Or maybe you just have a good teacher," he said.

She looked fondly over at Richard, who was showing Moric an ancient hide-bound book. "The best."

Quinn lowered his voice. "So, why didn't you tell me?"

"I didn't know if I could trust you." Veena looked away from him, and brushed her fingers on the edge of the table. "I still don't know that."

"My loyalty is to the Enclave now. I think that puts us on the same side."

"This is the same Enclave that recently withdrew Richard's protections?"

He winced. "Yeah. Sorry about that. Kiara forced my hand."

"What made you turn against them?"

He shrugged. "I guess you could say I figured out what I really wanted."

Veena gave him a Mona Lisa smile. "I hear she's lovely."

"Jesus, can no one keep a secret around here?"

She laughed. It was *good* to hear her laughing again. "So, what have you been doing for Richard?"

"Proving my loyalty. Remember that wyvern we encountered on the first mission?"

"How could I forget?"

"I lured one of those to the camp outside the gateway cave. It was absolute chaos."

"Gods." She shook her head. "It's a good thing you're on our side."

"You know, that's what I keep telling people."

Quinn emerged from the cold darkness on a grassy hillock beneath a perfect azure sky. He drew in a long breath, savoring the familiar smells of dew-laden grass and wildflowers and the faint taste of salt in the air. "It's good to be back."

"For once, we agree on something," Moric said.

"You want to tell me what you hope to find in the archives?"

"Not until I'm certain."

"Jillaine and I will do our best to carry on mischief in the Quinn-Moric tradition."

Moric jabbed a finger toward him. "If she comes

to harm, so do you." He stalked off in the direction of the library.

I guess we're not walking together.

Quinn didn't have a lot of time, but he went to the infirmary first. Passed through the waiting room where he'd waited for news after Leward got hurt. The place was empty now, which he took either for good news or very bad news. He left and took the road down into the center of the island, to a plain single-story building with woven arches over the doorway. The chandlery's door hung open. Soft orange candlelight glowed from within. He crossed the threshold, letting the warm air and dozens of scents wash over him. There was cinnamon, lavender, and lilac. Sea breeze laced with wildflowers.

And roses. Roses most of all.

Jillaine stood on a ladder, placing a pale windmill-shaped candle on the highest shelf. She wore, of all things, the biker chick getup they'd found for her in Caralis. She didn't look as he approached, but she said, "I thought I felt trouble approaching."

He grinned. "How much for the windmill?"

"It's not for sale." She pouted, but it was an act. "I thought you'd forgotten about me."

"That's impossible, and you know it." Sweet lord, he was glad to see her again. To hear her voice. "How's Leward?"

"Up and about. He's been wondering where you were."

"What about you?"

"He knew where I was."

"You know what I meant." He strode over and helped her climb down from the ladder. He let his hands linger on her waist.

"So, you're back. What for?"

"For you, actually. I need your help."

"On what?"

"Rich—that is, the Valteroni Prime wants us to cause a disruption in the company's communication network."

She laughed. "Am I supposed to understand what that means?"

How do I put this in understandable terms? "We have to destroy two buildings in two different places at exactly the same time. If we do that, the invaders won't be able to talk to one another."

"Why do you need me?"

"Because I trust you more than anyone else." He winked. "Come on, it'll be fun. There are still places you haven't seen."

The uncertainty played across her face again. "I don't know."

"Fine, you can stay here. Where should I look for Leward?"

She gave him an affronted glare. "You've put him through enough."

"Well, I need *someone*."

"Fine." She waved a hand, snuffing out every candle

in the room. Dozens of little puffs of smoke drifted up to the ceiling. "Where are we going?"

"The Valteroni palace, first. We have to pick up our protective detail."

"Ooh, an escort? That's exciting."

He laughed on the outside, and groaned inwardly. "Try to hold on to that enthusiasm."

"To our knowledge, Alissia has never suffered a massive armed conflict or an epidemic of infectious disease. One has to wonder if there are other, stabilizing influences at play."

—R. Holt, "Questions on Alissian Magic"

CHAPTER 24

SWAMP THINGS

Quinn couldn't believe his luck that a mission in the heart of Tion involved none of their "smart mules" whatsoever. Holt couldn't spare four of them, and indicated that the terrain might require travel by foot in any case.

By the second hour of wading through ankle-deep marsh water, Quinn would have given a fortune for even a Tioni smart mule to ride on. The mud sucked on his boots with each squelching step. Nearly an inch of it covered his feet, making them about twice as heavy. His legs were leaden, but he'd be damned if he uttered a complaint in his present company. Alethea and her knife-throwing colleague, whose name was Bita, acted like they were out for a pleasure stroll.

"When you said you'd show me other parts of the world, this is hardly what I had in mind," Jillaine said.

"Apparently, the company likes to put their installations in the worst possible terrain," Quinn said. "Something about natural defenses." *Or cost savings.*

Alethea had run ahead to scout the terrain, and now splashed back to the rest of the group with an air of excitement. "There's firm ground ahead."

"It's about time," Quinn muttered.

Alethea gave him a mock-sympathetic look. "Is this too hard on you?" She fell into step beside her sister.

"We can drop you somewhere nicer, if you need some time to recover," Jillaine said.

Oh, good. She and the Tukalu have found a common interest—picking on me. He ignored the barbs. "How about dropping us at the actual place that we're supposed to be going?"

The amusement slid away from her face. "It doesn't work like that."

"Maybe you should tell me how it works."

"Traveling from one place to another is the hardest thing to learn."

"All the reason to start now," he said.

"Sorry, my father says you're not ready. And I agree."

"Come on, Jillaine, I'm making progress."

"Progress is not control. And that is the most important part of magic."

"Then teach me control," he said, knowing what rejoinder she'd have next.

"It can't be taught."

Worth a shot. "Well, I'm working on it." He imagined an invisible pair of fingers pinching her in the side, right where she was ticklish.

A laugh escaped her lips, and she skipped a step, splashing muddy water on both of them. "Stop that!"

"Quiet, you two." Alethea scrambled up a weed-ridden bank and crouched low, peering ahead. "There's a structure ahead."

"Good," Quinn said. "Maybe we can—"

She silenced him with a hiss and a sharp gesture. "Something's moving."

Quinn shut his mouth, and pulled himself up on the bank beside her. Ahead, a low stone building had emerged almost reluctantly from the solid ground. Vines and creeping lilies covered most of the structure, but it was undoubtedly a company installation. The angles were too perfect, and a roof made of naturally occurring materials would have collapsed years ago. It appeared intact, but getting in would take either an act of God or a solid half hour of ripping back vines. And the half-dozen stocky lizard-like monsters sunning themselves on the stone might take issue with that.

"What are *those?*" Quinn whispered.

"Three-toed ridgebacks," Alethea said. "Highly venomous."

They retreated forty yards back into the muck to confer.

"Please tell me they scare easily," Quinn said.

"They don't have any natural predators in Tion, so what do you think?"

Why must there always be a problem? "Wish I'd brought my bow."

"Unless you can shoot six of them in under thirty seconds, it wouldn't have mattered."

"I could probably do that."

Bita snorted. "Men."

"A shame that we'll never know," Alethea said.

"How well do you know these creatures?" Jillaine asked.

"We have the nonvenomous version on Tukalu. Even they are dangerous," Alethea said.

"What are their weaknesses?"

"Outside of mating season? None that I know."

"You said they don't have any natural predators in Tion," Jillaine said. "Do they have any predators at all?"

"Mountain wyverns consider them prey."

"Mountain wyverns consider everything prey," Quinn said.

"Maybe you should have kept the one from Felara."

"I don't think a hatchling would have helped much. We need an adult, and good luck getting one here."

"Tell me what they're like," Jillaine said.

"Kind of like those things over there, but longer and thinner," Quinn said. "Triangular head, big wings, and a scream that can wake the dead."

"Like this?" Jillaine held out her hand, and conjured an image of a winged lizard. It was only the size of a shoebox, but looked astonishingly real. Even with the proportions off.

Quinn fought the urge to ask her how she'd done it. "The neck should be longer."

She wiggled her fingers and stretched the image out.

"Better," Quinn said. "The eyes should be scarier."

Jillaine snorted. "Scarier?"

"Narrow at the top and bottom, you know. Like it's a great big bird that thinks you're a worm."

"I think I can manage that." She didn't move, but the eyes grew tall and narrower.

"Just like that," Quinn said. "Now, I need you to make this two hundred times bigger."

"Oh, is that all?" She laughed. "I could probably pull that off."

"This is fantastic, but it's probably not enough," Quinn said. "The thing that really terrifies you is the scream. Like the world's biggest bird of prey."

"How does it sound?"

"Well, I'm not sure I can do it justice, but it's like this." Quinn made a half-hiss, half-scream that sounded nothing like a wyvern.

All three women burst out laughing.

"If you make that again when the ridgebacks can hear, they're more likely to try mating with you than running away," Alethea said.

I'll give it another shot. "All right, it's more like . . ." and he tried a deeper scream with a curdling quality. It choked him up and ended up putting him in a coughing fit. Not so much that he couldn't hear the laughter, though. He cleared his throat. "I can't get my voice high enough."

"That was pretty high." Jillaine looked to the other women. "Was he even close?"

"I doubt it," Alethea said. "Bita?"

The other woman took a deep breath and unleashed an earsplitting shriek that made Quinn cover his ears. *Sweet Jesus, it sounds just like the real thing.*

"Now *that* is terrifying," Jillaine said.

Quinn laughed. "You said it. That, with your image, might do the trick."

"We will not have long," Alethea said. "Even spooked by a predator, the ridgebacks will look to reclaim their sunning grounds, and there isn't another solid place for miles."

"If we do this right, there won't be anything to return to," Quinn said. "Let's get a look at the second location." *Maybe it wouldn't prove as challenging.*

They joined hands in a sweaty, muddy circle. Jillaine closed her eyes, spoke a word, and took them away.

Ten leagues southeast of Bayport in New Kestani, a ghost village looked out upon the ocean. Twenty wood-and-clay houses with thatch roofs, give or take, clustered around a few common buildings. A mill, an old forge, a two-story stone inn with a small stable attached. It held the promise of a burgeoning new settlement in a prime location, overlooking one of the calmest stretches of ocean on the western coast. Or did, once upon a time. Quinn kept watching it for signs of life as they approached, and saw nothing.

"Is that it?" Jillaine asked.

"Has to be."

"It feels . . . off, somehow. Muted."

More like haunted. "I know what you mean."

Other telling details revealed themselves—doors left open to the elements, drifts of fine-powder sand that blocked the paths between the cottages. Not a wisp of smoke curled up from any of the chimneys. The numb silence in the area spoke loudest of all, though. No birds, no insects. Not even the sound of waves hitting the shoreline could be heard as Quinn, Jillaine, and their Tukalu guards approached the settlement.

Alethea jogged back toward them, her face stonier than usual. "I didn't see anyone, but it would be the perfect place to set an ambush. Wait here."

Quinn and Jillaine halted while she and her sister ran ahead. Bita took up a position outside the nearest cottage door. Alethea drew her long knife and crept inside, keeping low against the wall. Bita followed three seconds later, but backed in, watching the entryway. They emerged a moment later and moved to the next cottage, clearing it in similar fashion.

"Oh, man." Quinn shook his head. "They're methodical, aren't they?"

"They're a lot of things," Jillaine said.

Oh, look, an invitation to poke the bear. No thanks. Quinn closed his mouth and kept it that way.

Ten minutes later, Alethea and Bita jogged back to where they waited.

"Anything?" Quinn asked.

Alethea shook her head, and then a circular gesture with an open hand, almost like she was crossing herself against some hidden evil. "This place makes me want to take a bath."

"We might as well get it over with, then," Quinn said.

"Where do you want to start looking?"

"The inn." It was the tallest structure, offering the best protection against the elements. And the only one with a familiar-looking weather vane on the roof.

They had to pass several cottages to reach the inn,

and it made Quinn glad that the Tukalu had checked them already. Their doors and windows hung open like wounds, and the air around them held an odd stillness. He checked his sword again to make sure it wouldn't stick in the scabbard.

They entered the inn by the front door, which opened into a sort of dining room with three round tables. Five stools per table. Everyone had a place setting—tin plate, two-tined fork, round glass tankard—beneath a light coating of cobwebs. Maybe it was Quinn's imagination, but he could have sworn there was still *ale* in one of the tankards. Curiosity got the better of him, and he lifted one of them up. It was half-full of amber liquid, but somehow lighter than he'd expected. Softer, too. "What the hell?"

He inverted the mug and nothing spilled out. He righted it, and tried to dip his fingers, but met only the soft, yielding surface of a plastic seal. "I'll be damned. It's a prop."

"What's a prop?" Jillaine asked.

"A stage prop. Fake." He gestured out at the place settings and the tankards.

Alethea used her knife to tip over another tankard. It clunked softly against the table, but nothing spilled out. She took a step back and repeated the warding gesture.

"It's all fake," Quinn said.

Jillaine edged back from the tables. "Why would someone do this?"

"Because we're in the right place. Come on." He walked beyond the tables and through the door on the far wall. The room beyond had a rectangular prep table, a hearth, and two stone ovens. A smaller door led into a narrow storeroom stocked with barrels and sacks of grain. Fake grain, probably, or else rodents would have eaten it long ago.

"Do you see what you're looking for?" Jillaine tiptoed up behind him. The Tukalu seemed content to stay in the common room near the door, as far away from the tables as possible.

"Not yet, but I'm sure it's in here somewhere. It'll be a door with a rectangular plate on it." *How the hell do I describe a keypad?* "Little buttons you can push, with symbols on them. But don't push any."

He checked the storeroom first. The grain sacks were light as pillows, probably filled with one of CASE Global's many synthetic foam products. The barrels looked real, but were made of some kind of plastic resin. He shoved it all out of the way to reach the back wall, which was plain. Featureless. He knocked on the wood, and it sounded solid. "Well, crap."

"I think I found something," Jillaine called.

She stood in front of the hearth, peering into one of the stone ovens above the hearth. The smaller one, about one foot tall and two feet wide. It was too shallow to be practically useful, which was the first clue. But the rectangular keypad against the back wall was the dead giveaway. Quinn inspected the hearth itself. A vertical seam ran right down the middle of it, as if the stone had been cut in half and put back together. He followed it around to the side where the hearthstone met the wall, and found three large steel hinges. "Bingo. It's a hidden door."

"This is it, then?"

"Absolutely. There should be a panel just like it inside that structure in the marsh."

"What if we can't find it?"

"Just ask the ridgebacks where it is."

She rolled her eyes. "Always helpful."

"I do what I can."

He started to head back to common room.

"Quinn." She caught his arm and pulled him back around.

"What?"

She stood on her toes and kissed him quickly. Surprisingly. Right on the lips, but she pulled away before he could kiss her back. "Good luck."

"Thanks." He treasured the soft impression her lips left behind. "You, too."

They walked out and reclaimed their guards. Bita, having the more effective wyvern cry, would go with Jillaine back to the Tioni marshes.

"Once you push the wrong buttons enough, you'll hear a loud noise. Then you have half a minute to get clear." The CASE Global fail-safe would do the rest.

"What about the timing?" Jillaine asked. "The Prime said to disable them both at the same time."

"Try and do it the moment the sun disappears below the horizon." *Not exactly synchronized watches, but it'll have to do.*

"We will." She looked to Bita. "Are you ready?"

The woman gave a nod, touched Alethea's shoulder in farewell, and stepped up beside Jillaine.

"Be careful," Quinn said.

"*You* be careful."

Alethea sidled up next to Quinn and took his arm. "Don't worry, Jillaine. I'll keep a *very* close eye on him."

Lord help me. Quinn brushed her hand off his arm, but she only laughed.

Jillaine gave her a cold stare. "Not too close. I'd hate to forget your sister in the marshes." She took hold of Bita's wrist and closed her eyes. They both vanished.

Quinn gave Alethea a side look. "You just love getting me into trouble, don't you?"

"What trouble? I only said I'd keep an eye on you."

"A *close* eye," he said. "I think she read something into that."

"We still have an hour until the sun sets." She took his arm again, and leaned in close. "Whatever will we do to pass the time?"

Thunder rumbled off in the distance, a fitting omen for Jillaine's inevitable fury. *Somehow this is going to be my fault, too.* The thunder didn't fade, but grew louder. "Do you hear that?"

The mischievous grin fell away from Alethea's face. She hissed.

"I was afraid of that."

Hoofbeats. Someone's coming.

"Even in our modern world, magic has its true
believers. Or, as I like to call them, easy marks."

—**Art of Illusion, February 11**

CHAPTER 25

COMPLICATIONS

Quinn eased his head over the ridge to sneak a
glance at the approaching horsemen. "I count six," he
whispered.

Alethea looked up at him from where she lay prone
against the sandy slope. They'd hidden just below
the crest of a sand dune between the village and the
water. Behind them, the ground plunged downward
into the churning surf.

"Are they armed?"

"Probably."

The riders wore light cloaks, but the ocean breeze brushed the lead one's back enough to show the hilt of a sword beneath. And above that, something even more disconcerting: the coal-black glint of flexsteel armor. "Make that definitely."

"Maybe they'll pass through."

"Maybe." Quinn tried not to let his doubtfulness show. CASE Global mercenaries showing up at one of their communications relays could not be a coincidence. Sure enough, they reined in right in front of the inn with the weather vane on its roof. They didn't search the houses around it, which meant they were either in a rush, or were confident they had nothing to fear. Two men dismounted and walked inside.

I hope they don't notice someone's been in there.

No such luck. A shout came from within, a summons. The other four dismounted; two ran inside while the other two stayed with the horses.

Quinn pounded a fist into the sand. "Damn it!"

"The sun will go down in half an hour," Alethea said.

"What are we going to do?"

She crept up to the ridge and peered over it. "Those are the biggest horses I've ever seen."

"Arabians, I'm pretty sure. Our adversaries spare no expense," Quinn said.

"They're not hitched to anything, though."

"No. Why, what are you thinking?"

She eased back, crouched, and crept down the

slope to where it was rockier. There, she began flip-
ping over stones. "Help me!"

Quinn scrambled down after her. "Want to tell me
what we're looking for?"

"Here." She'd gotten her hands under the edge of
a flat boulder the size of a trash can lid. He moved
next to her, and they heaved it over. "There you are!"
She hoisted a snake that had to be three feet long.

"Jesus!" Quinn fell over backward trying to get
away from it. "Is that thing poisonous?"

"Only a little." She held it by the neck, and the
thing wrapped its tail around her arm like a boa con-
strictor. "Cute, isn't he?"

She's crazy. "If you're going to kill me, I'd prefer
something faster."

"Don't worry, tenderfoot. This is for the horses."

Once Quinn understood it, he had to admit that
it was a clever idea. They climbed back up the dune
and worked their way along it to put some houses
between them and the inn's entrance. The sun moved
inexorably toward the horizon. Quinn checked it and
gritted his teeth together. *Twenty minutes left. At best.*

"You want to toss this under the horses, or watch
from here?" Alethea asked.

"What do you think?"

"Keep out of sight then, and be ready." She climbed
up the last few feet of the dune and sprinted across the
hard-packed sand to the edge of the nearest cottage.
She pressed her back against it and went absolutely

still. Quinn strained his ears, but heard no sound of alarm. He edged back to where he could see around the cottage to the inn's entrance. Both mercenaries milled in the open space outside the inn, talking low while they waited for the others to return.

He gave Alethea a thumbs-up. She skirted the cottage and moved up to the next one, keeping the structure between her and the guards. Her dun-leather garb blended perfectly with the clay walls. Then she sprinted up to the inn, melting into the shadows beside it. Which only served to remind Quinn how little time they had left—nearly half of the sun had disappeared beneath the horizon.

Alethea edged up to the corner and stole a glance around it. Probably to gauge the distance, because she began twirling the snake by its tail. Then she fox-tailed it around the corner, right into the feet of the nearest horses.

Their reaction was immediate.

The animals snorted and stamped in alarm. Quinn seized at his magic and made little pokes at their ankles, just to help sell it. A horse reared back, churning its legs. The two mercenaries fought to settle them, but as Alethea pointed out, these were big, strong horses in a full-blown panic. They took the bits in their teeth and bolted in three different directions.

One man was dragged a good thirty yards before he managed to let go. He found his feet after that and ran after them. His companion ran to the inn's door, shouted something, and took off after them. Mercenaries came flying out to help with the chase. *One, two, three . . . where's the fourth?* Hell, one of them stayed inside for whatever reason. It didn't matter. The minute the other three were out of view, Quinn jumped up and started running. He followed the route Alethea had taken, using the buildings for cover. It felt a lot slower, louder, and more awkward than she had been.

He threw himself into the wall of the inn, panting. "Made it."

"About time."

"How many came out?"

"I counted three."

He cursed. "I was afraid of that."

"What's the problem? We can handle one."

"Not if he raises the alarm." Lost horses would be a much lower priority than a security intrusion, and those men could be back here in seconds.

"We can take him by surprise."

"What if it's someone I know?" Causing trouble for CASE Global was one thing; you could argue that he'd been doing that even before he switched sides. But killing mercenaries in cold blood . . . *I don't think I'm hard enough for this.*

"Do you have a better solution?" Alethea asked.

Even without a heads-up, he had only a few minutes until Jillaine and Bita would be entering their destruction code. Holt had cautioned them that both stations had to be taken down at around the same time, or the network would be able to compensate. Even if he and Alethea ran in there weapons-hot, there was no guarantee they'd get to the keypad fast enough. It was so close, too. *If only I were still on the payroll.* He sucked in a sharp breath. "I've got an idea."

She drew her long knife. "Me, too."

"No, I want to try talking first."

"Talking?"

"I can be very persuasive. Don't come in, unless I call you."

She made a face that said *I don't take orders from you,* but she nodded.

He straightened himself, threw back his cloak, and strolled into the front door of the inn with a casual air. "Hello? Anybody home?"

The last mercenary, the fourth man, popped up from behind the bar. Quinn didn't recognize him, but he was almost as big as Logan and had the same haircut. His eyes narrowed when he saw Quinn. His hand drifted to his sword-hilt.

Quinn gave him an easy grin. "Sorry to drop in, but the lieutenant's busting my chops about checking these panels. Where's the rest of your patrol?"

"Something spooked the horses."

Quinn blew air across his lips. "Probably a snake. They're really bad around here. You need a hand getting them back?"

"My men are on it." His hand still hadn't moved from his sword-hilt. "Did you say the lieutenant—"

"Oh, she's all over me," Quinn broke in. *Can't let him get in a question.* "You having any trouble with the panel?" He pointed back to the kitchen and just walked back there. Not hurrying, but not taking his time, either.

"No. Where did you come from?"

"Bayport," Quinn called over his shoulder. He'd nearly reached the threshold. *Thirty more seconds.*

"Wait a minute!" the man said.

"It's all right, I know where it is." He gained the threshold and went right for the oven. Hoped he wouldn't hear the other man draw his sword and come charging in. *Keep him talking, man.* "You hear what happened down south?"

The mercenary came to the kitchen door, right as Quinn reached the hearth. "No one tells me anything. Matter of fact, no one told me you were coming."

"I'm trying to keep ahead of schedule. Kiara's been breathing down my neck about these upgrades." He reached into the oven, found the panel. *1. 2. 3.*

"What are you doing?"

"Just a little sound check. Getting a feel for the button tones, you know?" *4. 5.* How many was it going to take? A loud buzzer answered that question for him.

The mercenary made a surprised sound.

"Perfect," Quinn said. "Let me just put in the override."

1. 2. 3. 4. 5. Another resounding buzzer. Two beats, this time. "Whoops. Hit the wrong number." He started in again. *1, 2.*

"Hey! Stop that." The hand had gone back to the sword. "Who are you? What's your identification code?"

"Like I said, I'm the panel guy," Quinn said. "And my code is . . ." *3. 4.*

A metallic *click* announced two unfortunate facts: the man had a crossbow, and he'd just taken off the safety. "Don't move an inch," the man said.

Quinn froze. "What's wrong?"

"Get your hand away from the panel."

"I'm just—"

"Now!"

Quinn sighed, but complied and put his hands up in the air.

"Turn around."

Quinn obeyed, nice and slow. Sure enough, the guy had a crossbow on him. He must have had it tucked behind the bar or something. *That's what I get for not clearing the rest of the room.* Now this guy had the drop on him. Right when he was so goddamn close, too. He could call in Alethea, but then the man was certain to shoot one of them. Probably her, and he'd be damned if he was going to let that happen.

He didn't know what to do, so he kept pushing the story. "We both know a crossbow won't penetrate flexsteel armor."

"Good point." The man lifted it, so that the bolt was pointing right at Quinn's face. "How's that?"

Quinn laughed to himself. "The lieutenant's going to be *so* pissed about this."

"Stop talking about the lieutenant, and tell me your goddamn name."

"Julian Miller," Quinn said, making a gamble. The real Julian Miller ran the prototyping lab on the island facility. Odds were, this mercenary hadn't met him. "And I promise you I'm supposed to be here. Call it in if you want."

The man's eyes widened just a fraction when he heard the name. He recognized it. And the fact that he didn't pull the trigger meant that the gamble had paid off. This guy must be a new recruit, not senior enough to have met the engineering team. He took one hand off the crossbow and brought it up to his ear to activate the comm unit. That left only one hand holding the weapon. Quinn's magic screamed to be used. He let the power fill him, and brought an invisible hand swinging in to smash into the mercenary from one side.

The crossbow fired, but the bolt missed Quinn by a good foot. He turned and jabbed a finger at the number five. The buzzer sounded three times, then kept going in quickening beats. *Thirty seconds.* The mercenary hit the wall but kept his feet, and fumbled for his sword. Quinn yelled and shoved the prep table into him, pinning the man into the corner. Then he flew out the door, ducking beneath it. Halfway across the common room, he managed to shout "I'm coming out hot!" *Twenty-five.* The table scraped in the kitchen. Then boot steps pounded after him. He sailed out the main door and around the corner. The mercenary charged out the doorway. Alethea swung one of the prop tankards. It smashed his face with a wet *thud.* He collapsed on the dirt. *Twenty.*

Quinn ran back and grabbed his arm to drag him clear. *Damn, he's heavy.* "Help me!"

"We don't have time for this," Alethea said.

"Just grab his arm."

She mumbled something that might have been a curse, dropped the mug, and took the mercenary's other arm. They dragged him across the dirt as the beeping grew louder and more insistent.

"That doesn't sound good."

"Ten seconds," Quinn panted.

They dragged him clear of the houses and headed toward the dunes. Every breath burned Quinn's lungs. *Three, two, one . . .*

Nothing happened. They reached the top of the dune. Quinn paused and glanced back. "Maybe we're—"

The building exploded, and sent him tumbling over the dune into a blinding white wall of pain.

"Few things are more vital to our in-world operations than our ability to communicate."

—R. Holt, "Investment in Alissia"

CHAPTER 26

WINDS OF WAR

Logan hated to leave Port Morgan, but he couldn't delay any longer. He'd done the goat hunt and the fish fry. Jass had stocked their skiff with two weeks of fresh provisions, a barrel of clean spring water, and even a jug of his son's moonshine. When Logan tried to pay him, he waved it off.

"You did enough for us on the hunt this morning."

"Come on, I only got one," Logan said.

Jass guffawed. "You took out the herd's sentry. We'd never have gotten close otherwise."

"We both know you let me take that shot out of politeness." Logan looked at him with narrowed eyes. "I think you could have taken him yourself."

"Maybe," Jass allowed. He'd hung back and let the younger men take most of the shots that morning, but he knew his way around a bow. "Not from forty paces, though."

"Call it a lucky shot."

"Five goats in a single trip." Jass blew out his mustache. "Luck hardly begins to describe it."

"Remember that, when it turns sour," Logan said. Jass was sixty-two, above Kiara's arbitrary cutoff, but if he so much as touched a weapon when the CASE Global fleet arrived, he'd be a dead man. Logan wished he could warn him, but he didn't dare take the risk. *I've done all I can.* "Thanks for bringing me along."

"We were glad to have you." Jass offered his hand. "Look after the lads, will you?"

Logan shook it. "Trust me, they're doing me a favor." It had taken a lot of promises of money and adventure, but he'd convinced every man younger than Jass to take a trip to Valteron City. Six of them in total. *Let it be known I've taken out every able-bodied man in Port Morgan.* He'd simply added *on my ship* to that particular order. It might be playing with words, but he'd take his chances with the lieutenant.

Besides, he could use the extra manpower in any case. And they were already aboard the ship, getting it ready to sail.

Jass turned and Logan dropped a couple of coins into his pocket using a little move Bradley once showed him. When was that, on the way through Landor? It seemed like half a lifetime ago. Logan kind of missed having the magician around. *Now I know I'm getting soft.*

They rowed back to their pirated Valteroni vessel. Ralf and Snicket must have been in high spirits, because they volunteered to handle the oars. Logan didn't protest—the huge midday meal of fried fish and sea potatoes had him in a comfortable half-coma. Mendez lounged opposite him in the bow of the skiff, looking relaxed for the first time since they'd lost Chaudri.

"How come I didn't get to go hunting?" he asked.

"You?" Logan laughed. "We had to wake you for lunch."

Mendez grimaced. "Too much moonshine."

"It's strong stuff," Snicket said. "I tried to warn him."

"Speaking of warnings, why didn't you tell us you're from here?" Logan asked.

Snicket watched the village recede. "It's not something I like to bring up."

"You know, when we first met, I thought you were Tioni."

Ralf snorted. "He wishes."

They climbed back aboard the Valteroni ship and hauled the skiff up on its crane. It was midmorning, overcast, but with a steady breeze out of the west as they got under way.

If I grew up in a place like this, I'd never leave. Logan mused on this while they glided along the cliffs and out toward the open sea. Mendez vaulted up to the wheeldeck. "Good sailing weather."

"The best," Logan said.

The land fell away on the northerly side of the harbor, revealing a wide line of blue-green ocean. Not a ship in sight to the north. *Good.* He'd just started to relax when he noticed the knot of confusion on Mendez's face.

"What's the matter?"

Wordlessly, Mendez pointed the other way, to the south. They'd just cleared the southern point of the harbor. Beyond that, on the horizon, a long line of jagged white clouds hung low over the water. This alone wasn't unusual—Alissian weather certainly had its oddities—but these clouds formed a steady line from left to right as far as he could see. A few of them shifted to one side, moving independently of the others. But they all were getting larger. Getting *closer*.

That's when he focused on one shape and realized his mistake. They weren't clouds. They were goddamn *sails*.

"Shit!" He swung the wheel around and hoped they had enough momentum to coast back into the harbor.

Snicket ran up to the wheeldeck. "S'wrong?"

"Look south."

Snicket ran to the rail, shaded his eyes, and whistled. "Where'd they come from?"

Logan had a suspicion, but he brought out his field glasses to be certain. *Blue-and-white banners. Damn.* "Valteron. Get ready to reef sails."

They coasted back behind the southern cliffs. Not as far back as Logan would have liked, but they didn't have much time. Mendez and Ralf climbed up in the rigging to take down canvas.

"Take the banners down, too!" he shouted.

"No one will know our colors if we do that," Snicket said.

"That's how I want it." The ship's hull and mast would be hard to spot against a brown coastline, but the sails stood out like highway billboards.

"The old duck and cover, eh?"

"Something like that."

Snicket ran and started climbing the mainmast.

Logan prayed that no one in the Valteroni fleet had spotted them. Out of the way or not, Port Morgan had to be on the Valteroni navy's maps, and they'd be suspicious of a deepwater vessel in its harbor.

Mendez dropped out of the rigging. "You sure they're from Valteron?"

"Blue-and-white banners. Must be his entire fleet," Logan said.

"Son of a bitch. What's he up to?"

"A preemptive strike." Logan shook his head. "He must know Kiara's coming by sea."

"Did you already set the beacon?"

"Yeah, right before we left."

Mendez grunted.

The worried grunt. "What?" Logan asked.

"If she sails right into the Valteroni fleet, it's not going to look good," Mendez said.

"You think we should warn her?"

"Unless you *want* her thinking we set a trap."

"Hell, you're right." Logan jogged up to the wheeldeck and put his comm unit in burst mode. "Logan to HQ."

The comm unit buzzed in his ear, then gave two soft beeps. *Transmission failure.* Maybe he'd hit the wrong button. He tapped it again. "Logan to Kiara, come in."

Three beeps this time. The code for *network outage*. "Of all the goddamn times!" He climbed down and found Mendez near the bow, taking a depth measurement. Which was good thinking, given how far they'd drifted toward the cliffs.

"Is your comm unit working?" Logan asked. "I can't raise Command."

Mendez handed Logan the sounding-chain and put his hand to his ear. "Mendez to HQ." He shook his head. "I'm getting beeps."

Logan's heart sank. "I think the network might be out."

"Huh." Mendez drummed his fingers on the rail. "And they don't know this fleet is coming?"

"How could they? We're the only team this far south."

"Well, I'd say they're probably screwed."

"Pretty much," Logan said. *And so are we.*

Logan stood in the crow's nest with his binoculars, counting wave upon wave of Valteroni ships. First were the scouting ships with shallow drafts that zigzagged across the water looking for trouble. One of these, a little two-master, came within about a half mile of the harbor. Logan shouted down for Ralf and Snicket to "look busy" like they were repairing something with the rudder, just to hedge his bets. The ship didn't give them so much as a second glance.

The mast shook as someone climbed up to join him. Mendez. "Any joy with the comms?" he asked.

"Nothing. It's like I'm talking to dead air," Logan said.

Mendez stared out at the approaching sails. "Never seen so many ships in my life."

"They're well disciplined, too. Something tells me the admiral came back out of retirement for this one."

"So he survived, eh?"

"That's the rumor."

"When his keep burned down, I figured he was done."

What a nightmare that raid was. First losing Chaudri, and then learning that Kiara had set the place to burn down. "Did you know the lieutenant was going to torch it before we left?"

Mendez pretended not to hear him and looked away, the classic avoidance technique for when you knew something but weren't allowed to say it.

"She doesn't have munitions training, the last time I checked," Logan pressed.

"No, she doesn't."

"But you do."

Mendez looked at him. "So do you."

"I didn't help her. I'm laying that out right now," Logan said.

Mendez still didn't answer.

Hell, he was *involved.* What a goddamn mess.

Logan scanned the next line with his field glasses. "I make another twelve in this set. Riding light like the others." That worried him as much as the sheer numbers did. A ship riding high in the water didn't have a hold full of cargo. *But men and weapons are light.*

One of the ships in this set stood out. Logan didn't notice it on the first count, but it caught his eye on the double check. She was a two-master with clean lines, and her sails perfectly taut with the wind. Looked brand-new, and somehow familiar. Either Holt had trained his shipwrights with modern techniques, or. . . . *No. It couldn't be.* "I think they might have drugged me last night."

"Why?"

"Cause I'm hallucinating, that's why."

"What do you see?"

Something that can't be real. Logan handed him the field glasses. "Check out the two-master at twelve o'clock. Fifth ship in."

"One . . . two . . . three . . . four . . . all right, I see it. What am I looking—son of a bitch, is that one of ours?"

"It's the gods-damned *Victoria*."

"I thought it sank with all hands."

"We *all* thought that. I was part of the search and rescue team. I'm telling you, there wasn't even a scrap of wreckage."

"Forgot to frisk Holt, I guess, huh?"

Logan shook his head. "He was out there with us. Had three members of the research team aboard. He'd have gone himself, except he and Relling didn't get along."

"You think she's aboard that ship?"

"I don't know. I'd sure as hell like to find out, though."

"Too bad our mission is to find Holt."

"Yeah." Logan looked again through his binoculars. "I'll be damned, I think I just saw him."

"You spotted Holt," Mendez said, in a tone laced with disbelief. "With these field glasses."

"Sure as hell looked like him."

"I don't know, man."

"I think this fleet is probably the biggest threat to CASE Global at the moment."

Mendez looked back out at the flotilla. "I can't argue with that."

"Once the last ships are past, we'll loop in behind them. Pretend to be a straggler trying to catch up."

"How you going to break it to the motley twins?"

Logan smiled. "I'm planning to order an inferior officer to do it."

"They'll take it better if it comes from you. One ship, one captain."

He had a point, but that didn't make Logan look forward to breaking the news. He climbed down the mast. Ralf and Snicket lounged in the shade of the foredeck, playing a game with six wooden dice. Looked like Maiden's Tear, a sort of craps-Yahtzee hybrid that normally involved a lot of drinking. They were sober as priests, though, since Logan had tossed every drop of liquor and moonshine overboard the moment they took the ship. Instead of drinks, they took punches in the shoulder from one another. A man's game. A classic.

"Sorry to break up the game, but we should prepare to get under way," Logan said.

"You'll want to let that fleet pass for a while," Snicket said. "They could have a rear guard."

"They'll have one, all right. Us. We're going to slip out and trail after them."

"What about Valteron City?"

"There's been a change of plans."

Snicket threw another pair of dice. Sixes. "Thought we were going to Valteron City. Didn't you, Ralf?"

"Sure thought so," Ralf said.

Logan bit his tongue, took a breath, and made his voice level. "Like I said, our plans changed. We need to follow the Valteroni fleet."

"You might've forgotten, we're on a stolen Valteroni ship," Snicket said.

"And you might've forgotten that I'm the captain. We'll stay back from the main body of the fleet. Barely within visible range."

"If we can see them, they can see us."

"That fleet's going somewhere. They won't care about a single ship lagging behind. Especially a Valteroni one."

"We were going to pick up a new berth in Valteron City," Snicket said.

Ralf grunted agreement.

Logan pointed to the ships. "There aren't any berths in Valteron City. Every ship with a Valteroni flag is right out there."

"Fair point. Maybe we're better off back in Port Morgan."

"Sure, if you want to become a fisherman."

"It beats ending up in some admiral's brig."

He wasn't wrong, but Logan and Mendez wouldn't be able to run the ship without him. Certainly not for night-and-day sailing that would be required to keep up with the fleet. *Not like I can compel them to stay aboard, though.* And he hated to lose the skiff. "What would it take to keep you on board to help follow the fleet?"

"How about double pay?"

Logan should have seen that one coming. "I think I can manage that."

"For us, *and* the lads."

"Fine." It would leave him nearly broke, though. Not a lot of padding for supplies or emergencies.

Ralf elbowed Snicket. "The other thing, too."

"All right, I was getting to it." Snicket straightened. "We want one more piece o' compensation. A favor from you, when this is over."

Alarm bells went off in Logan's head. "What sort of favor?"

"Don't know just yet. We'll name it when the time comes."

"I can't just promise you something without knowing what it is." *I'm not a fool.*

"On our word, it'll be something within your power. An inconvenience, nothing more."

Knowing these two, it would undoubtedly fall under the *major inconvenience* category but there was little Logan could do about that. He needed them, and this was their price. Well, this and about all that remained of his gold. He sighed. "Fine, a single favor within reason that I have the power to grant you. But you can't ask it until the mission's over."

"What do you think, Ralf?" Snicket asked.

Ralf stood and spat in his right hand by way of answer. Snicket copied him, as did Logan. They all shook to seal the deal.

"Glad we got that sorted," Snicket said.

Oh, I'm sure. Logan couldn't dismiss the lingering suspicion that he'd just been played. Not much he could do about it now. "Raise anchor and get us ready to sail. We've got a fleet to follow."

> "It serves us to remember that every Alissian is
> the hero of his own story."
>
> —R. Holt, "Primer on Alissian
> Cultural Immersion"

CHAPTER 27

SHADOWS

Logan would have killed to get a closer look at the
Victoria. He caught glimpses of the elegant ship as
they shadowed the fleet north, but not enough to pick
out who might be aboard. Even with the field glasses,
which Ralf and Snicket had probably noticed by now.
Neither had said anything, but they'd begun actively
not looking at the field glasses whenever Logan had
them out. They might as well have pointed and asked,
what you got there, anyway?

He'd locked most of their weapons and other gear away in the small armory in the captain's cabin. For emergencies only, and he hoped things wouldn't get that desperate.

The Valteroni fleet sailed unerringly north and kept consistently within the sight of land. With the prevailing wind out of the west, this required changing tack every couple of hours. First, the signal flags went up on every vessel, indicating the change of bearing. Then a long trumpet blast sounded, and like magic, every ship came about to the new heading simultaneously. The first time it happened, Logan wasn't even ready for it, and they nearly bumbled right into the path of one of the stout merchantmen that made up the rear guard.

The redirects continued at night, with lantern signals instead of flags. It required constant vigilance to watch for the change, and then some hustling up in the rigging to get the ship ready. The only good news was that it reinforced Logan's decision to keep Ralf and Snicket on board at any cost. Without them, they'd never have kept up with the fleet.

The morning of the third day, the steady pattern of tack-sail-tack-sail broke down without warning. Mendez was on fleetwatch duty up in the crow's nest, and called down. "Heads up! The formation's changing!"

"How?" Logan shouted back. He wished he'd thought to bring a second pair of field glasses.

"They're spreading out. Ships on either side of the line are falling back a bit."

A half-circle, then. *That's a defensive formation.* A cold thought intruded. "Do you think they're on to us?" There would be no escape if the fleet decided to capture them. The admiral would have sent ships to circle back around hours ago, to box them in against the mainland.

"Nah, they've still got their backs to us."

"Even so, we should fall back a bit until we know what's happening."

"Good idea."

For Mendez to take a position on something, he must really be concerned. Logan spun the wheel, bringing the ship to port and more into the wind. He stopped when the mainsail began to flap. It cut their speed by several knots, with the advantage that he could turn back and speed up again if he needed it.

Logan's comm unit crackled in his ear. A short, distinct burst of static. *Oh, please tell me.* "You hear that?" he shouted.

"A bit of static? Yeah, copied. Hope that's good news."

"You and me both." Logan covered his comm unit with his hand, willing it to connect. *Come on, baby. Give me some tone.*

A long, soft beep rewarded his prayer. *Network online.* "Yes!" He went for his burst-transmit button, but the lieutenant beat him to it.

"Op Command to Alpha Team, status report."

He shouldn't have felt so much relief at the sound of Kiara's voice, given what she'd done. Yet the downtime and the comms outage had somehow muted the red anger that boiled inside of him. At least if he could talk to her, he had a connection to the gateway back to Earth. A path forward. A chance at seeing his girls again. "Good to hear your voice, Lieutenant. What the hell happened?"

"Network imbalance. We lost two of the north-south relays within ten minutes of each other. The techs think it was a planned attack."

"Well, you've got a bigger problem. There's a massive Valteroni fleet sailing north right into your twenty."

"How many ships?"

He gave her a rundown of the tallies he and Mendez had done.

"That's a lot." There was a grim tone to her voice.

"Recommend you evade or redirect pronto."

She remained silent so long, he thought he'd lost the comm network again. No doubt, she was getting a situation report from the other officers in the fleet. *And probably chewing out half of her crew as well.*

"It's too late," she said at last. "They just came into visual range, which means they've probably spotted us as well."

Damn. "I would have warned you sooner, but the comms were down."

"I'm sure that was part of the plan."

Irritating as it was, the disruption won some grudging admiration from Logan. To achieve that kind of coordination, in a world without satellites or even wired communications, represented a major accomplishment. Weeks of planning, certainly, and well-trained personnel to carry out the sabotage. It had to be one of Holt's bigger plays, and he'd saved it for the perfect moment.

"Guess you'd better retreat until you can regroup," Logan said.

"Negative. We're engaging."

"You're outnumbered five to one!"

"I've had worse odds. If we move fast, we might be able to sneak to the windward side."

She thought she had hundreds of years of warfare knowledge and technology over the Valteroni fleet. But she hadn't seen them sailing for the past two days, as Logan had. They coordinated as well as any modern navy could dream of doing. Better, perhaps, given the tight formations. *Hell, I should just tell her.* "Listen, Lieutenant. Can you go triple-Omaha?" That was one of their codes, a request for one-on-one communication. Hopefully she knew he wouldn't ask unless it was important.

"Give me a minute," she said.

He changed his mind three times during the brief wait.

"All right, Logan, we're triple-Omaha. Go ahead."

What do I even say? Well, all things being equal, the lieutenant valued directness. "We're shadowing the Valteroni fleet. The *Victoria* is with them."

"Say again, over." Her voice had no emotion to it, as if under complete restraint.

"The *Victoria* is with the Valteroni fleet."

"Are you certain?"

"One hundred percent."

A pause. "And the crew?"

"Unknown. I don't want to risk getting that close."

"Where is it right now?"

"Rear of the fleet, seaward side."

"Keep it in visual range."

"What are you thinking?"

"No matter who's on it, that ship is company property. I want it back."

"I think the two hundred Valteroni ships between you might have something to say about that."

"How close are you?"

"To what?"

"The *Victoria*."

"I don't know, three quarters of a mile? But we've got a skeleton crew that can barely sail this ship." He knew better than to tell her about the boys from Port Morgan. "I forgot my boarding party on my other boat."

"Get as close as you can. Maybe you'll think of something."

Unless it's suicide, my position will be the same. "I'll

see what I can do. But don't do anything brash, Lieutenant. It's been ten years. I'm sure she's not aboard."

"This isn't about her."

"Sure it isn't."

"This is about operational security. I want to know how our state-of-the-art sailing yacht that we thought had sunk fell into enemy hands."

Logan started to say that the Valteroni weren't the *enemy*, but caught himself. "Let me paint a picture for you." He knew some of his irritation slipped into his tone, but he didn't care. "The *Victoria* sails out of radio contact and gets into trouble. Maybe they run aground, and a pirate ship happens along. Someone takes the ship, and leaves no survivors. Otherwise I think we'd have heard from at least a few of them."

"There are too many unknowns."

"What do you want me to do?"

She sighed. "Something you won't like."

That sums up this whole gods-damned mission.

"**M**endez!" Logan shouted.

"Right behind you," Mendez said.

Logan jumped. "Damn, you're a sneaky bastard."

"I learned from the best."

Yeah, you did. "How much of that did you hear?"

"Just your side of it."

"You want to take a guess at what she wants?"

"Her ship back."

"Bingo."

"And a list of everyone on board."

"One name in particular."

"Oh, man." Mendez shook his head. "Did you know her? The sister?"

"A little. We only overlapped a couple of years, and I was at the bottom of the pecking order."

Mendez gave him a dubious look, like he didn't believe that was possible. "What was she like?"

"Picture the lieutenant, then go two degrees colder."

"I'm pretty sure that's below freezing."

"She was a good officer, though. A lot of our security practices were instituted in her time."

"Well, she can't be that clever, if she agreed to hire you."

Logan offered a thin smile. "That was more of the lieutenant's doing. Relling herself didn't make mistakes."

Mendez had the field glasses up. "I don't know, man. I think I'm looking at one of her mistakes right now."

"I stand corrected."

"Do you really think the captain's still alive?"

"I don't see how she could be. She loved that ship more than anything." He didn't add that someone would have had to kill her to take it away. Ironically, Relling wasn't even slated to command the *Victoria's* maiden voyage. That should have been Kiara's gig, but Relling wanted it and had the rank to enforce her will. "I'd love to know how it ended up the flagship of the Valteroni fleet."

"There's one way to find out."

"That's what she said," Logan said.

"We might have a chance here in a minute. A new signal just went up."

Now or never. "Get us more sail. We're going to need maximum speed to catch up."

"Don't forget the hat," Mendez said.

"Aw, really?"

"It'll help sell it."

"The thing smells funny," Logan said.

"How about you go raise the topsail, and I'll be the captain?"

Well, when you put it like that. "Fine." Logan tugged the floppy felt hat on his head and tried not to think about how ridiculous it looked. The feathers had to add a foot and a half in height, long enough to catch the wind whenever it guested. How Valteron had come to dominate Alissian seas while its captains wore these things he couldn't begin to understand.

The line of officer ships shifted into a sort of wedge formation, with the *Victoria* in the van. The fleet's entire attention was forward. No one took notice when Logan slid their ship into the end of the line. The clangs of distant bells drifted across the water, and with them, the unmistakable scent of burning wood.

"Never sail farther out than you can row back."

—**Pirean saying**

CHAPTER 28

FORCE MULTIPLIER

"I've got smoke ahead," Mendez called. He'd climbed back up to the crow's nest to get a look at what lay beyond the line of Valteroni ships.

"Where there's smoke, there's fire," Logan muttered to himself.

"All right, we're coming up on the rest of the fleet," Mendez called. "Make that two fleets."

Some of the other ships in the wedge peeled off to either side to protect the flanks. Logan slid into the gap, drawing them closer to the *Victoria*. Now she was a quarter mile distant, and he could begin to make out figures moving on the deck. "Talk to me, Mendez!"

"I make twenty or thirty on board. Can't see the pilot from this angle."

Damn. "Any sign of Holt? Or Relling?"

"Negative."

"Keep looking."

The *Victoria* disappeared behind a screen of drifting smoke. Orange light sparkled on the horizon, the eerie dance of fire at sea. Logan said a prayer and steered to bring them closer. Distant *whumps* sounded from across the sea ahead, followed by the crash of shattering wood.

"What is that?" Logan demanded.

"Siege equipment."

"Ours or theirs?" Granted, at this moment, the distinction between *us* seemed a little gray. They were in a Valteroni ship sailing with the Valteroni fleet. *How will Kiara recognize us as friendlies?*

"Uh, both," Mendez said. "Logan, you'd better get up here."

Shit. "Snicket!"

"Yeah, boss?"

"Take the wheel for a minute."

The man jogged up to the wheeldeck in an uncharacteristic hurry. Logan pointed at the *Victoria*'s stern. "Keep us in view of that vessel." He glanced at the Port Morgan boys, who sat near the stern sewing bits of canvas into an extra sail. "Get the lads below until we know what we're getting into."

"You got it."

Logan climbed up the mast to the crow's nest. "What's the situation?"

Mendez handed him the binoculars. "Have a look."

The sea battle ranged over more than a mile square. Catapult-flung stones and arrow volleys arced between the lines of ships—the tall Valteroni vessels on one side, and a motley assembly of northern vessels on the other. The former outnumbered the latter by a fair margin, and had spread out in a great half-circle to pen them in. Aboard the northern vessels, tiny figures in familiar black armor scrambled to find cover from the relentless assault. Every now and then, one of Kiara's ships managed to fire one of the modular catapults mounted atop the ship.

"Why aren't they firing more?" Logan asked.

"They were at first. Maybe they ran out of payload."

It made a cruel kind of sense. Kiara's gambit for the Valteroni raid had relied on speed and secrecy. They'd have brought men and swords and horses. None of which really helped in a naval engagement. "Holt caught 'em napping. That's why he knocked out the comms."

"So how did he know about the raid?"

Logan shrugged. "Better intel."

That reminded him to scope out the *Victoria* from this higher vantage point. The other Valteroni ships gave way so that she come to the forefront. *What are they up to?* Then two things happened at once: a deafening *clack-thrum* sounded as the *Victoria* launched a spear-like projectile into the CASE Global fleet. It snapped the mast off one ship before slamming into the hull of another. Wood and steel exploded, leaving a yawning hole three feet across. A crippling blow for one ship, and certain death for the other.

Yet Logan hardly watched the carnage, because the *Victoria* veered to starboard for another shot and he saw *her* at the helm. She wore Alissian garb—a long, belted jacket over dark leggings—but the stance and the bearing gave her away. Only two women Logan knew had an air of command that came from stance alone, and they happened to be sisters. "Son of a bitch."

"What?" Mendez asked.

"I've got to call it in." He found his comm unit and flipped it on. "Logan to Kiara." Code names be damned, this was too important.

The *Victoria* fired its ballista again, clipping the topspars of two ships and then sinking a third. The northern fleet had drawn together for some cover against the encroaching ships, and it was only making things worse. *It's like shooting fish in a barrel for the Valteroni.*

"I'm a little busy at the moment," Kiara came back.

"I know, but this is priority one. Captain Relling is aboard the *Victoria*."

No response came for a full five seconds. "How do you know?"

"I can goddamned see her, that's how," Logan said. "We're right on her five o'clock."

He brought up the binoculars again, just to be certain he wasn't hallucinating. Which is how he saw Relling press her finger to her ear, and then turn to look directly at him. *Oh, holy hell. She's got a comm unit.* "Lieutenant, we got a fox in the henhouse." He shook Mendez's shoulder and whispered. "We're blown. We gotta move!"

The *Victoria* started to turn toward them. Relling was shouting at the men on the ballista. Logan threw himself onto the ladder and slid down. On the wheeldeck, he shoved Snicket aside. "They know we're here. We're going to have to make a run for it."

Kiara's voice bloomed in his ear. "Logan, hold your position."

He paused midturn. "What?"

"Hold your position in that vector."

They were sailing practically broadside to the *Victoria*, maybe doing twenty knots. As perfect a wide-open target as anyone could wish for.

"We're sitting ducks here." Even as he watched, two began turning the *Victoria*'s ballista around toward him. It already had a nasty-looking bolt loaded and ready.

"Stay on your vector. That's an order," Kiara said.

What the hell for? He saw it then, a huge Felaran three-master that had broken free of the clumped-up northern fleet. An icebreaker ship, judging by the set of nasty iron spikes protruding from the bow at the waterline. Four others like it swung out to form a wedge. *It was a ruse.* The chaos, the tangled-up ships.

"What are you planning?" he asked.

"What didn't work in Damascus," she said.

Damascus. That was a half a lifetime ago, and a mission he'd just as soon not remember. The operative goal being to "cut the head off the snake" to destabilize a terrorist group. That was what she planned. To take out the flagship. The Valteroni ships might have something to say about that, though. They rained catapult fire down on the icebreakers from both sides.

Even worse, his and Mendez's role in her plan was simply to act as bait. Distract the *Victoria* so she can get in close.

Orders be damned.

He spun the wheel hard to starboard, using the wind to push him around. That put the stern toward the *Victoria*, and made them a smaller target.

"Damn it, Logan!" Kiara crackled in his ear.

Not that it mattered, at this range. They were so close, he *heard* Relling give the order to fire.

"Hit the deck!" he shouted, and followed his own order.

He crashed hard against the unyielding wood. It stank of tar and stale seawater. But it saved his life. The ballista bolt shattered the wheel housing where he'd stood a second before. Jagged splinters rained down on him. He covered his head. *Damn, that was close.*

He forced himself up to his knees to assess the damage. The wheel was entirely gone, but the bolt had mercifully spared the mainmast. They'd lost a crossbeam or two. The sails would probably hold. Mendez, Ralf, and Snicket scrambled up into the rigging to fix what they could. He didn't even have to order it. They knew the top priority without being told: get away from the ballista as fast as possible.

Trouble was, they had no tiller control. Only the steering cables remained in the remnants of the wheelhouse, and these were tangled up with the slats and broken spars left behind by the ballista bolt. No steering. *Shit.*

"Steering's out!" He shouted. "Where's the rudder?" Unless it were dead-on straight, they'd be stuck traveling in a circle.

Ralf ran along a topspar toward the stern and looked down. "Ten points to starboard."

"Damn." He did some quick estimation. They'd loop in a great big circle and end up at the back of the CASE Global fleet. In a Valteroni ship, no less.

Logan climbed back to the highdeck on the stern, where Ralf and Snicket were working to free the tiller from the wheel cables. "How bad is it?"

"We might be able to put in a makeshift tiller," Snicket said. "Won't give us the same control of the wheel, but it'll let us turn."

"What do you need?"

"Half an hour, and the longest piece of wood you got."

In half an hour, this will all be over.

But he ran down to the hold anyway, even though part of him knew it was pointless. The boys looked at him, the fear and anxiety on their faces.

"What's going on?" one asked.

"We took a hit." He knew he should leave them here in the safety of the hold, but they were able-bodied and he needed the help. "Get up on deck and see if you can help Ralf and Snicket."

He made a quick search. There was a spare mast, but that was too large and would take an hour to maneuver out of the hold anyway. No dice. He ran back on deck and searched for something to cannibalize. The best option was a bottom-spar on the secondary mainsail. He hated to lose the canvas, but it was worthless if they couldn't get the tiller under control. He drew his belt knife and cut it free from the fastenings, wincing at the way the freed canvas flapped in the wind. He ran it back to Ralf and Snicket. "Will this work?"

"It'll have to." Snicket took it and held it fast against an upright bar that protruded from the back of the boat. Ralf lashed it fast with cord, working as fast as Logan had ever seen him.

Logan almost did a double take. *He can really move when his life depends on it.*

"That should do it," Snicket said at last. "You'll have to put one of us on the tiller, though, if you want to navigate from the wheeldeck."

"Let's give it a whirl." Logan climbed back up to the wheeldeck, which offered a better vantage point but little else, with the wheelhouse gone. They'd sailed a few hundred yards from the main action. "Bring us about."

"What?"

"We need to get closer to those two ships."

"Are you mad?"

"We'll stay clear of the ballista."

Snicket muttered a few mutinous things, but brought the makeshift tiller around.

Smoke from the burning hulls of ships obscured much of the battlefield, but from what Logan could see, CASE Global was losing. The Valteroni ships still held their formation, drawing the northern fleet deeper and deeper into their firing zone. Kiara's attack force had been reduced from five ships to two. As he watched, her last escort took a direct hit of catapult fire and burst into flames. Still Kiara kept coming. Two Valteroni ships moved in to cut her off from reaching the *Victoria*. Even with a sturdy ship, there was no way she'd break through.

Logan hit the transmit button. "This isn't going to work, Lieutenant. You need a new plan."

"Yes, listen to Sergeant Logan, dear sister," Relling chimed in.

Son of a bitch, she can even transmit. Eavesdropping on their frequency was a simple hack. Broadcasting to it took that to a whole new level. Maybe Holt had some sophisticated tech gear, but more likely, he'd gotten hold of a *new* comm unit.

The only question was who it once belonged to.

But then Logan heard something he didn't expect: gunfire.

Crack. Crack. A high-powered rifle, judging by the sound. Probably a sniper up in the crow's nest of the Felaran vessel. *Pretty sure that's a violation of the technology ban, Lieutenant.* The Valteroni interceptors faltered as their navigators slumped at the wheel. Then the icebreaker put on a burst of speed so unnatural that it had to mean electric propulsion. On an in-world vessel.

"Lord help us," Logan whispered. Make that two violations.

Kiara's icebreaker slipped between the drifting Valteroni ships and came right at Relling. It would have rammed her, maybe, if she'd kept the *Victoria* where it was. Instead, she turned it in a neat half-circle, a feat that would have snapped the keel of a native ship. That brought the *Victoria* quartering-to as Kiara's icebreaker passed the second ship.

"Lieutenant, watch the ballista!" Logan shouted, but his warning was lost in the *clack-thrum* of the siege engine firing. The bolt ripped a gaping hole in the icebreaker's hull. It lurched downward, gorging itself on seawater. Still Kiara refused to change her bearing.

"Had enough yet?" Relling broadcasted.

The crack of gunfire answered her. One of the men working the ballista fell. But there was another bolt loaded already. *How in the hell?* Relling herself appeared behind the machine and took aim. "You never did know when to quit."

Oh, no.

The next bolt took out Kiara's mast, sending wood and canvas plummeting to the deck. Then two more bolts widened the hole in the hull to a cavernous mouth. It drank in cold seawater like a man dying of thirst. Flexsteel armor-clad mercenaries struggled to get clear of the canvas as the ship took on a serious list. It lost momentum as the electric motor gave out.

"Five points to starboard!" Logan shouted. The *Victoria* moved off to engage two more Felaran ships that had made it through the Valteroni barrage. Even so, he'd just as soon keep astern of her where the ballista wouldn't reach. Kiara's icebreaker was two-thirds under water already, amid a mess of floating debris. Nothing moved out there among the waves. It didn't look good.

Damn it all. "Get us closer," Logan snapped.

"Boss—" Ralf started.

"Just do it!"

They passed one of the smaller piles of floating wreckage, and suddenly, there she was. Clinging to a timber like a half-drowned rat. "Lieutenant!" He tore loose one of the halyards from the secondary mainsail and threw one end to her.

She looked up at him, as if not comprehending. Then she let go of the wreckage and moved out toward it, treading water. She spun in a slow circle. He knew what she saw. Her men dead, most of her fleet destroyed. Nothing left to command. Logan had been there before. He understood the darkness that came with it. Part of him wanted to leave her there to suffer it, for what she'd threatened to do. But he still needed her. "Grab on, Kiara."

She met his eyes then. Really *looked* at him. "Remember your orders, Logan." She went still, and sank into the blue depths.

"No!" Logan started to climb the rail, but two pairs of arms held him fast. Ralf and Snicket. "Let me go!"

"She's lost, boss," Snicket said.

"I can get to her."

Ralf put a calming hand on his shoulder. "Let her go."

They're right. And they were too strong for him. He slumped against the rail.

Mendez ran up. "What happened? Where's the lieutenant?"

"Gone," Logan managed to say. He stared at the place where the ships had gone down, still not believing it himself.

Mendez whispered something and crossed himself. "And the strike force?"

Every ship that Logan could see flew the Valteroni flag. The rest had fled, sunk, or were adrift and burning. "Gone."

"Shit. What do we do now?"

Logan stared at the soot-covered water where the ships had disappeared. "I don't know."

Mendez half-carried Logan to the wheeldeck. Snicket rousted his kinsmen from the hold now that the main danger was past, and sent them up to work in the sails.

Logan lowered himself to the deck and closed his eyes. *Please, let this be a nightmare.* It was a few minutes before he could bring himself to speak. "She was right in front of me."

"Nothing you could have done, man." Mendez sank to the deck beside him.

"I doubt the brass will see it that way."

Mendez let out a long breath. "Relling had a comm unit. The whole mission was compromised."

"How the hell did she get one?"

"She was working with Holt, so probably from him."

"It had our frequencies, though. The *new* ones."

"I know. That's the one part I can't figure out."

Mendez paused. "We didn't see Veena go under the water."

That's what he's getting at. "Mendez . . ."

"I'm serious. What if Holt's people captured her?"

"We'd have heard something. A ransom demand, or another ultimatum."

Mendez grunted. He had a wide grunt vocabulary, and this particular one meant *not sure I buy it.*

"What?" Logan asked.

"There's only one way to know for sure. One person, I mean."

"Oh, come on. *Him?*"

"Doesn't hurt to ask."

"We're still under orders, and they don't include chatting him up."

"Man, screw the orders. Kiara's gone. The whole chain of command is broken."

He's right. "Guess that means I'm in charge." They had contingencies set up for this kind of thing, and unless a superior officer appeared, operational decisions fell to Logan. On this side of the gateway, at least.

"What do you want to do?"

Central command would probably be expecting a report soon, with this raid in progress. Without the lieutenant's tablet, there was no way to get in touch to let them know what had happened. *What will they think, when Kiara doesn't report in?* They'd probably assume the worst. Hell, they might even pin the blame on Logan for this disaster, if he didn't go there himself to set the story straight. "Probably best we return to base, and let the top brass reevaluate our options."

"*You* can return to base." Mendez gripped the rail and looked down at the water. "I'm going to Valteron City."

"I was afraid you were going to say that."

"I'm sorry, Logan. I've got to know."

"What about your family?" They'd been *invited* to the CASE Global's island facility just as Logan's girls had.

"You'll do me a solid on that front, won't you?"

Logan sighed. The forty-plus member Mendez clan complicated his plans by an order of magnitude. "Of course."

"So, where you want us to drop you off?"

Logan guffawed. "Oh, you think you're taking the ship?"

"I've got farther to go. And it's through Tion. A nightmare to go overland."

"I guess you could drop me at Bayport."

Mendez grinned. "What a pal."

Snicket spoke up, startling them both. "Hate to break up these lovely little plans, but neither of you'll be taking the ship."

Logan turned around to find Snicket and Ralf

both holding loaded crossbows on him and Mendez. The Port Morgan boys stood behind them, looking a bit nervous but otherwise committed.

"I see you found the armory," Logan said.

"Figured we should arm ourselves as long as you insisted on suicide missions."

"How about putting them back, since we're out of danger?"

"Oh, we're not out of danger." Snicket turned to Ralf. "Where's the danger, Ralf?"

"Right here on deck."

"I'm thinking the same. We'll be a lot safer once you lot are gone."

What's he playing at? "If I didn't know better, I'd think you were hinting at insubordination."

"We like to call it *renegotiation*."

Well, at least they were Logan's kind of scum. He couldn't afford to double their pay, but in a negotiation, everyone gave a little. "What do you want?"

"We'll start with the ship," Snicket said.

"That's a little awkward, isn't it?" Logan asked. "We're standing on it out in the middle of the ocean."

"I got a solution for that, too." Snicket grinned, and it was a wicked thing to behold.

"I certainly hope that you're reading my reports. We have worked too hard for too long to be ignored."

—R. Holt, "A Decade Devoted"

CHAPTER 29

THE COALITION

Quinn, Jillaine, and their Tukalu escorts were among the first to arrive to Valteron City. His ears still rang from the explosion, but at least the headache was gone. They gained entry through the side-door without any extra "security" questions. Alethea—who seemed no worse for wear after the mission—conferred with one of her warriors inside the wall for a moment, then rejoined the group.

"We're meeting out on the terrace," she said.

Good to know. Traveling with a couple of Holt's personal guards certainly had its perks. They could go just about anywhere with hardly a security challenge, and Alethea was *plugged in*. Plus there was the whole protection-with-threats service that Tukalu delivered with brutal efficiency.

"Is that out in the open?" he asked.

"Just inside the seawall. The word around the palace is that the sea threat has . . . abated."

What's that supposed to mean? "I hope that's good news."

"We're also the first to arrive, which means we probably have a few hours." Alethea smiled wickedly. "The Prime has arranged rooms for you."

Quinn marked the use of the plural, and quietly cursed his luck. If there was going to be any downtime, he'd have preferred to spend it with a bathtub and Jillaine. In that order. Hell, at the same time wouldn't be so bad either, if she'd let him. After that kiss during the mission, he thought the possibility might be there. If only they were in Pirea, where men and women sometimes shared bathhouses. This was Valteron, though, and Holt seemed a little more old-fashioned.

Alethea and Bita passed him off to two of their Tukalu sisters. Which was fine, of course—Quinn didn't mind having someone to show him around the mazelike palace—but after spending nearly every minute with Alethea for the past few days, he already kind of missed her. She added a spark to things, that was for damn sure. And, she and Jillaine even seemed to have worked through the alpha-female-rivalry or whatever it was.

As much as he'd have liked for it to be about *him*, it wasn't.

Well, it *probably* wasn't.

Even so, when the Tukalu guards showed them to two rooms in the same hallway, that felt like an opportunity. He lingered outside his doorway a moment to make sure that he knew which room was hers. She glanced back and saw him looking. Held his eye a minute, but didn't exactly beckon. It was more of a neutral look that could have gone either way.

Quinn preferred to see the world as a glass half-full.

He hustled into his temporary room, which resembled the high roller suite in a five-star hotel. A low fire burned cheerily in the hearth, the flames dancing in hypnotic concert with those on four oil lamps set about the room. In the middle of it, two plush divans with hand-embroidered pillows flanked a low marble table. A heavy pitcher waited there with two porcelain cups. Steam drifted out of its rim, filling the chamber with the rich aroma of Landorian brew. *Now there's a nice touch.* Knowing Holt, every detail here had been carefully chosen to echo a certain theme, to convey specific information, to shape his thinking a certain way.

Quinn had no time for that. He found the bath,

stripped, and settled into it for a deep scrubbing. A light linen towel waited by the tub, and next to that, a fresh set of men's clothing. He recognized the weave and the fabric, too. The flame-resistant materials had a faint sheen to them, though an untrained eye would probably mistake them for in-world garb. How Holt had managed to have company-issued garments in his size was a mystery. Maybe he'd raided one of the hidden bolt-holes before he blew them up. In any case, Quinn had a short window and didn't want curiosity to ruin it. He dressed and made himself presentable. Considered shaving, but decided it was best to forgo that luxury for a bit longer. A lot of these missions required him to blend in with the crowd, and a great many Alissian men seemed to be allergic to razors.

He left the flexsteel armor off as well. It felt good to be clean and dressed and out of danger for a brief moment. Even better, he'd only burned about forty minutes. He yanked open the door to the hall, only to find his Tukalu guard leaning against the wall opposite. They had this thing about leaning, the Tukalu. They did it constantly, as if standing unassisted was against the law. He'd even wondered if it was a form of laziness, that they always found something to bend against. Turns out, it was none of those things. That casual foot against the wall behind them served as a launchpad if they needed to move quickly. Quinn had watched Alethea leap from the lean-back position into a full-on forward roll. They *trained* on different moves that started in those relaxed positions. It looked casual because they wanted it to. Because it made adversaries take them less seriously.

And that, right there, was what made Tukalu warriors so dangerous: they worked very hard to conceal how good they really were.

So when Quinn saw the guard leaning right opposite his door, he knew she was on full alert. Which raised the question of why Holt thought invited guests needed protection inside the walls of his own palace. He swallowed, took a right, and strolled down the corridor toward Jillaine's room. He didn't have to look to know the guard would trail after him.

Jillaine's Tukalu guard eased off the wall as he approached her door.

This ought to be interesting. He raised his hand to knock, but the woman pointedly cleared her throat. He gave her a questioning look. "Yes?"

"She asked not to be disturbed until the others arrive."

Quinn tried his best smile on her. "I don't think she meant me, so . . ."

"She specifically mentioned you."

"Say what now?" There was no way Jillaine would have done that. *Maybe Alethea's still playing games.*

The guard jerked a thumb toward Quinn's room and made her voice about two octaves higher. " 'That includes Quinn,' were her exact words."

Burned. "I see." He was half-tempted to knock

anyway, to hear this from Jillaine herself, but this woman would probably break his arm if he tried. Besides, that would only hang a lantern on the private shame. He didn't need that.

So he spun on his heel and returned to his own chambers. The Landorian brew helped a little, but he still couldn't get why Jillaine delighted in toying with him. The way she kissed him, right before the split up to take out the CASE Global comm relays . . . well, maybe there wasn't as much promise there as he'd thought. Or maybe she really *was* tired and needed some alone time.

He couldn't know for sure and hadn't had the guts to ask, so he gave up and sprawled out on one of the divans. His body ached with fatigue, but sleep eluded him. Probably because of the Landorian brew. *Well, as long as I can't sleep, I might as well sweep the room.* That's what Logan would want him to do, no matter the level of trust or the guard stationed outside. He found no hidden assassins, no traps, no surveillance equipment. The only thing his search turned up was a little square of folded parchment tucked beneath one leg of the marble table. He unfolded it, and recognized the handwriting right away.

Bravo, Quinn! Logan taught you well.-R.

"He sure did," Quinn said. Truth be told, he kind of missed the big man's ball-busting approach to training. *I'm even missing Logan. That's how screwed up things are right now.*

Someone banged on the door to Quinn's chambers, rousing him from a half-doze. He stumbled over and jerked it open, half-expecting to see Logan waiting to escort him down to the armory for more training. Instead, he found Alethea tapping her foot with impatience. She'd changed into fresh clothes and rebraided her hair. There was even a faint perfume about her, a scent of lilies.

"About time," she said. "I thought maybe you'd dropped dead in there." She didn't put the usual energy into her snark, though. If anything, her eyes were hooded.

"What's wrong?" he asked. "Is everyone here yet?"

"Everyone who will be. They're gathering on the terrace."

He buckled on his sword-belt. "Let's go."

They took two sets of staircases and emerged on a wide outdoor patio the size of an Olympic swimming pool. Beyond its beveled edge lay a spectacular vista of Valteron City's plaza, the merchant districts, and then the harbor. Moric and Anton were in deep conversation to one side. Holt and Veena chatted with Jillaine beside a massive wooden table laden with maps and scrolls and, strangely, a single empty tankard. All three of them fell silent and looked at Quinn as he emerged from the double door. Five Tukalu guardswomen lounged in a loose half-circle around them, far enough away to offer some privacy but unmistakably a security detail. They all made the same gesture, kissing two fingers and touching them to the forehead.

Quinn glanced back at Alethea, who walked a half-step behind him. "Hey, I'm getting salutes from your guardswomen now."

She pressed her lips together, but didn't quite smile. "I believe that was directed at me."

"You sure?"

"Comfortably."

He paused and took stock of the other coalition members. Moric and Anton, too, had spotted him and clamped their mouths shut. "Who gets the awkward silence?"

"That's all yours." Alethea jogged off to join her sisters.

Holt put on a smile and spread his hands out in greeting. "Well, it's my favorite troublemaker. Welcome back."

"Thank you. Glad to have made it in once piece." Quinn met his eyes, and Veena's, but pretended not to notice Jillaine. *Wouldn't want to disturb her.*

Jillaine saw right through this and jabbed him in the side with a finger. He gasped, but couldn't keep from smiling. Especially when she smiled back. *All right, I forgive you.*

"I did hear there were complications," Holt said.

Quinn remembered the look on the mercenary's face when he couldn't get out, as the inn was about to blow. *I'll probably never forget that, either.* "A few. Please tell me it worked."

Holt nodded. "Everyone should hear this." He raised his voice. "Everyone? If you'd be so kind." He gestured at the table. They all settled in. Quinn gave Moric and Anton a nod from across the table.

"Thanks to the speed and courage of the Valteroni fleet, we caught the invading strike force as they rounded the tip of New Kestani and engaged them at sea," Holt began. "I don't think they knew we were coming, which suggests that the communications disruption was a success."

Quinn nodded as if this were all normal and expected, while allowing a small fist-pump of celebration under the table. *Yes!*

"It was a victory, but a costly one," Holt said. "Nineteen of our vessels were sunk or destroyed. Six were disabled. Another three were captured by enemy forces and managed to escape. Whether that was a desperate stab at survival, or a coordinated plan, remains to be seen."

"Knowing Kiara, it's probably the latter," Quinn said.

"Lieutenant Kiara is dead."

Those four words brought a chill to Quinn's core. "What?"

"Her flagship rammed the *Victoria*. Both vessels sank, and she was not among the survivors."

Lieutenant Kiara is dead. The words kept echoing in Quinn's head, and while he knew their meaning, it still didn't seem possible. "Captain Relling?"

"Pursuing the remnants of the CASE Global force as we speak," Holt said.

"What about our mutual . . . friends?"

"If you mean Logan and Mendez, your guess is as good as mine," Holt said.

Quinn looked at Veena. Her eyes were red-rimmed, like she'd been crying. *Well, I know what she thinks.* "At least we won. We *did* win, didn't we?"

Holt raised his eyebrows. "This battle? Absolutely. But this engagement also demonstrated just how far CASE Global is willing to go. Navigators on at least two of our ships were killed by high-speed projectiles, from well out of bow range."

"A sniper rifle," Quinn said.

"That was my thinking, too. As formidable of an adversary Kiara was, she was also the biggest proponent of the gateway technology ban. Without her, and given our decisive victory, we must assume the company will resort to a draconian response. A full-scale invasion with modern weaponry and equipment."

Machine guns mowing down villages. Mortar shells lobbed at the Enclave from offshore boats. Quinn forced himself to unclench his jaw. "Do we even have a chance?"

"Perhaps. Moric?"

Moric cleared his throat and made a big deal of straightening out his robe. "After seeing it up close, and some digging in our oldest archives, I believe the gateway may have been created by Enclave magicians."

"How is that possible?" Quinn asked. "You didn't even know of its existence until I told you."

"That's not entirely true. We knew there was a third great enchantment cast by the Enclave's founders."

The third miracle. It made sense the more Quinn thought about it, but all he knew of the folklore were the bits and pieces he'd picked up from Moric and Sella. "I wish we knew for certain."

"You're a doubting Thomas, which I myself can appreciate," Holt said. "I felt the same, until I saw these." He dug into one of the piles of parchment and extracted a wide sheet covered with charcoal sketches. "Do you recognize these?"

The symbols *did* look familiar. The last time Quinn'd seen them, they were etched in stone, and the frigid air had discouraged him from taking a closer look. "They look like the stuff on the walls of the gateway cave."

Veena nodded. "That's what I thought, too." She nudged Holt. "See? They bear a distinct resemblance."

"They look like runes," Quinn said. "You know, magical symbols."

"That's an apt way to describe them," Moric said. "These are afterimages left by supremely powerful enchantments. Except they are not from your cave, but were left on another of the founders' legacy."

It took Quinn a moment to connect the dots. "The Enclave towers? You've got to be kidding me."

"Mags herself copied these from the foundations."

That's one hell of a coincidence, if it's true. "All right, let's say for the sake of argument that the gateway is the third great magic miracle. How does that help us?"

"It tells us that we're not dealing with a natural phenomenon, but a magical construct. Having had some time to study it, I believe that construct has three parts: the gateway in our world, the gateway in their world, and the link between them."

"Sounds familiar," Anton said.

"That's what I thought, too," Moric said.

Holt cleared his throat. "Perhaps you could explain, for the non-magicians among us?"

"It's reminiscent of how magicians transport themselves from one place to another. In essence, we create a temporary link between two places."

"Now that I think about it, walking through the gateway and being transported feel the same," Quinn said.

"We wondered as much, when you spoke of it at your trial," Moric said.

"Trial?" Holt asked.

"It was really more of a hearing," Quinn said.

"Not his first one, it must be said," Anton added.

Holt knitted his eyebrows at this, but pressed on. "It sounds like you have some inkling of the nature of the gateway. Can it be controlled, to dictate who comes and goes?"

"Probably not," Moric said.

"But what magic can create, magic can destroy," Anton said.

Moric pointed at him. "Exactly."

Quinn held up a hand. "Wait a minute. If we destroy it, how can those of us who aren't from here get back to where we came from?"

A ring of sad, silent faces answered him.

"Oh." *That's why we're all here.* But it wasn't just him, either. He looked to Veena. "You don't want to go back?"

She shrugged. "I spent most of my career studying Alissia. For most of that time, I was afraid to set foot here."

"You simply needed a little push," Holt said.

She gave him a warm smile. "Yes, I did." She looked back to Quinn. "My place is here."

But destroy the gateway? It seemed so extreme, so gods-damned *final*. "Is there no other way?"

"Every moment we delay, CASE Global brings more troops and weaponry through the gateway," Richard said. "At some point, their resources will outstrip ours."

And then they'd lose everything. Alissian independence, the pristine landscape, the Enclave. All of that would come to an end when CASE Global subjugated the populace. Quinn had seen their security practices too often, and from too close, to believe otherwise.

He could feel everyone's eyes on him. Holt wouldn't care about returning, so he was really the only one who had a shot at talking his way back through the gateway. And hell, he had things waiting for him on the other side. *My own ticket in Vegas.* Fame and money and influence, in the town where those things mattered most.

Of course, that was also a one-way ticket. Kiara had lobbied for him to join the second mission, and gotten approval from all the higher-ups. Logan indicated more than once that this wasn't an entirely popular decision. Her successor on the Gateway Project might not see a Vegas stage magician as useful. Especially one who'd gone off the grid for a few weeks at a vital time.

But who am I kidding? If that's what he really wanted, he'd have bolted for the gateway a long time ago. "If that's what we need to do to win, let's do it."

"Are you sure?" Moric asked.

"The Enclave is my home now." He looked from Moric to Anton. "If they'll have me."

Moric and Anton shared a glance, but this had clearly already been decided. "Due in no small part to your actions for the coalition, not to mention the testimony of some of your biggest supporters, the council has voted to restore your membership."

"Then I'm all in," Quinn said. *No better way to say it than that.*

Holt pulled out another, larger sheet of parchment that showed a blown-up version of the CASE Global parchmap in bright, beautiful detail. A gasp escaped Jillaine's lips upon seeing it. "In that case, let us formulate our plan to strike at the gateway cave itself. Or as I like to call it, Operation Closed Door."

"You know what, if I'm staying, I'd really like to be consulted on all op names," Quinn said. "You guys are killing me with this stuff."

"Duly noted," Holt said. "No matter the name we choose, this is a two-stage operation. The first stage begins tomorrow, so I'll need all of you to be well rested. We depart at first light."

"Sometimes we are blind to the most obvious things."

—R. Holt, "Reevaluating Alissian Assumptions"

CHAPTER 30

IN-LAWS

"I think that went well," Veena said.

"Yes. Almost surprisingly so," Richard said.

They strolled through the lamplit gardens in the center of the palace, shadowed by Tukalu guards, en route to the wing that housed the palace-within-a-palace, the residence of the Valteroni Prime. This was a freestanding castle in the courtyard near a miniature stone plaza. It had its own walls, its own staircase, its own wide terrace and schooner-shaped structure. A copy of the massive building in miniature. Veena found it a bit pompous, even for Valteron. Richard himself hadn't seemed to notice.

"When did you figure out that the gateway had magical origins?" she asked.

"As much as I'd like to claim credit for that, it was Moric's breakthrough. I didn't believe it until he showed me the sketches from the Enclave." He sighed and shook his head. "What I would give to spend just an hour on that island."

"Maybe when this is over."

He barked a laugh. "They'll continue to dangle that in front of me like a carrot in front of a donkey. I imagine I'll never go, unless I somehow manifest the ability."

"Like Quinn did."

"That would be nice, wouldn't it? How long do you think he's had it?"

"He didn't say. Frankly, I have trouble telling where the illusions end, and the real magic begins."

"I feel the same way." They crossed the little drawbridge across the moat to the miniature palace. Richard stooped to cross beneath the points of the portcullis. Two of the Tukalu positioned themselves at the foot of the bridge, while two others jogged around to cover other access points.

Veena didn't often get private moments with Richard. She had to make this count. "I don't think you should go with them."

Richard smiled. "I really have no choice. Alliance

or no, the Valteroni army will have trouble taking orders from the Caralissian nobility."

He meant Anton, who'd stepped up to command the army of mercenary guards that marched under the Caralissian flag toward Nevil's Gap. For the first time in almost a generation, not a single cask of Caralissian wine was en route anywhere. *The greatest sacrifice we've ever made,* Anton called it, to the wry amusement of most others in the coalition.

"Even so, we've no idea what kind of weapons CASE Global will bring to bear. You're too important to lose."

"No one is too important, when the future of this world is at stake." He always had a grandiose response to her cogent arguments. It was like he sat around thinking them up for future conversations.

"I'm worried about Valteron, too. They need their leader."

"They'll have something better." He made a flourishing bow at her. "The *legendary* Dahlia."

"I wish I shared your confidence in everything. My part especially."

"You've learned so much in such a short time." He put a hand on her shoulder. "You're ready."

"What if no one listens to me?"

"They'll listen. They've seen what you did in Tion, not to mention Caralis."

"I wish they believed in me half as much as you did."

Richard didn't stop in his sitting room as he usually did. Instead, he opened the door to the inner chamber. The *bedchamber*. A place she'd never been, even as his top advisor. He went in. She bit her lip and scurried after him.

"No one knows your potential as well as I do." He looked back at her and smiled. "You'll go far here."

"Richard." She reached out and grabbed his arm, making him face her. "I may not have another chance to tell you this."

"What's wrong?"

"Nothing. And everything," she said.

He smiled. "That sounds like a contradiction."

"When we came back to Alissia for the second mission, everyone had a reason. Do you know mine?"

"You'd fallen for this world, just as I did."

"That's part of it. I love being in Alissia." She took a breath. "But not nearly as much as I love sharing it with you."

"I feel the same way. You appreciate this world as only a fellow scholar can."

"It's more than that. For me, at least. Is it for you?"

A cloud passed over his face. "There's something I must tell you."

She eased a bit closer to him. "Tell me."

"When I discovered this world, when I saw its potential, I knew I had to devote my life to studying it. As part of that, I promised myself I would never let personal relationships get in the way of the work."

Now you tell me.

"But I broke that promise," Richard said.

She put a hand on his arm. "It's all right."

"You don't understand, Veena. I'm the Prime of Valteron. Personal entanglements only make me more vulnerable."

"They make you *human*, Richard."

He shook his head. "I wish I'd been strong enough to resist. For the sake of Alissia."

She gave his arm a squeeze. "You can tell me."

"I suppose I can. If there is anyone who should know, it's you."

Here it came, at last. Veena closed her eyes and inhaled slowly, to calm her too-fast-beating heart.

"I'm in love," he said. "And have been for a while. Years, in fact."

This was hard for him. She could see it, but she still had to hear it for herself. "And with whom are you in love?" *Say my name*, she thought.

"A Landorian woman."

Veena opened her eyes and broke free of her reverie. "Excuse me?"

"We met on my second year as head of the research team. I knew right away to be careful with her, to conceal her existence from the company." He smiled at her. "I didn't count on your cleverness. Comparing my journals to the travel logs, looking for a pattern of disparities. A bright flashing arrow to her hometown."

What was he talking about? The only person she'd tracked in that fashion was the witch in that little valley, the one who'd captured Veena, Quinn, and Julio with her intoxicating smoke. "You don't mean Iridessa?" The woman certainly possessed a certain allure, but she had more years on Richard than he had on Veena.

"She's a firecracker, isn't she? I suppose I could do worse for a mother-in-law."

Mother. In-law. The meaning of the syllables sunk in with excruciating slowness. "You're *married*? To *her* daughter?"

He laughed, his eyes still distant. "Hard to believe, isn't it?"

She was such a fool. "Almost impossible."

"We have a child together, too. A son. He'll be fourteen in the spring, and I hardly know him."

"I feel like I hardly know *you*."

"Touché. I hope you understand the need for dire secrecy. But by the gods, it feels good to share this with someone I can trust."

She should have seen it, should have known. It was all falling into place now—the way he'd kept himself distant, his blindness to Veena and how she felt about him. His desperation to escape into this world and save it from the threat CASE Global presented. Now, at least, she understood why he'd so blithely ignored her clear devotion. Why he'd politely refused her countless unspoken invitations. He wasn't married to his job. He was just plain married.

Strange, how that gut-wrenching revelation shifted her worldview a full ninety degrees. "Thank you for sharing this with me, Richard. I should go."

"Of course. I didn't realize how late it was," he said, still totally blind to the crushed woman before him. "Will you come to see us off tomorrow?"

All of her mistakes and missteps were laid bare before her. Maybe it wasn't too late to correct some of them. She owed it to herself to try. "I'll think about it."

"My biggest problem is knowing when to give up."

—Art of Illusion, October 20

CHAPTER 31

BARRED DOORS

Quinn trudged back down to the guest wing of the Valteroni palace, his mind still spinning with troop numbers, attack plans, and Moric's magical theories. A soft footfall behind him announced the presence of a Tukalu escort. He hadn't even thought to wait for one. It was Alethea again. *It's like I keep winning the Tukalu lottery.*

He slowed to let her catch up. "I must be pretty important, to draw the best Tukalu warrior so often."

"That's one way to read it," she said.

"Is there any other way?"

"Maybe you have a tendency to need more supervision."

He laughed. "Is that what Richard thinks?"

"The Prime doesn't make our individual assignments."

So it's more of a personal interest. "Good to know." He decided to take a different angle. "How did you fall in with him, anyway?"

"He came to Tukalu himself, years ago. More recently, he sent his ambassador. The one called Dahlia."

Also known as Veena Chaudri. "And she hired you?"

"She negotiated an agreement," she said.

Finally, a hint at the origins of the odd relationship between Valteron and the Tukalu. "You provide your services, and he provides . . . what?"

"A number of things. But primarily, independence for our island and its people."

He glanced back, because that almost sounded like a joke, but her face was serious. Hopeful, even. "Are you not independent now?"

"Tukalu is currently a protectorate of Valteron."

"Really? I'd never have guessed." He didn't add that granting independence to an already self-sufficient region cost Holt very little. In return, he got some of the best fighters in Alissia to serve as personal guards.

The guy is a goddamn genius. And bravo to Veena sealing that deal. She'd certainly been busy since turning her coat. "You said you got a number of things in return. What else?"

"Nothing I can share with you." She gestured ahead. "And here are your chambers. Bar your door, as we can't spare a guard tonight. I want everyone rested for tomorrow."

"No problem. See you at sunrise." He went in and pushed the door shut behind him. He'd barely unbuckled the sword-belt when she knocked on the door again. He yanked it back open. "Can I at least take off my belt before I—" and he trailed off when he saw it was Jillaine. "Oh. Hey."

She locked eyes with him and he couldn't move. She advanced through the open door and let it swing shut behind her. "Before you what?"

She moved close to him, filling the world with the scent of roses. *So close.*

He eased back a step or two, just to give her space. It seemed like the polite thing to do. "Bar the, um . . ." His mouth was having trouble forming cohesive words. "Door. I'm supposed to bar the door."

She curled a finger without even looking, and the bar slid home. "It's barred. Do you do everything Alethea tells you?" She advanced on him again, and her eyes glittered with the promise of violence.

Uh-oh. "Whoa." He held up his hands. "She's just a friend."

She slid between his hands. Grabbed the front of his shirt and kissed him. A long, lingering kind of kiss that made him dizzy.

"What am I?" she whispered.

"So much more." He pulled her up against him.

"Preparation and vigilance offer more protection than force of arms."

—R. Holt, "The Dangers of the Other World"

CHAPTER 32

THE BROTHER

It took Logan six hours to row to shore in the tiny skiff Ralf and Snicket put him and Mendez in at crossbow-point. No food. No water. Just the clothes on their backs and the little bit of gold that Logan kept hidden about his person. Not even their goddamn swords. *That's what I get for turning my back on thieves I had to threaten to work with us in the first place.*

Still, it wouldn't have happened if Kiara had listened to one damn thing he said to her in the past month. *Don't move the troops by sea. Don't engage the*

Valteroni fleet. Turn and run, when you know you're beaten. She always put the mission first, no matter the consequences. No matter whose family she had to hold at ransom.

Mendez was heading south toward Valteron City, and planned to reequip at a CASE Global hidey-hole near Bayport. Provided that Holt's little game of sabotage hadn't spread that far north yet, of course. Within a day of parting with Logan, Mendez had already "borrowed" a sword and a horse, according to their last chat before going radio silent.

Sneaky bastard.

Logan had no such luck on the two-week trek northeast across New Kestani. He *hated* not having more than a knife to defend himself, but he hadn't had a chance to nab something better. Even the tiniest settlements here were on high alert and distrustful of strangers. After the third village denied him refuge for the night, he no longer bothered to try.

Only the little monastery from the peace-loving Friars of the Star let him stay a night. They even gave him a hot bowl of soup to eat, and were kind enough not to ask too many questions. Logan felt bad about nicking one of their robes.

Now, as he crouched between two dark boulders and surveyed the Kestani encampment in the vale before of him, he was glad he'd taken it. A hundred and fifty tents, give or take, stood in neat rows along the floor of it. Soldiers crouched around the bright-burning cook fires between the rows, sharing a midday meal. He marked about seventy-five men, most of them armored, each with a sword or mace on his belt. Beyond them stretched a massive dirt-and-pike wall that ran from one steep mountainside to the other, blocking off the entirety of Nevil's Gap. An equal number of men stood on duty along the wall or manned the double-cart gate where the road came through and continued down into Felara.

Kiara wasn't kidding when she said they'd closed the border. The gate was closed, and the complete absence of travelers heading to or from suggested it had been for some time.

This is the only way north, too. "Damn."

He wouldn't chance the Landorian route through the mountains again, at least not until they did something about the smugglers that controlled passage—especially since he had no more money to bribe his way through. The only other way into Felara lay more than a hundred leagues to the west, practically to the coast of the ocean. Logan didn't want to lose another two weeks. CASE Global would already be in panic mode when they lost contact with the fleet. Who knew what orders Kiara left behind, in case she dropped out of contact. And if the executives thought Logan played a role in her death . . .

No. I won't think about that.

He just needed to get there, make sure his family was safe, and explain what had happened.

Going by sea would have been faster and avoided the Gap, but Logan vowed to never chance the Alissian seas ever again. Not after watching Kiara battling her sister, and then letting his hired hands get the drop on him. He tugged the robe on, and tucked everything in so no one would get a glimpse of the flexsteel armor. He couldn't hide the boots, so he smeared them with mud on the walk up to the Kestani camp.

He drew the hood and slouched as he walked. Kept his eyes on the road, too. If any soldiers crouched around the cookfires noticed him, they said nothing. He made it all the way to the central gate before an officer stepped out to bar his way.

"Where you headed, brother?" He had a long mustache, dark-oiled in the Kestani style, and his uniform was spotless. Not even a snowflake on it, and they'd just seen a blizzard.

"North," Logan said. "North, in search of peace."

"The last place you'll find peace is Felara."

"Unfortunately, that is not for me to decide," Logan said.

"I'm sorry, brother. You'll have to go a different way."

Logan wrinkled his brow, as if confused. "Has there been an avalanche?"

"No, but the Gap is closed."

Hoofbeats sounded, and the soldiers on either side of the wooden gates pulled them open to admit a party of four riders in Kestani uniforms. A patrol, most likely.

Logan watched them dismount and lead their horses away toward the stable at the western rim. "It looks open to me."

"If we don't send out patrols, we won't know when the next attack is coming. The Gap is crawling with Felarans."

"The conflict between you is disappointing." Logan let the officer chew on that for a moment. *Got a comeback? Didn't think so.* "But it doesn't concern the Order."

"Are you armed?" the man asked.

"No." He figured he had to sell it, so he added, "My wits and my faith are the only weapons I need."

"That may not be enough. The Felarans are desperate."

"What can they take from me?"

"Your life."

They'd left the gate open after the horses came through. The soldier tasked with closing it had stepped over to warm his hands by the nearest fire. The second he came back, the gate would be shut, and then Logan would have no shot at getting through. *What would Bradley do?* That was easy. Bradley would do what he wanted, and ask for permission later.

"I appreciate the warning." Logan stepped around the officer and walked toward the open gate, which was thirty yards distant.

"Brother, wait!" the officer called after him.

Logan kept walking. "Peace will not wait."

The officer strode and grabbed him by the arm. "You're a dead man if you walk down the Gap alone."

"All men die." Logan looked pointedly at the man's hand on his arm, and frowned until he lifted it. "Perhaps my time has come." He turned on his heel and kept going.

"Stop, or I'll signal the archers!"

Logan didn't dare stop. "And have them shoot a Brother of the Star in the back?" he called. "That's what Felarans would do."

He strode through the gate without another word. Not rushing, not slacking, just keeping a steady pace. Straining his ears to hear what the officer did next. Bracing himself to hear that order given. He wouldn't run for it, even if they did. Running was a sign of guilt. He was not guilty. He was a Brother of the Star, and he had somewhere to be.

"Stage magicians are night creatures. But then again, so is most of Vegas."

—Art of Illusion, January 4

CHAPTER 33

DEPARTURES

Trumpets made an enemy of Quinn Bradley that morning. They announced daybreak to the Valteroni palace, a rousting of everyone who would join the expedition to the cold north. Quinn had too little sleep under his belt, and could not be less ready. His clothes were strewn across two different rooms in his chambers. He found his shirt on the solid marble table, and one of his boots beneath the tipped-over divan.

If this were a five-star hotel, I'd be losing my deposit right now.

He gathered everything slowly and dressed in layers for the cold—light linen shirt, flexsteel armor, second linen shirt. He buckled on his sword, and strapped the quiver over his shoulder. It felt good to hold his bow again, though he wished he'd found some time to practice shooting. If all went well, he wouldn't have to use it. Then again, when was the last time everything *didn't* go to hell? Shaking his head, he draped the heavy cloak over his arm and walked out. Jillaine waited in the hallway. She'd tied back her hair, and wore the bounty hunter garb from Caralis. Leathers and all. He felt the big grin on his face. "I dig it."

"You . . . like it."

"Exactly. Hey, you remembered."

"I like your alien way of speaking."

"Alien?"

She shrugged. "You *are* from another world."

"How do you feel about that?" *Not sure I ever asked.*

She gave his hand a squeeze and leaned against him. "I dig it."

They left the palace proper and made their way back to the stable yard. The air was cool, but downright balmy compared to what they'd face in northern Alissia. Wisps of fog drifted over the ground. Richard Holt stood over by the stables, scooping grain for three horses. It was interesting to see the Valteroni Prime doing such menial work. Quinn looked around. No Veena, for once. He knew she had to stay here to run Valteron, but he kind of hoped he'd get to see her again. *Oh well.*

He gave Jillaine a little nudge. "See those animals over there? They're called *horses.* Kind of like Tioni smart mules, but way better."

She laughed. "Yes, I've heard of them. But don't let a mule hear you say that."

Alethea and her guardswomen stood nearby, thumbing the handles of their weapons. For once, they weren't leaning against something, or lounging on the ground. *They must be nervous.* Escorting the Prime to another part of the continent, a war zone, would have had him sweating, too.

Quinn looked around some more, but didn't see Moric or Anton, either. "Where is everyone?"

Jillaine's eyes lost focus for a moment. She pushed Quinn over by the fence.

"What?" he asked.

"Someone is coming."

Moric and Anton appeared out of thin air in the middle of the yard. Anton released Moric's shoulder and breathed deeply, the Caralissian noble's equivalent of bending over double with exertion. Apparently, Moric had let him handle the transportation for both of them.

Now there's something you don't see very day. Moric saving his strength. "Morning!" Quinn called. "I didn't realize you were gone."

"We had to get something," Anton said.

Quinn saw no packages, no bundles, no weapons. Just four empty hands. "What?"

Moric smiled. "Reinforcements."

Sella winked into existence between them. "Well, don't just stand there." She chivvied Moric and Anton off toward the fence as other Enclave magicians began appearing in the yard. Every council member, every person with magical talent on the island that Quinn knew showed up to join the coalition's most important mission.

"Hey, there's Leward!" Quinn waved to his Pirean friend, who hurried over with his younger brother in tow.

"Quinn!" They wore identical grins as they shook his hand.

"Hey, guys. Welcome to Valteron City." He shook their hands. "Everett, how are those lessons coming?"

"I'm still alive," Everett said.

"That's the spirit."

Richard emerged from the stables on a massive bay stallion. He held the reins but hardly used them, preferring to nudge the animal with his knees. "If I may have your attention, everyone? Find yourself a mount and meet in the center of the yard."

Quinn pulled Jillaine over toward the stables. "Come on, I don't want to end up with a mule this time." They reached the door, only to find a stable boy coming out with a pair of mounts.

"I think these will suit you both," Richard said over his shoulder.

Quinn made no claims of horse expertise, but he knew a thoroughbred bloodline when he saw it. Both animals had them, and the one on the left had a familiar face. "Hey, that's my mare!"

"We found her in a stable in the city," Holt said. "I wondered if she was yours."

"That was very thoughtful," Quinn said. He patted the mare's head, and wondered if she recognized him. Most horses didn't give him the time of day. He expected this would be no different, so it was a pleasant surprise when she turned to nuzzle his hand. "Aw, you *do* remember me."

Everyone mounted and assembled in the center of the yard. An odd silence fell over them as Sella began the enchantment. The rising power of it made the hair on Quinn's arms rise. He'd never really thought about how powerful a magician she was. *Imagine if I'd really pissed her off.*

Her voice rose. The wind swirled in a tempest around them. Quinn grabbed Jillaine's hand, just to reassure himself. Then the world jerked sideways into cold darkness. White light bloomed, revealing a wintry landscape of evergreens coated in snow. More of the white stuff fell heavily with the biting-cold wind, nearly obscuring the dark mountain range that loomed to the north. The mare was shaking like a leaf. He put a hand against her neck and made shushing noises to calm her. By the time he was done, his fingers were starting to numb. He chuckled.

We're in Felara, all right.

If he wasn't mistaken, Wenthrop should be right . . . *Sweet Jesus, what the hell is that?* The village was there, all right—with a newly built inn, no less— but surrounded by a vast tent city five times its size. Horses and wagons and armor-clad soldiers occupied every patch of open ground. A haze of smoke hung over the encampment, seemingly held up by the dark columns from dozens of campfires. He ducked around his mare and found Jillaine, who stared up at the sky. "Hey. You all right?"

A look of wonder spread across her face. "Look at it."

All he saw was a featureless gray sky and the promise of a blizzard. "What?"

"So much *snow.*"

"You've seen snow before."

"Not falling like this." She held out her hand, palm up. "It's enchanting."

"So are you." He leaned down and kissed her. This was war, and the future wasn't assured. He simply didn't give a damn about who might see it.

"And you said Felara was cold," she said.

He looked back at the thickening snow. "I just hope it doesn't make us blind."

The blizzard worsened as they made the trek north into the mountains. Quinn and Jillaine rode with most of the Enclave magicians behind the main forces. The two columns of infantry—one Valteroni, one Caralissian—stretched for a quarter mile in front of them. Richard and Anton led the van, and crested a ridge that looked down into the valley beyond. Not the gateway valley—that remained a half-day's ride farther north, but a valley. Anton signaled.

"What does that mean?" Quinn asked.

"They don't see anyone," Sella said.

Well, there's some good news. Maybe they'd be able to get right to the gateway without any confrontation.

Anton and Richard disappeared from view as they led the column forward and down. Every sound came muted because of the snow. More and more of the infantry lines disappeared beyond the far ridge.

"It's hard to believe that the third great enchantment lies hidden up here in the mountains," Jillaine said.

"You know, if we succeed here, you're going to be down to two."

"Not really."

"How do you figure?"

"Look at how much it's changed our world." She pointed ahead. "Armies from Valteron and Caralis marching side by side. Enclave magicians getting out and *doing* something for once." She brushed aside an errant strand of hair and looked at him. "And then there's you."

He grinned. "And then there's me."

They reached the top of the ridge and could see all the way down to the front of the lines, which reached nearly to the far end of the vale. He recognized this area, too. That meant the gateway cave wasn't far. But the valley looked a little different than he remembered it. Huge snowdrifts piled up on the sides, obscuring most of the boulders. The slopes were narrower, too, forcing the two lines to march more closely together. *Maybe it's not the same valley.* It was, though—he recognized a pile of three boulders that looked like Stonehenge. A distinctive landmark, but the landscape around it had . . . shifted. "Whoa." Quinn pulled back on his reins. The mare snorted, but stopped short.

Sella cursed. "Stop, please!" This was directed at the mule. "Give us a warning if you're going to stop, boy!"

Jillaine must have seen the concern on his face. "What's the matter?" she asked.

"Something doesn't feel right." He scanned the valley's rim, trying to pick out the differences. Which is how he saw the glint of metal up high on the right-hand side. *What in the hell?* A distant percussion sounded, then another right on top of it. A high-pitched whine filled the air.

"Ambush!" Quinn shouted. The men at the end

of the line, which had advanced about thirty yards, looked back in puzzlement.

Then they disappeared in an explosion of smoke and earth.

Quinn's mare reared back, screaming, and nearly trampled over Sella. Another explosion rocked the ground deeper in the vale. Then gunfire erupted from the rims of the vale. The soldiers scattered from their lines.

Quinn half-fell out of his saddle. "Take cover!" He dragged his mare backward by the reins. She tossed her head, fighting him. Jillaine struggled to do the same with her mount. Moric and Sella didn't have to even ask the Tioni mules to run back; they fled over the ridge on their own.

More gunfire erupted. Anton and Moric must have given an order, because both armies began a charge up the right-hand side of the vale to get at the attackers. Arrows flew and were met by gunfire. Quinn freed his bow and quiver from their lashings and nocked an arrow. He crept over the ridge. He could see the attackers now; they wore white-and-gray snow camouflage and lay prone against the un-natural snow embankments. The nearest one was no more than forty yards distant. A reachable shot. He had a long-barrel rifle and kept firing, over and over. Quinn felt himself draw the arrow to his cheek. He took aim in slow motion. Gauged distance, held his breath, found the pin, and released.

His arrow took the sniper in the throat. Blood splattered the snow in a wide arc. He tumbled over with a gurgled scream. Bullets struck the snow at Quinn's feet. *Shit!* He dove back over the ridge into cover. Soldiers charged up toward the ambushers, but it was slow going up the steep, snow-covered slopes. Sella whispered a word and gestured. One of the false embankments shuddered and fell apart, revealing four camouflaged mercenaries behind it. They scrambled for cover, but Valteroni bowmen fired a volley and dropped two of them. The others made it behind a second embankment. Sella leveled *that* one a heartbeat later. Another deep percussion sounded. This time, Jillaine was ready—she made a sweeping movement and spoke a word. A white, glittering shell formed like a roof above the soldiers' heads. The mortar shells struck it and detonated, showering fragments down below but doing no more harm than that.

Anton appeared out of nowhere, with a man clutched in his arms. "Help us!"

Quinn hurried forward and helped him lower the other man to the ground. Blood stained his robes, and each breath came with a wheezed. He'd been shot at least once in the torso. Then Quinn looked at his face, and cold realization came. It was Richard Holt. *Oh, gods.*

"Moric!"

The balding magician appeared at his side. "Gods," he whispered, echoing Quinn's thoughts.

Holt's eyes opened. He smiled, albeit weakly. "Just a scratch, old friend."

Moric closed his eyes and put his hands on the man's stomach. Quinn stood back.

Anton's eyes had a haunted look to them. "What is this madness?"

"Alien weapons," Quinn said.

"He was standing right next to me when they hit him. They're slaughtering our men like sheep."

"Can you get out of the vale?"

"They have reinforcements coming out of the next valley. We're going to be penned in before long."

Quinn's mind raced. *We're drawing them away from the cave.*

Moric finished his delving magic and stood back. His face was grim. "I have never seen injuries like this before. There's . . ." he trailed off and shook his head.

"Nothing you can do," Holt finished.

How can this be happening? Quinn knelt beside him. Tried putting pressure on the wounds, but his clothes were just soaked with blood. Just soaked with it. Then he felt Richard's hand around his wrist.

"Quinn." A haze of pain had settled on Richard's face, but his eyes were bright. "You know what you have to do."

Quinn shook his head. "I'm sorry. Anton said there are reinforcements coming down from the gateway valley." *No way out.*

"Exactly. We're—" he broke off in a fit of wet

coughs. When they ended, he drew a long, rattling breath. "Now's your chance."

More gunfire sounded as the mercenaries made another coordinated attack. Two dozen soldiers went down. Anton cursed. "I need to get back down there."

"Wait!" Quinn put a hand on his shoulder. "Hold them as long as you can."

"That may well be suicide." He made a face. "But the Valteroni lines are holding, and so will we." He disappeared without another word.

"Moric, you've seen the cave, haven't you?" Quinn asked. "Could you take us there?"

"I'm not going anywhere," Moric said. "There has to be something we can do for him."

"There isn't," Quinn said.

"How can you be so cold?"

"I'm not—this might be our only chance."

Holt reached out and found Moric's hand. "Go, Moric. He's right."

Moric looked up at Quinn. "It's tight in there, and I'll need most of my strength to work on the gateway."

Quinn stood and drew his sword. "You also need someone to watch your back."

Moric put a hand on Richard's chest. They shared a look, a silent farewell. Then Moric stood and reached out to clasp Quinn's shoulder. "Are you ready?"

He knew he shouldn't have, but he looked at Jillaine anyway. Her eyes were down in the vale, and he could sense the power of the magic coursing through her. He willed her to look at him, and she did. Her beautiful forehead furrowed in confusion. Then realization dawned. She set her jaw. Took a step toward them.

Quinn wished he had time to tell her once more how perfect she was, but there was no way she'd be on board with this desperate plan. Worse, she'd insist to come along. Neither was all right. Quinn gave her a sad smile, blew her a kiss, and said to Moric, "Let's go."

The world jerked sideways into darkness and then back into dim daylight. They stood an inch away from the stone cave wall with the crazy markings on it.

"Cutting it a little close, don't you think?" Quinn whispered.

"I told you, it's tight in here," Moric said.

Quinn eased his sword out of the scabbard and slipped around him, taking the front position as they crept into the chamber that held the gateway. It was empty, but for the flickering dome-shaped portal that led back to Earth. *There it is.* His hackles rose when he saw it. He felt the ball of magic inside of him pulsing in rhythm with the flickers across the surface. "I sense it now."

Moric approached the gateway slowly, almost with a reverence. He touched the stone just to the side of it. "Gods, what a creation. It almost seems a shame to destroy it."

"Can I help you?"

Moric sat cross-legged on the floor. "Tell me about the place where the gateway opens on your world."

Quinn sat beside him. "It's a cave, kind of like this one. The main cavern is larger, but the stone looks about the same. The company built a whole complex around it." *How the hell do I describe* that? Probably better not to even try. "The cave itself is on a small island. A tropical island, deep in a southern ocean. It's much warmer there than here. Like summer compared to winter."

"The same, but different."

"That's a good way to put it."

Moric reached out and took both of his hands. His grip was like dry parchment. "Picture the place in your mind."

Quinn closed his eyes and did just that, trying to ignore the buzz of magic that was growing between them. He called up his image of the gateway the last time he'd seen it, hidden behind double Plexiglas doors in a room filled with computers and equipment. He remembered the massive armory with its host of medieval weapons. The prototyping lab, where he'd perfected some of his equipment. Kiara's austere office.

"Good," Moric said. "Very good. I believe I understand your gateway and ours. And the link between them . . . gods, it's a thing of beauty."

"I'm sure it's lovely, but can you do something about it before someone finds us here?"

"I'll try. Make sure that I'm not interrupted." Moric took a breath, and began chanting in a low voice.

Quinn felt the power begin to grow in him. He heard something in the narrow tunnel that led to outside. A scrape of leather against stone. A heavy footstep, then another. *Crap.* He raised his sword and crept out into the corridor . . .

"Don't lie to your audience all the time. Lie when
it counts most."

—**Art of Illusion, May 3**

CHAPTER 34

DEAD MAN TALKING

Logan watched the last of the CASE Global mercenaries run over the crest of the gateway valley's rim,
heading south. Each carried a rifle. The Alissian army
marching up this way was about to get a rude awakening. The mercs hadn't even left a sentry outside
the gateway. He shook his head at the total lapse in
security as he shimmied out from behind the boulder
he'd used to hide. *This is what happens when I'm not
running things.*

Well, that was someone else's problem now. The

executives were no doubt falling over themselves to find a replacement for Kiara. Hell, they'd probably offer it to Logan once he finished his debrief. He'd be sure to tell them exactly where and how far to shove it.

He jogged up the slope to the cave itself and paused just inside the opening to let his eyes adjust. He shouldn't rush this. He had to be deliberate and composed when he walked back into that air lock. Give his identification, answer the challenge questions. Do whatever it takes to avoid the gas protocol. The second they let him through the inner gate, though, watch out. He'd make a goddamn beeline for his girls and gut anyone who tried to stop him.

He took a few breaths to settle himself, then walked around the corner into the corridor, where he came face-to-face with a man holding a sword. "Whoa." He held up his hands. Then he got a look at the other guy's face and couldn't believe it. *There's just no way.* "You've got to be shitting me. *Bradley?*"

Quinn Bradley grinned and lowered the sword, though not entirely. He looked haggard, but his smile was the usual hundred watts. "Well, look what the cat dragged in! I thought you were dead."

Nearly was, about six different times. "Likewise. What the hell happened to you?"

"Oh, man, you wouldn't believe it if I told you. Kiara's sister showed up and beat the crap out of me."

"You saw Relling? Me, too!"

Bradley shook his head in disbelief. "She's a piece of work, isn't she? Took my comm unit and everything."

Well, that explains that. Sorry, Mendez. "That's not the half of what she's done. She went native on us, and attacked our fleet as it headed south. Damn near wiped us out."

"Do they know they missed one?"

Logan laughed. "I'll send a memo later." Man, it was good to see a friendly face after all this long. "What have you been doing all this time?"

Bradley shrugged. "Pretty much just running from one threat into the arms of another. Trying to stay alive."

"You did that somehow." Logan gestured at the sword. "And here you are, getting the drop on me. I'm almost proud."

"Aw, thanks, coach!"

Distant gunfire echoed from the snow-covered valley. It sounded like the latest recruits had found some targets for their rifles. *Probably shooting some fish in a barrel.* "There's a battle happening about half a mile from here. We'd better get back before any of that spills over here."

He started into the tunnel, but Bradley held up a hand. "Ooh, hold on. About that."

"What's the problem?" Then Logan heard a man's voice from deeper in the cavern. Almost sounded like singing. "Is someone else back there? Move aside!"

He stepped forward again, but Bradley took two steps back and raised his sword tip to Logan's chest. "Sorry, man. You need to walk away."

What the hell is he thinking? Then a dark thought intruded, and the more Logan considered it, the more it made sense. Bradley, so eager to get back. Dropping off the radar at a crucial moment. Back here at the gateway while someone was attacking. *It all adds up, but I don't want to believe it.* "Wait a minute. Are you with *them?*"

"What? You're crazy." Bradley tried to play it off, but he'd waited just a second too long.

The realization hit Logan like a draft of cold air. "You *are.*" *I tried to warn them, too.* "Why would you do that?"

Bradley shrugged. "Got a better offer."

"Good for you. Now get the hell out of my way."

"No."

What a fool. Logan shook his head, and drew the sword he'd borrowed from an unsuspecting foot soldier two days back. It didn't have the lightness or perfect edge of a company-issued blade, but it was more than enough to mop the floor with Bradley. "You know how this is going to end."

The walls shook suddenly, like a mini earthquake, showering both of them with dust from the roof. *I don't have time for this.*

Bradley took a fighting stance, but his balance

was off-center and his sword tip too low. "I think we should establish some ground rules for—"

Logan leaped at him and made a brutal slash, aiming at his neck. Bradley barely got his sword up to deflect it into the stone. But he was off balance and Logan hit him like a center tackle, shoulder-to-chest. The impact sent Bradley tumbling into the cavern behind him. He hit the floor and groaned. Logan walked in and spotted the source of the chanting, a bald guy in robes who sat with his back to the wall. His voice lilted higher, and the walls shook again. More dust. He could have sworn the gateway seized a moment. "What are you doing, Mr. Clean?"

The man didn't answer. Didn't even seem to hear him. Logan started over, but caught a flash of movement out of the corner of his eye. He whirled to find Bradley winding up with a knife. He sent it flailing toward Logan's stomach, but Logan batted it aside with the sword. *Amateur.*

Bradley roared and charged him, swinging hard with the sword. Logan had to take a step back to find his stance, then deflected one swipe, dodged another. Bradley *was* fast, but unless Logan made a stupid mistake, there was no real danger. *And I don't make stupid mistakes.* The air thickened, and a rumbling noise came from the wall around the gateway. It was time to finish this. Logan found his stance, predicted Bradley's next move. *Slide over. Parry. Wait for the opening.*

He jammed up Bradley's blade with his own and shoulder-barged him against the cavern wall. The magician hit hard and kept his footing, but his sword went clattering down behind him, almost to the gateway. And the kid still wasn't giving up. He eyed it like he might go for it. Bigger pieces began raining down from the ceiling. The distant rumble rose to a deep roar.

"Don't be stupid," Logan shouted. He circled to put himself between Bradley and his sword. "You can never beat me in a fair fight."

Bradley's shoulders drooped, and he took a long breath. "I know." Then he looked up and actually *grinned*. "Good thing I never fight fair." He held out his open hand and closed it into a fist.

Heavy air pressed around Logan. An invisible force pinned his arms to his sides. He couldn't move. Couldn't get his sword up. *What the absolute hell?* "What is . . . this?"

"Sorry, my friend. This is goodbye." Bradley charged.

Logan couldn't do a damn thing. They collided, and then Logan was tumbling over backward. The cool-air slice of the gateway washed over him for a long moment. Then harsh fluorescent light bloomed, and he fell against the back of the air lock. Earthside. Suddenly he could move again. He climbed to his feet, but the gateway looked strange. Black lines spiderwebbed out from the middle of it, shattering the luminescence. Then the soft glow faded away, and Logan found himself staring at a featureless rock wall. He reached out and touched it—not quite believing his eyes—and felt only cold, rough limestone.

The gateway was gone.

"If you have to show your cards, you'd better have the winning hand."

—Art of Illusion, November 10

CHAPTER 35

THE LINK

Quinn sank to his knees and stared at the stone wall where the gateway had been. He couldn't believe how close that was. Wouldn't have believed it, if the screaming pain in his back and shoulders wasn't here to remind him. He fumbled to pick up his sword and half-crawled over to Moric, who leaned back against the wall like a drunkard. "You did it!"

Moric hardly seemed to hear him. Quinn shook his shoulder. "Moric?" He ducked as another huge chunk of stone fell and shattered on the floor behind him. "Come on, we've got to get out of here."

He grabbed Moric and tried to lift him, but the man was like a rag doll and Quinn's muscles weren't up for it. He fell back on top of him.

Moric's eyes flickered open. "Is it done?"

"Yes, but this whole place is about to come down."

"Leave me, and get out of here. Go, run!"

No way in hell. Quinn bent down and took his arm. "Come on, I'll help you."

They gave it another try. He got Moric's arm over his shoulder and they started making stutter steps up the tunnel. The walls shook again, and sent a great pile of rocks showering down in front of them. They tumbled over backward to avoid being crushed. Quinn coughed, half-blind from the dust. It settled enough that he could see through the dimness. Boulders and debris blocked the way. "No!" He stumbled forward and tried digging through, but it was no use. Everything was wedged in.

He turned around and found his way back to Moric. "We're blocked in. Can you take us out of here?"

Moric looked up at the ceiling. He tried to sit up, winced in pain, and sagged back against the wall. "I have nothing left."

"No magic?"

"No."

Quinn pounded his fist against the ground "Damn it!"

"You have to go," Moric said. "Someone must tell them about the gateway."

"I don't think either of us gets to tell them anything." He put his hand on Moric's shoulder. "I'm sorry."

"Don't be." Moric tried to sit up. "You can take us out of here."

Another avalanche tumbled down right beside them.

Jesus. Quinn shielded his head with his arm. "I can't, Moric. I never learned how."

"You already know how. Think!"

This is pointless. But he closed his eyes, and tried to remember what he could of the traveling spell. The tendrils of magic, joining one place to another. The magic pulsed inside of him with the memory. He felt the power growing. "But I don't know where to go."

"Yes, you do." Moric fumbled for Quinn's hand. He found it, and pressed it against his chest. Pinpricks of magic danced up Quinn's arm and shot away into the darkness. It pulled his senses along like a cord. Pulled him, pulsing, to another place.

"The bond," Moric whispered. "Do you feel the bond?"

The family bond. "That's her?"

"Yes. Go to her." Moric squeezed his hand tight. "And be good to her, Quinn."

More thunder shook the walls around him. This time, it didn't stop. The ceiling began to cave in. *Now or never.*

"Hold on!" Quinn shouted. He let the magic fill

him, seized the invisible cord, and thrust them sideways into the darkness.

Darkness enveloped Quinn. Cold, consuming darkness. A pinprick of light appeared, infinitely far away. He stretched for it. The light grew. Widened. Stretched out until it consumed his entire world, and he spilled into it. He tumbled out onto the snow, with his sword in one hand and Moric in the other. They'd emerged on the snow-covered ridge behind Jillaine and Sella and the other magicians. He drew in a painful breath. *I did it.*

"Quinn! Father!" Jillaine half-fell into the snow beside them.

"He's hurt," he managed. That was a lie of omission, though. Moric was beyond hurt.

Gunfire echoed up from the valley. Distant screams. The clash of steel. *Why are they still fighting?* He struggled to his feet as Sella came over to examine Moric. He took one excruciating step toward the valley rim, then another. He didn't want to look, but he had to.

He saw only carnage. Armor-clad bodies and bloody snow painted the valley floor as far as he could see. *Hundreds* of them. And still they fought in clusters and small groups. Struggled for life and death in the snow. They must not know about the gateway. More gunfire, down to the left.

"No," he said. The magic boiled up from within him until it roared in his ears. He stumbled over the ridge and down into the valley. He was distantly aware of the glow about him, the firelight. The electric power of pure magic. His steps shook the earth. He lifted his sword. Lightning danced along the blade. "No!" He stabbed down into the snow. A great crevice shot forth. Light bloomed from it, and rocked the floor of the vale. Everyone tumbled to the ground. They followed the crevice to their eyes. Saw him towering like a giant, with the power of the world flowing through him.

"Drop your weapons!" he boomed. He felt their eyes on him. The soldiers, the mercenaries, the magicians. All of them. "Do it!"

The two words delivered a shock wave that knocked over the few who'd managed to stand again.

Then all across the vale, swords and rifles and spears tumbled to the bloody snow. A white heavy silence settled upon them.

"The gateway is gone," Quinn said. *And so am I.*

He let go of the magic, and tumbled down into oblivion.

"We should not underestimate the unifying potential of this world's polyglossia."

—R. Holt, "Alissia: Political Overview"

CHAPTER 36

GHOSTS OF THE PAST

Veena told herself that she must, above all, be strong.

Richard is dead. She weighed the words in her mind and took their meaning, but refused to accept their reality. He couldn't have died on the verge of victory over CASE Global. He couldn't have died with so much work left to do. He couldn't have died thinking that she regretted her choice. She wanted to scream, and to cry, but she could do neither. Too many people were watching.

She had to get out of the palace, at least for a little while. Clear her head. Everything she saw reminded her of him. She left the palace by the side-gate, with Belladonna as her shadow. Even with Richard gone, the Tukalu held up their end of the agreement. Veena hoped Valteron would still honor their side.

They took a long alley toward the merchant district, mostly to avoid the wide steps that led down to the city square. People had been gathering there since daybreak, clamoring for news. The death of Richard Holt remained a secret, officially speaking, but rumors were already circulating. They couldn't put off the announcement much longer, no matter the uncertainty of how the people would take it. Veena could only pray that the transition wouldn't be bloody. The scars of the last one hadn't fully healed.

Belladonna grabbed her shoulder without warning and pulled her a step back. Three men emerged from a side-alley.

"Dahlia," said the one in the middle.

Veena recognized the voice of admiral Blackwell, and relaxed a fraction. "It's all right," she told Belladonna. She took a step forward. "Admiral."

"Is it true? Is the Prime dead?"

"Why should you care? You're retired from Valteron's service, if memory serves."

Irritation flashed across his face, but then it disappeared, and he dropped his head. "I regret that. But Richard is my friend."

He seemed genuinely sad, and Veena felt for him. He and the former Prime knew Richard even before she did. "He died saving our world."

Blackwell sighed. "That sounds like him. Yet I fear what it means for Valteron."

"I've spoken to his other advisors. We're going to make the announcement today."

The admiral didn't seem to hear her. "The transition of power must be quick. And unambiguous." He spoke a word to his men, who drew their swords.

Veena backed away as the men advanced. "What are you doing?"

"The people will choose me, but the name Dahlia is on too many lips for my comfort."

"We can work something out," Veena said quickly. "Talk it over."

"Talking is your way. This is mine." He nodded to his men. "Take them."

His two henchmen came forward. Belladonna slid in front of Veena, a knife in each hand. "Run, Veena!"

Veena backed away slowly. She couldn't believe that the admiral would *dare* try to harm her. Not until one of his henchmen slashed at Belladonna with his sword. The warrior leaned aside just enough for the blade to miss her. She closed the distance in a heartbeat, blades flashing. The man went down, his neck fountaining blood. The other man shouted and leaped at her. She danced backward.

The swordsman made a wide swing at her. She backpedaled but lost her footing and almost fell. The man snarled and raised his sword over his head to slash down at her. She pivoted and sprang forward, slashing upward. Opening a gash across his gut so wide that his bowels spilled out. She turned back and shouted, "Veena, *go!*" Then she stiffened, as a bloody blade emerged from her chest. Blackwell's sword. He'd stabbed her from behind. Her legs gave out beneath her. Blackwell jerked his sword free and kicked her aside.

Oh no oh no oh no. Veena backed away in horror. Belladonna shuddered once, then lay still. Blackwell stepped over her like a man out for a stroll. His sword dripped blood as he approached Veena. She turned to run, but her cloak tangled her legs. She fell and hit the ground *hard*. Pain shot through her palms. She rolled over to find Blackwell standing over her. She scrabbled backward across the cobblestones, but it was no use. He was too fast. Too brutal.

"Sorry about this, Dahlia." He raised his sword high and brought it down.

It came to a crashing halt five inches above Veena's face. Another sword barred the way, held by a figure in a hooded cloak. "Let her be."

Blackwell's lip curled into a sneer. "This is none of your concern, sellsword."

The man shoved back the admiral's blade and advanced, putting himself between Blackwell and Veena. "I said, *let her be*, Admiral Blackwell."

Blackwell pursed his lips. "So you know my name. I'd like to know yours, before I bring you to heel."

The man lowered the hood of his cloak. "Julio Mendez."

Oh my God, Veena thought. *Julio.*

"What a strange name. Who are you?" Blackwell demanded.

Mendez grinned. "I'm the one who burned your keep."

Blackwell's casual sneer twisted into a feral snarl. He attacked. Julio parried once, twice. Then went on the offensive himself. His sword was a shining blur. He backed the admiral against the wall of the alley. Slammed back his sword so that sparks flew from the stone. Kneed him brutally in the crotch. Blackwell grunted and doubled over. Julio took a step back and brought his sword down with both hands, severing the admiral's head in a single stroke. It thumped wetly to the pavement, followed by a heavier thud from the rest of him. Julio crouched down to clean his sword on the admiral's jacket, then sheathed it in a single, fluid movement.

"This is the guy who almost beat Logan?" He

shook his head. "The old man must be getting soft." He stalked over and pulled Veena to her feet.

She tottered and would have fallen if he hadn't held her up. "What are you doing here?"

"Following a hunch." He released her wrist and looked away. "Didn't want to believe it, but here you are."

"Julio—"

"I thought you were *dead*, Veena. Or should I call you *Dahlia*?"

The look on his face broke her heart a little. "It was the only way. I'm so sorry."

"You made your choice."

I chose wrong, she wanted to say. But that was half a lie. She didn't regret what she'd done for Valteron. For Alissia. "How did you find me?"

He nodded back toward Blackwell's body. "I followed him. Figured he'd make a play like this, with Holt gone."

With Holt gone. The words hit her like a hammer. She threw her arms around him and held him tight. Then the tears came, unbidden but uncontrollable once they started. She cried for Richard, and for Belladonna, but most of all for Julio.

Veena wasn't certain how long she cried in Julio's arms. At last, he'd gently insisted that she return inside the palace walls. Somehow he talked his way in as well, and told the Tukalu of what happened to Belladonna. Suddenly a phalanx of the warrior women had taken up positions around where Veena sat in the midst of the garden, while Alethea led yet another contingent to secure the alley.

All the while, Julio stayed with her, his mere presence a comfort until she recovered herself enough to speak.

"I can't believe you came back," she said. Her voice sounded as raw as her throat felt.

"What can I say? I have a thing for powerful women." He looked at her face, and smiled. He had a wonderful smile, all warmth and affection. She missed it more than she'd realized.

"You can call me either, but it won't make me powerful."

He snorted as if amused.

"Well, it won't," she said. "I'm nobody, now that he's gone."

He smiled again. "You don't get it, do you?"

"Get what, exactly?"

"Everything I heard in the streets and the common rooms was about you. Dahlia brokered the new alliance with Valteron. Dahlia kept the city fed while the Prime was away."

"I've been busy."

"And then there was the part where Blackwell tried to assassinate you, and you killed him instead."

She narrowed her eyes. "That was you."

"Me? Oh no. I was just an eyewitness. In fact, you saved my life." His smile faded. He took her hand in his own. "You really did save me, you know."

"I feel like I'm getting credit for too many things other people did."

He laughed. "Welcome to politics. Lucky for you, I can stick around for a while to help out with what happens now."

She sighed. "I don't know what's going to happen now." Nothing was certain with Richard gone.

"You're going to be the next Prime of Valteron," Julio said.

"What?"

He shrugged. "The people have pretty much already decided. And with the admiral dead, no one will dare to oppose you."

"Oh my God," she whispered.

"I think you mean *gods*," he said.

"Veena Chaudri, the Valteroni Prime." She smiled and patted his hand. "You know what? I think I like the sound of that."

"How many magic users are there? How do they learn it? And most importantly, what are their full capabilities? Let us hope we never find out."

—R. Holt, "Questions on Alissian Magic"

CHAPTER 37

SUCCESSIONS

Without his training, Logan might never have gotten out of the air lock, much less out of the room that CASE Global had built around the gateway. His old drill sergeant used to number off the lessons.

Lesson one. Keep your cool, soldier.

He knelt and gave his name. "Sergeant Major Logan. Alpha Team." Gave his passcode, too. Kept a stony face on when the controllers went through his security identification questions over the two-way speaker box.

"What are the make and model of your first car?"

"Chevy Corsica."

"How long was your deployment to Kandahar?"

"Which one?"

"The first one."

"Nine months." The second tour, they got the job done in six. Of course, *done* was a gray area. No job in the Middle East was ever truly done.

Lesson two. Do everything by the book.

He tugged off his filthy leather boots, then stripped off all his outer clothes. Those went into one air lock compartment. The borrowed sword went into another. He waited for all the seals to turn green, then stepped forward for scans and sanitation. Standard procedure. As much as he wanted to barge through the doors and burn a hot path to his family, he followed *standard procedure*. So did the guys on the other side of the Plexiglas, to their credit. It took a lot of training not to hit the mic button and shout *what the hell happened over there?*

The final gate slid open. The two guys in the room, Mathias and Goldberg, were half of Charlie Team. Also known as the cleanup crew. They only went in to clean up messes that Alpha and Bravo teams left behind. Generally *after* the danger was long gone. Mathias was forty-five, Goldberg close to fifty. Family men with kids in college who wanted the paycheck but not the hazard pay.

Damn, it's good to see them, though. At least a couple

of friendly faces had gotten back to this side of the gateway before it disappeared. Leaving Bradley on the other side, where he'd never have to answer about a hundred questions Logan would've liked to ask him. *Can't think about that now.* He waited for the buzzer to give them a rueful smile. "Am I clear?"

"All clear," Goldberg said. He hit a button on a control console, probably to notify the execs that Logan had returned. A response beep came back almost instantaneously. "Briefing room one."

"Roger that."

Mathias pulled out the bins and loaded them on a cart to bring down to processing. He gave Logan an eyebrow-raise, like *what the hell happens now?* Logan answered with a shrug. He didn't know what to say. That problem was above his pay grade. He and Mathias were just a couple of jarheads trying to keep their helmets pulled low while the crap hit the fan above them.

Lesson three, deal with the problem in front of you.

The way Bradley had immobilized him in the cave with his goddamn hand. That strange priest's chanting. The gateway flickering and turning to stone. All of those were problems, but not in front of him. Not things he could change. Hell, not things he could even explain. He'd have to come up with something, though. The executives wanted answers, and he was the only one who could give them.

For now, he had a simple, practical problem: getting through the two levels of steel bunker and miles of red tape that separated him from his girls. That meant keeping his cool. Doing the debrief. Acting like the very *idea* of CASE Global threatening his family didn't make him blind with rage. No, he had to play this just right. The small Logan family and the massive Mendez clan all needed him to deliver.

You know who'd be good at this? Goddamn Bradley, that's who. Talk about a guy who could keep winning cards close to his chest and play them at the perfect moment. Even though it eventually got Logan home, it still burned that Bradley had gotten the drop on him.

"How long do I have?" he asked.

Goldberg checked the console. "Ten minutes."

He spent the first eight in a steaming-hot shower, and it was glorious. He dressed in clean clothes, hustled down to the briefing room, and yanked open the door with ten seconds to spare. He'd never been in briefing room one himself before; this was where the lieutenant used to come to brief the executives. Part of him expected to see the suits right there in the room. But no, there was a small conference table with chairs on the near side, all of them empty. A videoconference screen lined the far wall, and showed the live image of another conference room—this one far more luxurious—with five suits seated around a wide mahogany table. Three men and two women, all staring at him like a panel of judges. And guessing from their facial expressions, all of them were beyond pissed.

This is going to suck. He pulled out a chair and took a seat.

The suits all looked behind him at the closed door, waiting. When no one came, their faces grew grim.

The woman in chair two finally broke the silence. "Where's Kiara?"

"Lieutenant Kiara is dead," Logan said.

They frowned and muttered at one another, but betrayed no hint of surprise. They already suspected.

"How?" asked the guy in chair three, a silver-haired fox who was tan as a surfer. A Californian, probably.

"Holt's navy ambushed them at sea." Whereupon Kiara spotted her long-lost sister on the long-lost ship, and decided to force a little family reunion, he didn't add. *I couldn't save her from herself.* What if he'd kept sailing south, though, instead of taking a two-day R & R at Port Morgan? What if he'd warned her about the Valteroni fleet while there was still time to run? There were so many what-ifs.

None of which actually mattered anymore.

"You were supposed to take care of Holt," said the silver fox.

Yes, let's talk about that. Logan leaned forward and put his elbows on the table. "Are you referring to the part where you ordered me to kill a civilian in cold blood?"

"Alissia is not Earth. Ordinary laws don't apply."

He couldn't resist a little jab. "Neither does the technology ban, apparently."

"Necessary precautions. We had to protect our investment."

"I don't know if you've looked in the gateway cavern this morning, but your investment's gone."

"Charlie Team says the gateway disappeared right after you entered. What did you do?"

Lost a fight with Bradley, that's what. He cheated like hell, but he beat me.

Logan could throw him to the wolves right here, right now. All he had to do was say the word. It's not like the magician could turn up to dispute it. The suits would *love* to make him a scapegoat for this whole debacle. They'd make good on their vague threats to the magician's distant relatives. Pile the blame on him. Smear the name he'd started to make for himself in Vegas, out of pure spite. It would make Logan's life easier. But there was no honor in it, and honor was about all he had left.

Besides, he wanted to remember his friend the way he was. Friend. That's what Bradley had called him, at the end. Weirdly enough, Logan felt the same way. *I'm definitely too soft.*

What would Bradley do, if he were in Logan's shoes right now? He'd probably just rewrite the story and make himself the hero.

"I followed protocol," Logan said. "There was an

earthquake, and the whole mountain started to come down. The tunnel collapsed on top of me." He stood, turned around, and lifted his shirt to reveal the nasty bruise on his back, from when Bradley had thrown him into the air lock.

"Oh my God," the woman in chair one whispered.

"I put my ass on the line to get back here and make my report. *That's* what I did."

"We … we appreciate your service, Sergeant Major Logan," said the Californian, who seemed to be in charge.

"You're welcome. Now, who's in charge of the Gateway Project?"

The suits looked at each other. It was hard to read their faces. Then the man in the middle looked at him and said, "You are."

"I'm in charge," Logan said, in a doubtful tone. *Maybe I heard wrong.*

"You're the highest-ranking soldier we have left, and there's a lot of work to do."

Logan shoved back his chair, stood, and walked to the door. "Find someone else to do it."

"Wait!"

He paused and looked back, irritated. "What?"

Their eyes had whites showing, and they whispered back and forth with an air of desperation. The woman in chair one looked at him. "We need you, Logan. Name your price."

"I'm not doing anything until I see my family."

"Go ahead. They're up at the resort, enjoying a free vacation."

Free vacation, my ass. "They fly home as soon as they want. The Mendez family, too." Logan pointed right at the guy's face. "And we don't pull that crap ever again."

The man looked left and right to his colleagues, then said, "Agreed."

Logan walked back to his chair. "I have a few more conditions."

If anyone had told Logan the amount of paperwork that awaited him on Kiara's desk, he'd never have taken the job. He should have known by how quickly the execs agreed to his conditions. *Should have asked for more. A lot more.* Too late for that. Now he had two months of work to come through for a project that no longer served a purpose. The reports began to shed a light on the extent of CASE Global's incursion into Alissia. The horses, weapons, and siege engines alone must have cost millions, and that didn't include the salaries for four hundred highly trained mercenaries.

Salaries, and now death benefits as well. Logan had insisted on that, as one of his conditions. Those men weren't coming back, and their families needed taking care of. It was only right, since the company had put them in harm's way. These were military families. They knew the risks. That didn't make it any easier not to have a loved one come home. The money would help.

There were also reports he had to verify and sign out. Every I dotted, every T crossed. The executives wanted nice complete records. Why, he couldn't figure. Considering that they'd probably shove them in a records building somewhere made it even more ridiculous, but they still wanted them.

So he worked through the older stuff first—the last few weeks before he'd come back were still too painful to relive—and did the best he could. Sometimes the numbers didn't line up, and usually the people responsible had ended up on the wrong side of the gateway when it closed. But no one was really around to dispute his reports, and Logan learned he was a fairly decent fiction writer.

That only took care of those who weren't on Earth anymore, which wasn't the case for the Charlie Team. Logan read the mission report twice just to make sure he wasn't mistaken. Then he brought up the comm panel on the closest projection screen and made a call. Someone answered on the first ring.

"Mathias here."

"It's Logan. How's the great disassembly going?" Goldberg and Mathias, by simple merit of being on duty when Logan came back through, won the dubious honor of getting to disassemble the equipment in the gateway room.

"The big money stuff's already crated up. We're about to demo the workstations."

The air lock and its integrated scanners still represented state of the art in travel security. CASE Global would find a purpose for them somewhere. The computers, not so much. They got the hammer and magnet treatment on their way to the landfill.

"Got a question for you about your last recovery mission. The one for Bravo Team." The sting of those losses had faded a little, but not entirely. Logan trained Bravo Team himself, and always figured they'd step up when he was ready to retire. Instead, they'd been wiped out almost to a man by Raptor Tech mercenaries. He'd seen the aftermath, and left a beacon for the cleanup crew to do a recovery.

"What about it?" Mathias asked.

"Says here you didn't recover Magrini's body."

"Right."

"You want to tell me why?" They never left anyone behind. That was part of the deal. At least, it had been when they still had a functional gateway. Which Charlie Team did for the mission he was discussing now.

"Couldn't find him," Mathias said.

"You obviously found the box canyon."

"And recovered the others, yes. We did a half-mile sweep, found nobody else. I figured you got the location wrong."

"You sure he was completely gone?"

Mathias paused. "You sure he was completely dead?"

Pretty damn sure. "I was the one who found him."

"It's a magical world, man. Anything can happen."

Logan snorted. "So what the hell am I supposed to put in the final report?"

"Fudge it."

"You know, I'm starting to understand why you never got promoted."

"Just trying to help, boss."

"Enjoy the sledgehammers. Logan out."

Mathias had a valid point about Alissia. Anything could and did happen in that place. Logan had seen Magrini's body; he could have sworn he'd checked for vitals, but now he didn't know. *Who knows? Maybe Hank the Tank lives after all.* He changed the soldier's status from KIA to MIA and moved on.

An hour later, the comm panel lit up. Intercom from the woman working the island's reception desk. "Sergeant Major? I have Lieutenant Kiara's attorneys for you."

Well, that was fast. "Transfer them to legal."

"Sorry sir, but he's actually here."

"On the island?"

"Affirmative."

"How the hell did they find the island?"

"They filed a request to pick up Lieutenant Kiara's personal effects last week."

Logan had approved it, too. He must have missed the part about them coming in person. "All right, give them whatever they need."

"They're asking to speak to you, sir."

What the hell for? There was only one way to find out. "Put them in briefing room two. I'll be up in a minute."

He hustled up two flights of stairs and down the corridor, arriving just a moment after them. Two knocks on the door, and then he let himself in. A middle-aged man in a pin-striped suit sat in the chair facing the door. Late forties, receding hairline, half-moon glasses. He had a nice face, though, and he was smiling. Most lawyers Logan knew never smiled.

"Hello," Logan said. "I'm—"

He got a look at the woman on the right, and his words faltered. She looked *so much* like Kiara. Same hawk-like features, same dun-brown hair. Maybe a little rounder and softer in the face, but the resemblance was startling. *It's like seeing a goddamn ghost.* He coughed and found his voice again. "Paul Logan."

"I'm Eva," She shook his hand. A soft handshake, and warm. Definitely not military. "This is my husband, Stephen."

Logan shook the man's hand, which was, above all things, sweaty. "I'm sorry. They said you were attorneys."

Eva waved at her husband. "Stephen is the attorney of record for Lynn's affairs."

Lynn Kiara. Logan hadn't heard her called that in years. "And you . . ."

She smiled, though it was sad. "I'm her sister.'

He remembered himself then, and his duty. "I can't begin to say how sorry I am for your loss. She was a great officer."

"Thank you," Eva said. "Were you with her when she . . ."

Logan already had the cover story memorized. The execs cautioned him not to stray from the script, but he already liked these people and felt it deserved a special touch. He nodded. "She put herself in harm's way, to try and protect the rest of her team. It's what she did."

"That sounds like something she'd say about you."

"Oh, she mentioned me, did she?"

"All the time. She loved working with you."

He laughed. "Now I know you're lying."

"I'm serious. Every phone call was Logan this, Logan that."

"Only good stories, I'm sure."

"For the most part." Something flickered across her face. "I think she felt bad about some of the things you had to do. It weighed on her." She brightened. "Well, I don't need to tell you this. You knew her well."

Not as well as I thought. "She had a hard job. I'm appreciating that more and more every day."

"You've taken over her post then?"

He waved it off. "Only temporarily."

"She would like that."

"They're big shoes to fill," Logan said. "She left quite a legacy behind."

Eva looked at Stephen, who cleared his throat. "That's part of why we're here. Eva and I are the executors of Lynn's estate."

"Of course." They'd need the paperwork to get things through probate. "Happy to help. Let us know what you need, and we'll take care of it."

"It's the other way around, really. My sister left something to you, in her estate." Eva slid an envelope across. Business size, with *SERGEANT MAJOR PAUL LOGAN* typed across the front.

Orders. Logan knew the minute he saw it. How very like Kiara to have a contingency plan for anything. "Thank you." He took the envelope and slid it in front of him.

"Go ahead, you can open it," Eva said.

"Right. Of course." He felt an awkward moment coming. Hopefully they wouldn't complain when he told them it was private, whatever it was. Top secret, eyes only.

The envelope felt a little light. At least there wouldn't be a ton of orders. He slit the side with his finger and unfolded a single sheet of paper. But there were no code names, no ciphered messages. It was simply a check from Grand Cayman Bank. Made out to Paul Logan. For a very, very large amount. "I—I don't understand."

"She had a sizable estate, even before your company made good on the death benefits."

Logan shook his head. "This should stay with you."

"Don't worry, she took very good care of us." Eva *harrumphed*. "I don't think she ever spent a dime on herself."

"But you're her family."

"So were you, Logan." Eva put a hand on top of his. "She always said it was an honor to serve with you."

No, Lieutenant. The honor was mine.

Logan planned to call it a day after Kiara's sister left, but the message indicator was blinking red in his office when he returned. *Damn, so close.* He pulled it up on one of the monitors. Apparently a development company had approached CASE Global's real estate division to make an offer to buy the island. Normally the executives would have laughed this away, but with the wall in the gateway room fixed into stone, the island was basically a hole in the water into which the company had poured a lot of money.

Even more interestingly, CASE Global's forensic accounting division had traced the development company back to a shell corporation controlled by none other than Raptor Tech. Their curiosity about what was hidden on this island knew no limits. Hell, they'd even put up millions to find out.

"You know what? They can have it." No one deserved this rock more than Raptor Tech.

It wouldn't put the Gateway Project in the black, but it helped salve the wound. He wrote up a memo with his recommendation, sent it off, then slipped out before more work could catch him. He jogged up the stairs, saluted the guards at the security entrance, and walked out into the breezy warmth of a pretty decent afternoon. With the weather this fine, they'd probably still be at the beach.

He took the shell road that started at the stables, meandered underneath the cliffs where CASE Global tested siege equipment, and eventually wound its way to the beach on the western shore.

"Daddy! Daddy!" His girls came flying out of the main cabana to greet him. He took a knee to catch them, hugged them tight, and hoisted them up in the air. They screamed and giggled.

Sharon slinked over in that dark orange dress that made her look like a goddess. "Hi, baby! How was your day?"

Logan leaned down to kiss her. *Damn, I love getting to do this every day.* "Good," he said. "Weird, but good."

"When do you think you'll be done? It's kind of lonely around here without the Mendez clan."

Julio's forty-one-member family had all been granted permanent visas, and been shipped off to start a new life in the States. Yet another part of the deal with CASE Global's executives. It felt good to do right by Mendez. Logan sure hoped he'd found what he was looking for. "How does tomorrow sound?"

"Do you mean it?" She pointed a threatening finger at him. "Don't toy with me, Paul Logan."

"I mean it, babe. Let's get off this rock."

He set down the girls and put his arm around her for the walk back to the cabana. "And that's Lieutenant Paul Logan, to you." *Soon to be retired.*

"The truly magical things in life don't use magic at all."

—**Art of Illusion, final entry**

CHAPTER 38

BEGINNINGS AND ENDS

Quinn Bradley had cheated at cards and dice and virtually every form of gambling he'd ever tried. None of that compared to cheating death one more time. As grateful as he was to have survived, there were many others who hadn't been so lucky. Too many others. Good people on both sides. But the battle for Alissia had robbed the world of two of its greatest champions. Moric, who alone had managed to destroy something that took three of the greatest magicians ever to create. And Richard Holt, who arguably understood the world better than anyone else.

Jillaine softened the pain of losing them. She'd been there when he woke, a week after the battle of northern Felara, with eyes still red from crying. He felt her through the magic bond that joined them now. He knew she was there before he opened his eyes, in the same way that he knew Moric was gone.

The Enclave held no funeral for Moric. Pireans didn't believe in them, apparently. They sent the departed out to sea in a floating funeral pyre, and afterward referred to them as "out fishing." In Moric's case, they couldn't even do that. Instead, there was a feast in his honor in the Pirean common room. No expenses spared. They roasted mutton, of course—the intoxicating smell of that specialty permeated the tower even before Quinn got out of bed. And they threw open their doors to anyone who wanted to come celebrate Moric's life. Or tell stories about him. Quinn learned more about Moric in three hours than he'd picked up over the course of several months.

But he'd mainly come to sit by Jillaine and try to lighten her spirits. She probably thought he didn't hear her crying at night, even though they had rooms right next to one another in the Pirean tower. But this world had done the impossible: it made Quinn Bradley a light sleeper. He didn't bring it up, but he tried to ease her pain in a hundred tiny ways every day.

Everyone came to pay their respects. Even Sella, who'd oscillated between serving as Moric's staunchest ally and his most vocal critic.

She plunked down on the bench beside Quinn and sighed. "I keep expecting him to walk through that door as if nothing ever happened."

Jillaine glanced up at the door, but wistfully.

Quinn gave her hand a little squeeze. "That would be nice."

"He was always up to something. Hatching a plan of some kind."

"I kind of liked that about him."

"Ha!" She gripped her walking stick as if she might use it on him. "You would. Only the gods know how many of them we'll unravel before it's all said and done."

"I just hope he didn't have any books on loan from the library. Old Mags will go nuts."

"That reminds me," Sella said. "I've begun a little project, and I'd like help from both of you."

"What kind of project?" Quinn asked, with some hesitation. Sella's idea of fun often put him a hair's breadth from bodily harm.

"The story of Moric's life, including his role in breaking the third great enchantment."

"What a great idea," Quinn said.

Jillaine wiped her eyes with dainty fingers. "It does sound nice. A tribute."

"He'll be a legend among our kind for generations

no matter what," Sella said. "We might as well make sure they get it right."

"So, would this be a book?" Quinn asked.

Sella gestured to the crowded room. "I'm sure there's enough material."

"And you'd put a copy in the Enclave library?"

"Certainly."

"The story of Moric, in the keeping of Old Mags," Quinn said. Just saying it made him feel warm inside. "I can't imagine anything he'd love more than that."

They'd just finished breakfast in the Pirean common room when Anton found them. He was dressed for travel, in a flawless crimson jacket beneath a gray riding cloak. He paused on the threshold, then took three steps inside the door. Whatever he saw made him decidedly uncomfortable, to Quinn's great amusement.

"Anton!" He waved the man over. "You hungry?"

Anton approached the table, eyed the selection of breads and berries—a traditional Pirean light breakfast—and frowned. "No, thank you."

"It's going to be a long day."

"Yes," Jillaine said. "We'd hate to see you faint in the heat."

"Valteron has nothing on Caralis when it comes to heat," Anton said. "That being said, we should be on our way."

Quinn stood and tugged on his riding cloak, which now seemed dingy by comparison. *I need to meet Anton's tailor.* They went outside before traveling. It seemed to help, to be outside. He still didn't quite understand why that was. Sella had told him he had to be "perfectly in tune" with his surroundings and "seriously focused" on the destination before he tried to move somewhere. It remained a work in progress.

"You want me to try taking us there?" Quinn asked.

Anton shook his head. "It's a long way to Valteron."

"I'm ninety percent sure I can get it right this time."

"As tempting as that is, I think I will handle the necessary magic," Anton said. "Stand ready."

Fine. At least I won't wear myself out.

He put a hand on their shoulders and closed his eyes. Quinn sensed the magic building in him, from a gentle rain to a tempest. Then the cold darkness yanked him sideways. They emerged in the sweltering heat. The air was thick enough to taste the salt in it. They stood at the mouth of an alley overlooking the city square. Mourners packed it to the gills.

"Gods," Jillaine breathed. "I've never seen so many people in one place."

"It looks like half the world turned out for this," Quinn said. The only time he'd seen it nearly as crowded was the day Holt had come into power. The same day Moric had discovered him and whisked him off to the Enclave. *It feels like so long ago.* And they were gone now, both of them, leaving a hollow part inside of Quinn that he knew he'd never fill.

"More than half, I'd say." Anton pointed to the closest corner. "Those are Tioni banners. And over there, Landorians. I see every nation but Felara."

"They still have a lot to figure out." *Like where to resettle hundreds of displaced mercenaries.* Thank the gods that Veena had contacts almost everywhere in Felara. How she'd gotten them, he didn't know. She and Sella had begun the difficult tasks of integrating modern soldiers into a medieval world.

Valteron City's normally vibrant avenues waited in muted silence. Black cloths draped every window, and the banners that normally fluttered over the palace of the Prime were bound tightly against their poles. Quinn was grateful for the back entrance to the palace of the Prime, because they'd never have made it through the massive throng of people to the front steps. Bita let them in the side-gate and took them straight to the wide balcony. The same balcony where Richard Holt had brought so many disparate groups together. *That feels like ages ago.*

"Quinn!" Veena excused herself from a cluster of dusty-looking bureaucrats and ran over to hug him tight.

"Hey, Veena." He hugged her, then drew back. "Or should I say . . . Your Eminence?"

She slapped his arm in a playful way. "Hush, you. It's not official yet."

She embraced Jillaine, and even hugged Anton, to his visible consternation. "Thank you both for coming."

Anton cleared his throat and made several unnecessary adjustments to his cloak. "It's an honor to be here."

"I'd like to introduce you to my new minister of security," Veena said.

Quinn didn't notice someone coming up behind him, but suddenly felt the pressure of something sharp against his back. Right over the left kidney. He froze. "Um—"

"Got you again, rookie," a man said.

I know that voice. "No way!" He turned and laughed, because it sure as hell was Julio Mendez. "Well, well. Rico Suave."

"I heard a rumor you were still alive." Mendez offered his hand and gave him a bro-hug. He introduced himself to Jillaine and Anton. Then he came back to Quinn. "You got a minute?" He gave the hand signal for *private*.

"Sure." Quinn followed him over to a quiet spot along the rail. Which brought the full extent of mourners into view. There had to be thousands of them. "Man, that's a lot of people." He looked at Mendez and grinned. "So, what happened? You get lost on the way home?"

"I never got lost, man. That's *your* thing."

"Hey, I can't help it. I've been kidnapped more times than I can count."

"Yeah, you've got the record. That's for sure." The smile faded from Mendez's face. "I was wondering if you ran into our mutual friend. Big black guy, likes to hit things?"

"Hm." Quinn put on a pensive expression. "That does sound like someone I encountered recently."

"So where is he? He's not on the list of in-world personnel. Last I heard, he was headed for the gateway."

Quinn laughed. "Oh, he got there. Right when we were trying to destroy the damn thing. I had to hold him off myself."

"Oh, *man*. How are you still standing here?"

Quinn gave a casual shrug. "We fought, I won, and then I shoved him through the gateway."

Mendez gave him a flat look. "You beat Logan."

"Yep." Quinn kept his face still.

"In a real fight."

"With swords and everything."

Mendez pursed his lips and pondered this for a moment. "You cheated, didn't you?"

Quinn laughed. "For all I was worth!"

"That sounds more like it." Mendez paused. "So he got back, huh?"

"I think so."

"Good."

Quinn gave him a serious look. "I'm surprised you didn't want to go back, too."

"I had a pretty good reason to stay." He looked over at Veena.

"Didn't she kind of . . . leave you in the lurch?" *For another man,* he didn't add.

"She did what she had to. And she got away *clean.* Not even you can make that claim."

"It was a hell of a performance, I'll give her that." And her defection was just the warm-up. Everyone had played a role in defeating CASE Global, but Veena's was bigger than most.

"She was worth coming back for," Mendez said.

"Good for you, man." Quinn nudged him in the shoulder. "Got to be honest, though. You might've bitten off more than you can chew."

Mendez smirked. "I hear that's going around."

Quinn followed his gaze, and saw he was looking at Jillaine. Gods, she was as lovely as the day he'd first met her, atop that pile of boulders at the Enclave. Being with her was like riding a ship into the eye of a hurricane. And he wouldn't want it any other way.

"Veena told me something else about you," Mendez said. "I'm not sure I believe it."

"Yeah? What's that?"

"She said you're a magician now. Like, a *real* one."

How long have I waited to hear that? He used to dream of proving himself to the world. Of seeing his name in the neon lights and knowing he deserved the title of magician. Now the word carried a different meaning. It meant the Enclave was his home, and the magicians were his family. Strange how much that seemed to matter now. Yet it was a private sort of feeling, a thing best left unsaid.

And Quinn Bradley still had a reputation to maintain.

"Oh, Mendez." Quinn clapped a hand on his shoulder and walked with him back toward the others. "I've *always* been a real magician."

AUTHOR'S NOTE

Dear Reader,

You made it! Thank you so much for reading my series from start to finish. And it is finished, as far as I know. As much as I love Alissia, I've always seen this as a story with three parts. Feel free to assume that every character you've come to love lives happily ever after. I'm still writing, of course, but I have other stories to tell. If you'd like to hear about them, please join my mailing list here:

http://dankoboldt.com/subscribe

My e-mail followers get other perks, too, like free stories and some juicy contest details.

If you enjoyed my books, I hope you'll consider rating them on HC.com, Amazon, Goodreads, or your online bookstore of choice. Even a short review helps other readers find my book and decide if it's something they'd like.

For a quick primer on how to write a book review, visit this page on my author website:

http://dankoboldt.com/reviews

ACKNOWLEDGMENTS

I'm grateful to so many people for helping this book become a reality. To my family, for their unconditional support of my writing. To my editor, David Pomerico, for his sharp editorial eye. To the publicity and marketing teams at Harper Voyager, for helping my books reach a wider audience. To my agent, Paul Stevens, for his constant support and career guidance. To my critique partners, Dannie Morin and Mike Mammay, for ferreting out my writing weaknesses.

I would never have come this far without the support of the writing community. Special thanks to my friends in The Clubhouse, Codex Writers, the Pitch Wars community, and Impulse Authors Unite. If I still have my sanity, it's because of you.

Last but not least, I'm grateful to my readers for taking a final trip through the gateway to Alissia. I hope it was everything you wanted, and more.

ABOUT THE AUTHOR

DAN KOBOLDT is a genetics researcher and fantasy/science-fiction author. He has coauthored more than sixty publications in *Nature, Human Mutation, Genome Research, The New England Journal of Medicine, Cell,* and other scientific journals. Dan is also an avid hunter and outdoorsman. Every fall, he disappears into the woods to pursue whitetail deer with bow and arrow. He lives with his wife and children in Ohio, where the deer take their revenge by eating the flowers in his backyard.

You can find him online at http://dankoboldt.com and on Twitter @DanKoboldt.

Discover great authors, exclusive offers, and more at hc.com.